Omie's Well

Rebecca Holbrook

Dancing Heron
Publishing

Book Covers by Michael Mabe, Amy Leonard

Editor Gary Nelson

Printed in the United States

Dancing Heron Publishing Hoodsport, Washington

dancingheronpub@gmail.com

ISBN 9798218254223 (paperback)

ISBN 9798218254230 (ebook)

Acknowledgements

Many thanks to those who've been on this journey with me. There are too many to name, but your encouragement was essential to seeing this book through. I owe a great deal to my mother and her sisters for the stories that inspired me to write this novel. To family and friends who read the first drafts and made me believe that I'm a writer worth reading, Much Love.

Thanks to Ilana Lehman, Strong Paulson and Sierra Gaelan, members of my author's group, Write On of Lacey, for all your invaluable help. Deep appreciation to my brother Mark Holbrook and his husband Michael Mabe for their input. My thanks to Michael also for designing the front cover. Thanks to Amy Leonard for designing the back cover. Also, thanks to my Dream Team beta readers.

Hugs to my step-daughter Emma Mitchell, my first editor and fan. Most of all, my undying gratitude to my husband, Gary Nelson, for his support and amazing final edits. You are the light of my life.

Kate Lee   Frank Lee

|

Omie Lee—Nate Silar   ***Emmie Lee— Caleb Decker***

| |

Ada Kate—James Dillon   ***Bitsy***

Tess Jacob Cyrus Olivia Naomi   ***Danny***

Bartie—Shadrack Cain   ***Aaron***

Lilly

Frank Thomas

Ezra

Georgia Rose

Grace

Chapter 1

1904

Omie stepped up to the lip of the well and touched the stones. Closing her eyes, she took a deep breath and leaned over, a small mirror in her trembling hand. When she allowed herself to look, a ripple passed through the mirror's reflection, as though from a mild breeze. The water stilled, and in the mirror's frame a figure walked along a road, lean as a stick, not much more than a boy. He was dressed in overalls and a slouch hat. A shiver ran through her, a slight tingling that preceded the *Sight,* causing her to step away from the well.

This was the man who would hold her future.

It was a sweltering June day in a month of uncompromising drought. Omie, her sister Emmie, and their friends were restless and bored. The girls turned listless faces toward Mrs. Lee as she came in the back door, surveying them with a shake of her head.

"All right you girls, now gather round and I will tell you what's special about this day," Omie's mamma said. "This is the longest day of the year and today, only today, if you shine a mirror down a well, in its reflection you'll see the face of the man you are goin' to marry."

The girls started chattering like excited magpies. Mamma said, "Now, it has to be right when the sun is overhead, and I reckon it's about that time. Besides, I got a lady comin' for a readin', so y'all need to scoot."

Emmie grabbed her hand mirror and the girls raced outside, the sun-baked Georgia clay burning like hot bricks beneath their feet.

Mrs. Kate Lee had been giving readings for folks in the county since she was a young woman. Somehow though, *the Sight* did not allow her to predict for her daughters. Kate smiled and shook her head, hoping whatever the girls saw would take place far in the future.

Emmie, the oldest at fifteen, staked her claim as first at the well's narrow opening, lifting the wooden cover and setting it at her feet. The water below, lower now from the drought but still deep and dependable, shined up a blue reflection of the sky. She held her mirror in the midst of all that sky.

The girls gathered near with shouts of, *What do you see? Is he there? Who is he?*

After a time, she still saw nothing but her own hopeful reflection in the water beside the mirror. Not to be outdone in case the others had more luck, she said "I don't know who he is but he's dark-haired and has a handsome moustache."

"Me next!" Silvey shouted, and Emmie moved aside to let her look. After a few moments, a frown came to Silvey's face, as this youngest friend let out a low moan. "Not Silas, he's the dumbest boy in school! He can't even tell time."

"Well, but he's sweet," encouraged Omie, "and his family owns the best land in Effingham County. You could do worse."

Next up was Cora, tentatively peeking over the edge. "I don't know, maybe it's best not to know if you feel sure to be disappointed." Curiosity overcame her. As she gazed into the water, a slow smile spread across her face. She set the mirror down and started running for the barn. Emmie and Sylvie ran after her, shouting *Who? Who?* like a couple of owls, leaving Omie alone.

The man who would hold my future. . . Dazed for a moment by the vision she'd had, Omie wondered, *Should I look again? Might I have imagined him?*

She stepped back up to the well, pondering what this might mean for her. The others may have seen who they hoped—or dreaded—would appear. But she didn't know this person.

As she heard the girls returning from the barn, Omie slid the cover back in place.

"Guess who Cora saw," cried Emmie. "Her third cousin Benjamin from over at Ebeneezer!"

Ben was a handsome young teacher who taught at the school near the old church.

"Well, you won't be rich, but you sure will make some purty babies," Omie declared.

The girls then clamored around Omie, asking, *What happened? Did you see anyone? Somebody we know?*

She shook her head and turned to walk back to the house. Later, she confessed to Emmie about the man in the mirror and her confused feelings.

Emmie told her not to worry, she was just too young at thirteen to think about such things.

"Anyway," Emmie had soothed, "by the time I can go to secretarial school, we'll run away to Savannah and meet some fine young gentlemen there. We can leave this sorry little back woods town. Not even a town at all!"

1939

JUNE 18

With the warm stones against her back and the sun edging over the tree line, Omie drifted into a doze. A mockingbird sang in a nearby tree, mimicking a redbird, a robin, and the mule's bray. Omie smiled when she felt a small hand on her shoulder.

"Grandma, are you ok?"

"I'm fine, Lilly." She sighed. "Just needed a little rest, is all. Come sit here by me."

Omie was resting on a bench nestled beside the well, where buckets were set to fill. It was a peaceful place, and she sometimes paused there during the day to gather her thoughts.

"Your grandaddy built this bench for me."

Lilly settled her head on her grandma's shoulder and said, "Are you very sad? Is that why you're up here at the old house instead of down there with everybody? People keep bringing food. I don't know where we'll put it all."

"Mostly, I'm just remembering, child. You know, this well is really where my life with your grandaddy started."

"That story you told earlier, this is the well where you saw him?"

"It is. Seen many other things in it too. Some I did and some I didn't want to."

Omie turned to look at her granddaughter. "Your mamma tells me you been *Seein'* some things yourself."

Lilly looked toward the house a moment before she replied, "I don't rightly know what it means, Grandma. I was hopin' you might be able to help me. I could spend the summer with you. Mamma doesn't want me to, but I feel like I need to be here. Maybe learn some of your healin' ways? I could be a help to you too, now Grandaddy has passed."

Both looked up as a raucous group of crows settled into the trees nearby.

"Wish I could have known him. Fifty seems kinda' young for him to pass."

"He put a lot of hard living into those years, Lilly. Probably did cheat himself of more. Cheated us too."

"I wonder if Mamma is sorry they didn't make peace now that they can't."

Omie put her hand over the girl's.

"Mamma don't have a good thing to say about him. She won't tell me why." Lilly let out an exasperated sound. "I want a chance to know my family. What's wrong with that? Would you talk to her?"

"Let me think on it, Hon. You are always welcome here, you know that. Your mamma's feelin's about your grandaddy . . ." Omie shook her head sadly. "They've cast a shadow on everything about this place, not just him, and we'll have to convince her to separate the two."

"But what happened?"

Omie considered what to say. "I never saw two people who took such pleasure in each other as your mamma and her daddy. When you love that deep, what feels like a betrayal makes scars inside you that never heal, the way the flesh does. This is not a story for me to tell, without she agrees to it. I'll talk to her. Your grandaddy was a hard man later in his life, but he wasn't always. There was much more to him than that."

Omie closed her eyes for a moment more. *Had Mamma been able to read the leaves in the bottom of my cup, would I have done different?*

"Mamma, Lilly, come eat!" Bartie, Lilly's mamma, called from the house below. Omie thought her daughter was lovely as she stood on the porch with the early afternoon light shining on her fair hair. Her dark funeral dress seemed out of place here, where she had once been such a lively, laughing young girl.

Lilly took her grandma's hand and they walked down the hill.

Bartie smiled to see her mamma and Lilly hand in hand. As they stepped onto the porch, she offered, "If you want to sit out here Mamma, I'll bring you a plate. Lilly, come help."

Omie settled in a rocker.

"Hey, sister." Emmie came out of the house and took up residence in the remaining rocker. "How you holding up?"

Omie smiled. "I believe I'm all right. Got a world of things going through my mind, though. Feels like only part of me is here. Lilly has so many questions and I can't figure where to begin."

Emmie's daughter, Bitsy, came up on the porch and gave Omie a hug. "I'm sorry to have to leave so soon, Aunt Omie. Mamma and I have deliveries of fabrics coming from Europe and someone has to be in Savannah to receive them."

Omie patted her niece's hand. "I know, Hon. You go take care of the shop. Thank you for letting me have my sister for a few more days. Eat something before you go, though."

"I will."

Bartie, Lilly and Bitsy returned with plates of food. After making sure Omie had what she needed, they sat on the steps to eat their own dinners.

Talk turned to stories of Omie's and Emmie's childhoods on the farm. When Bartie's daddy, Nate, was brought up, Bartie stood to pick up the dishes and carried them inside to wash.

A look passed between the sisters that was not missed by Lilly. Before the child could ask what it meant, Omie began to speak.

"Honey, I wish you could have known our mamma. I named my first girl, Ada Kate after her. A finer person never lived. She had such healing in her hands."

Emmie nodded and added, "And she had the *Sight.* She couldn't predict our futures, said family was too close, but she always knew what we were up to . Your grandmamma here took after her, learned how to birth babies and mix potions for the sick. She got the *Sight* too. I sure didn't want it! She and Mamma could see spirits and talk to them."

Omie winked at her granddaughter. "Whether *I* wanted to or not. Though, never was anybody as good at those things as Mamma."

"True," Emmie agreed. "I had my heart set on other things, other places. Didn't realize at the time what a fine life I had here."

"Tried to tell you!" Omie laughed as Emmie stuck out her tongue.

A soft, warm breeze rose up and brushed the sisters' cheeks.

Chapter 2

1904

Emmie always dreamed of bigger, better things, but Omie didn't mind the farm so much.

She loved the smell of pines in the hot sun and the sweet-eyed cows lying about the pasture. Now that she was thirteen—nearly fourteen—she was allowed to milk Dinah by herself, rather than sitting on Mamma's lap. Leaning her head against the cow's warm, round belly, squirting a stream of milk toward the hopeful cats—this was entertainment enough. She could tame anything from chickens to raccoons and always had some critter or other scampering at her feet.

Most days, Kate had people come to the door asking for help with ailments, physical or otherwise. There might be a sick child, a missing object, a wandering husband. Some just needed a bit of reassurance, a respite from loneliness. Mamma never turned anyone away, no matter what she was in the middle of at the time. Her tonics and teas had a wide reputation for their healing powers, but Omie knew that there was something more to them than the plants alone could give. Something passed from her mamma's hands to whatever she touched, some kind of shimmer Omie could just see around the outline of her fingers. The quiet peace on Kate's face as she was working spoke of a deep, spiritual communion with all things.

That was the foundation of her being.

On the table where her mamma made her potions was a book Omie's Grandmamma Ida Ruth had made for the recipes she used in healing. It was a collection of pages cut from brown butcher paper, covered in sketches and notes—first in German, then in later years, English. Pieces of newspaper were tucked among the pages, and tucked inside these were dried plants and flowers. Some of this knowledge came from the native women she encountered as she foraged. There were some plants common to both Austria and Georgia. Omie recognized drawings of nettle and yarrow, rosehips and elderberry blooms.

"Mornin', honey." Omie's mamma kissed her on the forehead. "Would you hand me that big pot on the drainboard? I want to cover it with cheesecloth and strain these nettles through it. No matter how I try not to handle them much, they still manage to set my hands on fire. Worth it though, there's a whole gallon of tea right here! Thank you, baby."

Mamma spends so many hours gathering and steeping these plants, just to get what seems like a small return.

"Mamma, is it true that Mrs. Wilson's husband will come home if she puts a pair of his shoes on the porch facin' the house? I mean, he always comes back anyway."

"I know child. But she needs to feel like she has some say in what he does, and it's a small comfort. Now, Naomi Lee, have you and your sister been listening under the window again? I've asked you not to do that, it's disrespectful. You may think people's troubles are small, but what weighs down a soul may be something you can't understand. Disease begins when there is dis-ease, remember that. Promise me you'll not be snoopin' again."

"I'm sorry Mamma, I won't," Omie said, seriously.

I can't speak for Snoopy Emmie though.

"It's not that we're makin' fun of anyone, leastways I'm not, but I just want to understand what it is you do. Folks always seem to leave better than when they came."

"Well, you can start by helpin' me pound these mullein leaves and I'll show you how to make a poultice. That's a good start. It's not just your hands that make these things work, Omie. It's also what's in your heart when you do it. Never set yourself to these tasks if you harbor anger or fear. Nothing that might be of a harmful nature must ever pass from you into their making. Do you understand?"

"Yes ma'am, I think so. I will do my best," she promised.

Kate loved seeing the gentle concentration of her daughter's movements, light flickering around her young, deft hands. She smiled and turned back to her labors, and they worked side by side until a tentative knock at the door signaled another soul in need.

Omie quietly slipped out the back door and headed for the barn, looking for her daddy and Emmie. In the cool shade below the hay loft, she saw him bending down beside Emmie, showing her how to plait leather strips to make bridles and such. Her sister sat on a stack of hay bales, back straight and proper as ever, completely absorbed in her work. Omie thought how pretty Emmie was with the slanted light from the hayloft window shining on the reds and browns of her hair.

The same colors as their father's, she realized. Deciding not to disturb them, Omie turned instead toward the fields to make daisy chains for the goats to wear around their necks.

Fall descended on the fields with a heavy hand, folding the leaves beneath a caul of brittle frost. It came early this year, putting the thirsty plants out of their misery as if to make up for the summer's relentless heat. The weather had become more extreme recently, shortening the weeks of spring and fall, giving folks little time to get acclimated in between.

Omie walked between the darkened rows of plants as the sun began to rise, taking note of the patterns of frost on gate and fence posts, of frozen dew drops gleaming in spider webs.

Like Mamma says, gifts of beauty to ease the passing of life.

Maple and sweetgum trees would soon put on a parade of color before dropping their leaves to swirl among the river's currents. Sumac berries had already turned a velvety red and sassafras trees mingled peach, rose and gold all on a single leaf.

The smells of fall, more than any other season, stirred memories for Omie. She felt the sense of another year soon put to rest. An unnameable longing would come upon her suddenly when certain scents filled her nostrils, making her stop in her tracks to wonder at it.

Soon, the kitchen would fill with the spicy smells of winter baking. She, Emmie and their mamma would have time to sit by the woodstove, talking while tending to the tasks of mending and piecing of quilt tops. Clothes that could service no more would give up their seams to be refashioned into quilts that not only brought warmth from their delicious weight, but also from the brightness of their colors against the early darkness of winter. Most of these pieces had begun their journey as flour sacks that came in flowery prints, to be turned into clothes. One might have a shirt, skirt, and underclothes, all from the same cloth.

Omie was old enough, and skilled enough now, to join the ladies and her sister at quilting circles in the community. Laughter and news of the past year kept cadence with the flashing of needles around kerosene lamps.

Quilt frames were supported on the backs of two chairs and Omie remembered crawling with other young ones beneath them amongst a forest of legs and shoes. The children were watched by everyone there. Heavy-breasted women nursed any child who had a need. Ample laps cushioned sleepy babies, lulled by the hum of voices and the warmth of bodies.

This would be Omie's last year of school, the last time she'd spend her days inhaling the scents of paste and chalk, while being among the other young folks she'd grown up with. Soon, many of them would be too busy becoming adults, ready or not, some already having a head start because of their difficult lives. Here at school, at least, you could count on a hot meal once a day. Each family contributed what they could, a ham or a side of venison, fruit and vegetables or fresh-baked bread.

The time had come to wrap chilled feet for the trek to the schoolhouse. Some children managed with just rags, slipping a carved piece of wood or bark inside to protect against sharp ice. Omie counted her hand-me-down boots from Emmie as a blessing. She never recalled a time of being cold or hungry or without the basic things a body needs, and often felt she had more than her due.

"Omie, come look!" Silas Miller called across the schoolyard, "What you reckon that is?"

Omie looked at the strange, red-capped fungus by Silas' feet and said, "Why Silas, that's a fairy's hat. You wait here long enough and he'll be back to claim it!"

"Naw, really?" Silas exclaimed and stood there watching until the end of recess when Omie took his arm and pulled him toward the schoolhouse.

"I'm sorry Silas," she said, laughing. "I was just teasing you."

"Well, that would have been somethin' to see!" He smiled back good-naturedly.

Silvey walked up beside Omie and rolled her eyes, then asked, "Omie, does that well always tell the truth? Does it have to be Silas?!"

"I don't rightly know, Silvey," she replied. "Mamma says even her readings are generally true in the moment, but a body can make one decision, even a small one, and change the course of everything. Like if you was to take a path through the woods to get home rather than walk the road, you'd still end up in the same place eventually, but something completely unexpected could happen to you along the way, depending on how you chose."

"But if Silas is the one I'll eventually come to, what does it matter?"

"Maybe marriage is just the place you'll come to," Omie offered.

"Well, if that ain't true, I might just choose to be an old maid." Silvey scowled.

"Still, Silvey and Silas has a nice sound to it."

Silvey yanked Omie's braid and they ran laughing into the classroom.

Later, Omie wondered. *If you knew your destiny and it was not a pleasing thing, how could you go about your life and enjoy the day at hand?*

She decided then and there that she would not follow in her mamma's footsteps and do readings for folks, though she knew she could.

Surely, there were other ways to use this gift of knowing things.

Silvey would marry Silas two years out of school. His sweet nature and generosity won her over and, for a time, she was happy.

Winter came and went with little to recommend it. However, a snowstorm arrived near Christmas, so that they woke to a different scene than the one they had known at bedtime. Omie marveled at the quietness of the world. The only sound was her soft footsteps as she went to feed the animals, checking the water troughs to see if they were frozen over. She could count on one hand the number of times she'd witnessed snow. The deepest cold usually presented itself as troublesome ice or hail, beautiful in their own way.

Walking to school, Omie encountered a handful of children engaged in a furious snowball fight, scraping what they could from the few inches on the ground.

"Omie!"

"No...!" she shouted as they attacked her from all sides. Omie joined in until ammunition ran low, then sang out.

"Snow angels! Everybody join hands."

The children plopped down on their backs to fan their arms and legs back and forth so that when they stood up, the joined angels looked like a string of paper dolls. They ran in a laughing, wet mob, toward the schoolhouse, knowing they'd be late.

Miss Landers stood in the doorway waiting for them with her hands on her hips. They ducked their heads, expecting a scolding from the teacher, but were surprised when she, and the other students, ran out and started pelting the newcomers with snowballs.

Finally, she called them all inside to take off their wet coats and gather around the woodstove for cups of hot chocolate. Miss Landers reckoned as how it was so close to the Christmas break and so hard to concentrate on schoolwork with the wonder of snow outside, they might as well begin their celebration now.

The boys had cut a cedar tree and set it in a bucket of sand by the window. The older children popped corn and taught the younger ones to string it into garlands to lay amongst the branches. They made paper chains, tied ribbons to prickly sweetgum balls and to small clusters of berry-laden holly, then placed it all on the tree. For the tree top, Silas attached a silver star he had cut from a tin can. They all sang carols until it was time to go home.

Somehow Miss Landers had been able to buy enough oranges for each child to have one. For many, this was the first they had ever tasted such sweetness. A few saved part of theirs to take home and share, while others couldn't help but gobble the whole orange down. Miss Landers told them to put the peels in a pot of water on the woodstove when they got home, to sweeten the air in the whole house.

Omie looked around at the familiar faces.

This is a day I will hold close in memory for the rest of my life. A gift of pure joy.

For some of the children, this day was the only gift they would receive.

Chapter 3

1905

Between winter's chores and preparations for this spring's planting, Omie had all but forgotten the adventure at the well until she heard of Cora's engagement to her cousin Benjamin.

While feeding the chickens, she thought of the images she and the other girls had seen reflected in the water.

Would they all come true?

Her mamma's *Sight* was usually dependable, but Omie wasn't sure about her own.

What if I conjured him up out of my imagination?

Spring had come early to Georgia this year, tempting the azaleas to bud before the camellias began to drop their blooms. Omie finished her chores and went to find Emmie to tell her of Cora's news.

She was hoping they might walk down to the creek for a swim before dinnertime. The mornings were still cool but by noon the heat began uncoiling, foretelling another hot, dry season in the months ahead. Only April, and already the skies were stingy with rain.

This was a year for cicadas, the thirteen-year kind, and Omie could feel the woods swell with the sound of them mating. She'd been finding their molted little shells everywhere and could see the holes in the ground where they'd crawled out from their long waiting. Omie tried to imagine what it would be like to fall to the ground and burrow under to sleep for thirteen years. The length of her life.

Could they hear what went on above them? Did they have dreams of wind and wings? Or was it just a dark slumber?

Omie had fastened eight of the little dry husks onto her fingers and waggled them at Emmie, making her squeal and run, shouting, "You keep those awful monsters away from me or I'll never speak to you again!"

Maybe the idea of a cool swim could be a peace offering. Emmie can hold a grudge for days, though. Acts like she grew up on Bull Street in Savannah, instead of on a tobacco farm pulling worms off the plants all her life. She's sure determined to be a lady.

Omie found Emmie in the tobacco barn sneaking a smoke from the rolled leaf of a young deer tongue plant. Her big sister had started smoking the year before and had now run out of last year's hidden tobacco leaves. Deer tongue was a poor substitute for tobacco, but it was something. Emmie looked long and hard at Omie as she blew out a cloud of smoke, then sniped, "Well, I guess you'll go running to Mamma about this."

"Naw, Emmie. I won't. But did you hear about Cora's engagement? Ain't it exciting? She'll be the first of our friends to be a married woman."

Emmie didn't respond, pretending she knew all about it.

Omie sighed, "Come on and let's get us a cool dip in the creek. You know after supper Mamma will put us to workin' the tobacco sets and we'll never get a minute's rest. Ain't you hot?"

Emmie scowled, considered the gesture of solidarity, then gave in. She crushed the cigarette between her thumb and finger. "Ok. But no more of them bug puppets, you hear me?"

They laughed and ran for the woods. After a short swim, they walked toward the house, watching their shadows lengthen before them.

Mamma shouted, "Girls, you need to go ahead and make sure those tobacco sets are covered good before dinner! I reckon we're in for a little blackberry winter."

"Yes'm," Omie called.

"How does she know that?" Emmie asked, "I'm sweating like it's June already. Anyways, I wonder why they call it dogwood winter and blackberry winter?"

"There's always just a little bit of winter that don't want to give up," Omie replied. "Just when you get all happy to see the dogwood trees in bloom, winter gets jealous and sneaks back around. Then, when the blackberries blossom and you can just taste the pies to come, winter nips at your heels again on its way north."

The girls pulled old feed sacks over the rows of young tobacco plants, then walked toward the house. Along the way Omie stopped to look at what was blooming in the grass, taking her sweet time.

"What are you looking at?" Emmie exclaimed. "Sometimes you are slow as molasses, and if you don't come on there won't be anything left to eat but molasses and biscuits."

"I love the tiny flowers best of all, Emmie. Seems like they just bloom for the joy of the season turning. They're too little even for the bees to take notice. But they have some of the most beautiful, perfect little faces. See?" She held up a tiny violet flower striped with dark purple.

Emmie bent down and gobbled up the blossom from her sister's fingers, then grabbed Omie's hand, laughing as she pulled her toward the back porch and the wash basin.

"About time, girls!" Frank Lee said, with a mock frown on his face. Emmie put her arms around her daddy's neck, bending to kiss his stubbly cheek. Omie plopped down on his lap and grabbed his hat off the chair back, plunking it down on her own head.

"No hats on in the house!" he joked, and tickled her until she slid off his lap onto the floor. "You are getting just about too big for my lap. Guess you must have a birthday comin' up soon!"

Omie grinned and replied, "I'll never be too big for your lap, Daddy. You just best get used to that!"

"I swear," Kate remarked, "y'all are like a bunch of baby goats! Now get over here and carry these bowls to the table."

They sat down to dinner and, as Frank said grace, Kate looked around her table, saying a silent prayer of her own.

Lord, you have truly blessed this family. If there is hardship to come, I know that you will help us through it. But please, Lord, don't give me the knowin' of it beforehand. Bless me with the bliss of that ignorance I pray. Amen.

The four of them tucked into their dinner, talking about the events of the day as the light slipped away across the fields, gathering up into the darkening pines.

Chapter 4

Omie's fourteenth birthday came and went, leaving her feeling as if little had changed. She thought the world would look different somehow, as if this landmark birthday would nudge some internal clock hand forward, revealing what she was supposed to do from here on. She had gone as far in school as possible without going to the city.

Mamma and Daddy don't have enough money for me and Emmie to go. I don't want to, anyhow. Everything I know and love is right here.

She wondered if this absence of curiosity about the bigger world was a flaw, if it meant she had a lack of imagination or intelligence. Emmie certainly had the hunger to leave though. All the folks Omie knew who were scheming to leave New Abercorn, to go out into the unknown, always seemed be dissatisfied with life. Always looking in the distance for the one true thing that would make them happy.

Omie figured she'd accept this gift of contentment and stay close to home, learn all she could about the healing properties of plants from her mamma. She couldn't think of a more satisfying way to be part of God's plan, if there was one.

"Omie darlin', would you like to go with me on my rounds this morning? I need to deliver these tonics and check on some folks." Kate handed the girl a basket.

Omie had been helping her mamma more often of late, crafting the medicines she needed. It seemed as if Mamma recognized in her a talent for the work. The offer to observe firsthand how Mamma worked with patients seemed like a big vote of confidence. Maybe turning fourteen meant being more grown-up than she'd thought.

As they walked, Kate pointed out plants that she used in her practice. "You recognize that dark green, low growing plant there, daughter? Has these red berries in summer?"

Omie crushed a leaf between her fingers. "Yes Ma'am, wintergreen. We put it in our iced tea."

"It has healing uses too. Crushed up and made into poultices, it's good for aches and pains. Especially toothaches, put right on the gums. This grows the year round, real useful when nothing else is ready."

Omie's mamma showed her other plants whose leaves would soon be big enough to harvest.

"Now you know where to look for them, I'd like to send you out to gather for me when the time comes. Some plants will have to wait 'til the roots are mature enough, or the berries are ready. I'll teach you those later."

These outings were pure joy for Omie. She loved learning from her mamma and having time for just the two of them. The folks they ministered to came to know Kate's daughter and soon became comfortable with her presence.

Sometimes on these visits, Omie's vision would become clouded with images, like bits of a dream, half-remembered. She wasn't sure what they meant. Occasionally a person would hug her or touch her arm and she would suddenly have a pain in some part of her body, followed by a sense of uneasiness.

Mamma's here, so why does this happen to me? Can't I just help her with the medicines and leave the knowin' of things to her?

Omie posed these questions to her mamma after one particularly strong episode.

Kate sighed. "I was about your age when the *Sight* came to me, honey. I knew my mamma had it and her mamma before her, but I didn't really understand what they experienced. I didn't know what to do with what I sensed either. It scared me a good bit, actually."

Kate stopped and turned to face Omie.

"Does everybody have the *Sight*?" Omie asked. "What if I don't want to have this? What if I *See* awful things coming to people. Things I don't want to tell them?"

Kate took Omie's hands in hers.

"I don't know why some of us have it and others don't. Babies born with a caul across their face are most likely to; folks sometimes call this 'the veil', believing that the child will be able to see beyond this world into the next. When a girl has her first menses, the *Sight* comes on stronger, that's why this seems so sudden to you. Yours will start soon."

"Was I born with a caul across my face?"

"No, but my mother was."

"Do boys ever have the *Sight?*"

"I've not known any, but some boys are more sensitive to things than most. Do you remember your uncle Tobias? You met him when you were small, but he and his wife moved way south once they married. He and my mamma were so close they could send pictures to each other in their minds. One always knew if the other was in need or just missin' them. Mamma never needed a letter to know how he was."

Kate smiled for a moment at the memory. She tilted Omie's face up to look in her eyes.

"I understand why you might not want to know about all the pains and woes we come across, daughter. It's not easy. You've not had enough of life to understand many of these trials, but they will become clearer. Try to separate other folks' feelings and fears from your own. I don't mean you're not to care, Omie, just know their burdens are not yours to carry."

Kate put her arm across the girl's slight shoulders as they walked.

"Most problems solve themselves eventually or open the way to a new life. Some, you just got to leave in God's hands. When an ailment is hard to figure out though, it's useful to have this gift, so don't ignore it completely. You may not always have a say in what comes to you, but do your best with it and ask for God's help. He has His reasons for choosing you."

"Yes Ma'am." Omie replied.

Chapter 5

Omie curled up in the hollow trunk of an old sweet gum tree that had gone down in a windstorm many years ago. The shell of wood that remained had harbored many a small creature. She could tell by the tiny bones and berry seeds left behind. The opening of the trunk faced the deep, cool woods, and Omie settled into it as she pulled her harmonica from her apron pocket.

She began to play a slow, sweet melody born of the shadows of dancing leaves, and the low hum of insects rising from the grass. As her breath rose and fell through the reeds, tunes seemed to move through her as if drawn from a river of notes, a stream momentarily diverted until it found its way back to the source. Some tunes were kept in her head to play for her mamma and daddy. Some were released into the air to float away, soft as dandelion seeds.

The harmonica had been all she'd asked for on her birthday, so daddy had taken her to the dry goods store in New Abercorn to buy it. Omie found she had a natural ability to play almost any instrument, given a little time to find her way across the keyboard or fingerboard. Grown-ups were happy to share their guitars, fiddles, banjos, whatever was at hand,

and show her things when they gathered at the church for a sing. But she loved having an instrument so small she could tuck it into a pocket. Omie was delighted when deer and other wild creatures were drawn toward the music, if she stayed still and only moved as much as it took to play. Music, for her, was the voice of God and was a way to feel a part of Him, though some of the voices raised in praise at church might test that theory.

Today she left the shelter of her tree to walk toward Silvey's folks' farm, something pulling her in that direction. Just past the road leading to Mr. Shaver's fields, Omie felt a tightening in her throat. A gurgling, choking sound came to her.

What is that? There's something over the fence that's in trouble.

She ducked between the barbed wire and saw young Amos Hawthorn lying on his side, gasping and crying. White foam flecked his mouth and cheeks. Omie thought at first he'd been snake bit by one of the timber rattlers that grew as big as a man's leg in these parts. When she called to Amos, he gave her such a look of desperation that she knew there was something more urgent to it. He struggled to speak and Omie leaned in closer to hear him.

"Berries," he whispered. "Sam and Fern."

Omie ran up the drive to where blackberries grew densely by the creek. Beside them, the children were curled up where they'd fallen, berry juice and white foam on their small faces. Flies had already begun to buzz around their mouths and open eyes. Omie said a quick prayer before she ran back to Amos, and pulled him up, half-carrying him toward the field where the workers were chopping weeds in the corn rows.

"What's this?" Mr. Shaver ran out from behind his wagon in the shade where he had a water can and lunch buckets waiting for the mid-day break.

"It's the Hawthorn kids, Mr. Shaver. Somethin' horrible has happened! The two littlest ones are down by the berry patch dead, and I got to get Amos to my mamma before he dies too."

Mr. Shaver stood there looking stunned, and Omie yelled, "Help me git him on the wagon. Please!" After they laid him on the seat, Omie climbed up and grabbed the reins, urging the horses into a gallop while buckets flew everywhere.

"Hey!" Mr. Shaver yelled, but all she heard was the pounding of her heart and the ragged breathing of the boy beside her.

Her mamma was already at the gate waiting when Omie pulled up. Kate took one look at Amos, then told Omie. "Get my deer stone and crush some into powder. Mix it in a cup of water. Hurry!"

Kate carried the boy to the sofa in the front room, laying him gently on his side. She covered him with a heavy blanket for warmth, wiping his face until Omie brought her the grainy- looking water. Together they held Amos up while Kate spooned the liquid down his throat.

"I couldn't crush it any finer mamma, my hands were shaking so!"

"You did good daughter. His throat is pretty closed, but I believe there's room enough to get this down him. I just hope it's enough to draw out the poison. Do you know how long since he ate it?" Kate asked.

"No mamma, but I don't think it was very long." Omie sobbed as she told her mamma about the two little forms lying under the brambles, their hands still full of berries.

They heard a carriage outside and voices. Someone brought Mr. Shaver to the Lee's to retrieve his wagon. Omie heard them asking her daddy to return with them in his own wagon and help bring the children's bodies back to Kate.

Frank stepped up to the screen door. "Kate, I'll be home soon's I can."

Mr. Shaver stuck his head inside to ask about Amos.

Kate walked over to him, looking hard into his eyes. The old man ducked his head, hurried out the door and jumped up on his wagon, taking the reins with shaking hands. She turned back to Omie with a deep sorrow in her eyes and her mouth drawn into a hard line of anger.

"He did this, didn't he Mamma?" Omie asked, already sure of the answer.

"Yes, child. There is evil in this world we can't begin to imagine, and that old man has just delivered his soul to the devil. Well, I reckon we'll know the truth of it soon enough."

Kate sat beside the boy, putting her hand on his trembling chest.

"Only the Lord can decide Amos' fate now. We'll do the best we can, but I expect it will be touch and go. His poor soul may decide it doesn't want to stay in a world that would do such a thing to his baby brother and sister. Since their mamma died, there seems to have been nothin' but hardship and they had little else to start with. You remember Mrs. Hawthorn?"

"Yes ma'am," Omie replied. "I thought when she died, *that* was the saddest thing I ever saw."

Kate sighed as she rose heavily.

Sometime before sundown, Frank returned in the wagon with the two small bodies wrapped in sheets on their daddy's lap. Mr. Hawthorn was in such a deep despair, Kate took the children one by one from him, as he couldn't seem to move from the wagon seat. She laid them on the bed where she and Frank slept and came back out before preparing something for Mr. Hawthorn himself.

"Help him down Frank. He needs to see his boy is still alive. They are going to have to find a way to get through this together if Amos lives."

Kate made the man a cup of strong black coffee with a few drops of St. John's Wort in it to help dull his grief enough to be able to hear her.

"Samuel, you're going to have to sit by this boy's side tonight and give him spoonfuls of this breathing tonic. A little at a time. I'll be nearby if you need me, but most of all what he needs is his daddy's love and prayers. Whatever happened to those little ones was not his fault, and he needs you to tell him so."

Kate squeezed the man's bony shoulder, then stoked the fire for the evening. No one had an appetite, so the girls went on to bed. Frank left to sleep in the barn so Kate could prepare the children for burial in the bedroom.

Omie curled up next to Emmie, crying until she fell into an exhausted sleep. Emmie lay awake all the night stroking her sister's hair as her own tears slipped down to mingle with Omie's on the pillow.

In the night, Amos' eyes fluttered open to see his father looking down at him with such love and sorrow that he thought he must have died and gone on to heaven. His father's rough grizzled face had never shown such a tenderness toward Amos in all his eleven years.

"Oh, son," his daddy cried, as he rocked Amos in his arms. "Oh, son."

Mr. Shaver was found near the grange trying to hop on one of the trains carrying sorghum and corn away. He was so tired from running that he just fell to his knees, confessing everything. He hadn't meant to kill the children, he said, he just wanted them to stop interrupting their daddy's work in his fields. Every day, they came through his land, picking blackberries and making a nuisance of themselves. He'd dusted the berries with arsenic used to kill tobacco worms, thinking it would only make them sick so they wouldn't come around anymore.

Mr. Shaver was taken to the county jail. His nights were filled with nightmares of the Hawthorn children coming to haunt him and his days were filled with the fear of what was to become of him. On his third day behind bars, he asked the sheriff for paper and pen.

"What would you be wanting with that?" The sheriff glared at him.

"I just want to write a letter to Mr. Hawthorn and his boy to tell them how sorry I am, Sheriff. Could I trouble you to take it to them?"

When Amos could breathe well enough to speak, he told them, "Fern and Sam wanted to run ahead and I thought it would be ok, Daddy. I had just got there and ate a few berries when they fell to the ground jerkin around with sumthin' terrible comin' out their mouths. I thought it would be quicker to find somebody if I ran for the road, but I got sick too." He buried his face in his daddy's chest and sobbed, gasping for air.

"Son, I know, and ever'body here knows, it was not your fault. Believe that."

Mr. Hawthorn held the boy in his arms and the family left them alone to grieve.

Sheriff Turner knocked softly at the Lee's door. When Omie answered, he removed his hat and held out the letter.

"It's for the Hawthorns from Shaver."

After she took it, he turned and left quietly. Omie walked over to Mr. Hawthorn and handed him the envelope.

"From Mr. Shaver."

He opened the door of the woodstove and threw it in, unopened, then put his head in his hands.

Sam and Fern were buried next to their mamma in the churchyard. All the field hands and most of the town were there to mourn the senseless deaths of the Hawthorn children. Everyone knew they had not been a problem for their daddy.

Old Mr. Shaver had wanted every ounce of sweat he could wring from his workers, not caring that the children had no one else but their father to look after them. The little food they could buy with their father's wages was supplemented by what they could forage—poke salad, wild onions, berries and fox grapes.

Folks had taken up a collection to have a simple stone made with the children's names on it as well as their mother's. *Sam, Fern, and Ruth Hawthorn*. The monument maker had carved two little lambs over the children's names, with "In God's Hands" inscribed below.

Omie played her harmonica while people sang *Amazing Grace*, then *Closer to Thee.*

These are such somber songs for ones too young to have the stain of sin on them yet.

Then she played a softer, sweeter melody that she'd written in her hollow tree for them. After the last note faded, she felt their little spirits beside her, a small hand in each of her own. As she left the grave side, Omie looked back to see the faintest outlines of the children watching their father and brother walking away, looking as if they wanted to go with them. Slowly, they moved toward the grave where their mother rested and faded away.

Father and son stayed with the Lees long enough for Amos to recover as best he could before they set off walking toward Samuel's sister's place in north Georgia. The Lees tried to get them to rest a while longer, but Mr. Hawthorn said it just wasn't in him to stay. They had buried three of their family in this clay. There was nothing left here for them now but sorrow.

Chapter 6

During a break when all the planting was done, Omie was sent to deliver packages of herbs to her mamma's customers. In the curve of the road ahead, she saw old man Souther walking behind his pet pig Ruby.

Everyone thought the old-timer crazy to go hungry at times when he had a perfectly good side of bacon in front of him wherever he went. Omie knew, though, that deep in the cypress swamp where Mr. Souther lived, Ruby had saved him many a time from the shifting quicksand that could swallow a man bit by bit, sinking him into a certain and solitary death. Though the swamp was dangerous, it kept unwelcome visitors away, and he trusted the pig's sensitive snout, for the wild hogs survived by their ability to avoid sand traps. Mr. Souther had found the little piglet after shooting her mamma one fall day, and she had been with him ever since.

"Mornin' Omie," he said, doffing his hat in her direction. Knowing of her fondness for the wild things of the woods, he sometimes brought her injured birds and other critters. Once, it was a half-grown hawk with a piece of arrow stuck through its wing. She extracted the shaft and cared for the hawk until it was healed enough to fly again.

Ruby allowed Omie to scratch behind her ears. "Where you headed to, Mr. Souther?"

"Ta' get more meal and salt. I reckoned me and Ruby needed ta' git some sunlight on us a'fore we start gettin' mossy as the oaks!" He laughed. "Skeeters don't seem to have taken a break this year, nor the ticks neither. Gonna' be a hot dry one."

"Did you happen to notice any horsetail growing near the swamp, Mr. Souther? Mamma needs some. She's teaching me to become a healer too!"

The pride in Omie's voice made him smile.

"I surely did, Miss Omie, just down that dirt track. It's not too fur a piece."

"We thank you, Mr. Souther. Bye, Ruby!" she called, as the pair ambled off in the direction of town.

Drawing close to the house with her arms full of skinny horsetail stalks, Omie saw her mamma out back hanging wash on the line and went to help pin up the heavy sheets. She could smell lye soap with lavender mixed in. Mamma was always experimenting with her herbs and flowers to get different scents. Omie had the sweetest dreams when she slept beneath the freshly washed, sun drenched sheets.

Today she felt a weighty distraction on her mamma's mind.

"Daughter," Mamma said, "I saw somethin' today. At that crossroads on the way to Miss Lila's there were three male robins fightin' in the road. One pecked another one pure to death, and I got the saddest feeling that it was a sign of somethin' to come. I don't know what or who." She sighed. "Sometimes this knowin' is just short of a curse to me."

They finished hanging the wash in silence and climbed the porch steps. Kate set down the basket and took a seat in the rockers.

"Honey, why don't you get your mouth harp and play a tune to settle me."

Omie pulled the little harmonica out of her pocket and started on a familiar hymn she knew her mamma liked to sing.

Swing low, sweet chariot, comin' for to carry me home.

Kate's premonition at the crossroads proved true in the years following, when the husbands of three of Emmie and Omie's childhood friends were stumbling home from a backwoods roadhouse. The men commenced to arguing over some woman two of them had been carrying on with. Silvey's husband Silas got between them to break it up and was stabbed to death. The men left him by the side of the road where the turkey vultures drew attention to him. They didn't even remember who had done the deed, which they weren't sure was a blessing or a punishment all its own.

After Silas' death, Omie walked through a blur of tears to lay a bunch of flowers at the spot where her schoolmate had died.

Silas, are you still here at the crossroads trying to find your way home?

Omie would encounter many a lost soul throughout her life, wanderers with no idea they had passed out of the world, dwelling in confusion at its edges. Most had some unresolved business or an attachment to a loved one that couldn't let them go. She did her best to soothe these weary spirits, assuring them that it was time to move on to a place of peace, where all would be understood.

Violent deaths had the strongest hold of all, weighing the soul down with anguish. These *shades* appeared in changing hues of cobalt and smoke, trembling in the darkness.

Early that winter, folks started seeing Ruby without old man Souther walking behind her. The pig would be looking for acorns in the cemetery under the shelter of oaks, with a skinny rooster foraging alongside her. A few of the men ventured out to see if they could find the old man's stilted shack, but the quicksand proved too daunting. Finally, they just decided to let him be, as he preferred, figuring he'd succumbed to some mosquito-borne fever or just the ailments of age. There came a time when no one saw Ruby or her cockerel friend again. Years after, when Omie and her mamma walked back from town in the shimmery light of dusk, they would occasionally catch a glimpse of the silvery-gray shades of Ruby and Mr. Souther winding through the cypress knees.

1939

JUNE 18

Things had gotten quiet on the porch. Omie rose and stretched, needing to move her bones after the weight of all these memories.

"Let's get us a glass of cold tea. Emmie, I don't know how we got along before you gifted us that electric icebox."

They slowly gathered themselves and moved into the house.

Bartie stood at the sink washing dishes. Lilly went to help her mamma, telling her she'd missed out on so many stories. Bartie just turned to give her a small smile and handed Lilly a drying cloth.

Bartie had come home for her daddy's funeral all cinched up tight, with storms brewing behind her eyes. Omie ached for her second oldest. She imagined all the emotions fighting to surface, and Bartie doing her best to keep them contained.

Time. The best we can do is give her time. Her big sister is the one she'll unravel those feelings with. She always did.

At that moment, Omie's oldest daughter Ada Kate came through the door with her brood. The children clustered around their grandma, smothering her with hugs and kisses.

"Oh Lord, young'uns! Let me look at you all. Just so clean and shiny!"

Ada Kate gave her mamma a kiss and said, "That was no small feat, let me tell you! Like catchin' frogs. Soon's I put one in the tub, another one jumps out."

Omie laughed. "Ya'll mind your mamma, hear? Now why don't you take your cousin Lilly out and show her around?"

"Will you tell us more stories later, Grandmamma? I have a lot of catchin' up to do!" Lilly cast a sideways look at her mamma.

Ada's oldest, Tess, looked at Omie. "I don't even know how you and grandaddy met. "Was it really him you saw in the well that day?"

"Yes, Hon. Later."

Tess grabbed Lilly's hand and pulled her outside. Her little sisters and brothers ran to the rope swing under the old oak.

Ada Kate stepped in to take her niece's place at the sink. Her sister's presence seemed to quiet the crackling lights around Bartie. Omie watched them together, knowing that much more was passing between them than housework.

"Where is everybody, Mamma?" Ada Kate asked.

"They'll be here directly. Everybody needed to go their own way for a while after the service. Be with their own thoughts about your daddy's passing. Your brothers will come to eat up all this food, believe me."

Omie looked at the bowls and platters covering the sideboard. *Funny how the occasion of a death can bring out a person's appetite. I reckon the body wants to remind us that we are still here, upright and taking nourishment, as they say.*

"Best put on a big pot of coffee, it's likely going to be a long evening," Bartie muttered.

In no time, Lilly and Tess tired of watching the young ones and returned.

"Is there enough of that tea for us, Grandmamma?" Lilly sat down next to Omie. "We're hot. Would you tell us some more stories?"

"About you and Grandaddy," Tess prompted.

Ada Kate caught her sister's eye and said, "Walk down to the house with me. You've never seen it and I know James is eager to say hello. He's seeing to a new calf that chose this mornin' of all days to come into the world."

Bartie dried her hands and walked out the door, linking arms with Ada Kate as they headed down the field road.

Chapter 7

1905

At sixteen, Nate had finally endured enough of watching his mamma disappear a little more each day, like an old flour-sack shirt washed thread-bare. The man who was and wasn't his father had beaten them both down to the point where he had to make his break.

If I stayed any longer, I'd have to kill the man, and where would that get me?

Deep in the Georgia night, he'd thrown on his hat and overalls and slipped away, taking his only possessions: an old Tree Brand pocket knife and a broken pocket watch he'd had since he could remember. Nate had set off in a generally eastern direction following deer trails and dirt roads until he'd lost all sense of familiarity with his surroundings.

If there is hope of getting anything from this life, it is not to be found where I come from.

The three days he'd been traveling began to merge into a haze like heat coming off the road. The midday sun was high overhead, seeming to burn up all the air around him.

Up ahead, he saw a man with a pair of piebald mules wrestling to pull a pine stump from a newly cut plot of ground.

"'Excuse me, sir. I'm wonderin' could you use a hand there? All I'd ask is a cool drink of water and any leftover lunch you might spare."

Frank Lee leaned back on the traces, signaling the mules to stop. He looked at the bone-thin boy standing on the road.

He might not be of much help, but he could surely use something to eat. The sooner the better.

Frank wiped his face with a worn bandana. "Well, I reckon we could all use a break. This stump ain't goin' nowhere anytime soon."

He turned the mules out to graze by the roadside and directed Nate toward a stand of sweet gums by a small creek.

"There's a spring yonder, drink your fill. It's one of the few that hasn't dried up in this blasted drought."

Nate found the spring and splashed cool water on his face and neck after a long drink. Frank watched him, noting the lean, hard muscles on the young man's body. He was used to hard work, that was clear, but hadn't reaped much from it, judging by his gaunt frame.

Here's a hard story. Not much of a child in this boy.

Frank opened his lunch bucket and portioned up the beans, ham, and cornbread Kate had packed for him, giving Nate the greater share.

Nate sat down, looked hungrily at the food, then up at Frank.

"Go ahead and eat," Frank said. "You'll need it for the job ahead. There's a stump to pull for near 'bout every bite. I cain't hardly eat in this heat."

They worked in tandem long into the afternoon in comfortable silence, broken only by an occasional click of tongue to signal the mules and the jingle of harness.

Frank had managed to coax the boy's name from between mouthfuls of food.

"Nathaniel Green Silar, sir. Folks just call me Nate."

The girls will get the rest of his story out of the boy, I reckon. No denying those females anything they want. Kate will know it all in a heartbeat anyway. Damndest thing, that Knowin' of hers. Good thing I'm an honest man.

Toward evening, Kate looked out the window for the girls.

Funny how two human beings from the same womb could be so different.

Emmie came into the world looking affronted at her circumstances, like she'd bought the wrong train ticket. Omie, on the other hand, was maybe too much like Kate. Her youngest daughter seemed happy in her lot, but would soon know more about people and the sorrows of this world than she might want.

Kate could see the spark of recognition in Omie's eyes when someone laid a hand on her shoulder or hugged her. It was as if she had the knowing of everyone and everything bottled up inside her, waiting to be seen as soon as a physical connection was made. But over time, she would have seen enough that experience and common sense would blur the lines of intuition, and Omie would just know things with no contact at all. Kate remembered how it had been so for herself.

Round about dark, she slid the biscuits out of the oven and placed them on the table. Out the door, Kate saw Frank putting up the mules with a strange boy at his side. Slight but tall, the young man tended to the animals in the lot with a practiced hand, seeming perfectly at home with Frank.

She got that familiar tingle in her spine and temples. Her heart felt weighted with a dark inevitability. Just then, the girls came from the tobacco field, and Kate saw Omie catch hold of the fence rail and stop dead still. She couldn't hear what Emmie said to her sister, but it was plainly upsetting.

"Omie," Emmie gasped. "That's the fella you saw in the well, the one you're meant to marry!"

Omie turned away from her sister and ran to the chicken house.

Emmie soon found her in the coop with a chicken in her lap.

"Honey, you got to come out of here," she said gently. "You can't hide forever. What's to be will be. If he's not what you want, you can still come with me to Savannah."

Omie considered Emmie's advice, then reluctantly set the chicken down and crawled out of the coop. The girls slowly made their way to the back porch to wash up for supper.

Frank introduced the boy as they gathered at the table. Omie fell into an uneasy shyness around Nate, wondering if he would be with them for a while. She didn't know where to rest her eyes in his presence, though he didn't seem to take much notice. In the days that followed, he became like a familiar but distant melody she couldn't quite name. Or a dream nearly remembered. He disquieted her, but tugged at her curiosity as well.

Nate watched a hawk circle over the chicken coop. He'd finished helping Mr. Lee with the cows and had been washing up on the back porch when he heard the hawk's high keening.

Outside the chicken pen, a young pullet was trying to find its way back in, not smart enough to remember how it got out in the first place. Just as the hawk made its dive, Nate jumped down from the porch, grabbed a rock, and with a sure shot, clipped the hawk on the back of its neck before it got its talons extended. With a squawk of indignation, the hawk swerved, then flapped up into the branches of a nearby pine. Nate grabbed the pullet and shoved it through the coop's door.

Omie stood inside the kitchen, skimming cream off the top of the day's milk for Daddy's coffee. She did not understand how hot coffee could cool a body down in this heat, but he swore it was true. Nate's actions caught her eye and she moved to the door, watching him rescue the young bird.

This boy might not lay claim to much in this world, but I reckon a kind heart toward the lesser creatures makes him worth more than some.

The tightness in her stomach lessened a bit.

As the weeks went by, the family grew accustomed to the addition of Nate at their table. He'd made himself comfortable in the barn loft and asked for little else. There seemed to be no question of him staying for as long as he wished, for the young man certainly was a help to Frank. The addition of another male seemed pleasing as well.

Chapter 8

1906

Frank looked to the sky for signs of what the day might bring. He'd felt an odd change in the air. A salty wind blew inland from the coast and a seagull or two rode it west. He wondered if this was just a storm brewing up, or a portent of the start of hurricane season.

Twice in his life Frank had seen the power of hurricanes.

When he was eight, the first of them spun off a twister that lifted his family's house right off its foundation and set it down five feet away. Not a bale of hay nor a stalk of corn was disturbed. It took him and his brother Thomas all day to round up the chickens and put them in a makeshift pen, their coop having been set about halfway up in an old live oak. Afterwards, the boys would hide out in the tree-coop sometimes when their folks were looking for them.

Six years later, a hurricane spared the farm again but took his fool brother Thomas, who had gone fishing out near Tybee Island. His body was never found, just the oars and pieces of the boat. Frank was left to tend the farm with his younger brothers and sisters with little time for grieving.

He missed Thomas yet.

I guess the dead are always with us. I wonder if there's good fishin' in heaven.

He was pulled from his memories when he saw Nate leading the mules to the barn.

"I'm not likin' the looks of that sky," Nate said. "The colors are all wrong and there's not a bird to be heard."

Frank looked to the west where a bank of dark clouds was lumbering toward them, casting the orange color of the clay onto the light, giving everything a strange glow.

"Best let them know at the house that we might be in for bad weather," Frank said. "Make ready to git in the root cellar."

Frank put the mules and cows in the barn, then stored everything that might blow away from a heavy wind inside as well. He took one last look around, making sure the doors were securely latched.

Kate and the girls walked by carrying water and kerosene lamps to the cellar.

It would be a tight fit. With the water table so high, Frank had only been able to dig the cellar deep enough to stoop inside. Still, there was enough room to hold five adults and, he suspected, whatever critters Omie had attached to her today.

As the wind picked up and scattered raindrops began to fall, Frank called, "Hurry, get inside!"

Lightning had begun to scratch at the sky with veins of horizontal and vertical streaks. After all were accounted for, Frank pulled on the door, fighting the wind. He heard the bleating of a goat and suddenly Omie was on her feet headed up the steps, trying to push past him. He grabbed her and she shouted.

"No, Daddy, that's Mollie's kid. They'll both get hurt outside and she won't go in the barn without him!"

Frank shook his head and nearly got back out when a gust slammed the heavy door against his leg. He went down with a cry, unable to push the door open to free himself.

Nate put his back to the heavy wood. They all reached up and pushed where they could, shoving outward. Suddenly it flew open, causing Frank to fall to the dirt floor, holding his leg in pain.

Nate ran out to get the little goat, slapped Mollie on the rump and shoved her toward the barn. He handed the shaking kid to Omie, then managed to get the door closed when the wind shifted.

Kate lit a lamp and inspected Frank's leg. It wasn't good.

Just below the knee, the bone was protruding and he was losing a good bit of blood. She took off her shawl to bind the open wound, then looked up at Omie.

"Here, hold this lamp. I got to get this bone back in place. Best do it now so I can stop the bleeding. Nate, hold him. It's gonna hurt like the dickens. Emmie, stop cryin' and get me that jug of hard cider hid back in the corner behind those jugs of tea. Yes Frank, I knowed it was there. Now take a deep drought for me."

Frank took the jug with a sheepish look on his pale face and did as he was told.

"At least it ain't corn likker," Kate remarked.

Nate and Emmie looked away as Kate positioned herself to set the bone. Omie stared in fascination as her mamma's sure hands found their places.

"All right, on the count of three," she said. "One, two," and there was a loud crack. Frank screamed as the bone slid into place.

"Damn, woman!" Frank panted, "I thought you could count!"

They positioned Frank more comfortably on the floor, and Emmie covered him with her shawl.

Kate bound up the wound as best she could. Finally, the bleeding slowed to a seep. She moved so Frank could rest his head on her lap, running her gentle fingers through his hair until his breathing slowed and became regular.

Omie left the lamp beside them and crawled to the corner. She gathered the baby goat into her lap, stroking it much like Mamma caressed her daddy.

Nate sat beside her, and in a few minutes said, "I never thought I'd wish I was a goat." She smiled at him, thanking him for saving her daddy and the goats, then settled back against his shoulder.

Outside, the wind screamed. They could hear things hitting the wooden door as time passed with no way to mark it. Suddenly, a dead calm descended.

"It's the eye, children. We got to stay put. Everybody ok?" Kate asked.

Shortly, the howling winds soon resumed with greater force. Talking was not possible above the noise, so each turned to their own thoughts.

Finally, calm descended once more. The four of them slowly unwound their stiff limbs, then pushed the door open. Omie and Kate helped Nate carry Frank up the steps, moving him as gently as was possible. There was no way to avoid causing pain. Every cry broke their hearts.

Emmie kept saying, "Just a little further Daddy," as if he didn't know where he was.

When Frank was settled into bed under the ministrations of his wife and daughters, Nate went out to assess the damage. A big tree was down in the pasture. Pieces of tin were torn from the barn's roof. A tornado, spun off from the hurricane, had tossed the outhouse to the very end of a wide flattened swath running through the corn.

Nate returned to the house, reporting the damage. Frank grinned slowly through the haze of laudanum Kate had given him and said, "I reckon it's time to dig a new hole anyhow."

In the days that followed the storm, it became apparent that Frank's leg was going to take quite some time to heal, so the bulk of farm work would go to Nate. Kate and Emmie got the garden replanted. Most of the damage was due to hail. A few tomato plants, tied to the fence, remained unbroken. The pea brush, set for young plants to climb, needed to be replaced, but downed branches were plentiful.

Omie worked side by side with Nate in the fields, hilling up the rows of corn that were salvageable, replanting what was not. The tobacco plants were mostly spared. The young people road mules down the rows, shaking sacks filled with arsenic powder over the leaves to kill hornworms.

As soon as Frank was able to get around with a crutch, he spent days on the porch repairing harnesses and helping Kate. She found him busywork he could do outside the kitchen, where he was more hindrance than help.

His pain gave way to impatience, so he figured out a way to mount the mule. After that, he took to riding out of a morning, coming back at dinner worn out but far more tolerable.

Chapter 9

Kate placed a knot of fat lighter under the wash pot and laid kindling, plus a few small logs, on top. Once the fat lighter caught, she went to the well to fill buckets for washing. She poured a dipper of cold water over her head, then looked up, noticing Omie and Nate talking by the feed lot.

Omie certainly has changed in these past few months since the boy came. Was it a good idea to let him stay? It isn't that he's done anything to earn my distrust. Lord knows he's been a help to Frank, such that he more than pays for his keep.

But he had difficulty meeting her eyes and, polite as he was, she felt the slow smoldering anger of a beaten animal nearly emanating from his skin. Nate was beginning to fill out some, looking more like a man than a boy now. This hadn't escaped Emmie's notice, and had Omie, by turns, giggly and moody. Omie had recently got her monthly menses, which worried Kate considerably. She sighed.

I'll have to talk to Frank about making sure there's no idle time for these two to sneak off alone.

Emmie came to help, taking one of the buckets from Kate. She motioned toward Nate and Omie, saying, "You might as well try to stop a runaway mule as to keep those two apart. Did she ever tell you that he's the one she saw in the well?"

Kate shook her head.

"She wasn't too sure about him then, Mamma. Looks like that's changed though."

Turning away before Emmie caught sight of her tears, Kate stirred the heavy laundry with a paddle.

It's a wonder how childhood folds its wings so quickly when love comes, setting free a different bird altogether.

She thought of her own courtship and marriage to Frank. They had been blessed with a good life together, though sometimes she regretted not being able to give him more children. Especially a boy to carry on his name.

I might have liked to have had a few more carefree years. Maybe even gone as far as Charleston or Atlanta when I was young and pretty. Well, maybe Emmie will get to experience some exciting things if we can save enough money to get her into secretarial school in Savannah.

On the following day, as Frank was washing up on the porch, Kate stepped outside to throw out a pan of dishwater. He said slowly, "I think it's time we talked to them young'uns about marryin', Kate. I got a feelin' if we don't do it soon, Omie's goin' to end up with the big belly. I cain't watch them all the time."

She replied softly, "I know we were married at their age, but it feels too soon. Omie's still fresh as a kid in this big old world. Seems too young for the things she'll face with a husband and children, but then, she knows a lot secondhand from helping me tend to families. And from the *Sight*. It's just...I don't know Frank, what do we really know about that boy? There's bad blood twixt him and his family, that's plain."

"Yeah," Frank nodded, "you ain't got to have the *Sight* to see that." He dried his hands and neck. Just then, Emmie, Nate, and Omie came into view. "Let's give it till the end of the season. They're too busy to get into much mischief yet."

Nate and Omie moved in a world of their own, walking out to work in the hazy morning light and returning in the evenings as the sun drew particles of red dust into the air, casting the fields and trees into an incandescent green. In between, they came to know each other, weaving bits of their past along with their shared days like a nest around them. Omie gathered the dark strands of Nate's sorrow, tucking them in along with the bright colors of her joy.

They filled this nest with their love of the land, the smells of hot earth and sweat, the sound of June bugs buzzing about their heads, and all manner of snakes, birds and four legged creatures, tempting them away from their chores.

He made a scarecrow in the cornfield, then she dressed it, using a stolen pair of Emmie's proud bloomers and an old shirt Nate had outgrown. Omie also wove a hat for it out of palmetto fronds while they ate their lunch beneath the trees. At last, they pronounced it the silliest scarecrow in Effingham County. It was good to hear Nate laugh. She found ways to weave his laughter into that nest too. By summer's end, their familiarity led to the touch of hands, the brush of lips on cheek. Finally, the temptation to lay down in this nest and know the mysteries of each other became too strong to resist.

Nate stroked her hair and said, "I'm talkin' to your folks tonight, darlin'. We're gettin' married and that's that."

They came back from the fields a little early, anxious that they might lose their nerve. Frank and Kate were sitting on the porch with glasses of tea, shelling the last of the butter beans.

Omie sat by her mamma and picked up an apron full of beans while Nate stood turning his hat in his hands.

"Mr. and Mrs. Lee, Omie and me want to ask your permission to become man and wife. I know we're young and all, but I believe I've shown I can work hard and take care of her. I will always show her the respect you give your missus, Sir, and Ma'am, I love her with all my heart. We just cain't see why to wait any longer."

Kate looked at Omie, who blushed and tucked her chin, signaling that they could, indeed, not wait any longer.

Frank gazed at Nate for a full measure and said, "Have a seat, son. Omie's mamma and me have know'd this was comin' for a while. We appreciate all you've done here and we can see how it is with you two. You're already like family to us, Nate, but we don't know nothin' about you, who your folks are, where you come from. Don't you think it's about time you told us?"

Nate looked up and blew out a breath. Omie and Kate could see prickly lights dancing around him now. Kate went into the kitchen to fetch them all tea, as it looked like a long, difficult tale was about to be told. She put lemon balm in it to soothe the spirit, and a bit of mullein for courage. Emmie sat down quietly at Omie's side.

Nate leaned on the porch rail across from Omie.

"Well," he began, "I guess you know my full name is Nathaniel Green Silar. But the man who raised me, if you can call it raisin'—more like I was a dog he liked to kick around—was not my real daddy. My mamma is named Kate, like you, ma'am. She's a real purty woman, or at least she was. Mr. Silar beat her down something awful too." He turned his face away.

"I never could figure out what I done wrong until I heard fellas at the co-op talkin' when they didn't know I was near. Seems there was a rich man in town who was sweet on Mamma. To get Mr. Silar out of the way so he could have her, the man made up a story that Mr. Silar had stole one of his pigs. He had some men bury the entrails on our farm to prove it. Mamma's husband was arrested, then put in jail for a year. Meantime, Mamma was caring for Mr. Silar's elderly mother, without much to get by on."

A sneer had come to Nate's's face, and the prickly lights buzzed stronger around his head.

"So, this *Mr. Moneypants*, out of the *kindness of his heart,* took care of them, making sure they had food and a hired man to keep up the place. I guess Mamma felt she had to give him what he wanted or they'd starve. Anyways, about nine months later, here I come. When Mr. Silar got out of jail, I guess I was a real slap in his face. Ever since then, he's been a mean drunk, and anythin' Mamma and I put on our backs or in our bellies was up to us. One day I just couldn't take it no more. Mamma said she didn't have it in her to leave. Besides, who would take care of old Mrs. Silar? My hateful 'step-daddy' sure wouldn't."

Nate stood and looked at the Lees.

"There you have it. I'm a bastard with not much to offer but a strong back and a will to do everythin' I can to give Omie a good life. Y'all have been mighty good to me and I don't want to repay you with sorrow, but Omie and me mean to get married with your blessin's, or set out on our own."

Everything was quiet for a moment. A crow called from the pines. A breeze carried the scent of night jasmine, just beginning to open up its blooms around the porch posts. It seemed the weight of Nate's words settled like a mantle on all of them, as much what wasn't said as what was.

Frank stood up, leaning on his cane, and said, "Come on, son, let's have us a little walk."

They went down the steps, heading toward the root cellar.

"Mhm," Kate murmured, "A real *little* walk," but a smile tugged at her mouth. She put down the pan of beans and turned to Omie. "Baby girl, are you sure this is what you want? You've got a few years yet before you're an old maid."

Omie replied, "I know, Mamma, but we are set on this course. I feel it in my bones. It might as well be now. Daddy needs us, and I don't want to be anywhere but here with you, so please say it will be all right with you both."

"You know I can't predict for you, child, but I have a feelin' you're going to have a hard row to hoe. I reckon all marriages take some work, though, and I'd love to be able to hold and tend those sweet babies. Reckon I'll get my chance next spring."

With that she got up to fetch them some more tea, verbena in it this time, for a hopeful future. Omie took her sister's hand and sat there, with her heart soaring up into the darkening Georgia sky.

Chapter 10

The wedding ceremony would take place that fall after the crops were in. A brush arbor was built for them in a sunny spot near the river. Nate didn't have much truck with churches, but he had to consent to a preacher.

"Those churchy folks never showed no Christian concern for me and Mamma when we was goin' without. I don't reckon I need their blessin' on this."

As dawn brushed the sky azure and amber, Omie got up to bathe and wash her hair. Her daddy had heated a tub of water before he went down to the barn to give the women some privacy. Her mamma washed and rinsed Omie's hair in a sweet-smelling mixture of steeped herbs and flowers she'd picked just for today. The scent reminded Omie of all the walks they'd shared collecting things for Mamma's healing potions, and for the sachets she slipped into their cedar hope chests. Daddy had made one for each of the girls when they were born.

Kate had sewn linens and stacked them neatly inside the chests for the girls to take to their own homes one day. For this special day, she'd made a lovely nightgown for Omie out of soft cotton and bits of lace collected over the years. The back fastened with mother of pearl buttons, and the bodice was decorated in patterns of wildflowers sewn with tiny stitches. Kate lifted it gently from the chest and presented it to her daughter. Omie gasped, tracing the gown's delicate embroidery with her fingertips. Speechless, she buried her face in her mamma's lap and wept.

"Now, now, child," Mamma crooned. "You deserve to have somethin' purty in this life. I only wish it could show how much I love you. You are my own heart's darling girl and ever will be. Now dry them eyes and let me comb out your hair."

Being the first to marry, Omie would wear the dress her mamma was married in, *something old,* with a little letting out of the seams to allow for the slight swelling around her waist. When her hair had dried, Omie slipped on the wedding dress and Emmie's white Sunday dress shoes. *Something borrowed.* Taking a deep breath, she gazed at herself in the mirror, hardly believing the reflection looking back.

Emmie twined one of her ribbons into Omie's hair, *something blue,* along with the tiny pale blooms of joe-pye weed, purple ironweed, and yellow daisies. In her hands, Omie would carry the loveliest of mamma's roses, their stems wrapped with a bit of lace taken from the hem of an old gown. Nate had carved a tiny wooden heart and strung it on a fine cord, which he slipped over her head before they parted for bed the night before. *Something new.*

Kate held Omie close for a moment, then looked deeply into her eyes. She asked, "Now, is there anything you want to ask me before I go?"

Omie blushed and assured her mamma that she was ready.

When Kate opened the door and stepped outside, Omie caught a glimpse of her daddy waiting for her.

She closed her eyes and took a few breaths, checked herself in the mirror once more, then walked to the door. Stepping out into the morning light, Omie tucked her hand under her daddy's waiting arm.

"You are the most beautiful bride I ever saw," he whispered. "Don't tell your mamma I said that, but it's true. If ever he don't treat you right, if ever you need me, you just send word and your daddy will be right there. I promise."

Frank stopped and kissed her forehead before walking her up to stand beside Nate.

Nate was stunned when he saw Omie walking toward him. She was radiant in the clear fall sunlight.

Will this truly be my wife?

The minister began to speak. When he asked who gave this woman to be married, Frank looked firmly into his soon to be son-in-law's eyes, then answered.

"Her mamma and I do." He kissed his daughter on the cheek and took his seat beside Kate.

Nate began to weep quietly. He tried with all his might to stop the tears, but they kept on coming. Omie took his hands in hers as they were asked to repeat their vows, sending him all the calming energy her love could carry.

"Nate Silar, do you take this woman to be your lawfully wedded wife?"

"Yessir. Yessir, I do."

"Naomi Lee, do you take this man to be your lawfully wedded husband?"

"For always."

As they kissed, a cheer went up and the young couple were surrounded by well-wishers. The fiddler struck up a waltz, leading Nate and Omie into their very first dance together.

It was a glorious day. The fields were stubbled with gold, and the fences were lined with wild daisies and purple butterfly weed. Tables were set up, laden with the best of the harvest. Bowls of butterbeans, squash, and greens cooked with ham hocks, sat beside platters piled high with fried chicken, cracklin' cornbread, and buttermilk biscuits. Crocks of fresh butter nestled up to jars of homemade jams. The last of summer's bright red tomatoes lay sliced and sprinkled with a liberal dose of salt and pepper.

A whole separate table boasted the apple and sweet potato pies ladies had baked, trying their best not to suffer too much the sin of pride. Even the poorest among them contributed a shoo-fly pie made from the year's sorghum crop.

A pig had been cooked in the ground all night, tended by the young men who'd tried to cajole Nate into sipping some celebratory whiskey. He'd thanked them, but said he'd been around more of that in his lifetime than he liked to recall. They good-naturedly offered a toast to him anyway, clapping him on the back.

Omie thought of her daddy's words many times as the years went by, wishing sometimes that he had lived long enough to fulfill his promise. Still, just the memory of him carried her through the hard spells.

1939

JUNE 18

'Aunt' Phoebee, Omie's dear friend and neighbor, came walking down the hill to join the family.

"Hey there, ladies. What kind of yarns are y'all tellin' these young'uns? If they been talkin' 'bout me, girls, don't you believe a word of it."

Tess scooted over to make room at the table. "Come sit with us. Grandma just told us how Grandaddy found her."

"Oh Grandmamma, that was so romantic!" Lilly declared.

"Y'all are just a pair of silly geese!" Omie laughed.

Emmie smiled at her sister. "It was a lovely ceremony. Your grandmamma was beautiful, and your grandaddy was a handsome boy. They were both just children, really."

"I gained a husband and lost my sister not long after," Omie groused.

"You did not lose me!" Emmie gazed out at the back door. "I was hardly grown myself the day I learned about the opportunity in Savannah. Remember? You and Mamma were out there hanging up laundry behind the old house."

"I do," Omie replied. "Like to have broke my heart. Mamma's too."

Emmie squeezed her hand.

"Dang, I never heard any of this, girls. It was before my time." Phoebee looked at Emmie and grinned. "I was around for Caleb an' Emmie's courtin' days though."

Lilly cried, "Tell us, Aunt Emmie! Please?"

"Oh, it was so long ago . . ."

"By the time you came back from Savannah to visit, both our lives were different," Omie said quietly.

"Yes, you were so busy becoming a mamma, you didn't visit me for the longest time."

Lilly stared pointedly at her great-aunt, and Emmie began.

Chapter 11

1907

Emmie came back from New Abercorn flushed and soaked through her good cotton dress, which was so unlike her that Omie wondered what trouble her sister might have run into on the road.

"You all right, Emmie?" she asked.

"I'm fine, I'm fine. Where's Mamma?"

"Out back hanging up sheets. What...?" But Emmie was out the door before Omie could finish.

Emmie found her mother elbows deep in laundry, humming a tune around the clothes pins in her mouth. Kate took in Emmie's breathless agitation and stopped to remove the pins.

"Why child," she said. "What has got you in such a state?"

"Well Mamma, you know Mrs. O'Dell at the dry goods store has a sister in Savannah, right?"

Kate smiled, thinking of all the times Mrs. O'Dell had made certain that whenever Kate was in earshot, she heard all the latest news of the well-to-do sister who had 'married her a doctor and owned her own business in Savannah'.

"Mhmm," Kate responded, turning back to the laundry. She placed the pins back in her mouth now that she knew no trouble had followed Emmie home.

"Well, Mrs. O'Dell said that her sister wants to find a young woman to train as help with her millinery business. Says the job comes with room and board above the shop, and a small stipend as well. Her sister saw some of the needlework I did for Mrs. O'Dell, when she was last here for a visit, and told her to speak to me. I really want to do this, Mamma, it would be like getting paid to go to school! You and daddy wouldn't have to help me at all like you would if I went to the secretarial school. I know I'd be good at this, Mamma. She sews the latest fashions and makes the most beautiful hats, I'm told. She ships them all the way to New York City. Oh please, Mamma, you got to say it's all right and convince Daddy to say so too!"

Emmie was out of breath and so exhausted with excitement that she sat right down on the ground at her mamma's feet. She saw Omie then, just on the other side of the clothesline, with sad, damp eyes.

"Omie, come sit by me." Emmie held out her hand. Omie took it, sitting down quietly and looking at the ground. "Be happy for me honey, you knew this was going to come someday. It's just a bit sooner than we thought. You have a husband beside you now, you'll hardly miss me."

"When does this woman need an answer from you, daughter?" Kate asked softly.

"She would like me to start in a week if I could," Emmie said. "The holiday season will be here in a few months. All the ladies there in Savannah want new dresses for parties and dances."

Emmie turned to her sister. "Maybe you all could come visit me and see the Christmas decorations down on Victory Drive. Mrs. O'Dell got to go last year and said it was the most beautiful sight she'd ever seen!"

"Well, one thing at a time, girls," their mamma said. "I cain't promise your daddy will cotton to the idea of you leavin' us so soon, Emmie, but I will do my best. We know you want to go darlin', but we'll need to talk with this lady. We need to know what kind of place you'll be living and working in. Hush now, I know you might not want us tagging along to see you off to your new life, but we'll not feel easy about it until we see for ourselves. Besides, it's been many a-year since I been to the city. Maybe we all need a treat."

Emmie jumped up and hugged her mamma so hard the pins popped out of Kate's mouth. She ran to the house, feet barely touching the ground.

Omie looked at her mamma and saw the same loss in her eyes.

"I know, child. I know," Kate murmured.

Nate stayed to tend the farm while Kate, Frank, and Omie accompanied Emmie to her new destination. Frank borrowed a buggy from one of the neighbors so as not to mortify Emmie by arriving in Savannah in the farm wagon. It was a pleasant day with just a touch of fall in the air and a recent rain had calmed the dust of the road. They shared a lunch along the way that Kate had made for them. Emmie was too excited to take more than a few mouthfuls.

Omie was quiet for most of the trip, but when signs of the city started coming into view, she couldn't help but catch some of Emmie's excitement.

At night it must all seem like something out of a storybook.

The homes were lovely. Cobblestone streets outlined lush parks laid out in a series of squares in the middle of the city. The arching necks of gas lights stood sentry over walkways. Wrought iron gates separated private gardens from passersby.

"This is it, Daddy!" Emmie could hardly resist jumping from the buggy before it had fully stopped, but reminded herself that she must comport herself in the manner of a city woman now.

They stopped in front of a two-story building with a glass-fronted shop at the street level. Omie marveled at the dresses in the windows.

Oh my! How many yards of fancy material and lace did each dress take to make?

Tiny buttons and glass beads adorned the bodices. There were shoes with elegant purses to match and hats of the most astounding varieties.

I know this is where you belong, Emmie. But how do I let you go?

A handsome woman opened the door and smiled up at the family. "Why, you must be Mr. and Mrs. Lee. And you, of course, are Emmie! So glad you were able to come. This must be your younger sister, Omie. My own sister has told me much about you both. I'm Elizabeth Campbell. Please, everyone, come into the store and I'll have some tea brought to us."

Frank eased his way down from the buggy and assisted Kate, then the girls. Omie thought he seemed a bit lost and unsure of himself, faced with all this fanciness and three women-folk to contend with.

A young woman with caramel colored skin and dark eyes came down the stairs at the back of the shop, carrying tea and pastries. They all settled at a table in the corner to be served. Frank looked too big for the delicate chair, and Omie loved him all the more for his vulnerability.

"Everyone, this is Maizie. She and her husband Thomas take care of the house and everything else around this place." Mrs. Campbell put a hand on Maizie's arm. "I don't know how we'd manage without them."

Maizie patted Elizabeth's hand and then offered hers to each of the family as they introduced themselves.

The Lees talked for nearly an hour with Mrs. Campbell, who excused herself from time to time to attend a customer. Emmie's eyes followed the woman wherever she went, taking in her mannerisms, the way she put the ladies at ease and inspired their confidence.

Kate looked at Frank and an unspoken approval passed between them.

He said, "Well, I guess we should be getting back on the road if we're to get home before dark." Frank went out to the buggy to unload Emmie's trunk while Kate and Omie said goodbye to her. Kate thanked Mrs. Campbell for giving Emmie this opportunity.

"Please know that I will take good care of your daughter, Mr. and Mrs. Lee, and I will make sure she writes you regularly."

She looked into Omie's eyes and touched her cheek. "I know how hard it is to miss your only sister, child, but it's not so far away after all. I promise I'll bring her with me when I come to visit my own sister."

Emmie hugged her family, then stood with Mrs. Campbell in the doorway, waving goodbye. Omie turned around to look at them for as long as she could, then settled into her own thoughts as Savannah faded from sight.

"Well, she seems like a right kind woman." Frank said and reached over to pat Kate's hand.

Kate smiled up at him with wet eyes and replied, "I know she'll be fine. I just miss her already."

Me too.

Omie knew that something had already changed. The Emmie they'd just left behind would not be the same one that came to visit.

Chapter 12

Kate felt Emmie's absence every day, but knew she should feel happy for her daughter most of all. Keeping busy with customers and potions filled the time, so the ache in her heart did not rule her thoughts.

On a lingering fall day, she walked home in the early evening after tending several neighbors. Some needed a bit of her potions. Some, just the touch of her healing hands to give them ease. Often as not, the goods she was given as payment went to another neighbor in need along the way, but Kate believed that she would be provided for when she had needs of her own. It was the natural way of things. She'd been fortunate to have such a good life thus far, much better than many folks.

The summer had been busy, delivering seven new babies in the community. Most were fairly easy births but one had been stillborn. The infant had been a tiny little thing, due to lack of enough food to keep the mamma and baby both alive. A shame, really, that the family didn't let anyone know how bad things were on their hardscrabble farm. Everyone fell on lean times sooner or later. It was a farmer's fate. Folks were willing to lend a hand if they could.

This baby had died for the sin of pride.

She sighed and hung her bonnet up on a peg by the door. Her last visit that day had been to old Grady Rhymes' house. His land bordered theirs to the south, nearer the river, where the bottom land was rich and it was easy to get water to crops. Nate had occasionally helped Mr. Rhymes in his fields as the widower grew less able to do all the work himself. Less and less of his fields were planted as time went by. Nate couldn't stand to see so much fertile land go fallow, so at the end of his and Frank's long days, he would go over to work Mr. Rhymes' fields for half-shares.

The Rhymes had not been blessed with children, none that lived at least. The last baby had taken the life of his wife Sarah, too. The infant was a change of life baby, one more attempt to fill their empty arms.

The bereaved man never remarried, just pulled deeper into himself and only spoke to the Lees when they stopped by with food to share. His pride fell quickly before the likes of Kate's cooking.

When Kate had walked up to the porch, she saw Mr. Rhymes sitting in his rocking chair, hands on top of his cane. Though it was only mid-afternoon, he looked as if he'd been of a mind to return to the fields, but could only get as far as the porch, and settled for gazing forlornly out at them instead.

"I cain't go it no more, Kate," he said. "I fell out by the hog pen yesterday, and today I feel like every bone in my old body hurts. Thank the Lord I went down outside the pen or them hogs'd have had me for supper!"

He looked across his land and toward the barn with a defeated expression on his face. "This place is all I ever knowed. I was borned here. My daddy cleared every tree and stump from those fields. He built this house out of lumber he milled hisself. And Sarah is here. I just cain't see as how I can leave it. Besides, I got no kin left to take me in. I just don't know what I'm gonna do."

They sat and rocked awhile, listening to the mourning doves coo in their nests under the eaves, until the orange glow of dusk hung in the air.

Finally, Kate said, “Let me talk to Frank and the young’un’s, Grady. Between us we’ll figure somethin’ out.”

At suppertime Nate and Omie came through the back door to find the stove cold and Kate and Frank deep in discussion at the kitchen table. Her parents looked up and motioned for the young people to join them.

By the end of the week, Mr. Rhymes was set up in Emmie’s old room at the front of the Lee's house nearest the fireplace. The young couple moved down the hill, happy to be in a house of their own. They would give Mr. Rhymes rent money after selling the crops he and Nate had grown, which he in turn would give the Lees for room and board, so as not to feel like a charity case.

Nate would come get him of an evening and take him over in the wagon to see how things were faring in the fields and feed lot. This seemed to satisfy his homesickness. Frank tried to reason with the old man, telling him he didn’t need to pay them, they were grateful for the opportunity he was giving the newlyweds. But Grady was a stubborn old soul, and so they let him have his way. Kate tucked his rent money away for him in the event that he had something or somewhere he decided to see before his time came.

Pneumonia took him late that winter, though, and they found in his small possessions a letter willing his place to Nate and Omie. He had signed with his “X” and folded the paper around a ten-dollar bill, meant to buy him a simple coffin and headstone.

With the money Kate saved for him, she had a nicely carved stone made with both Grady and Sarah’s names engraved. They laid him beside his wife on the rise looking out across their land to the Savannah River.

Chapter 13

Nate sounded a soft cluck to get the mules started up again after the noon break, enjoying the autumn sun. Things were going fairly well, crops nearly all in. Omie had gone to town with her mamma for supplies and a much-needed day off, as Nate prepared the fields for winter, turning under stubs of corn stalks left by the deer and other critters.

It felt good to move the plow through willing ground. The work was so much easier after a couple of seasons mixing a good portion of straw, manure, and sand into the clay to break it up. He'd turn the fields again when winter took hold, so the clods would dry in the wind, breaking up easily into soil next spring.

Nate felt layers of cool and warm air mingling and separating as he went from sun to shade, low spot to high. This had always been his favorite time of year, especially if all had gone well through the growing months. He thought now, though, that might change. The coming of winter's respite brought to mind pictures of his and Omie's little house, *our very own,* with its small woodstove and her fine quilts on the bed.

Finer than her own mamma's, or any others I ever seen.

Omie took old feed sacks and bits of worn-out clothes and made them into something like pictures on a page. All the colors fit just so. Mostly, he was thinking of how their warm bodies fit together so well beneath those quilts, with her head on his shoulder and her arm slung across his chest. She snored soft as a puppy with breath just as sweet.

Mornings when the five o'clock train whistle woke Nate, it was too early to rise and too late to go back to sleep, so he would lift Omie's hair and snuffle the back of her neck until she giggled and turned to him, still half asleep. Then they would find all the ways love could express itself through their young bodies, Nate learning the power of tenderness and Omie knowing the joy of receiving it.

He was pulled from his reveries when the plow dropped into a hole. "Whoa, girl." An old stump had rotted and left a hole in the ground. Tucked inside a furry nest, was a late-season batch of baby rabbits. He reached down and felt the warmth of their bodies.

A sudden memory took him to the previous winter when, shortly after they'd married, Omie miscarried. Thank goodness they were still living with her folks. When Nate got home after cutting firewood one day and saw blood spots on the porch floor, he ran inside, heart bursting in his chest. Frank had just come in the door and was listening to Kate's awful news. Nate looked at them and rushed to the bedroom where he found Omie in a deep sleep.

Kate walked in behind him. "I had to give her a sleeping draught, Nate. She lost a good bit of blood along with the baby. I can't begin to tell you how sorry I am." She hugged him, then explained, "It happened so sudden. I didn't have time to come get you."

"Mamma?" Omie stood outside the screen door. Her face was chalky white and blood colored the hem of her dress and apron.

"Oh no, child." Kate ran out in time to catch her daughter as she slumped to the porch floor. "Let me get you inside."

She laid Omie across her bed, making soothing noises as the girl whimpered. When Kate parted Omie's legs, a small bloody bundle slipped out onto the quilt.

Omie started crying in earnest, knowing what this meant from the miscarriages of other women she had witnessed at her mamma's side. Being a midwife brought with it as much sorrow as joy, she'd learned.

"But it can't be, Mamma!" she sobbed. "I'm four months on."

Kate cleaned Omie gently and wrapped the tiny remains in a clean towel. She moved to the head of the bed and gathered her daughter into her arms, rocking her.

"Honey, losing your first baby is not unusual. It happened to me as well. I truly believe that little soul stays close to help watch over the babies that follow."

"Thank you, Mrs. Lee." Nate dropped to his knees and took Omie's hand, holding it to his lips. His shoulders began to shake and Kate left the room, giving them privacy.

Frank sat at the kitchen table, tears sliding down his face. "I shore hoped they wouldn't have to face this sorrow like we did, Kate."

She went over to him and pulled his head close, running her fingers through his hair. "Let's just pray this is the only time."

In the following days, Omie and Nate both cried and held each other like children, lost in their grief. Kate made herb teas to calm them both, and a tonic for Omie to help bring her menses back again.

Eventually her mamma's reassurances that there would be other healthy babies encouraged the two young people to try again, praying they soon would get another chance. Nate found his thoughts constantly returning to the child that might have been though, feeling he would always carry the sense of that lost life close to his heart.

Returning to the present, he tucked the bundle of nest and bunnies into the bib of his overalls to carry home.

Something must have just gotten the mamma rabbit. Surprised these three survived. I'm a fool. They'll probably grow up to eat all the greens in the garden.

He'd try to get them to take some water from a wet cloth twisted up like a sugar tit. Maybe Omie would know how to fan the flame of life still in them when she got home. She always knew what to do. These babies would give her something to mother until a baby of their own began to grow in her belly again.

Nate took a minute to wipe the sweat from his face in the shade of some pines edging the field. All in all, life had taken a sweet turn when he'd wandered into the lives of the Lees. He hoped this was what normal was supposed to feel like—simple, solid, and as happy as he knew how to be. Hoped too, that it was enough to turn his back on his past to earn this life.

He wondered then if that past might instead sneak up on him one day, like the dark dreams which sometimes robbed him of sleep.

Will it make me out to be nothing but a bastard and a fool after all, like my 'daddy' said?

Chapter 14

Gathering plants to dry, Omie walked down the field road toward the river, noticing how the shadows were growing longer as the days grew shorter. She felt the change coming before the temperatures began their erratic fall. Something about the light made the world seem clearer, more at ease with itself. Summer, with its incessant chorus of frogs and insects, the weight of moisture in the air, and the casual conversation between grass and feet, had given over to the anticipation of leaner times. Of sleepier rhythms.

She noticed the number of crows scavenging the cornfield for leftovers from the harvest.

Crows used to not travel in such big, noisy bunches.

In the near dusk, she could hear a rain crow calling, though the sky showed nary a cloud.

Strange portents. I'll have to ask Mamma what it means.

Her mamma seemed to be privy to habits in nature that most folks missed.

The crows reminded her of an old song, and she began to sing.

As time draws near my dearest dear when you and I must part
How little you know of the grief and woe in my poor aching heart
Each night I suffer for your sake, you're the girl I love so dear
I wish that I was going with you or you were staying here

I wish my breast were made of glass wherein you might behold
Upon my heart your name lies wrote in letters made of gold
In letters made of gold my love, believe me when I say
You are the one that I will adore until my dying day

The blackest crow that ever flew would surely turn to white
If ever I prove false to you bright day will turn to night
Bright day will turn to night my love, the elements will mourn
If ever I prove false to you the seas will rage and burn

Omie looked for muscadine grapes, thinking of making jelly. She decided to gather herbs alongside the field at the edge of their property where she might find jewel weed and other plants that loved the sun and upturned ground. Climbing over the fence near the river, Omie recalled the first time she had crossed at this corner, years ago. She'd come upon an old burial ground, barely recognizable as such. Only the sunken areas, in somewhat orderly rows, gave a clue to what lay beneath an ancient grove of live oaks. No headstones gave it Grace, no iron fence set it apart as a place of rest. Here, dust had surely turned to dust, and though gnarling roots claimed some of the graves, drooping limbs seemed to shelter others. Wild Cherokee roses grew in abundance on the far side, and just beyond that grew the wild ginger she searched for.

Omie reckoned some settlement had been here before her people arrived, maybe some of the first white settlers in these low lands. They likely fell prey to fevers carried by mosquitoes and ticks and such. Strange how some of the tiniest of God's creatures were the deadliest, not killing only one person, but dooming whole families with a single bite. The few who survived did the best they could by the ones left behind in this inhospitable land.

A spring flowed among mossy stones, an artesian well smelling of sulphur, which left a slimy, white residue in the path of its flow. It gave Omie an eerie feeling, bubbling up endlessly in that still place. Birds seemed not to want to break the silence, neither did the sound of frogs nor insects carry here. This was not a place she was inclined to visit, but Mamma's stores of wild ginger had gotten low. Kate claimed she needed more for the bouts of nausea that afflicted some women when their menses came around. Omie also knew ginger was one of the things keeping these same women from having more children than they could possibly manage to care for.

After filling her sack, she turned to go as quickly as she could, but turned back when something caught her eye beneath the trees. Just a suggestion of movement there, a lightness against the dark grey bark. She stood still, waiting for whatever this was to state its need or to simply reach out to her in a wordless way, needing to connect with another being. Omie closed her eyes for a moment, trying to listen with her inner senses, but when she looked again, the light was gone. She walked home feeling a sense of loneliness, like an echo of her footsteps.

Deep in the night, Omie was tugged from her dreams by the sweet smell of wild ginger. She felt the warmth of Nate beside her, heard his rhythmic snoring, and wanted to slip back into a hard-earned sleep. But there was a presence, a thickening of the air near her, and she woke to find the form of a young woman leaning over her side of the bed, peering at Nate.

As Omie's awareness rose to the surface, the young woman smiled and said, "Mmmhmm, my mamma sure would like him!"

Omie looked at Nate and back at the woman, whose form had become more distinct. Long brown hair framed a lovely face with large hazel eyes.

Her slender neck rose from a white, high collared nightgown. Omie figured her to be maybe a couple of years older than herself, but of another time.

She sent a silent question to the girl. "Who might you be?"

The girl looked from Nate to Omie and said, "My name is Cecelia. Who are you?"

"My name is Omie Lee Silar, and this is my husband Nate. Do I know you?"

Cecelia gave a small laugh and said, "Don't reckon so. I lived around here a good bit before you was born. I saw you today, over in the graveyard."

Omie thought of the shimmery shape she'd seen.

"My mamma and I lived in a cabin over that rise beside Chinquapin Creek. Cabin's gone now, like most things from before the war. Not because it was burnt by Yankees, though. It was burned down because of the fever. My mamma was a healin' woman hereabouts. My daddy run off when I was little, so there was just me and her. She did like her men though, and this one," she nodded toward Nate, "would do her just fine, young as he is. Most of the men folk had gone off to the war, and those that didn't go died from the sickness."

"What sickness? What happened?"

"Well," Cecelia replied, "a cow died in the creek up above our settlement. Most folks' springs came off of that creek, so the drinkin' water went bad. No one knew that till folks started gettin' real sick. Mamma saved those she could. I wasn't one of them. It broke her heart. See, I was promised to marry a handsome fella named Evan when he got back from the fightin'. Mamma was so happy that I would have a good man to care for me if something happened to her. After I passed, another fever started takin' folks and Mamma caught it too. Those that survived burned the homes of the sick and moved on further away from the river."

Omie was considering this bit of history, trying to remember if she had heard anything about it. She would ask Mamma come morning.

Cecelia was quiet for a while, and Omie drifted back toward sleep, with the image of that sweet young face slipping away.

Omie told Nate about Cecelia in the morning, but he smiled and said, "Jest another one of your crazy dreams, darlin', I wouldn't put much store by it."

Omie remembered another 'dream' that Nate was referring to, something that had happened soon after they moved into the Rhymes' house. She'd been hearing the sound of boot heels walking up in the attic for several nights, but chose to ignore them, since Nate heard nothing. She was dozing on their bed one afternoon shortly after she'd lost the baby, back when she'd hardly had the energy to open her eyes. There was a pressure on the mattress beside her which startled her awake. Though she couldn't see anything there, Omie felt a presence beside her and told whatever was there to go away. But then, remembering how these lost souls sometimes came to her and Mamma for comfort, she said, "If you don't mean any harm, you can stay."

The ghost seemed to accept her invitation. Omie drifted into that listless place between waking and sleep. Soon, she had a vision of a young man, perhaps nineteen or twenty years old, with dark, shoulder length hair and grey eyes. His high cheekbones spoke to some Cherokee or Creek heritage. She asked him who he was, but instead of speaking, he suddenly wore a union soldier's coat, as if to show her something of himself and how he died. In the lengthening silence, Omie slid into the comfort of sleep.

Omie wondered now if that had been Cecelia's Evan, and did he ever know what had happened to his girl.

I hope that if he died in battle, he carried a living memory of Cecelia to his end instead of knowing she had passed.

Yet, if he did not know, Omie worried that his ghost might still be searching for Cecelia, that he might be held here by the powerful gravity of love unfulfilled.

Chapter 15

1908

By the first of the year, Omie felt certain a new life was growing inside her. She waited to tell Nate until she was confident it was not just something amiss with her menses, which had been somewhat irregular since she'd lost the first baby. But the tenderness in her breasts and the slight swell of her belly told her they had another blessing on the way. She prayed it would take this time. She wasn't sure they could go through such a loss again.

Ada Katherine was born on a fine summer day in June, with Omie's mamma and their old friend Aunt Julia in attendance. You would have thought it was the first baby they'd ever delivered by the fuss they made over her.

"A beautiful girl you got there, Miss Omie," Aunt Julia said. "About as purty as you was."

"She looks just like you, daughter," Mamma said with a tearful smile, handing the baby up to Nate.

He was afraid he'd drop her, his hands shook so. He cried for the second time in his adult life, the first being when Omie put her hand in his as his wife. Now she'd put this tiny delicate creature in his hands, too. He could hardly breathe for the fullness in his chest. The baby reached out to cling to his big rough thumb with her tiny fingers and he wept harder.

"Somethin' of your very own flesh, son," Kate said. "She's a miracle that nothing can take from you, no matter what happens."

"I will protect her with my life if need be. No harm will ever come to her, nor her mamma neither," Nate whispered. He laid the baby gently on Omie's breast and Ada's little mouth pursed hungrily, searching for the nipple.

"See that!" Aunt Julia said. 'She knows just what to do. They are tougher than you know, boy. I see this one having a long, healthy life."

The following days went by sweetly, with Omie nursing the baby and sleeping when possible. Kate came to stay for a few days and was never far from them afterwards.

Frank helped Nate work the fields, and it was all Kate and Omie could do to shoo them out the door in the mornings and after supper. Little Ada kept them both so enthralled, you would think she was the only child that ever did the things that all babies do. Ada's gaze followed the men whenever they were in the room, and she laughed when they rubbed the stubble of their chins against her tender cheeks. As the months went by, it seemed to Omie that Ada Kate had always been a part of their lives.

"Well, little Ada Kate," Frank said, the day she said her first words, which were *Da... da da da da da!* "I reckon now you'll be tellin' us both what to do, like the rest of the women in this house." He kissed her on the forehead, then kissed Kate and Omie, too. "Not that I'm complainin', mind you." With that, he went out the back door toward the barn to hitch up the mules.

Nate just stood in the kitchen with a grin on his face, and Omie said, “I think she’s tryin’ to tell you to git to work.” She kissed him, then sat down at the table as he headed out to join Frank.

Chapter 16

1909

"I can't believe she's so big, Mamma." Omie tucked a cloth beneath Ada's chin.

"Big!" Ada Kate declared, before accepting a spoonful of sweet potatoes.

"I'll be glad when she decides to quit nursing. She eats like a horse already."

"Not much fun when they latch on with those sharp little teeth, is it daughter? You like to have never turned loose!" Kate laughed.

Omie smiled and said, "She's gonna have to learn to let loose before Thanksgiving. I don't reckon I'll have enough milk for two."

Kate held out her arms and Omie fell into them, laughing.

"I'm so happy things are going well for you darlin'," Kate crooned into Omie's hair. "I sure wish we could have given you more sisters and brothers, but you fill up this house with young'uns and it will be enough for the both of us."

She was born to be a mamma. Frank smiled as he watched Omie dancing with the baby after she'd hung up the wash. *That carryin' basket ain't never far from her side.* He walked over to them and said, "May I have this dance, Miss Ada Kate?"

He whistled a tune as he waltzed Ada around the yard until he ran out of breath. Omie clapped and they sat on the ground laughing. Frank dangled the baby's feet over the grass so that it tickled her toes and she looked up at her grandpa, giggling.

"Oh, if they could just stay so little," he sighed. "I miss the days when I was dancing you around like this. What'd you have to go and get so growed up for?"

Omie reached for Ada and gave her daddy a peck on the cheek. Frank gave the baby his watch to play with.

"Daddy, did you worry a lot about how to keep us safe? If you were doin' things right? Mamma always seems to know what to do."

"That knowledge was hard earned, darlin'. I seen plenty of times when she was at her wits end. Lucky she had Aunt Julia for a friend. Me, I was terrified! You, darlin' . . . you will do just fine."

Frank retrieved his watch, winked at Omie and stood up. "Better get busy before your mamma takes a switch to me." He laughed as he walked away.

Omie felt a deep love for her daddy. He was a sweet man who gave everything he had to his family in his steady, gentle way.

I pray Nate learns to love like that. Maybe me and these babies will be able to soften him up. Someday he'll come to trust that we are never going to hurt him or desert him.

"You sure have your grandaddy wrapped around these little fingers, missy!"

Ada waved 'bye and smiled at her mamma, then the two of them went off to find Nate.

In the weeks before Thanksgiving, Omie was attempting to work around the old cookstove with her swollen belly, trying to curse quietly around Ada. That child heard everything that was said. She chattered on to anyone who would listen, mixing nonsensical words with those she had picked up.

The acorn didn't fall far from the tree. Nate would hear a fancy word and use it whether he knew its meaning or not. If there was not a human ear nearabout to be entertained by Ada, the chickens and the pigs heard their fill.

"Ada Kate, would you help your mamma wash these potatoes?" Omie set a bowl of water on the table, and with Ada perched on her lap, they began to scrub dirt from the skins. Ada got more water on herself than on the potatoes, but Omie didn't mind. This was one of their favorite things to do, carrying on with kitchen work.

When Omie set the toddler down and stood up, a pain shot through her belly all the way to her back and she cried out.

"Mamma?" Ada looked up into Omie's face, questioningly.

"It's all right, honey, mamma just got up too fast," Omie said. She looked around the kitchen for something to bite down on in case another pain was to follow. Reaching into the kindling box, she found a stick about the right size, then sat back down and pulled Ada close. Omie looked into Ada's little hazel eyes, calmed her voice and said, "Okay sweetie, we need to go see if your daddy is near about and tell him it's time for breakfast. Will you hold my hand and help me?"

Omie shuffled carefully to the door, trying to get her breathing regular and calm. They made it down the back steps and nearly to the barn when another pain hit her. She sank to her knees and squeezed Ada's hand. "Mamma, hurt!" Ada cried.

"I'm so sorry, honey," Omie gasped, "could you do something for Mamma and go to the barn to fetch your daddy?"

Ada looked unsure, but Omie said, "I bet he's in there feeding the mules." She took a slow breath. "He'll put you up on one!" Ada hesitated, then ran on her stubby legs to the barn.

She found her daddy harnessing the mules. He picked her up and swung her around, then noticed Omie had not joined them. "Where's your mamma, sweet pea?" Ada pointed out the door. Nate grabbed her back up and ran to the yard where Omie sat panting, trying to get up. "Omie, what's happenin'?"

"Don't make a fuss in front of Ada," she said, "but I think the baby's coming."

"No, no, it's too soon!" Nate exclaimed. "I thought we had another month!"

"Well, this baby says it's ready now. I need you to keep your head, Nate. Mamma and Daddy have gone to the store, and I don't know when they'll be back. Probably before the baby comes, though."

"Probably?" Nate shook his head. "Omie, what will we do if they ain't?"

"We'll do the best we can, that's what we'll do." Omie grunted, "I've helped Mamma with enough births to tell you what to do."

"Me?" exclaimed Nate.

"Help me up and get me back inside," Omie said. "Get some water boilin' on the stove. We'll need clean rags. You can tear up one of the older sheets."

Nate picked Omie up and carried her inside with Ada clinging to his pants leg. The child asked, “Ride mule?”

“When we can, baby girl. Right now, we got to get your mamma comfortable in case your little brother or sister comes.”

Nate laid Omie on their bed, then hastily drew some water from the well. He carried it to the cookstove and poured it into the big canning pot. Ada stood with her fingers in her mouth and watched as her daddy quickly ripped up an old sheet.

“Come here, honey,” Omie called and held out her hand to Ada. “You want a little baby brother or sister, don’t you?” Ada nodded. Omie smiled, then gasped as another pain hit her.

Hours went by with Omie’s pains coming faster and harder and her folks still had not returned. Nate kept looking out the window toward the house up the hill, but saw no sign of their wagon.

“Nate, I need you to see if the baby is in position yet,” Omie said through clenched teeth. “Just feel inside and let me know if the head is coming out first. Wash real good with hot water and soap first, and bring a clean cloth with you.”

Nate did as he was told, tucking the cloth up under Omie and taking a deep breath.

“You’ve helped Daddy deliver many a calf before, you know what to do,” she said tiredly.

He slowly reached inside to feel the crown of the baby’s head, and when he withdrew his fingers, a lock of long, reddish hair came out too.

“Oh my gosh, Omie, she’s got hair already! It has to be a girl. I never saw such!”

Omie gave a short laugh. “That’s good, darlin’, she’s close to comin’. Now, I’m goin’ to start pushin’ and you get ready to catch her. But first, fetch me that piece of kindlin’ to bite down on.” She looked up. “This is goin' to scare Ada. You have to soothe her and get her to watch the baby come instead of watchin' me."

With each push, Omie seemed to grow weaker.

"Nate," she panted, "I need you to push on my belly and help me do this."

"Ada," he said, "you stand here and tell me when you see the baby's head coming out." Ada nodded and stared at where the lock of hair stuck out.

"All right, darlin'," Nate said, "count of three."

Omie pushed as Nate pressed and Ada cried, "Baby!"

Nate hurried to catch the baby as it slipped from between Omie's knees. He gently wiped her little body with a clean cloth while Ada jumped up and down beside him.

"You got yourself a baby sister, Ada Kate!" he announced.

"Are you happy with that?" Omie asked softly, gazing at Nate.

"I couldn't be happier, honey."

Omie instructed Nate how to cut and tie the cord.

He wrapped the baby in a blanket, then laid the tiny bundle in her mamma's arms.

"She's ours, and that's all that matters."

"I'd like to call her Bartie if you don't mind."

"Miss Bartie." Nate smiled. "What you think of that, chicken?"

He picked Ada up so she could see the baby more closely.

"Baby ride mule?" Ada asked, and they both laughed.

"She's got to get big enough to sit up first," Nate said. "When your gramma and grampa get home, you and me will go for a little ride though."

After Bartie nursed, baby and mamma fell fast asleep.

Nate put Ada Kate on his back and went to tend the animals. After pitching one last fork of hay into the stalls, he picked her up again.

"You are such a big help, Sweet Pea."

They walked back to the house with Ada's small voice singing out, "We got a baby, we got a baby."

Around dusk, Kate came hurrying in the back door.

"Oh, my heavens!" she cried. "When I got home, I knew something had happened. Let me see that little one."

Omie handed the baby to her mamma with a tired smile. Kate looked questioningly at Nate.

"He did a fine job, Mamma," Omie said.

"I can see that, darlin." Kate wrapped her free arm around Nate. "You're a good man, son."

Nate turned his weary face away, but Kate could see how pleased he was with their praise.

"How about you and me ride that mule up to fetch Grampa, Ada?" Nate asked. The two of them walked hand in hand back toward the barn, and Kate smiled at her daughter.

"My precious girl," she said, and wiped Omie's moist face with a cool cloth. "Emmie is going to be some disappointed at missing another one of her nieces being born."

Omie laughed. "Truth be told, Mamma, she probably would have passed out, and Nate would have had to tend to her too."

Chapter 17

Emmie spent her days in wonderment discovering Savannah's remarkable, restless beauty. Lovely homes graced tree-lined streets and verdant parks created a latticework, defining the more affluent part of the city. Many squares boasted grand statues of persons who had shaped the destiny of Savannah. The casual air of finery trailing the gentry mesmerized Emmie, as if these were creatures from another world entirely. She felt as if she'd come home to the place where her true self could finally find its expression. This feeling had only grown stronger in the two and a half years she'd lived here.

Emmie's hands were quick to learn the delicacies of the finest stitching. Her eye for detail and style elevated her quickly in the esteem of Mrs. Campbell and her customers. After her first year of apprenticing, she had been trusted with much of the work, so that Mrs. Campbell was free to devote her attention to the ladies who graced her shop. They gathered to gossip as well as peruse the latest fashions. As the women were mostly unaware of her presence, Emmie learned much about the workings of Savannah society; who the oldest and most influential families were, the latest improprieties and the difficulties of running a proper household.

Having come from a life requiring dogged determination to simply provide for the needs of day-to-day life, she found these concerns a bit ludicrous. But Emmie learned to turn an agreeable and sympathetic face to their chatter.

Occasionally Dr. Campbell would stick his head in, but if there was a gathering of women, he was quick to offer greetings and be on his way. At other times, when Emmie and Mrs. Campbell had the shop to themselves, he would linger over the lunch Maizie prepared and talk with them about their day, sharing news his patients brought that he thought might interest them. Emmie could tell he adored his wife and was truly interested in her opinions. They had engaging conversations, and Emmie admired the fact that though they did not always agree, they were respectful of each other's thoughts.

This is the kind of life I would like to have for myself one day, a comfortable life where one has the luxury of time for conversation with a beloved partner.

As preparations for holiday orders began, the doctor came into the shop with a letter for Emmie. It was from her sister. Emmie opened it quickly, fearful of what it might contain.

"Oh no," she cried, dropping the hand holding the letter to her side.

"Oh dear, bad news?" Mrs. Campbell asked.

"Just that I missed the birth of my second niece, too. She came early. I had hoped Omie would have her at Thanksgiving, while I was home."

"I trust that mother and babe are well though?" Dr. Campbell asked.

"Oh, yes sir. I can't wait to see them."

"Well, why don't you surprise them with an early visit!" Mrs. Campbell exclaimed. "We will get Maizie's husband Thomas to drive you."

"But what about all the sewing to be done?" Emmie asked. "I have so much lace to make before Christmas!"

"Well, I expect you can make it there as well as you can here, dear. Go see your family."

And with that, all was settled so that Emmie could leave the following day.

"I have truly grown fond of that young woman," Elizabeth told her husband as they waved their goodbyes.

"I can see she feels much the same about you," Dr. Campbell observed. "It's good that she's worked out well and can take some of the load off your shoulders. I like having you more to myself." He kissed the top of her head. "I'm considering taking on an assistant myself, a young doctor just out of training. He seems to have considerable skill and a hunger for learning. I would enjoy mentoring, passing on some of the knowledge gained from my experiences. Though sometimes it seems I've forgotten more than I remember. He may have a few things to teach me as well."

"I think that sounds wonderful, dear. I wouldn't mind having you more to myself too. Where did this young man come from? A family here we know?" Elizabeth asked.

"He says he's from Statesboro, a community I'm not familiar with," Daniel replied. "His background speaks even more about his determination to follow the calling to medicine, I think. It must not have been easy to rise to the challenge, coming from a small-town education."

"Well, we must have him to dinner soon." Elizabeth smiled. "What is the young man's name?"

"His name is Caleb Decker, darling. Now, I must be off. I still have a long day ahead." With a quick peck on her cheek, he was out the door.

She stood in the doorway watching him go. Turning her face to the sun, Elizabeth felt a change in the breeze dancing with the moss amongst the stately old oaks. Something indefinable, but comforting for all its mystery.

They were not old, she and Daniel, but they had gotten so caught up in their businesses that time had passed more quickly than they realized.

I suppose work has filled the space where a family might have been.

It was not for lack of trying that their big house was so quiet, but they had finally accepted their childlessness and turned their hands to other things.

We really are very fortunate to adore each other so.

Elizabeth smiled to herself as she turned back into the shop.

Chapter 18

I quite like being an aunt. Emmie smiled to herself. *Omie's children are sweet and so much like their mother.*

It had done her heart good to see them all together—her folks, Nate, Omie, and the little ones. Even Nate surprised her with a hug. The closed look he wore for most everyone but Omie changed completely when his children were near. A tenderness she hadn't known he possessed came over him.

Perhaps our earlier misgivings about him have resolved under Omie's gentle persuasions.

There was much to give thanks for this year. The Campbell's driver, Thomas, had come to fetch her from the farm and left her to her thoughts as he guided the horses toward home.

Emmie pulled her wrap tighter, glad to see the soft gas lamps of Savannah glowing in the foggy distance. Savannah *was* home to her now, she realized. How quickly she had left behind the self that was familiar to the rhythms and ways of the farm, having found a cadence of her own in the lively streets of the city.

There isn't anything wrong with the life I've come from, but it never seemed like my true life.

Savannah was where she breathed best, despite the odor of coal fires, horse manure and chamber pots being dumped into alleys.

It smells of life, big, bustling and full of infinite possibilities.

Reining up in front of the shop, Thomas helped Emmie down, and she thanked him for coming to get her. His big smile was heartwarming. Though they spoke little on these trips, they shared a comfortable silence.

I miss the quiet times like this I've spent with Pappa. Those have been too few of late. I'll have to remedy that somehow.

There was a note on the door from the Campbells asking Emmie to join them for dinner if she wasn't too tired from her trip. She washed off the dust and changed into one of her latest creations—a soft, dove-gray dress that would do for most any occasion. She re-pinned her hair and gave her face a thoughtful looking-over in the mirror.

A simple kind of prettiness perhaps, much like my dress.

Emmie pulled on her coat to walk the few blocks to the Campbell's home, enjoying the exercise after riding in the wagon for two hours. She could see the Campbells seated at their dining table through the latticed windows of their lovely home. Another figure sat at the table with his back to her, a man she did not recognize. She paused at the door for a moment, then knocked, wondering who the stranger was. Maizie opened the door and welcomed her inside, then showed her to the dining room.

"I hope I'm not too late. I hate to interrupt your dinner," Emmie said.

Dr. Campbell stood, as Maizie took Emmie's coat. "Not at all, we were just sitting down. Come warm yourself."

Mrs. Campbell embraced the young woman. "The trip was not too tiring, then?"

"No, no, I'm fine." Emmie turned toward the man across the table as he rose to be introduced.

"Emmie Lee, this is Caleb Decker, my new associate at the clinic," Dr. Campbell said. "He has just joined me in my practice, and I must say, he is already making himself invaluable to me."

"Very nice to meet you, sir." Emmie offered her hand.

"My pleasure, Miss Lee, I'm sure." He smiled as he lifted her hand to his lips.

Goodness, what white teeth he has. And a handsome mustache.

She was taken aback for a moment by the long-ago memory of looking in a mirror's reflection down in the well.

I imagined this face!

"Is everything all right?" Mrs. Campbell asked.

"Oh yes, you just reminded me of someone for a moment, Dr. Decker. Forgive me." Emmie smiled up at him. Caleb held out a chair for her to be seated.

The three resumed the conversation they had been in the middle of when Emmie joined them, and Maizie brought her a plate of food.

"Dr. Decker here was just telling us about some of the home remedies his mother uses for various ailments. Quite interesting really," Dr. Campbell told her.

"Is your mother a healer, then? Mine is very familiar with the use of plants as well," Emmie said. "She and my sister are midwives and healers for our community."

"Indeed?" Caleb asked, interested. "Yes, my mother isn't formally trained but she has some skills. I learned from her that we shouldn't throw out the proven methods of folk medicine completely as we embrace modern practices. Many of the medicines we prescribe now are derived from plants, such as this new pain reliever known as aspirin. My mother has used white willow bark in a tea to help with aches and fever. Now you can get the same comfort in the form of a small tablet."

Dinner went along pleasantly. Afterward they all retired to the parlor for a brandy.

"I see that Christmas decorations have been placed in the parks while I was away," Emmie commented, as she settled near the fire.

"I was studying in Germany during Christmas once," Caleb remarked. "It's quite a sight, let me tell you. The Germans are known for their beautiful glass ornaments."

From there, the conversation turned to medicinal practices in other parts of the world and to travel in general. Emmie was content to listen and dream of perhaps having the opportunity to visit these places one day.

"I believe our young miss is growing tired," Dr. Campbell said. "Would you like me to walk you home?"

"Permit me to, if you please," Caleb offered. "I have some research to do tonight and should be retiring myself."

Thanking them for dinner and the lovely evening, Emmie stepped from the porch into the crisp night, accepting Caleb's arm as they walked down the avenue.

Dr. Campbell looked at his wife, sharing a conspiratorial smile as the two young people faded into the darkness.

Chapter 19

1910

"Mornin' Omie," Mrs. O'Dell said. "How's your mamma?"

"She's good, Mrs. O'Dell. She and Daddy have gone to visit Mamma's brother in Macon for a few weeks. His wife is poorly and Mamma hopes to be of some help."Omie fingered a new bolt of cloth by the counter while Mrs. O'Dell finished waiting on a customer. "Any letters from my sister today?"

"Why, yes! She's a good girl, that Emmie, and workin' out real well my sister says. She's got a talent for makin' them new fashions. Myself, I cain't see the sense in spendin' what amounts to most of a year in farm wages just for a frock."

"Different world from us, I suppose," Omie mused, "I'm not sure I'd trade places."

The bell tinkled as the customer left and Mrs. O'Dell came out from behind the counter, pulling Omie close as if there were still ears about.

"Omie, a man came in here askin' if I knowed of a Nate Silar. He stank of likker and looked like trouble so I didn't tell him nuthin', but it's just a matter of time until someone does."

Omie blinked and felt a cold shiver run up her spine, but turning a careful face to Mrs.O'Dell, she said, "I can't imagine who that would be. Did he give his name?"

"No, he wouldn't, and that cautioned me even more. I just thought I should let you know in case he comes skulkin' 'round."

"Well, we thank you, Mrs. O'Dell. I'll be sure to let Nate know." Distracted by the news, Omie quickly purchased her goods and left the worried shopkeeper gazing at her out the window.

Omie hurried home and found Nate in the barn pitching hay to the mules. She told him about Mrs. O'Dell's news of the man who was inquiring about him.

"Could he be your stepfather?"

Nate looked stunned for a moment. "Naw, Omie. Ain't no way he could've found me here. We're miles and miles from that place. Must have been someone lookin' for work, or there was some mistake on her part. Dunno. But Mr. Silar come here? I don't think so."

Omie let it be, but she could see it worried him. Not just the how but the why of it.

Why would the man look for him in the first place? There was no love lost between the two.

At dinner, Nate was quieter than his usual self, and Omie was pretty sure he'd come to the same conclusion she had.

Mr. Silar has found him. And he wants something.

In the evening, Nate told Omie he was going out to the barn to check on things. She knew by the old prickly lights she *saw* around him again, that he had some thinking and sorting out to do. She sat by the fire nursing Bartie and rocking Ada, testing the powers of her *Sight* to see if it would reveal anything about this news.

As Nate entered the barn and lit the lantern, one of the shadows moved. The face he hated most in the world stepped into the light.

"Well, well, if it ain't my bastard boy. Done right good for yerself these past few years, I see. You got a sweet little missus there. I followed her from the store today. She's a purty little thing. I cain't imagine what she sees in you."

"What the hell do you want?" Nate asked through gritted teeth.

"Why, cain't I even come to see my own son?" Silar asked with mock indignation. "The one I raised just like he was my own?"

"It's a damn good thing you didn't sire any of your own, if'n they were likely to turn out like you," Nate snarled.

"Now you just hold up there, boy. I whupped you before for that smart mouth and I'll whup you again."

"I don't think so." Nate walked nearer to the man, lantern in hand and growled, "I growed up a bit since you last laid a hand on me and I think you'll find yourself getting whupped this time."

Silar took in the changes in Nate, noting how he'd filled out.

"I doubt that's so," Silar sneered. "But I need you unmarked and of a piece so's you can go and claim what's rightly mine."

"And what would that be?" Nate asked, moving even closer.

"That son-of-a-bitch father of yours got hisself killed. And his mamma, the old biddy that still rules that family, well they thinks you ought to get a share of his *worldly goods*. They told me they ain't proud of what he did, and want to make it right. I told them I was the one they ought to be makin' things right by. They treated me like I was nuthin'. Called me a *low down drunk*. Said they wasn't givin' that money to nobody but you."

"I don't want their damn money. They can give it to my mamma so she can leave your sorry hide." Nate turned toward the stalls. "Now be on your way."

"Well, Mr. Proud-and-Mighty, that ain't gonna happen 'cause she's dead. And I say good riddance to the whore and her sorry son. The day you left was the best day of my life!" Silar spat on the ground.

"What?" Nate turned back to face him. "When? What did you do to her?"

Taking a step back, Silar said, "I didn't do nuthin. She and my mamma caught the in-flu-enza and died last winter. As if you cared."

Nate swung the lantern in a blind rage, knocking Silar out the back door into the feedlot. The lantern broke and kerosene sloshed onto the man's ragged old coat. He was on fire before Nate realized what had happened. Silar ran for the nearby water trough as flames spread to his hair and beard, throwing himself in. Nate grabbed his step-father's head and held it under. Silar flailed desperately, but Nate held him fast. In the churning water he saw images from the past—the beatings, the curses, the worn face of his mother. All the old rage rose up inside him, strengthening his grip, until he realized the body beneath his hands had ceased struggling.

"I use to think I wouldn't piss on you if you was on fire, but I guess this is the next best thing. You're welcome," Nate declared, as he pulled Silar out of the trough.

Nate opened the stall for one of the mules, then hooked a bridle over her head. The mule snorted and stamped at the strange, burnt smell as he hoisted the body over her back. The next hour or so passed as if in a dream, Nate walking the mule down to the river, shoving the body over the bank and watching the current carry it away.

I shoulda' filled his pockets with rocks. If he's found, maybe they'll just think he's some passing stranger who got lost in the dark and fell into the river to drown.

As darkness swallowed the body, Nate turned the mule back toward the barn, trying to calm himself and figure out what he was going to tell Omie.

Best just to tell her I went for a ride to clear my head, and the mule kicked the lantern when I went to take the bridle off her.

Omie got the children to sleep, wondering what had become of Nate. She'd heard a ruckus in the barn but couldn't leave the babies to investigate. She figured she would sense it for sure if Nate was hurt, but still her imagination conjured up all kinds of frightful scenes. She heard an owl call nearby. Never a good sign.

Finally, Nate walked in, sweaty and haggard looking.

"My Lord, Nate! What has happened?" she exclaimed.

"Nuthin'. I'm all right," He bent to rinse his face in the wash bowl.

"You are not all right," she cried. "I heard somethin' out there and you've been gone the longest time."

Nate told her his story about riding out on the mule, and the lantern breaking, hence all the dirt and smut on him from putting out the fire. But Omie knew it was mostly a falsehood.

What could be so awful that he would lie to me about it? He's held things back from me that he can't speak of, I know, but he's never outright lied to me before.

She crawled under the covers and waited for Nate to finish washing up. He took off his clothes and lay down on the bed, staring up at the ceiling. Omie laid a hand on his chest and said, "I know somethin's happened, Nate. What is it?"

"Let it be, Omie," he warned, and turned his back on her for the first time in their married life.

For days, Nate went about the business of the farm with a vengeance, taking care of tasks long overdue when his work in the fields was done. He couldn't be still. It seemed to him that nothing about the way he felt was how he imagined it would be after getting his hands on Silar and crushing the life right out of him. Nate had dreamed about killing the man often, and the various ways to go about it. There was no sense of relief, and he could not turn to Omie for comfort. Not even the grief for his mamma could be shared, or else she would know he'd spoken with Silar, would know this wildness unleashed in him came from the angry beast woken by Silar's presence. Omie knew something anyway, but he didn't want her accountable if he did get found out.

Nate took to buying a little moonshine from one of the men at the grange, someone he barely knew, so it wouldn't come as a surprise to men who knew him as a teetotaler. After dinner, he'd slip down by the river and have a few swigs just to ready his mind for sleep. In a short while, it took more than just a few. One night, he just kept walking the banks of the river in the dark until he got turned around and couldn't find his way back home.

Omie sat up all that night rocking the children and worrying about Nate. His behavior of late was so unlike him, she knew something terrible had taken place that night in the barn. And the likker on his breath recently had taken her completely by surprise.

I wish Mamma was back. If I could talk to her . . . no. This feels like something that needs to be kept between me and Nate.

One day soon after, the sheriff knocked softly at the door before Nate had come in from the fields.

"Hello, Miss Omie," he said, as she opened the screen door for him. "How you doin'?"

"Why, come in, Sheriff. We haven't seen you or Mrs. Turner in some time. Is there something I can do for you? Nate is still in the field, but I can go get him to watch the babies if your missus has a need of me."

"No, no, Vera's fine, she's just been off visiting our daughter and them grandbabies over to Guyton. I'm sure you know how it is, grandmas can't get enough."

"I do, and I'm ever grateful for it, too. I don't know how we'd manage without my mamma. Please, come in. Can I get you some tea or water?"

The sheriff took off his hat and stepped inside.

"A cool glass of tea would be most welcome, it's a hot one today."

They took their time catching up and talking about commonplace things. She knew the sheriff would get around to the reason for his visit when he was ready.

"Omie, I come here to ask if you'uns have seen a man in the last week or so, just called himself Silar? He'd been askin' folks around town about Nate. Down at the grange, the men wouldn't talk to him without he gave his full name or stated his business with you all. Nobody sent him your way, but they was worried. Something about him just didn't sit right."

"Silar?" Omie replied. "Well, Mrs. O'Dell at the store did mention a man to me, but she didn't know that was his name. We haven't seen any sign of him here. If he's trouble, I hope we never do."

The sheriff took a long drink of his tea and studied his glass for a moment.

"Not likely to happen, Omie. The man fell in the river and got hisself drowned. He got caught in a snag down by the Harper's place where their son was fishin' yesterday. The boy came to get me, and we pulled the fella out of the river. We put him in the wagon and carried him to Doc Pritchard's. Even the river couldn't wash all the whiskey stink from him so I imagine it was just an accident, him stumbling around in the dark and all. Funny though, part of his coat and hair was burnt."

"Oh my," Omie breathed out. "Poor man. Maybe he had a campfire and got into trouble and went looking for water."

Sheriff Turner looked at her and said, "Maybe so. Anyway, I need to ask Nate to come look at the body, see if he recognizes the man."

"Let me go get him for you."

Nate's story about the lantern fire jumped into her mind, but before she could get up, the sheriff stood and walked to the door.

"No, don't trouble yourself Omie. You stay with these babies, and I'll go talk to him."

He put on his hat as he walked out, and Omie put a hand over her eyes, doing her best to send a silent message to Nate.

Please be careful.

Nate had seen the sheriff's horse ride up as he was clearing a new field. He started toward the barn, then thought better of it and turned toward the woodshed.

"Hey, Sheriff Turner," he called. "What are you doin' out this way?" Nate grabbed the axe as if to deal with a troublesome root.

"Got some business I need to tend to that I might could use your help with," Turner said. "There's a body I need you to look at."

He watched Nate's face register the word body.

Nate leaned on the axe and looked the sheriff straight in the eyes. "A body! What in the world would I know about a body?"

"Oh, I'm just hopin' you can help me identify him, seein' as he's somebody that's been lookin' for you."

Nate shook his head slightly and said, "Well now, Omie did tell me there was mention of someone that came 'round to the store askin' for me. I cain't figure who that would be though."

"Just said his name was Silar to some men at the grange."

Nate straightened up. "My stepdaddy called himself that, but we hadn't had no truck with each other since I left home years ago. I don't know what he'd want with me."

Sheriff Turner thought it interesting that the young man showed no shock nor asked about how the man died, but it was evident that there was no love lost between them.

"Can you come with me now to see if it's him?"

He's not really askin', I reckon.

"Of course. Just let me put the mules up and tell Omie."

The two men had little to say on the ride to the undertaker's office in town. Nate wondered if this was the sheriff's way of trying to trap him, make Nate start talking from nervousness. Well, he would not give the man anything to fan his suspicions.

I got no regrets and no guilt. Let him think what he wants.

They pulled up to Mr. Obermeyer's funeral parlour, and Nate jumped down from the buggy, walking inside without looking back at the sheriff.

"Good day, Mr. Silar," Obermeyer greeted.

"Is it?" Nate replied, and followed the man back to where a body was laid on a cooling board, covered with a sheet.

The undertaker pulled the covering back to reveal Silar's bloated face.

Nate gazed impassively for a few seconds and said, "Yep, that's him." He walked out of the room, through the door and returned to the buggy.

The sheriff looked at Mr. Obermeyer for a moment. The man shrugged. Sheriff Turner followed Nate, got onto the driver's seat and they rode back to the farm in the same unyielding silence.

Omie paced between the crib and the door as the children napped, too agitated to sit and rock for long. The story of what had happened to Nate's stepfather began to reveal itself in half-formed pictures playing across her mind. Like pages of a book being turned too quickly to read.

Finally, she sat down and pieced it all together well enough. Now it was clear where Nate's nightly rambles took him. She could *See* the glint of moonlight on water and sensed the sinking of Nate's spirit.

I'll tell him these things, so he'll have nothing more to hide. Then we'll figure this out together.

She built a fire in the cookstove and began to make fried chicken and gravy to go with her biscuits that he loved so well.

I never saw a man could put away as many biscuits as Nate Silar. He 'bout smothers a half-dozen with gravy and finishes the rest off with sorghum syrup for dessert.

When Nate finally walked in the door, he smelled supper ready and waiting, right on time. His drawn face looked at her questioningly, wondering where the stream of angry questions were, she expected.

Omie took his hand and led him to a chair. She picked Bartie up and put her in his arms, set Ada Kate on his knee, then sat beside them and told him all she knew.

Nate shook his head slowly and said, "If I ever had my doubts about your gift of the *Sight*, they're gone now. I just wanted to keep you safe from the guilt of knowin' what I'd done if I got found out. I hate that I had to look on that devil again."

He set Ada down and, cradling the baby, sat on the floor at Omie's feet, laying his head on her lap. Nate began to sob as if he'd never stop, like his heart held more sorrow than his body could contain. Omie ran her hand through his hair, pulling the heaviness away from his aching head with each stroke. He felt the muscles in his shoulders begin to loosen and relax as his sobs finally slowed and quieted. A stillness came over him, a feeling of being washed clean through.

Nate imagined this must be what it's like to get saved and be baptized in the river.

But that river'll never be a place of peace for me now. I gave it my greatest sin.

He had a sense that no matter what came of all this, he and Omie and the girls would be fine. They were all that mattered.

That night, Omie woke to Nate shaking her, whispering, "Omie. You're havin' a nightmare. Wake up, darlin'."

She looked around at the familiar room and at Nate's face, lit by moonlight.

"I had an awful dream," she said. "It was so real. There was a man on a horse, riding on a path through the woods. Another man stepped out of the shadows and spooked the horse. On purpose. I smelled whiskey and evil on him, I swear. Don't remember what was said, but the rider tried to beat away the man on the ground, who grabbed the end of the whip, trying to pull the fella off his horse. Only his foot was caught in the stirrup. It was terrible, Nate. I still hear the man's laughter as he slapped the horse on the rump, and it galloped off, dragging the rider."

"Did you see either one of their faces?"

"No, it was dark in the dream. I never will forget that laugh though. I hope I never hear it again."

"Go back to sleep, darlin'. It was just a bad dream." Nate rubbed her back.

If it's who I think, you'll never have to worry about hearin' him again.

Kate closed her eyes, giving in to fatigue as she and Frank neared the end of their last long day of traveling.

"It sure will feel good to sleep in our own bed, won't it honey?"

Frank nodded. "It was good to see Collie and Ethel, but I hope not to make that trip again for many years. You did her a lot of good Kate. I know they appreciated us coming."

As they drew closer, Kate felt the hair on the back of her neck rise. Some kind of trouble had visited the farm while they were gone, but she couldn't get a clear picture of it in her mind. There was a smell in the air like singed hair, or sulphur.

All seemed well as Frank drew up to the barn. Omie came up the hill to meet them, with Ada Kate on her hip and Bartie in a basket.

"Let me take that little'un!" Kate exclaimed, as she stepped down from the wagon.

Frank jumped down and swung Ada into the air, then nuzzled her cheek against his beard.

Kate looked closely at her daughter, who did not meet her eyes.

"Everything all right while we were gone?" she asked.

"Just fine, Mamma."

There was a trace of the same scent around Omie that Kate had smelled earlier on the way home. Whatever the trouble had been seemed to have passed, and Omie was keeping it to herself.

Chapter 20

By the first haying, Omie was in her seventh month of pregnancy. Ada Kate had started putting an ear against her mamma's belly, talking to the baby and listening for a reply. Omie tried to explain that the sounds were just rumblings of her stomach, but Ada was convinced the baby was talking to her.

Omie was making dinner for the family, with Bartie on her hip and Ada Kate standing on a chair stirring a pot. Nate came in and slipped his arms around her from behind, rubbing one hand over her belly until she pushed him back into a chair.

"Enough of that Nate Silar, how do you think I got this belly?"

"Oh, I remember all right. I love feeling your sweet round belly. This time I can tell it's a boy!"

"Is that so?" Omie asked. "Well, let's just hope he doesn't have your appetite or I'll never get away from this dang hot stove!" Omie set Bartie on Nate's lap and fanned herself with her apron. "This one already starts kickin' when those biscuits come out of the oven." She laughed. "Where's Daddy?"

Nate jostled Bartie on his knee and replied, "He's raking up the last bit of hay. Said he'd be in directly."

Omie set dinner on the table and called out the door to where her mamma was hanging diapers on the line. "Come and eat!" She turned to Nate, "Watch the girls for a minute. I've got to get out of this hot kitchen. I'll go see what's keepin' Daddy."

Outside, a slight breeze lifted the curls from her neck, and Omie breathed a sigh of relief. She pushed the damp hair away from her forehead. Turning the corner at the barn, she saw the mule grazing by the fence, still hooked up to the hay rake.

"What in the world?" She looked toward the neat rows of hay and saw her father lying on his side on the ground. She ran toward him yelling, "Daddy, are you all right?", already knowing he was not. So many images passed through her mind in the short time it took to get to him. Omie knelt down and turned him toward her, feeling for a pulse, but there was none.

"Mamma! Nate!" she screamed.

Kate ran from around the house crying, "No! Oh Lord, no!"

Nate came outside with the girls in his arms and hurried over, seeing the still form of Frank on the ground. "Oh no, no no no!" he yelled. He sat the girls down beside their mamma and felt Frank's chest for movement. He put a hand over his face as tears began to course down his cheeks.

"It musta' been his heart," Nate said. "He was havin' trouble gettin' his breath this mornin'. I tried to get him to stop and go lay down, but your daddy said he was just a little tired and would rest after dinner. I never heard those words out of his mouth before. I shoulda' knowed something was wrong, I shoulda' made him quit!"

Kate lay down, resting her head beside Frank's. She turned his face to hers, kissing him and weeping. "No one has ever made this man do anything he didn't want to, Nate. You know that."

Nate rose and slowly made his way to the barn. In a walking dream, he hitched the mule to the wagon. Shakily, he climbed onto the seat. The mule seemed reluctant to approach the sad scene, slowly pulling up beside them. Somehow, they managed to get Frank's limp body up into the back. Nate led the mule as Omie walked behind with Bartie on her hip and Ada Kate's hand held tightly in her own. The children were quiet and uncertain about what they should do in the face of all these adult tears.

Ada looked up at her grandmamma with brimming eyes and asked, "Gam'pappa sleepin'?"

"Yes, child," Kate said softly. "He's sleepin' in the arms of the angels."

Ada tried her best to see the angels as Nate and Omie carried Frank's body into the Lee's house. They laid him on the bed that he had been born in, and Nate left to find the doctor.

Emmie. Come home.

It hit Emmie like a blow to the chest, hearing her mamma's voice calling to her. It was just as clear as if she were right next to her in the shop. Louder than the ladies' voices around her, louder than the noise from the street.

"*Daddy.*" She stood, gripping her sewing table. Mrs. Campbell glanced over and saw that Emmie had turned white as a sheet. Maizie had just stepped in to let them know lunch was ready and caught Emmie as she was about to fall.

Mrs. Campbell rushed over. "Get her some cold water please, Maizie! Emmie, what is it child? You look as though you've seen a ghost!"

Emmie started sobbing, and Mrs. Campbell wrapped her arms around her.

"I think it's my pappa," Emmie cried. "I heard my mamma clear as day calling me just now. I don't know how I know it, but I do. He's dead." She buried her head in Mrs. Campbell's shawl, shaking like a child.

Maizie returned with the water and set it on the table. She gently rubbed Emmie's back. Mrs. Campbell said, "Now, would you please fetch my husband from the clinic? Thank you so much."

Grabbing her shawl, the young housekeeper gave Emmie a curious glance and hurried out the door. Moments later Dr. Campbell rushed inside, looking questioningly at his wife.

"It seems there is a family emergency for Emmie, Daniel. She fears her father may have taken ill or worse. We need to have Thomas prepare the buggy and take her home."

"But...how do you know, Emmie? Are you sure?" He looked around for a messenger bearing the news.

"This is just something her woman's intuition tells her, dear. I should go with her and make sure she's all right."

Emmie raised a forlorn face and said, "No, Mrs. Campbell, you have the shop to tend. I'll send word as soon as I know something."

"Let me go with her, Missus," said Maizie. "I have family over that way to stay with. Thomas and I can come back for you if need be."

Elizabeth smoothed the tear-dampened hair from Emmie's face and said, "Are you sure Emmie? The shop can close for a few days."

"Thank you, ma'am, I'm sure. But I may need you to bring me some proper clothes and things later. I'm too worried to pack. I just want to go home. I don't know what I'll do without Pappa. Poor Mamma. Poor Omie!"

Thomas brought the carriage around and helped a tearful Emmie onto the seat. His wife climbed up beside her and put an arm around the girl's slumped shoulders. She simply held Emmie until her sobs quieted. Once Emmie had blown her nose and calmed down, Maizie asked softly, "You have the *Sight*, don't you?" .

Emmie looked up and saw the understanding and compassion in Maizie's deep, dark eyes. "I never thought so," Emmie said. "It's my mamma and sister who are blessed with the *Sight*. But I swear, I heard my mamma call to me like she was inside my head. This has never happened to me before."

"Reckon it's stronger in some folks than others. Maybe God lets us choose whether or not we want that gift. I don't know. Doesn't seem to be a choice for my Aunt Julia, though. I myself get little bits of it now and then, information about folks that I don't rightly know what to do with. Nothing important though, silly things like what a person is reading or what they had for lunch. Don't know why I'm bothered with it."

"Why, I may know Aunt Julia!" Emmie exclaimed. "Does she live in Thistle Town?"

"She does."

"She and my mamma have tended to many birthings together. They share information about the use of herbs and such. I've known Aunt Julia all my life. Is she really your aunt or do you just call her that, too?"

"Oh, she's my aunt all right. My great-aunt actually. She and my mamma never let up for a minute trying to educate me, turn me into a wise, worldly woman. I came to Savannah to study at the Black folks' college here, so as not to be too far from home. I needed to work while going to school, and I heard that Mrs. Campbell was looking for a housemaid. That's where I met this one here." She gave Thomas a jab with her elbow. "We married after my last year of school."

Thomas grinned down at her.

The young women talked quietly, with Maizie trying to distract Emmie from imagining the worst until they knew for certain how things were.

"What did you study?" Emmie asked.

"Got a teaching degree, but it seems no one wants a married school teacher. That's just silly to me. There's somethin' else I really want to do anyway, Miss Emmie. I've been writing about Aunt Julia's methods of healing with herbs and such. She has so much knowledge and there's really no one to pass it on to. Young folks don't seem to be interested in learnin' the old ways. What has inspired me even more are the stories she's shared about her life, and they've made me realize I want to be a writer."

Emmie thought for a moment about her mamma and Aunt Julia's long friendship. "I'm embarrassed to say that I never asked Aunt Julia about herself. She's just always been in our lives. I thought she was ancient when I was a child, I have no idea how old she is now."

"I'm not sure she knows either." Maizie smiled. "I only know that she's a treasure, and there are many more stories like hers that need to be told.

"I haven't considered what will happen if one of my nieces doesn't carry on Mamma and Omie's work. Maybe I can record some of their knowledge as well, Maizie."

Halfway to the farm, they met Nate riding up the road toward Savannah.

"Emmie!"

"Nate, what . . . ."

"I have some bad news about your daddy."

"I know." She started crying again.

"But how?" he asked. Maizie met his eyes for a moment, and he looked back at Emmie. "Well, I'll be danged," he said, and shook his head. "You too?"

"Best not to even ask," Thomas offered with a slight smile. They headed toward the farm in silence.

Emmie fell into her mamma's arms as soon as she climbed down from the carriage. Omie joined them, and the sisters sobbed like children. Kate's tears fell silently as she stroked her daughters' hair. There were no words that could offer comfort, only the strength of their love for each other held them up.

Frank's funeral was to be in two days' time. Emmie sent word back to the Campbells through Maizie and Thomas, asking Elizabeth to please bring her something suitable to wear. She knew they would want to attend the service and, deep down, hoped that Caleb might come as well.

The following days seemed to pass in a blur. Everyone went through the motions, doing what must be done for the funeral, feeling logy with the weight of grief. Maizie and Thomas returned as soon as possible to help Aunt Julia make food for the folks who would be coming over to pay their respects after the service. The Campbells would come later with Caleb.

Nate stayed in the barn making a coffin for Frank, refusing to eat or sleep until it was done. Omie understood his need to grieve in solitude and left plates of food for him just inside the barn doors, but they remained untouched.

Ada Kate searched out the lap of anyone sitting long enough to hold her, which was usually her grandmamma. Kate seemed to have no energy for anything else. While the two rocked together, Omie placed Bartie in their arms and asked Ada Kate to be her 'Little Mamma' while she worked. Tending the baby appeared to give them both a sense of purpose while the funeral preparations went on around them. Omie sensed Frank's spirit hovering near his wife and granddaughters.

She and Emmie had brought in flowers from their mamma's garden to brighten the tables laden with food. For Omie, however, their colors only reminded her of how much light had gone out of the world with her daddy's passing.

I reckon the smells of food and flowers together will always bring this memory back to me.

The day of the funeral was clear and cloudless, a day that seemed out of place. The small church where Frank was laid could not contain the number of mourners offering their condolences. Neighbors spoke to the family of kindnesses Frank had done for them, expressing love and appreciation for his good-heartedness.

The Campbells embraced Emmie when they arrived and offered their services if there was anything they might do to help. Caleb gently clasped hands with Kate and Omie as Emmie introduced him.

"Emmie's told me so much about you both. I'm terribly sorry that I didn't get to meet your husband, Mrs. Lee. I can tell from the way Emmie speaks of him that he was deeply cherished."

Kate thanked the young man and assured the Campbells that she would indeed let them know if they could help. When they had moved on, Omie looked at Emmie with a small smile.

Her sister frowned back, feeling her face redden.

Emmie stayed on with her family at the Campbell's insistence, miserable with grief and guilt, torn between the people she loved and the life she loved in Savannah.

One morning Kate took Emmie's hand and led her out onto the porch. "Sit with me a spell, daughter," she said. They were quiet for a while, watching purple martins doing their tricks of flight, catching bugs in the hazy sunlight. "I know you loved your daddy and you love us, honey, but it's time for you to go."

"No, Mamma, I can't leave you all to do daddy's share of the work. Maybe if I hadn't left, he wouldn't have worked himself to death." She sobbed as she leaned down and put her face in her hands.

Kate stroked Emmie's back like she had when Emmie was a small child, saying softly, "None of that now, Emmie. It was his time, and not you nor me nor anyone else was going to stop him from doing what he'd done all his life. That man loved hard work and that's the truth of it." Kate looked out across the fields and sighed. "We'll manage, sweet girl. I've saved every penny of the money you've sent us, for the day you get married. If we get in a bind, we'll hire some help with that money." Kate had no intention of ever doing such, but knew Emmie needed to feel like she was contributing something.

Emmie raised her face and wiped at her tears. "Are you sure, Mamma? Because I can stay as long as you need me. The Campbells said as much."

"Go, child. You have your work to do and your own life to live. And, I suspect, that young doctor will be missing you a good deal by now."

Emmie blushed and turned her face, but Kate saw a little half smile on her lips as she did so. "We'll see, Mamma. He seems a good man, but I hardly know anything about him, really."

"Well, you take your time. If he's right, you'll know."

Emmie looked quizzically at her mamma.

"I can't *See* for you, you know that. But I don't feel any misgivings either, and that bodes well. Some things a mamma just knows without the *Sight*."

The next day, Nate loaded Emmie's things into the wagon and helped her up onto the seat. "We won't be going in the style you're accustomed to, My Lady," Nate teased, "but I promise not to spit tobacco on the streets once we're in town proper."

"You can spit it right on James Oglethorpe's statue if you want to, brother!" Emmie gave Nate a hug, and he smiled with embarrassment and pleasure. "We have to take care of each other, Nate, and I want you to come get me if I'm needed. Promise me that."

"I will, Emmie. I will." He shook the reins and they pulled away from the house.

In the months following Frank's death, Nate threw himself into the farm chores with all his might. He was driven by anger born of grief, expressing himself in the only way he knew. Omie helped as much as she could, but with the baby due soon, she felt helpless to relieve him from the weight of chores. Also, from the weight in his heart.

Neighbors quickly helped build a room onto Nate and Omie's house for Kate to move into, so she could care for the children and Omie when the baby came. Kate was grateful for the needs of the little ones, as they gave her no time to sink into the well of sorrow that threatened to drown her.

When Omie's time came, Aunt Julia was called on again to assist in the delivery. On a bright August morning, Nate and the girls gathered near to witness the baby's entrance into their lives. This was the easiest of Omie's births, and Kate thanked the Lord for this blessing in the face of all they had been through these last weeks. A soft breeze blew through the window across Omie's damp face like a tender touch, carrying the smell of warm hay in the sun.

Omie held their tiny son against her breast and stroked his soft little cheek. Ada Kate and Bartie were up on the bed cuddled next to their mamma, watching him nurse. Nate sat beside her with an arm around Bartie.

"He's widdle!" Ada touched the baby's toes one by one.

"Have you picked out a name for him, Miss Omie?" Aunt Julia asked.

Omie looked up at Nate and replied, "We want to name him after Daddy. Frank Thomas Silar."

Nate nodded, his eyes full of joy, tinged with sadness.

Aunt Julia squeezed Kate's hand and said, "Sounds about right to me."

The baby was sweet-tempered, a joy for them all. His gentle eyes sought each of them out as if he knew their voices. Kate thought maybe there was some portion of her Frank in this new life, some gift bestowed on his little spirit by his grandfather, as they passed each other in their travels to and from heaven.

Nate seemed to recognize this, too, carrying the baby out with him at day's end to see all that had been done. The loss of Frank was like a current dragging him down into some darkness he had no time or desire to understand. His feelings for his father-in-law were as close to loving another man as he was ever likely to know again. This knowledge knit into his bones.

Chapter 21

The morning after returning to Savannah from her daddy's funeral, Emmie woke in her own room with the sun shining fully in her eyes.

"Oh, My Lord. What time is it?" she exclaimed, jumping out of bed.

Maizie heard Emmie rustling about and knocked at the door, bearing a tray with coffee and breakfast.

"Oh Maizie, that smells heavenly. Am I very late? Is Mrs. Campbell in the store already?"

Maizie turned to Emmie with a kind smile.

"Just don't you mind, Miss Emmie, you've been through a trial now, and you need to get your rest. Seems like a broken heart just pulls all the joy out of the world, and all your strength with it, too. Takes everything you got to put one foot in front of the other till time works its healin'. Mrs. Campbell wants you to go easy gettin' back to work. We all know what loss is around here."

"Thank you." Emmie touched the young woman's shoulder affectionately, then stretched and opened the curtains wider to take in the day, watching the bustle of activity on the streets.

"Dr. Decker has been askin' after you this mornin', too. Wants to know will you have lunch with him tomorrow, if you feel up to it."

Maizie left, closing the door behind her. Emmie was deep in thought about Dr. Decker when Mrs. Campbell tapped lightly and entered.

"I heard you were awake. How are you, dear?"

Emmie looked up with eyes so full of sadness that Elizabeth wrapped her arms around the girl and held her close. She knew there were no words that could truly take away Emmie's pain, and she was not one to indulge in banal condolences that only served to comfort the giver. Instead, Elizabeth just let her weep in peaceful silence. When Emmie had unburdened her heart enough that the sobs calmed to sniffles, Elizabeth stepped back and held Emmie's hands as she looked into her eyes.

"I am always here for you, honey. Never hesitate to call on me, you hear?"

Emmie looked back gratefully. "Thank you, Mrs. Campbell, thank you for everything."

"I believe we've been through enough together to move on from 'Mrs. Campbell' now, don't you agree? It's Elizabeth."

"I appreciate that...Elizabeth." Emmie smiled. "But perhaps in the store it would be best for me to address you as Mrs. Campbell."

"Whatever suits you, dear. Now go wash your face, and if you are feeling up to it, let me show you these new fabrics I ordered from London while you were gone."

Emmie was surprised at how quickly the days fell back into a familiar routine—waiting on customers in the shop, sewing special orders, and spending her evenings sketching designs for new dresses. That is, the evenings when she wasn't walking out on the arm of Dr. Decker. They dined often with the Campbells, and the four became easy companions despite their positions as employers and employees.

It wasn't that Emmie didn't think about her father and family. Once again, she had not been there for the birth of another of Omie's children, and this weighed on her heart. Sometimes the longing for them all came on her with such sudden intensity that she had to catch her breath.

I suppose this is the way of things. The measure of love one feels for people has its equal in the sorrow felt from their absence. It's time for another visit home.

Emmie mentioned this to Caleb one evening as they were strolling through the parks enjoying the first suggestion of fall in the breeze. Each verdant square had its own personality, a series of jewels in the heart of the city.

"Emmie, I didn't have an opportunity to get to know your family at the funeral, of course, but I could see how close you are. I'm sure your father was a good man who did all he could to give you everything you needed. More than that, to make sure you knew you were loved. It's fortunate indeed to have that love. I can't say the same of my father. I don't know if he thought a show of affection would make my brothers and me weak, or if that emotion just was not in him. He provided for us, of course, and he paid for my medical training, for which I will always be grateful. I would have liked more, but that's not who he was."

Emmie stopped and turned to face him. "You speak of him in the past tense?"

"Yes, we lost my father a couple of years ago."

"Caleb, I'm so sorry. I didn't know."

"Well, we haven't really had much time to know the details of each other's lives, have we? Though, having seen where you grew up, I feel I know much more about you."

"Not the sophisticated life I suppose you are used to." Emmie turned to resume their walk. Caleb held out a hand to stop her.

"Emmie, never be ashamed of your upbringing. It was an honest and admirable life. You had the most important things—a close family, acceptance, purpose. Things I never had. My mother grew up on a farm. Although she married into money, she does much to help the less fortunate in our town, feeling she should share some of her good fortune with others. Mother is a lady of grace and compassion. And great strength, which I attribute to the challenges of farm life."

He lifted her hand to his lips. "I see this strength in you as well. I often went along when she made visits to people in the outlying areas. Many times, try as she might, there were limits to what comfort she could give. That's where I found my purpose—to become a doctor. I determined to be able to do more for these folks who seemed more my people than my father's family."

Caleb touched her elbow and they resumed their walk as he continued, "Of course, all my father saw in my decision was a way for me to be successful and make a good living. A good reflection on him. He was none too happy to hear of my decision to come to Savannah and assist Dr. Campbell. He had bigger aspirations for me up north in some university hospital that ministered to those of higher means."

"How did he die, Caleb?" she asked quietly.

"Oh, my father was a man of many indulgences. I believe he had a heart condition which he chose to ignore. He fell from his horse and was dragged for some distance. I just pray his heart killed him first. Being a fine horseman, we can't imagine him falling for any other reason."

"How has your mother held up in his absence?"

"She has a reservoir of strength that is quite impressive. There's obviously sorrow within her, but I don't know if it's all for him or for what they didn't have. I heard them arguing once when I was small, something about his lack of affection toward her. She accused him of only truly loving one person in his life. He told her she was being ridiculous and given to histrionics, then he stormed out of the house. But he didn't deny it. It's not something she ever spoke of to us children, of course, even after we were grown men. I wonder sometimes of whom she spoke."

"I hadn't realized just how lucky I have been," Emmie said. "The love between my parents was always there to see. Other than Omie and me, they hardly needed anyone else in their lives, they enjoyed each other so. Humor was an important part of our life too. No matter the circumstances, they always managed to laugh about something in the face of adversity. And truly, there seems not to have been much struggle, other than my father's broken leg. Besides the typical concerns of a farmer, anyway. If I choose to marry, theirs is the kind of marriage I am determined to have." Emmie blushed. "Not that I'm suggesting anything, Caleb. You understand what I mean."

Caleb stopped beside a park bench and spread his coat for them to sit on. He turned to her. "I do understand, Emmie. I feel the same. Although my parents didn't have the kind of relationship as yours, I've seen it. Mostly in the lives of people with more children and much less means than we had. Their problems seem to bond them more than divide them. Perhaps, when love is all you have plenty of, love is enough."

He looked out into the gathering darkness for a few quiet moments. "Emmie, I had thought to speak of this later, but the time seems right for it." He stroked her cheek. "We don't know each other well, that's true. But I have so much admiration for you. You are your own person, intelligent, thoughtful, and as guileless as anyone I've ever known. Not to mention lovely."

He smiled at her, lifting her chin. "I would like to think that we could have that kind of life together, a love that spans a lifetime. I'm falling in love with you, you know. But most of all, I would rather be in your company than anyone else's. I suppose that's a good sign?"

He looked at her questioningly. "I'm asking if you would consider becoming my wife. Maybe this is presumptuous of me, as we've never spoken of our feelings for each other. But I believe I've sensed a similar affection from you. Please tell me if I'm wrong, and I will speak no further."

"No, Caleb, you are not wrong. I just don't know . . ." she began, and he took her hand.

"I'm not asking you to give me an answer now. Please think deeply about this before you do. One of the things I appreciate most about you, Emmie, is your independence and skill in your own profession. I would never ask you to give up anything you choose to do, and I don't believe you would ask that of me, either."

Emmie kissed his cheek and snuggled closer to him. She felt as if they were in a warm, secret place of their own with a window looking out onto the rest of the world.

1939

JUNE 18

Aunt Phoebee took the girls on a walk to gather wildflowers. She had promised to show them how to plait blooms into their hair.

The older women were grateful to be left to talk among themselves without interruption. Chatter and laughter coming from the yard were a soothing background for remembrances and tears being passed around the kitchen table. More than a few laughs were woven into their conversation as well. Love's balm for the ones left behind.

When the girls had gathered an armful each of daisies and other flowers, Aunt Phoebee said, "That should be plenty," motioning for them to sit. The oldest of them sat behind the youngest, which included Tess' two little sisters. They followed Phoebee's lead as the woman's small fingers deftly wove beebalm and daisies into Lilly's hair.

"Where are your brothers, Tess? Don't they want to hear Grandmamma's stories?"

"Naw," Tess replied. "The kind of stories they want to hear come from the uncles."

"Phoebee," Lilly asked, "are we related somehow? I never have heard. I don't know exactly what I should call you."

Phoebee finished and sat back to look at her handiwork.

"Why, Miss Lilly, you are a sight! Go show your grandmamma how purty you are!"

"But are you? Related, I mean?" Lilly turned to look at Phoebee and all eyes followed.

"Well, I reckon you could say we become chosen family. I was far away from mine when I come here and your Grandmamma's bunch took me in. That was before my Polly was borned. I been 'Aunt' Phoebee ever since."

"Tell us the story!" Lilly cried.

Tess turned to Lilly and said, "I know a secret about Aunt Phoebee. How she got her name."

"What's the secret?" Lilly asked.

"Well, for starters, it's spelled with two e's at the end." Tess smiled smugly.

Lilly arched an eyebrow in Aunt Phoebee's direction.

"I'll tell y'all everythin', but then we best go help with supper."

Chapter 22

1910

Nate came back from getting supplies in town followed by a couple in a wagon. He jumped down and fetched Omie and Kate from the house to introduce them to Ephram and Phoebee Miller, newly come to the area from Stone Mountain, Georgia. He said that they were looking for a place to settle and farm, and Nate reckoned with the Lee's house empty now, Kate might be willing to rent it to them.

Kate greeted the couple, taking in the girl's youth and the young man's charming smile. Something in that smile didn't sit quite right, but the girl beside him had a delicate, lovely light about her.

Kate nodded. "I reckon that would be all right. There's everything you might need there. No sense in it sittin' empty. I'll come up and air things out, see if there's anything I want to bring down here, and we'll get y'all settled."

Omie smiled up at the girl in the wagon, who she supposed to be fourteen or fifteen, and felt a sisterly protectiveness toward her. The women invited Phoebee into the house while the men went off to discuss details of the rent and fair shares of the crops Ephram planned to grow.

Phoebee cooed over the baby. The other children took to her like she was one of them. She was a small young woman, tiny boned and just a foot or so taller than Ada Kate. Omie couldn't imagine her as a farmer's wife, but didn't want to pry. It was apparent they hadn't been together long from the way Phoebee's eyes followed Ephram wherever he went.

The women and children traipsed up to the Lee's house with Phoebee carrying Frank Thomas. He couldn't take his little eyes from her face. By the time the men brought the Miller's wagon up, the house was clean and ready for the couple to move in.

The family left the couple alone to bring their things in and get comfortable, with a promise to send one of the children up later to fetch them for supper.

Omie and Kate had a few minutes to themselves as they hung wash out on the line, watching in the distance as Ephram and Phoebee moved between the wagon and the house.

"She's a sweet little thing," Kate said. "I'm of two minds about that young fellow, though. I expect we'll know soon enough what he's about."

"I agree, Mamma. It's nothing I can put my finger on yet, but there's an uneasiness to him. I suppose Nate learned enough about them in town to feel all right bringing them here. I don't sense Ephram is a bad man, but I think he needs watching. That little Phoebee, though, she's light as a hummingbird, isn't she?"

"Yes, daughter, there's something precious about her. As small as she is, she has a greatness of spirit shining all about her."

At supper, conversation was light, and Ephram seemed intent on diverting the talk away from why they'd left Stone Mountain. He just allowed that they had farmed a plot of land Phoebee's parents leased him, and things had not gone as well as they'd have liked. They decided to set out to find a place of their own in the less rocky lands close to the coast.

Nate and Ephram got on well. They were both hard-working men who could not stand to be idle. Omie thought perhaps that instead of relieving Nate of some of the workload, the two of them seemed to find more projects to work on together than ever before. Omie was glad for Nate to finally have a friend, especially someone his age. It seemed to ease the blow of losing Frank. Somewhat. She knew that Nate had felt the love and admiration for her father that he never could for his own, and hoped the short time they'd had together softened some of the scars of his childhood.

Chapter 23

Omie hummed a tune to herself as she waded through the tall grass at the pasture's edge, looking for mullein stalks to use for candle wicks. The flowers were dried up and gone from most, and the stalks stuck up from the leaves like torches. Her mamma said mullein stalks had been used for candles as far back as she could remember; some said they were used to keep witches away. Omie imagined it was the wise women who knew the uses of plants who were called witches, anyhow.

She realized there was another voice humming nearby besides her own, further into the woods. She slipped quietly between the trees and came upon a sight that made her take a sharp breath and drop her basket.

Phoebee was halfway up a sweetgum tree, barefoot and with her skirts hiked up. She was humming a low sweet tune as she dipped her hand into a hole in the tree's trunk, pulling out a piece of honeycomb as big as her fist. She tucked it into an open jar in her apron pocket and reached for more. The bees seemed not to know she was there as they flew about their business, in and out of the hole without even landing on Phoebee's arms. The humming of the bees blended in with the tone of Phoebee's voice, and Omie knew she was witnessing the miracle of a bee charmer before her. She didn't make a sound until Phoebee had come down out of the tree, so as not to startle her. When Phoebee saw her, she laughed with pleasure.

"Omie!" she cried, "how would you like some honeycomb? First I've found since we came here." She walked calmly over to Omie and extended a piece of comb with beautiful golden honey dripping from it. "This time of year, I reckon this is mostly sourwood honey. My favorite!"

Omie took a bite and moaned with pleasure. It was indeed some of the best honey she'd ever tasted. "Land's Sake, Phoebee, how did you ever learn to do that?"

"Oh, I reckon I just done it since I was big enough to climb a tree. My granny said it has to do with how I was borned."

"Why don't you come with me back to the house for some cold tea? I know Mamma will want to hear this story too!" Omie said in amazement.

The young women stepped up onto the porch where Kate was rocking Frank Thomas, and Phoebee held out the jar of honey toward her.

"Well, my goodness, what do we have here?" Kate unscrewed the lid and dipped her finger into the thick sweetness inside. "Sourwood!" She beamed up at Phoebee.

"Yes'm, that's what I reckoned, too."

"A bee charmer is what we've got here," Omie said. "Let me get us all some tea, and Phoebee is going to tell us her story."

Phoebee leaned over to peek at the baby and smiled as he took her finger in his little hand.

"Don't let him put your finger in his mouth, darlin. It's not good for babies to have honey until they are about a year or so old."

"I didn't know that! Why do you 'spose that is?"

"There's just something in their little bellies that don't take to it. I've heard of babies dying from eating it too young."

Phoebee snatched her finger away with a gasp, and Kate smiled at her. "It's all right, Phoebee. Just wash your hands, and you can hold him while we visit."

Phoebee jumped up and washed at the basin, then came back to cradle Frank Thomas in her arms. "I cain't wait to have one of my very own to hold," she said, looking adoringly into his face.

Kate felt a twitch of something in her belly as she looked at the young girl rocking in the chair. She was so small, her feet barely touched the floor. Before Kate could give it much consideration, Omie came onto the porch, bringing cool, sweet tea for them all. Bartie was clinging to her skirts while Ada Kate helped her little sister walk.

"So, let's hear the story of Phoebee the Bee Charmer!"

Omie smiled as the little girls settled beside her on the floor, staring at Phoebee.

"When my mamma was carrying me," Phoebee began, "she was washin' clothes down at the creek near our house. There was a log that lay across from bank to bank above the water that she draped clothes across to dry. Well, this one day, Mamma saw that a limb had broke off from the high waters we'd had that spring. She didn't notice the hole in the trunk it left, and as she went to lay a piece of wash over it, a bunch of bees flew out and started stinging her. Mamma laid down in the creek to get them off until it was safe to get out, then made her way back home to where her ma was makin' dinner. Granny said they was so many stings on mamma's poor face that she hardly knew her."

"What did she do, Phoebee?" Ada Kate asked.

"Right off, Granny laid her down and put poultices on all the welts, but mamma fainted and Granny couldn't wake her. Then I started to come. I guess all that poison just caused her body to want to get me out, to save me if'n it could. Mamma wasn't but seven months along, so even when she woke up with the pain, she couldn't push much. Granny said when I did come out, I was the tiniest, most pitiful thing she ever saw. They didn't expect me to live out the day, but somehow, I hung on. When daddy fetched the doctor, he said if mamma hadn't got down in the creek away from those bees when she did, she might have died and taken me with her. Granny said I didn't look much bigger than a bee, so she named me 'Phoe-bee'. And in all my days, I never have got stung by a bee. I could always hear them buzzin' when they flew over my head, and I'd follow them back to their tree. Seems like they was kinda tryin' to make up for me almost dyin', cause they never begrudged me a share of their honey."

"She even sounds like them when she hums," Omie said.

"Sound like a bee for us, Phoebee!" Ada Kate cried.

"Well, I best hand Frank Thomas over to his mamma first so he don't think I'm a bee come to get him!" Then she chased Ada Kate around the porch buzzing and nipping at her clothes until they both fell giggling to the floor.

Afterwards, Ada Kate danced around the yard buzzing like a bee, while Bartie slept on her mamma's lap. The women sat contentedly and talked as the sun tilted toward afternoon. Then, Phoebee went home to make some corn cakes to dip in the sweet treasure, for after dinner.

Phoebee began tagging along with Kate and Omie, learning about the plants they were gathering for medicines. Kate showed them both how poisonous plants often had their remedy growing close by. Jewelweed was usually found close to poison oak or poison ivy. The odd spikes of horsetail grew where stinging nettle waited to set fire to any creature who touched it.

Kate remarked, "It's said that the shape of a plant will tell you what part of the body it's meant to heal. Ginseng is the easiest. It looks like a man.

Good to strengthen the whole body, get the sugar in the blood right and almost as good as coffee to get a body movin'. 'Sang', as some call it, is like goldenseal though—you got to know when it's mature enough to pick, and you got to re-seed it yourself."

Phoebee was fascinated at Kate's knowledge of plants. She teased her and Omie both about being 'witchy women', until Omie pointed out that charming bees was as witchy as anything she'd ever seen.

"Honey cures ailments too," Phoebee told them. My Grandmamma used honey to ease stomach problems, put it on the skin for burns and cuts to keep infection away. Cain't beat it."

"You are absolutely right, child. I've been using your honey for those very things!"

Kate's praise made the girl's eyes shine, and she fairly skipped back to the house.

Nate had built a room on their back porch for the women to work in with their herbs. Kate began to see her customers there when Phoebee and Ephram moved into her house on the hill. This small space was a refuge for Kate, giving her a place to be alone with her thoughts at times. She invited Phoebee over occasionally to teach her some skills and enjoyed the company of the lively girl. When Omie joined them, laughter rang out across the fields.

1939

June 18

Supper was a loud, busy time, with the adults gathered around the table and children spilling out onto the porch. Omie's sons, Frank Thomas and Ezra, and Emmie's boys, Danny and Aaron, did a fair job of finishing off the food that neighbors had brought by.

Omie smiled as she watched them eat. *I bet there's not a chicken left in Effingham county that hasn't been fried or cooked up with dumplings. In times of sorrow, actions speak louder than words. I reckon food is the language of love.*

When not a crumb of pie or ounce of pound cake was left and the kitchen cleaned, everyone returned to the coolness of the porch.

"We want to hear more stories!" Lilly declared.

The little ones chorused, "We want to catch fireflies!"

Frank Thomas grinned. "C'mon. I know where Daddy kept his empty jars."

Ezra rolled his eyes, and they led the younger children out into the yard.

Danny looked at his brother. "There's gonna be girl talk."

"I'm outta' here!" Aaron announced.

Aunt Phoebee placed her small hand on Lilly's, smiling. "I want to hear more, too! Your grandma and Emmie was fully-growed women when I showed up."

Omie laughed. "Ha! I was just a couple years older than you. I got an earlier start on havin' a family is all."

From the back, Phoebee and Lilly looked to be the same age. Phoebee's hair was still dark brown without a trace of gray, despite her forty-some years.

Omie felt great affection for the slight woman who had been a part of her life now for decades. *I reckon Phoebee is as much a sister as Emmie, in her own way. I don't believe she'll ever grow old.*

Lilly placed her hand on top of Phoebee's. "I'm so glad I can call you my aunt too."

"Oh honey, I don't care what you call me, long as you call me to supper!"

Laughter was a welcome sound on this day of mixed emotions. Omie had to admit to some relief that Nate's suffering and turmoil were at an end. She was grateful for what they had between them in the past. Grateful for the children that came from that love. Sorrow for what came after.

The voices around her were a pleasing balm. She shared in telling tales of the childhood shared with Emmie, but mostly let herself drift into memories. She started at the sound of Lilly asking, "Grandma, are you ok? You went somewhere on us."

"Oh, sorry child. I guess I was in a deep remembrance. I was thinking on the day Emmie told us right here on this porch that she was getting hitched."

"I was only thinking of getting married then," Emmie corrected her sister.

Lilly and Tess cried, "Tell us more. Please?"

"I've told y'all about me and your Uncle Caleb before."

"Didn't he have some handsome brothers?" Tess nudged Lilly.

Omie closed her eyes, recalling the aftermath of that day, when Nate learned the truth about his future brother-in-law.

Emmie looked at her sister for a long moment. Then began to speak.

Chapter 24

1910

Under a clear blue fall sky, Thomas drove Emmie home to visit her family for the week. Sassafras trees and sumac bushes had already begun to turn various shades of peach, orange, and red, mingling with the soft yellow of sweetgums. There were layers of coolness and warmth in the air. The sun splashed light on everything. An indefinable smell announced autumn had arrived. Emmie took a deep breath.

This is the kind of day that makes me so glad just to be alive. A day perfect in all its elements.

She was preoccupied with thoughts of Caleb's proposal, and looked forward to sharing them with Omie and Mamma. She sighed and Thomas smiled at her.

Emmie smiled back, "What is it, Thomas?"

"Oh, nothin', Miss Emmie. You just seem in much better spirits since we last made this trip."

"Indeed, and I don't think I've ever thanked you and your wife for the kindness you showed me then."

"It was our pleasure. Losing a loved one is not something you should ever go through alone." He turned back to watching the horses. "That smile on your face wouldn't have somethin' to do with a young doctor I know of, would it?"

He laughed at the look she turned on him, and Emmie said, "That Maizie! What has she told you?"

"Just that you been keepin' company with him quite a bit lately, is all. 'Bout time, I say."

She went back to admiring the purples and yellows of the roadside flowers and lost herself in contented silence.

As they pulled up in the yard, Emmie noticed a diminutive young woman standing out back with Omie, reaching to pin clothes on the line.

"Well, hey!" the young woman called. "You must be Emmie!"

Emmie smiled back, thinking that Phoebee was as contagiously cheerful as Omie's letters had said.

"I am, and you must be Phoebee!" Thomas helped Emmie down from the wagon, and she hugged Omie, then was surprised to be caught up in a hug with Phoebee as well.

Kate came out of the house and held her arms out to Emmie saying, "Daughter, you've turned into quite a young woman these past few months! Come in here and tell us all the news of the big city." Kate tucked Emmie's hand beneath her elbow and smiled with pleasure at having both her girls home again.

Emmie noticed how much silver had begun to show in her mother's hair. Mamma had always had such a mane of dark shining waves, a nod to both her Creek Indian and Irish roots.

The autumn light glinting off the silver makes her even more lovely.

The sisters sat down as Thomas unloaded Emmie's bags and Kate packed him lunch for the return trip.

"Are you sure you can't stay for a bit?" Emmie asked him.

"No, ma'am," he said. "I promised the missus I would be home before dark, and I try never to cross that woman!" They all laughed, knowing how much he adored Maizie, and that he could not wait to get back to her.

"I'll see you in a week's time then, Thomas. Thank you so much," Emmie called as the carriage pulled away.

Nate and Ephram came in for dinner, and Emmie was introduced to Phoebee's handsome young husband. When Nate gave Emmie a quick peck on the cheek, Omie turned to him with a sweet smile. He kissed her as well, then went with Ephram to wash up for the meal.

Phoebee had many questions about the city. Emmie entertained them all with stories about life in Savannah, her work, and the Campbells. She casually brought up Dr. Caleb's name as if in passing, but Kate could see how much pleasure it gave Emmie just to hear herself say it. Once the men had gone back to work and the dishes were washed, the women sat at the table for a cup of tea.

Omie said, "Now, let's hear more about this Dr. Caleb," and wagged her eyebrows at Emmie.

"Not much to tell." Emmie smiled into her cup, but Omie would have none of it.

"Beans!" Omie said, "Spill 'em!"

"All right." Emmie grinned and told them about Caleb's proposal.

Phoebee piped up, "You will say yes, won't you? It's all so romantic and excitin' and...right somehow!" She looked up at Emmie with a concerned smile. "Not that I know what's best for you, Miss Emmie, but...it just is, that's all!" They laughed and Emmie could not be affronted at the girl's infectious enthusiasm.

The next days were lovely and long. Emmie spent time with her mother and the children. She took long walks with Omie and Phoebee. Once, Phoebee even showed her how she robbed the bees. Emmie was astounded and told her so. The girl promised to bring over some honey for Emmie to take back to Savannah with her.

Wait until I tell Caleb about Phoebee's story and how she's never suffered a single sting!

Too soon, it was time for Emmie to be on her way back. The evening before she left, they all gathered in front of the fireplace, enjoying the coolness in the air and the warmth of the fire. Nate brought out the last of the cider Frank had kept in the root cellar, and even Kate had a small cup. They toasted to all the blessings received in the year, the birth of Frank Thomas, the coming of Ephram and Phoebee, and the bountiful harvest made possible with the help of the Millers. Kate was quiet for a moment, and they saw dampness in her eyes.

"Mamma, what's wrong?" Omie asked softly.

"I'm just thinking how nice it would have been to share a sip of this cider with your daddy. I wish I had sometimes."

"Well, here's to Frank. I'm sure he's smiling down on us now, and if heaven is the kind of place it should be, he's having a drink with us, too." Nate said. They all raised their cups in a toast.

When the children were put to bed and the Millers had gone home, Kate said her goodnights also and went to bed.

"I have never in my life seen Mamma take a draught of any kind!" Emmie giggled as she and Omie sat in the rockers, finishing off the last bit of cider.

"Well, she certainly deserves to," Omie said. "She's carried so much on her shoulders this year."

"How is Mamma doing, really?" Emmie asked.

"Mostly she seems fine," Omie offered, "but sometimes I see her just sitting here, looking out across the fields, and I know she sees daddy everywhere. Not his ghost, but pictures from their past. I just let her be with her memories. She seems content to stay here with the children and make her tonics and such while I gather the plants and do her rounds for her. I'll never be the healer she is, but I try to do her justice with all she taught me. It's harder than it seems, Emmie. How she witnessed so much suffering without taking on the weight of it, I'll never know."

They rocked in silence for a while, then Omie asked, "Do you think you'll marry him, Emmie?"

"I believe I will, sister."

Omie got up to kneel beside Emmie and hugged her hard, glad for her happiness.

The following morning, Thomas returned to fetch Emmie for the trip back to Savannah. Everyone waved goodbye until she was out of sight, then Omie went to find Nate in the barn. She came up behind him, wrapping her arms around his waist.

"Well, now," he said, "what's put you in such a sweet mood?" He turned around and sat on a hay bale, pulling her into his lap.

"I guess I'm just so happy for Emmie, is all. It sounds like she's made up her mind to marry Caleb. He seems like a good man. Good catch, too! Mrs. Dr. Caleb Decker." She smiled.

Nate suddenly got very still. "Decker, did you say?" he asked.

"Yes. Why?"

"Do you know where he's from?" Nate asked with a tightness in his jaw.

"Somewhere west of here I believe. Statesboro?"

Nate rose quickly, nearly spilling Omie to the ground.

"Nate, what is it, what's wrong?" she cried.

"Damn those sonofabitches!" he said. "First one and then the other, I just cain't seem to get rid of 'em!" He kicked at a feed bucket and put his hands to his head.

"Decker, Omie. That was my real daddy's name. It's too close, he has to be related to him!"

Nate saddled the mule without a word, while Omie sat in stunned silence. He started out of the barn before she could respond.

"Nate!" She tried, but he was off and gone from sight.

Omie dragged herself up from the hay bale and slowly made her way to the house. Kate was in the yard dangling Frank Thomas by his arms, tickling his feet on the grass. She looked up as Omie came near and said, "What is it Omie, what's happened?"

Omie sat on the cool ground and took the baby onto her lap. "Oh Lord Mamma, I can't believe this. Caleb's last name is Decker."

"Yes, I recall that, but what...?"

"It's the same name as the man who got Nate's mamma pregnant with him. They may be brothers."

"Heavens." Kate sat beside Omie and they pondered the way things could change so quickly. "We'll have to give him time, is all," Kate said. "Caleb is not responsible for Nate's circumstances."

"I know, Mamma, but he feels like he just can't get ahead of his past."

"Nobody can, daughter. It's part of what makes us who we are. We just have to learn to live with it."

Nate did not come home that evening nor the next. Aunt Julia sent word that he was sleeping off a two-day drunk in her barn, and he and the mule were all right. She said when he was sober and cleaned up, she'd send him home with an earful of the Lord's Word. No one could deliver it like Aunt Julia. If you were not a believer before, you were afraid not to be after she got hold of you.

After a few days, Omie was prepared to go after him, but long about dinner time, she saw Nate ride the mule up to the barn, remove the saddle and hitch her to the plow. He went right out to the field without a look toward the house. Omie gave him a little time to sweat out some of the likker and emotions she knew must be fermenting in his blood as well.

She took him a plate of food and a glass of cold tea. He saw her coming and called, "whoa" to the mule, who looked relieved to see Omie. Nate turned to her, stoney-faced. She offered him the food and drink, and he said, "Well, ain't you going to fuss at me, too?"

"Naw, I reckon Aunt Julia did enough of that for the both of us. Come sit and eat."

They walked over to a grassy spot at the edge of the field and sat down. Nate held the plate in his lap but did not lift the fork to his mouth. Instead, he said, "I don't know if I can do this, Omie. Welcome a man into my home who shares the same blood as that bastard. I just don't know. I *do* want Emmie to be happy. You know that."

"I do." She sighed. "I don't know how, but we'll find our way through this, Nate. We don't know Caleb's history. We don't know that you share the same father. But if you do, Caleb may have suffered at that man's hands, too, and none of it his doing either."

"Well, blood will out, they say." He looked down and began to eat.

"Remember though, Nate, you both have as much of your mamma's blood in you as your daddy's. I know what a good man you are, darlin'. I think Caleb is, too."

After dinner, Nate found Ephram turning furrows under and raking the ground smooth to sow winter rye. He approached his friend, hat in hand.

"I'm sorry to leave you with this, Ephram. I had some sortin' out to do."

"No need to apologize. We all got things to work out, time to time." They shook hands and went to work. Omie watched out the window as the men found their pace, thanking the heavens once again for having sent Ephram as a companion to her husband.

Hard work seemed to erase some of the strain from Nate's face. He took to carrying Frank Thomas around with him again before supper, tucking his son inside his coat to keep him warm.

"This boy is growing fast as a shoat!" he said one evening, handing the baby to Omie. "He'll be big as Dapples before you know it."

"Maybe tomorrow I'll take him to meet the old pig."

Dapples was a boar they had raised from a little spotted runt into a five-hundred-pound hog. He was a good sire and mild-mannered for his size. Omie had tamed him so that he followed her everywhere until he grew too large to keep up. They could not bring themselves to have him slaughtered. Nate trimmed his tusks regularly, even though they doubted he would use them. It was best to be safe with the children around. Dapples even allowed the little ones to ride on his broad back, without complaint. He had a pen to himself beneath a big oak where there was plenty of shade and an abundance of acorns.

Omie stopped by Phoebee's the following day, and invited her to come with them and meet the old hog.

Frank Thomas gurgled when she touched his tiny feet to the animal's back. Dapples seemed to enjoy it as well.

Phoebee liked feeding the pig bits of honeycomb, to watch him chew and chew when it stuck to his teeth. "Looks like he's got a chaw of tobacco in his mouth!" Phoebee giggled, scratching his chin.

"Maybe we could get the men to chew honeycomb instead of tobacco so they wouldn't be spittin' that juice everywhere. Such nasty stuff!" Omie exclaimed.

"Yes, and their breath would be sweet as honey," Phoebee laughed.

"Maybe their dispositions, too."

The women looked out to where the men were standing by the fence, talking.

"Phoebee, I'm so thankful the two of you found us. For Nate's sake and mine. For us all."

The girl blushed and replied, "Nate's doin' better, ain't he."

Omie smiled. "Yes ma'am, I believe he is."

Chapter 25

Emmie fidgeted in the carriage, adjusting her hat every time the wind blew it askew and pinning stray strands of hair back in place.

"You may as well leave it be until we get close," Caleb chuckled. "Your arms are going to get mighty tired over the next six hours or so."

She looked at him sheepishly and said, "I know. I'm just so nervous, Caleb. I want to look my best, and I think by the time we get there, I'm going to look like I flew in on a broom."

"No chance, darling. You could never be anything but beautiful."

She looked at him sideways and said, "You might think so, but your mother may wonder what you're doing with this rag-tag farm girl. Oh, I wish we'd get there faster, I just want this meeting over with!"

"She'll love you too," he said, as he put a hand on hers and gave it a squeeze.

The day passed in a slow dream. Emmie was bundled up for the October chill, cozy against the warmth of Caleb's side. She fell asleep to the slow *clop clop* of horses' hooves, waking with her head on Caleb's shoulder, a line of her drool staining his topcoat.

"Oh, I'm so sorry!" she said, wiping at his shoulder with her handkerchief. "How long have I been asleep?"

"A goodly while. We don't have too much further to go."

They finished the last miles in a comfortable mix of conversation and silence. Emmie was pleased they didn't feel a need to fill every moment with words. The quiet spaces taught her nearly as much about him as the stories he told about his life. She watched how he took in the scenery going by, how he whistled softly under his breath and how he reached to touch her hand, even when he seemed deep in pleasant reverie. If this was how they were now, imagine how contented they could be in a home of their own with the small rituals of everyday life. She smiled at the thought, and he reached over to kiss her cheek.

"That's better," he said. "No more worried frown on your sweet face."

Emmie felt her brow wrinkle again as they pulled up beside a lovely Victorian house on a shady street. An older, colored gentleman in livery came out to take the reins from Caleb's hands, and Caleb gave him an affectionate clap on the shoulder.

"Thank you, Otis. How are you these days?"

"I'm jest fine, Dr. Decker. How are you?"

Emmie heard the affection in the older man's voice and was pleased for Caleb.

"This here must be Miss Lee. How do, ma'am?" Otis doffed his hat toward her.

She said, "Emmie, please."

"Aw'right, Miss Emmie. The missus is waiting for you in the parlour. I'll see to these fine horses."

After they stepped down from the carriage, Otis climbed up slowly onto the seat.

"Is he all right to take care of those beasts alone?" Emmie whispered, looking at the elderly servant with a little concern.

"Don't let his slowness fool you. He's still strong enough to take me over his knee again if he had a mind to."

Emmie laughed at the image of a grown Caleb being paddled by the old man.

As they walked up the steps, she took in the modest, but elegant lines of the house. Its most engaging feature was the wrap-around porch with ornamental moldings painted in tasteful colors. Large ferns hung between the posts, and leafy potted plants caught the afternoon sun.

"You boys must have spent all your time on this porch!"

Caleb replied, "Much mischief occurred on this very spot."

The door was opened by a sweet-faced, colored woman in a maid's uniform. Caleb introduced her as Cassie, Otis' wife.

"Why howdy, Miss Emmie. I'm pleased to meet you. Mrs. Decker is looking forward to meetin' you, too."

Cassie led the way to the parlour. A petite woman stood waiting for them, and Caleb scooped her up, swinging her around. She was lovely. Her thick brown hair was swept up into a coif on top of her head. Her laughing eyes were of a deep blue, like her son's.

"Mamma," he said, setting her down in front of Emmie, "this is the young lady I have been writing you about."

Mrs. Decker held out her hands and gave Emmie a kind smile. "I hope the trip wasn't too tiring, dear. So kind of you to come all this way to meet us. We're very glad to have you."

Emmie was relieved to find Caleb's mother trying to put her at ease. She had wondered whether she would be scrutinized and judged as to her suitability for the eldest son of the family, but she could sense the admiration and respect his mother had for her son, and for his choices.

They enjoyed a cup of tea as Cassie performed the final preparations for supper, and soon they were called to the table.

"Now, don't be scared by the ruffians I call my brothers," Caleb leaned over to tell her. "I made them promise to wear more than loin cloths to the table."

Emmie laughed and blushed slightly as two handsome young men came in through the kitchen door, arguing good-naturedly until they spied Emmie and stopped behind their chairs. They were like flip sides of a coin, one dark-haired and grey-eyed, the other blonde with blue eyes. Caleb seemed a mix of both.

"Well, would you look at that."

The dark-haired one was Marion, she recalled.

"Caleb has managed to find a pretty girl who feels sorry enough for him to join him for supper."

The youngest, Cyrus, winked at her and said, "We are very grateful for your kindness to our poor brother. We hope he did not bore you terribly on your journey!"

"Quite the opposite," Emmie countered. "He told me all about you two!"

They looked at each other and laughed, then gave their mother a kiss on the cheek and shook hands with Caleb.

After the meal, they all moved into the parlour for a glass of sherry before bedtime. Emmie could tell Cyrus and Marion joined them to be polite, but that their tastes ran to much stronger spirits. The banter between Caleb and his brothers was enjoyable for her, having had so little experience with the ways of boys.

She said as much to Mrs. Decker when the men went out to the porch to enjoy cigars. Emmie and their mother relaxed by the warm fire.

Mrs. Decker smiled. "I have been fortunate to be blessed with such good boys."

Emmie wasn't sure what to say for a moment, then she took a chance on seeming forward. "It can't have been easy for you, caring for them alone after Mr. Decker died. Caleb just recently told me of your loss. I hadn't known before."

"Ah well, my dear, they have mostly raised themselves. Their father seemed not to have much time for them, but they are the joy of my life."

After watching the flames for a time, Emmie offered, "My sister Omie and I were the only children my parents were able to have. I'm sure my father would've liked to have had a son, but he never let on if he was disappointed. Omie and her husband Nate have a dear little family that looks to be on its way to becoming a large one. Their latest is the sweetest little boy."

Emmie noticed that Mrs. Decker had become very still all of a sudden. Momentarily she smiled at Emmie and said, "Omie and Nate, what nice names."

Emmie felt a touch of nervousness for a moment and began talking to cover it. "Yes, Nathaniel Green Silar is his given name. I don't know if he was named after the general. His is a sad history from the little I do know about him. Apparently, the man who raised him was a cruel man, and Nate's life was a very hard one. He doesn't talk about it, but I heard him telling my parents about it when he asked for Omie's hand."

Mrs. Decker seemed lost in thought for a while, then turned a pained face to Emmie, saying, "I'm afraid I've developed a bit of a headache dear. They come upon me suddenly sometimes. I think I should retire early, and we can get to know one another more in the morning."

Caleb came in at that moment without his brothers, explaining that they wished him to say their goodnights to the ladies. The boys had some business in town and would see them tomorrow.

"Mm-hmm. Monkey business I suspect." His mother laughed, but it was a hollow laugh, and he looked at her with concern.

"It's nothing Caleb, just one of my headaches. It's been a long day, and the excitement of your coming has just tired me out, I'm afraid. Goodnight young people, I hope you sleep well. Emmie, Cassie will show you to your room."

With that she rose and walked out into the hallway.

Caleb turned and raised his eyebrows as he looked at Emmie.

"I'm not sure what I said," she replied to his gaze.

"I'm certain it wasn't anything to do with you. She used to get these headaches when my father was alive. I had hoped his passing would relieve her of them, but I suppose not."

Later that night, after a troubled attempt at sleep, Emmie got up to have a drink of water. As she made her way down the winding stairs toward the kitchen, she noticed a silhouette in the moonlight on one of the porch rockers. She slipped quietly out the door and saw Mrs. Decker sitting there.

"Is everything all right?" Emmie asked. "Is your headache very bad?"

Mrs. Decker looked at her with a tired smile and said, "Come sit with me, Emmie. I have something I need to tell you."

"Just a moment, let me get my shawl."

Momentarily she returned to the porch and sat quietly in the chair beside Caleb's mother.

Mrs. Decker sighed. "This has nothing to do with you, please don't worry. Life just plays some strange tricks on us sometimes. Whether there is a purpose behind them or if everything is random, I just can't say. I've never been a religious person, so I'm afraid I've never had something I turned to for answers."

Caleb's mother gazed out into the night for a moment, then said, "This young man that is married to your sister. What more do you know of his story?"

"What I heard was a pretty sordid tale of a wealthy gentleman who managed to have Nate's mother's husband—a poor farmer named Silar—put in jail so he could have her." Emmie blushed at the words. "When the man got out of jail, Nate was abandoned by his blood father. Silar was so angry at his wife when he found she'd had this child by the person who'd put him in prison, he beat and starved both boy and mother. Nate ran away. That's how he ended up at our farm. Why do you ask?"

"The man who abandoned him was my husband," Mrs. Decker said quietly.

Emmie sat stunned, not knowing what to say. "Are . . . are you certain?" she stammered.

Mrs. Decker looked down at her hands folded in her lap. Her words had a tight resentment behind them.

"People like to talk. It's a very small town, and everyone thinks it's their Christian duty to tell you things you may not want to know. I'm sure they imagine themselves as good, righteous people." She took a moment to calm herself. The expression on her face as she turned to look at Emmie, was one of deep sorrow mixed with resignation.

"I knew though. I knew from the beginning there was someone else Charles cared for, perhaps even loved. He knew her long before we met."

A night bird called from among the trees. The women listened to its lament until it fell silent.

"That's terribly unfair, Mrs. Decker."

"Call me Hazel, please." Emmie seemed about to protest, so she amended, "Miss Hazel if you must."

"Miss Hazel, then. Please continue."

"The girl was the daughter of a sharecropper who lived on some property Charles' family owned. Charles came from money you see, and his family forbade him to see her. I imagine he found ways. He always found ways to do what suited him."

Mrs. Decker looked away from Emmie and adjusted her tone, trying to subdue her fermented anger.

"I understand that the feelings were not mutual, however, and if the girl had not been such a lovely thing, Charles might have let it go. My husband was a vain man, though, and used to getting what he wanted. I think he courted me to spite her. Her name was Kathrine. Katie. She married a man people call Silar, and I thought that would be the end of his involvement with her."

Pale moonlight exposed the shadowed planes of grief carved into Hazel's lovely face.

She continued, "Charles and I married and began our family, but there was never a deep love between us. I had hoped there would be in time, but neither I nor our new baby seemed enough for him. He began to disappear for days at a time. Then I heard about the incident that put Mr. Silar in jail. There was a tenant on Charles' family's farm who raised pigs. I suppose he was afraid not to do my husband's bidding, so the tenant buried a pig's entrails on Silar's farm to incriminate him as a thief. Charles had Katie's husband incarcerated, then there was no one to stop him from taking advantage of Katie's desperate state. She had no support for herself or her elderly mother-in-law who lived with them."

Emmie was shocked at the deception Caleb's father was capable of. A man completely without a moral compass, it seemed. Her heart ached at the total disregard Mr. Decker had for his wife and family.

"I often suspected what we all now know. Nate was born two months before Mr. Silar was released and, when the poor man found out, he threatened to kill Charles. Of course, Charles was either related to, or in cahoots with, everyone of importance in this town, including the sheriff. I imagine they used some threats of their own."

Emmie raised damp eyes to look into Mrs. Decker's. "I am so sorry, ma'am. What a disappointment that must have been for you. For Caleb too."

"Charles was an unpredictable man. There were times when he was quiet, even kind. Then suddenly, he would be gone again. On his return, he would reek of liquor and shut himself in the library. All night, he would rant about God knows what." She raised her hands in exasperation. "The boys learned to read his moods, so that they knew when they could approach him and when to stay out of his way."

Emmie wondered if any of the Decker sons had inherited their father's traits.

As if she read her mind, Hazel turned to Emmie. "I truly don't believe you have anything to worry about with Caleb, dear. His father was challenging when I met him, before he was even twenty. I had hoped my love could have a calming effect on him." She shrugged.

"Anyway, Charles came to realize that a scandal would not further his reputation in the community. Likely his parents would have disinherited him as well, so his absences lessened, and we said nothing about it to each other. We managed to carry on as people are expected to do in this society."

Her voice softened, "Cyrus and Marion came along, and the three boys became the focus of my life. I could lavish upon them the love that my husband rejected, though he resented the attention I gave the boys. I felt I was merely property to him."

Hazel shook her head.

"I heard that Silar became a mean drunkard, that Nate and his mother suffered greatly under his fists. I was, and am, truly sorry for the boy and for her, too. I don't imagine she had much say in the matter."

She closed her eyes and took a long breath. "I feel I may have burdened you too much with this, Emmie, and for that I apologize. I wanted you to know the truth of things, though."

Emmie took the woman's hand. "Miss Hazel. I am so sorry to be a reminder of all that you've suffered. You look as though your head is pounding, perhaps you should lie down now."

"I will retire soon, Emmie. But there are some other things I want to say to you first. None of this is any reflection on you or your family. If anything, it must make you wonder about being part of this one. But I see how you and my son feel about each other, and it brings me such joy to see Caleb so happy and to know he's cared for. I will never regret having my boys, even if it took being in a loveless marriage to get them. But promise me, if you and Caleb do decide to make a life together, that you will not lose sight of who you are. Be a good wife and a good mother, but also be a good friend to yourself."

Emmie wrapped her shawl closer and contemplated these words.

Mrs. Decker gathered her thoughts for a moment and said, "Caleb has told me that your mother and sister are very gifted healers in their community. I admire that greatly. I had a passion once to learn about all the things the earth has to offer for healing whatever ails us. My grandmother knew medicinal plants well, and as a child, I used to follow her everywhere to watch while she gathered and concocted her remedies."

Emmie recalled her own forages with her mamma, though she feared her contribution simply resulted in the dismemberment of flowers.

"Once I married Charles, however, he discouraged any of those kinds of things. He thought it was beneath people of our station to resort to 'old-wives' tales and folk remedies when we had access to modern medicine. He was so proud when Caleb became a doctor. Not so much for Caleb's sake, but for his own ego."

Mrs. Decker stood. "I should like to meet your mother and sister one day."

"Please, may I help you inside?" Emmie asked.

"You're a kind girl, Emmie Lee, and I sense a strength in you that you have only begun to discover. I think that we shall be good friends."

She put her hands on either side of Emmie's face and kissed her forehead. "Goodnight, dear," she whispered as Emmie opened the door for her.

Emmie woke in the morning startled and confused about where she was. She tried to hold on to a dream that was slipping away. In the dim light she began to recognize the beautiful dressing table and mirror that she had noticed last night in the lamplight.

She lifted the curtain next to her bed to peer out at the sun rising over the stables and trees behind the house. The horses were already grazing in the pasture, steam rising off their backs in the cool dampness.

Hearing voices downstairs, she slipped into her clothes and shut the door quietly behind her. Caleb and his mother were seated at the kitchen table with cups of coffee. Caleb was holding both his mother's hands in his, listening intently to what she was saying.

They heard Emmie's footsteps and looked up.

Mrs. Decker smiled. "Good morning, Emmie dear, you're up early. Would you like some coffee?"

"I don't want to intrude," Emmie said hesitatingly.

Caleb stood to give her a kiss on the cheek.

"Not at all, darling. We were discussing you, actually."

Emmie sat in the chair he offered, then Caleb put a steaming cup in front of her.

"Thank you," she said, smiling up at him. Turning to his mother, she said, "Good morning. I do hope your headache is gone."

"I am just fine, dear. I trust you got some sleep?"

"I did," Emmie said. "But I woke from the strangest dream, and I can't seem to remember what it was about. Funny how the mood of it stays with you sometimes, even when the dream has disappeared."

"Mother has been telling me about the conversation you two had last night. I knew some of the story. I remember folks gossiping about my father when they thought I couldn't hear. I don't think most are mean-spirited. This is just a small town where very little happens worth gossiping about. How interesting, though, that your brother-in-law is part of it all. Somehow, that makes our meeting seem even more predestined."

Emmie looked at them both for a moment and said, "My mamma will know the portent of this all." At their quizzical looks, Emmie said, "It's hard to explain. She just seems to know things most of us don't. Omie too."

"Interesting," Mrs. Decker said. "My grandmother was like that, also. I could never get away with anything!"

"Is she still with you?" Emmie asked.

"No, she passed on years ago, but I still hear her fussing at me when I don't do the things I know I should." Mrs. Decker rose and said, "Like tending to the details of running this house and taking care of my family. I'll leave you two to talk, I'm sure you have much to discuss." She gave Caleb an affectionate pat on the cheek as he stood to let her by.

The two of them watched her leave, then sat again.

"I don't know what this will mean for Nate when he discovers who you are," Emmie mused. "He's a bit of a tinder box when it comes to his past."

"Let me be the one to talk to him, Emmie. It's our place to try and do what we can to repair the damages done by my father. Mother told me that my father's mother stated in her will Nate should be acknowledged and given a portion of my father's inheritance when she died, or father would get none of it. I don't think father tried very hard to seek him out. Mr. Silar claimed not to know Nate's whereabouts and wanted all the money himself, but the attorney told him, in no uncertain terms, that any trouble he made over this would land him back in jail."

"Will you tell your brothers?" Emmie asked.

"I'm not sure just yet. They think badly enough of father as it is. This can wait."

The rest of the visit went by comfortably. The Deckers did not want to overwhelm Emmie by introducing her to too much of the extended family. They all wanted time to get to know her themselves first, and by the day of their leaving, Emmie felt she was one of them. Caleb's brothers teased her as if Emmie were their sister, and she loved every minute of it. Surprising herself, she gave as well as she got.

As their carriage pulled away, Emmie and Caleb heard a raucous noise behind them and looked back to see strings of tin cans tied behind the wheels, clattering along the ground.

"Wait until we fix it up for the wedding!" The brothers laughed, running off before their mother could chide them.

Caleb just smiled and jumped down to cut the cans loose with his pocket knife. He waved to his mother and they set off to visit Emmie's family on the way back to Savannah.

"Well, they seem certain that I'm going to marry their poor pitiful brother," Emmie said, smiling.

"Are they right, Miss Lee?" He asked, looking at her.

"Much as I hate to admit that those two are right about anything, I believe they are." She leaned her head against his shoulder.

Emmie and Caleb were surrounded by the women and children as soon as they pulled up into Nate and Omie's yard. Letters had passed between them about the happy news, but this was the first time the family had seen the couple since Caleb had proposed.

As soon as Emmie was helped from the buggy, Omie linked arms with her, pulling her toward the house. Caleb asked where he might find Nate. Everyone stopped, and all were quiet a moment, then Omie nodded toward the barn.

"I believe you'll find him in there, Caleb," she said. He smiled his thanks and walked in that direction as the women pondered the outcome of this situation. They exchanged looks and resumed walking toward the house.

"You know, don't you?" Emmie asked.

Both Omie and their mamma nodded.

"Not from the *Sight* though, sister. I mentioned Caleb's last name to Nate and where he was from. Nate figured it out on his own."

Emmie looked at the barn. "Should I be concerned?"

Kate shook her head. "No, Hon. I wouldn't expect any brotherly love from Nate, though." Kate let the girls walk on ahead. *This rests in your hands, Lord. Cain't no one undo what's been done. I just pray there's a little bit of Nate that's not too blinded by rage to see the good in this man.*

Caleb found Nate sitting on a stool with one of the mule's hooves resting on his knee, cleaning it with a pick. He knew Nate had heard him come in by the stiffening of his back as he hacked at the tough clay caught in the animal's hoof. The mule apparently felt the change as well, snuffling around Nate's hat as if she might pluck it off his head.

"Cut it out, dammit!" Nate said, and moved his stool around to the other side of the mule, blocking his view of Caleb.

"Excuse me, Nate," Caleb said. "I wonder if I might have a word with you. I suppose some things have come to light since we met at your father-in-law's funeral, and I thought we might need to talk. Especially seeing as we're to be brothers-in-law."

Nate finished working the hoof and slowly stood, sliding his hand along the mule's back as he came face-to-face with Caleb. What Caleb saw in Nate's eyes made him take a step back, but he was determined not to be intimidated. This conversation needed to happen.

"Let me make this clear," Nate said quietly. "You and me will never be brothers of any kind, not through marriage and certainly not through your sorry sonofabitch father's blood. I can't keep Emmie from marryin' you, much as I wish I could. If you ever do anything, anything at all, to hurt her in any way, I'll take you out of this world and won't nobody ever know what became of you. Now get out of here, I got work to do."

Caleb stood in stunned silence as Nate moved further into the barn. He had expected that there might be hard words between them, but the intensity of Nate's dislike was palpable. He knew Omie's husband would make good on his threat.

After a deep breath, he walked a few steps toward Nate. "I'm sorry for the suffering my father's actions caused you, but I am not him. And yes, he was a sonofabitch."

Nate paused for a slight moment, then shook his head, and Caleb headed back toward the house.

"Well?" Emmie asked, as Caleb walked in the door with his hat in one hand, the other raking through his hair. "What did Nate say?"

"Not much, but enough," Caleb replied. "I can't expect him to like me, but maybe in time he'll at least come to accept me. That is, if he doesn't kill me first."

Everyone was caught up in hugs and congratulations about the engagement, not noticing how Omie went suddenly still. She looked out the window toward the barn. Nate's was walking toward the river with his head down and his fists in his pockets.

1939

June 18

"My goodness," Lilly said solemnly. "Grandaddy and Great-Uncle Caleb were related. What a small world."

"Truth be told, granddaughter, it *was* a small world here at that time. Where your grandaddy grew up is not as far as it seemed in the days before automobiles."

Omie leaned toward them. "Now, I trust that y'all won't talk about this story to folks outside our family. My husband did not want to own up to who his real daddy was. Neither this Mr. Decker nor his step-daddy were a good choice. Your grandpa did not want to be known as a bastard, so he chose to be known as Silar's son."

Bartie bit her lip, but remained silent.

Phoebee spoke up, "I have t' believe Caleb was sent by the Creator for this family. He saved us more times than I can count."

"Indeed, he did," Omie agreed. "Our precious Polly would not be alive if it weren't for Dr. Decker."

Lilly asked, "Did Caleb deliver your babies too, Grandma?"

"No darlin'. My mamma, our friend Aunt Julia—you've heard us speak of her?" The girls nodded. "And *twice*, your grandaddy did that. You know, the women in this family have been midwives and healers for generations. Your Aunt Phoebee's birthing, though—now, that was something only a trained doctor knew how to do."

"It was a miracle," Phoebee agreed. "If y'all hadn't taken me and Ephram in like you did, I most likely would be dead now."

"You were so tiny then, Phoebee." Omie said.

Lilly was astonished. "Tinier than now?"

"Indeed, she was. I was carrying your Uncle Ezra at the same time. Phoebee's belly was the only part of her that grew. Looked like she'd swallowed a watermelon!"

Emmie added, "Your grandmamma was to be my bridesmaid, but Ezra seemed like he was going to stay put until Polly came out."

"Thank goodness he decided to come when he did. I was goin' to be in that wedding if I had to birth him in the aisle!"

Chapter 26

1910

Omie stood at the window with Frank Thomas cradled in her arms, looking at the delicate snowflakes falling. Ada Kate and Bartie had never seen snow, this would be a day of wonderment for them. Perhaps Phoebee would take Ada outside to play in her stead. Bartie had a cold, and Omie feared Frank Thomas might become ill too, if he became chilled.

Phoebee tiptoed in the door, checking to see if the little girls were awake. Omie turned and grinned at the excitement on her friend's face.

Phoebee looked around. "Dang, they're still sleepin'? What if it stops, I don't want 'em to miss out."

"You mean you need a playmate!" Omie waved toward the bedroom. "Wake Ada Kate, but let Bartie sleep awhile more. She's not feeling well, so I don't want her to go out, but we can watch y'all from the window. Thank you."

Omie heard soft murmurs from the children's room, then giggles as Phoebee came out to the kitchen, with Ada wrapped in the blanket from her bed.

"Look! Christmas come early."

The women laughed as the little girl opened her mouth and eyes wide.

"Mamma, what is dat?"

"Snow, baby. The cold makes rain turn into tiny flakes of ice. See how they cover everything?"

"Purty, ain't it?" Phoebee hugged the child close. "Your mamma says I can take you out to play in it."

Big eyes looked up at Omie. "I can?"

"Let Aunt Phoebee put you in some warm clothes and I'll fix you a hot breakfast first."

They could hardly coax a few mouthfuls into Ada, but finally Omie relented and sent the two out the door. Bartie woke, noticed her sister missing and began calling, "Ay-Ay."

Omie laid Frank Thomas in his cradle and went in to scoop Bartie up.

"See? There's Ay-Ay." She pointed out the window.

Bartie laughed as Ada Kate and Phoebee danced beneath the white sky. Seeing the excitement in the eyes of her children, Omie felt as if this was her first snow also. The world was held in a spell of silence like nothing else. Time stopped. All the creatures normally going about their business seemed stilled and reverent, peering out from nests, burrows, and dens. She imagined the deer took shelter under cedars for warmth, gazing with their calm eyes at the unfamiliar wonder of it.

Even the mules capered in the crisp air. The world seemed made right somehow. It was as if angels were dusting them with some heavenly grace, tempting all into a respite from their labors, a reminder that all of importance was not effort. There was a time for quiet joy.

There was joy, most definitely, but quiet was not how the children expressed it. Their antics reminded Omie of how much she and Emmie loved these rare gifts of snow, and she missed her sister terribly.

I imagine Savannah is beautiful in the snow.

To take her mind off Emmie, Omie got several bowls from the kitchen and asked Phoebee to set them out to catch snow for 'snow cream' later. At this rate, most of the day would be needed to capture enough for them all to have a taste. Perhaps after dinner they'd have the sweetness of cream and Phoebee's honey to pour over the bowls, with a precious sprinkling of cinnamon atop.

Her first snowfall is probably what Ada Will remember most about this Christmas.

That same week, an extremely late-in-season calf had to be brought into the house and kept warm by the woodstove, delighting the girls. The animal needed to be fed often from a bottle and Ada Kate tried to help with the calf's care. Phoebee milked the mamma cow enough to relieve the soreness in her swollen teats, sometimes letting Ada Kate sit on her lap as she did so. Omie couldn't help but smile, remembering all the creatures her daddy teased her about bringing into the house. She wished he could see them now, Ada Kate growing tall and Bartie talking.

Bartie's features so resemble his.

She knew her mother talked with him often. Omie did as well, but mostly in her dreams. It gave her comfort to know that heaven was so close, for surely that was where her sweet daddy resided.

Omie placed a hand on her belly and wondered when she should inform Nate about the coming baby. It was early, but Omie knew she was pregnant again. Her mother knew too, of course. She'd tried to counsel Omie about the use of preventative measures, asking if she wouldn't like to delay having more children until Frank Thomas was older. Something in Omie told her it was not time to slow down, that having them when she was younger was important, and she trusted her instincts.

Chapter 27

Omie and her mother went to Savannah just before Christmas so Emmie could measure them for their dresses. though her wedding was to be in the fall of the following year, she knew she would need time to fit them in between orders for the shop.

Kate and Omie stayed a few days to shop for gifts for the children. Omie had saved enough from selling her own herbal tonics and teas to buy Nate a new pocket watch. He'd had his old broken one melted down to make their wedding rings.

Mamma went off in search of gifts for her daughters. Omie found a lovely gold locket just the right size to hold the small photograph of her daddy, which sat on the mantle at home. She imagined it would please her mother to carry his picture close to her heart.

"Mamma, what do you suppose we should get Ephram and Phoebee?" Omie asked, as they finished up with their purchases. "I'm thinking just some small gifts. He's mighty proud and might be offended if we give them too much."

Kate pondered this a moment. "Why don't we see if Mrs. Campbell and Emmie can spare some scraps of cloth for a quilt? We could buy the thread and such we don't already have and package it all up. When they open it, we can ask Phoebee to help us sew it, that way it's something they've had a hand in too. Nate can make them a quilting frame like your daddy made me. Ephram can be in charge of growing the cotton for the filling, and next year they'll be snug as bugs!"

"That's perfect, Mamma, I knew you'd think of the right thing." Omie kissed her mamma's cheek. They walked the windy streets back to the Campbells, enjoying the salty air blowing in from the coast.

Christmas Eve on the farm brought with it a light dusting of snow which settled on the pines like sugar icing. The women and children were so cheered at the sight that they all bundled up for a candlelight walk, singing carols as they strolled by Phoebee and Ephram's house. Phoebee ran out the door like an excited child, and they called to her to join them. She ran back inside for her shawl.

"Ephram, come with us!"

"Naw, I think I'll stay and tend the fire, maybe invite Nate over."

She noticed the bottle he was tending.

Well, no matter. I reckon he's gotta celebrate his own way.

Secretly, Phoebee was glad to be in just the company of women for a change. With less to do in winter, Ephram was becoming restless and irritable.

The moon broke through clouds scudding across the sky, lighting the way so that candles were no longer needed. Kate and Omie were glad to be able to tuck their hands back inside their shawls where the little ones were snugged in close.

"Sing with us, Aunt Phoebee!" Ada Kate called out, and they broke into a merry rendition of "The Twelve Days of Christmas".

When they were too chilled to stay out any longer, the group walked Phoebee to her house. They all stepped inside to make sure Ephram knew he and Phoebee were invited over for Christmas morning coffee and fruit-cake.

Omie told him, "Mamma's fruitcakes are soaked in so much whiskey, you'll feel some Christmas cheer for sure, but you might not be able to feel your toes!"

"Naomie Lee Silar!" Kate cried and blushed.

"Coun' me in fur sure then!" Ephram grinned.

The women pretended not to notice the slight slur of his words. The children called *Goodnight* and *Merry Christmas* as they went back out into the lovely evening.

Ada Kate was up early Christmas morning, trying to keep Bartie from pulling the wrappings off gifts under the tree.

Omie yawned as she stroked the baby's hair. "Ada Kate, you are such a good helper with your sister, thank you."

"Like a Santa elf?"

"Yes baby, just like an elf."

Kate was at the stove starting the fire. Soon, the smell of coffee drifted out, drawing the Millers down the hill. The adults settled at the kitchen table to watch the children open Santa's gifts. Ada Kate was given the job of handing out presents to the grown folks. She proudly presented the Millers with theirs first.

Phoebee was delighted with the quilt makings and could hardly wait to try her hand at it. Ephram too seemed pleased and not at all affronted.

Ephram had carved a wooden doll for the children. It was attached to a stick and had moving parts. He showed them how to make it dance on a narrow platform which rested on the knee. While Omie played her harmonica, the children taught the doll to buck dance.

Phoebee had saved an entire gallon of honey for the family, including comb that the children loved to chew.

"Why Phoebee, this tastes like pure summer to me!" Kate exclaimed. "It will ease the wait for spring." She held the girl's small face between her hands and kissed the top of her head. A deep affection passed between them. Phoebee's eyes shone with tears when she looked up at Kate's face.

She squeezed Kate's hand and declared brightly, "Why, I believe I need some more coffee to go with this wonderful cake!" She jumped up to put the kettle on. "Can I make some for everyone?"

Christmas day was a pleasant jumble of joy. After gifts were opened, the little girls played on a quilt beside the tree. Bellies were full and hearts as well. Spirits ran high until they ran down, and finally the Miller family stood to go, looking forward to a late afternoon nap.

Sitting beside her mamma, with the children sleeping on their laps, Omie reckoned she could feel the flow of time, of her place in it. She looked at the lines on her mamma's face, thinking how much her father would have loved growing old with Kate. Omie couldn't bear to think of the world without this wonderful woman in it, but she knew it would come to that. She knew, too, a part of her mamma longed for reunion with her daddy in heaven.

"Mamma, what are you thinking about?"

Kate turned her face toward the window and sighed.

"He loved Christmas most of all, you know. Took more pleasure in seeing you girls happy than receiving anything himself. It tickled Frank to pieces if he could surprise you with something you never expected. Put his mind to it all year long."

"I know." Omie smiled, taking her mamma's hand in her own. She traced the raised veins below the skin, work worn and dotted with age spots. "I love you," she said, kissing the warm palm.

Nate was well pleased with his pocket watch, Omie could tell.

They sat on the bed in their room the evening of Christmas day, after all was cleaned up and the exhausted children put to bed. Kate had retired early as well, with the locket Omie had given her pressed close to her bossom. Omie still missed her father so, and could only imagine what it must be like for her mother to have Christmas without him.

"Omie, this is a fine watch, darlin'," Nate said softly. "Much more than I deserve."

Omie took his hand as shadows of candle flames danced across his face. She noticed new lines had etched themselves along his weathered brow and settled at the corners of his mouth.

"I love you, Nate Silar, more than you know," she said earnestly. "You give so much to us all, me, the children, Mamma. And you gave up the only thing of any worth you had to make us our wedding rings. How do you *not* deserve it?".

"I found that old pocket watch in a dried up well. Didn't mean nothin'."

He moved closer to her. "I was savin' something special to give you when we were alone. This is my true gift for you, Omie Lee Silar." From behind his pillow, he pulled out a small box covered in velvet.

Omie looked up at him and said, "Nate, what have you done!"

Her eyes widened as she opened the lid of the box to find a delicate gold ring inside with a tiny diamond at its center.

"Emmie found this for me in Savannah." He smiled. "It ain't brand new. She got the ring at a second-hand jewelry store, but they promised it had hardly been worn. It was a bit too small for the lady, so her husband had another one made."

Omie slipped the ring on, pleased that it nestled perfectly up against her wedding band. She was quiet so long that Nate began to worry.

"If'n you don't like it, I'll take it back. I'm sorry I couldn't buy you something new, Omie."

"I love it, Nate." She looked into his eyes. "I have another gift for you, but it won't be here for some months yet."

His eyes widened and a grin split his face. "A baby?"

"Yep." Omie pushed him back on the quilt with a grin of her own.

“Is this all right?” he asked, a hand on her belly.

“I am absolutely sure it is,” she said, blowing out the candles.

Chapter 28

1911

The winter and much of early spring was taken up with the excitement of planning Emmie's wedding. After the Christmas holidays were over, Emmie began in earnest to sew her wedding gown, as well as bridesmaids' dresses for Omie and Elizabeth. Though Elizabeth felt much too old to be asked to stand alongside Emmie and her sister, Emmie begged until her friend relented.

Daniel was pleased Emmie had asked, and amused at Elizabeth's fussing about her "tired old face and thickened waist." He still thought her to be one of the loveliest women he'd known, felt time had only made her features more dear. If there were lines around her eyes and mouth, they were merely signs of the warm humor which was so appealing to him.

Omie was fair certain the baby would come in plenty of time for her to fit into her dress. The weight always fell away quickly after the babies were born and she would be sure to make it so this time, too. Emmie had sent a sketch of the bridesmaid's dress she planned to make her sister, along with a swath of material. Omie had never seen, much less owned, anything as lovely as this. It would take yards of satin, in a color Emmie called “Ashes of Roses.” The material had come all the way from Paris, a gift from the Campbells, as was the white satin for Emmie’s wedding gown. Mrs. Campbell had insisted on paying for her own dress and joined Emmie at the new sewing machines she had gifted them for Christmas. Kate’s dress would be elegant but simple, with a light jacket made of pale green to match her eyes.

All that winter, while Emmie was sewing their dresses in Savannah, Kate, Omie and Phoebee worked on the Miller's quilt at the farm. Ada Kate and Bartie played beneath the frame, reminding Omie of the cozy, hidden feeling she'd had as a child there. The dark winter days were made lighter by the glow of kerosene lamps, which brought out all the lovely colors and textures from the scraps they’d been given. Included were pieces leftover from Emmie’s wedding gown, as well as some from Omie’s and Kate’s dresses.

When the quilt was finished, Phoebee allowed as she had never touched anything so beautiful.

"I'm afraid to use it and get it dirty!"

“You certainly will use it, missy!” Omie teased. “After all this work, you better snuggle up in it with that handsome husband of yours.”

Kate wondered if this might be a good time to bring up the swelling she and Omie had noticed beneath Phoebee’s apron. The girl was so slight that the least bit of weight told the tale of a little one to come. Phoebee had not mentioned her lack of menses to them, and Kate wondered what the girl’s mamma had taught her about the facts of life. Omie seemed to read Kate’s mind.

She ventured, “This baby has me so tired I could fall asleep standing up.”

“Not me!” Phoebee exclaimed. “I feel like I could race right up the hill and down the other side without breakin’ a sweat.”

Omie laughed and said, "How long have you known?"

"Oh, 'bout a month now. I didn't want to say anything 'til more time passed, and I felt sure the baby took. My mamma lost babies in her first few weeks three times, and I didn't want to jinx this one. Silly, I reckon." She sighed and took Omie's hand. "Ain't it grand, Omie? Our babies will be born so close together they'll grow up like twins!"

Omie felt a sudden sense of misgiving and took both of Phoebee's hands in hers for a moment. "That will be wonderful, yes!" she said, and withdrew her hands, pretending to need to take a seat suddenly. She smiled to cover her worries, and Phoebee chatted on about the babies until the men came in for their supper.

When the supper dishes were done and the Millers had gone home, Omie sat at the table with her mother and asked if she also felt some warning signs about Phoebee's pregnancy.

"Yes, I recall once when she said how much she wanted a baby, I was on the verge of knowing that something was not right, but it slipped away. I s'pose I didn't want to pursue it further. Probably I should have done a reading for her to get clearer about it. Might have saved her some heartbreak. I don't know if she'd have accepted my cautioning anyway. Let's just watch her closely, Omie, and be ready to do what we can. Aunt Julia works wonders with difficult pregnancies. I'll let her know the situation as soon as I get a chance. She may have a better sense of things than I do."

As the days grew longer, the first blooms of spring braved the possibility of a late frost. Robins began to arrive by the dozens, pecking at the softening ground.

One bright morning, Omie , Kate and the children sat on the porch steps, baring their feet to the warm sun.

The heat felt good on Omie's belly as well. She could almost feel the baby purring like a cat in a patch of sunshine. Her pregnancy was another easy one in most ways, and she felt sure Frank Thomas would have himself a baby brother to play with. He often put his little hands on her belly and patty-caked a rhythm. Omie thought her boy would be a music maker like herself one day, so she determined to find him a small parlor guitar when he was big enough to hold one.

Phoebee joined them, glad to feel warm again. She put her hand on her own growing belly.

"Seems like this baby is swimmin' inside me. I think I got a pollywog in there!" They all laughed and began referring to the coming child as Phoebee's pollywog.

Omie felt dozy. She missed the luxury of naps and late mornings that winter allowed.

Phoebee looked at Kate. "Would you tell us stories 'bout how you learned all you know of plants and how to use 'em? I thought my mamma knew a bunch, but not compared to you."

"Oh, goodness," Kate replied. "My mamma, Ida Ruth, and Aunt Julia were my most important teachers. I learned a lot on my own, too. What worked. What didn't. Sometimes, when I couldn't help someone, I felt like my will and God's were at odds with each other." She shook her head. "Faith can be a difficult companion in the face of suffering. But without faith, life would seem a bitter burden for many, rather than a gift."

Aunt Julia stopped by that same afternoon. Clear skies had coaxed everyone outdoors, and the women had spread a quilt in the yard. They sat with their faces turned up to the sun as the girls romped all around them, delighted to be outside again. Frank Thomas was enthralled with a dragonfly perched on his tummy.

"How do, ladies?" Aunt Julia called out.

"Please, come join us!" Kate and Omie called, sliding over to make room.

Aunt Julia slowly lowered herself to the ground. "My, that sun feels good to these old bones. I had to get moving before I stiffened up like an old okra pod."

"We were just talking about you, actually," Omie said. "Mamma was telling us things she learned from you and Grandma Ida about herbs and such."

"Oh, your mamma had much to teach me," Aunt Julia said to Kate. "I was gone from here during the years I would have studied such things, and she took me under her wing when I returned." Aunt Julia patted Kate on the leg. "There was healing in her hands, no doubt."

"You helped her put a good bit of her book in English. I sure do appreciate that. I had a little German but not enough to read it."

"Book?" Phoebee asked.

Kate lifted her face to the sun for a moment. "I was just a little thing when my mamma started writing that book. She had all this knowledge handed down from her own mamma, but it was stored in her head. We were taking some of her jam to sell at the store—back then it was owned by the Kraymers, remember?"

Aunt Julia nodded. "One of the first families to come over."

"They were. Well, Mamma saw a roll of that brown paper Mr. Kraymer wrapped parcels in, and she got the idea to use it for writing and drawing plants on. They made a deal to trade her jams for a roll of it. She took that home, cut it into pages and bound it. Her daddy was a book binder by family trade, so she knew how. My Frank replaced the old cloth cover with leather he'd tanned from a deer. Softest thing. I've got it soiled now from carrying it to the fields."

Aunt Julia put her hand on Omie's. "That book is a treasure. You be sure to take care of it, Miss Omie, when it's passed to you."

"Oh, Mamma's going to outlive us all!" Everyone laughed, but Omie felt a tightening in her stomach at the thought of losing Kate. She pushed the thought from her mind as Phoebee asked Aunt Julia what she meant by *when she returned*.

"Aunt Julia," Phoebee asked, "where all did you go? Did you get sold off away from your folks before the war?"

Omie realized this was a part of Aunt Julia's life she had never heard about. It seemed like her mamma's friend had been old as long as she'd known her, and it had never occurred to Omie that Aunt Julia had been young once too.

"No sirree, child, my mamma and daddy bought our freedom from a man here in Effingham County just before the war. Their master had a gambling problem and would have likely lost us in a bet if it hadn't been for Daddy's skill with the fiddle. Daddy's playin' earned him enough on the sly so he was able to save some, along with Mamma's egg and butter money. He not only bought our freedom, but he bought a little piece of hardscrabble land to call our own. In the place you know as Thistle Town. That was a rare thing in those times, but my daddy was a smart man."

Aunt Julia seemed to look into the past with her soft clouded eyes.

"The land wasn't the best, but it was ours, and we made a living somehow. When I was 15, my folks sent me to work for a doctor and his wife up north in Pennsylvania who were abolitionists. They gave me a good life and an education, something I'll always be grateful for. Some of my healing skills were learned there. But I missed my home and family. My folks could not read or write, so the only news of them came from people moving north from Georgia, carrying messages to me. After I got married, I convinced my husband to come back here with me, to try making life better for those I'd left behind."

"Is your husband still with you?" Phoebee asked.

"No, darlin'. Amos passed from this world not ten years after we moved here. A fever took him and I couldn't save him. Nearly gave up my healing practice, my heart was so broken. I had a visit from an angel that changed my mind, though. Most beautiful sight I ever saw. Bright shining like the sun. Filled the air with music."

She turned to look into Phoebee's face. "Let me tell you, they are with us as sure as I'm sitting here. That angel said Amos had gone on to give me counsel from the other side, as I would have need of guidance for the challenges to come. I have heard him every day of my life since then, and some things he's said can't be repeated!" Aunt Julia laughed out loud.

Kate smiled to herself. She always remembered Aunt Julia holding her head high, making sure her children did too, calling on the Spirit to walk with them every day so they would follow in the footsteps of the righteous. The children were her pride and joy. When they left to go north for more schooling and opportunities, you never saw anyone sadder nor happier. Her apron pockets bulged with letters at all times, for most of them wrote to their mamma every week. After her husband died, Aunt Julia helped birth and raise many another woman's children. Often, she would be seen down by the river when there was a revival going on, bobbing up and down on the bank, preaching to the heavens with a half dozen children dancing around her like little chicks.

Chapter 29

April blossomed into May, bringing rich smells of earth and new life. Omie felt the heaviness of winter slipping away. Her days were filled with the making of spring tonics, giving her reason to slip away from the house to collect plants and breathe in some solitude.

As she neared the river one afternoon, an old ballad her mamma sang played in her mind. She began to sing.

I asked my love to take a walk
Just a little ways with me
And as we walked we would talk
All about our wedding day
Darlin' say that you'll be mine
In our home we'll happy be
Down beside where the waters flow
Down by the banks of the Ohio
I held a knife against her breast
As close into my arms she pressed,
She cried, "Oh Willie, don't you murder me!
I'm not prepared for eternity!"

She pulled her harmonica out of an apron pocket and played the rest. Tiring, she sat beneath the old willow tree. Another song, a favorite of her mamma's, came to mind.

Down in the willow garden
Where me and my love did meet
As we sat a-courtin'
My love fell off to sleep
I had a bottle of Burgundy wine
My love she did not know
So I poisoned that dear little girl
On the banks below

Omie shook her head at the absurdity of the lyrics.

Why do we love these old killin' songs so much? Always the man *takes the woman he supposedly* loves *down to a river to kill her. Not just one way, but with poison,* and *a knife, then he throws her in the river to make sure the job got done!*

Laying back against the warm trunk, she dozed until the sun slipped behind the trees on the far bank. She stood and stretched, thinking this might have been the best rest she'd had since the baby'd begun to move.

Reckon I need to sing to you more often, little one.

Soon, planting the garden, helping with the fieldwork, tending the children and house, left little time for music making.

Kate had begun rubbing her daughter's tired feet in the evenings before bed, knowing how it relaxed her body and mind. The evening after Omie's walk, Kate motioned for her to sit. "Got a new liniment I want to try." She pulled Omie's feet onto her lap, placed a cloth underneath, then began to work the mixture in from calves to toes.

"Mamma, that is pure heaven," Omie purred. What's in it?"

"Oh, the usual. Comfrey, yarrow, willow bark. This time I soaked the dried plants in witch hazel after I ground them fine. Gave them a few days to steep, then I added the caster oil and some peppermint oil to it."

"Mhm," Omie mumbled.

Kate kissed the bottoms of her girl's worn feet and shoo'ed her off to bed.

By the end of June, Omie was beginning to worry that she might not be able to get into her bridesmaid's gown in time for her sister's wedding. Fortunately, Ezra Green Silar decided to push his way into the world about four in the morning on the sixth of July, not much more than a week after Ada Kate's birthday. The baby was trying to come out feet first, as if to hit the ground running. Omie cried out in her sleep as her water broke, and Nate called for Kate.

"Stay with me, Nate," Omie whimpered, which scared the living daylights out of him. He'd never seen her afraid before when giving birth. No matter how much pain wracked her body, she had always remained calm in the face of it. This time something was different though. When she arrived, he looked to Kate for guidance.

Kate looked back at him with a glower that felt like a blow, but he wasn't sure what he was guilty of.

"You stay," she said. "I'll send someone else for help."

Kate woke Phoebee, who sent Ephram for Aunt Julia with instructions to tell her this was a breech baby. Aunt Julia hurried in the door not ten minutes after Ephram had ridden out, and when they all looked at her, she said, "Well, don't look so surprised. I been dreamin' about this child all night, and I figured he must be callin' me, so I just got up and came on.

Needs turnin', don't he?" It was not so much a question as a confirmation, and she washed her hands and got right to work.

Nate looked at Aunt Julia. "A boy?"

"Yessir. Now, Omie, I know you're a brave woman, and you know how to do this. Just relax so I can do my work." Aunt Julia looked at the worried faces of Nate and the girls.

"Nate, you put those young'uns back to bed. We'll let you all know when this baby is ready to meet you."

Nate looked at Omie, who gave him a tired nod, and he guided the children gently out the door. "Daddy, is Mamma goin' be all right?" Ada Kate asked.

"Honey, she always is. This time is just a little bit harder, but don't you worry. They's nothin' your grandma and Aunt Julia can't take care of. Now help me get Bartie to bed and let's check on Frank Thomas. I love you more than I can say, my big strong girl."

Nate finally got Bartie to sleep. Ada Kate promised to watch over them until the baby came. He knew she would fall into dreams as soon as her little head hit the pillow.

Nate whispered, "I'll leave the door open a crack so I can hear if you call to me. Thank you, angel."

He walked back toward the room where his wife struggled to give life to their newest child, fearing he might lose them both. Nate slid to the floor with his back against the door frame, Omie's cries tearing at his heart.

Aunt Julia gently reached her hand inside Omie and got a sense of which way the baby might be eased into position. Kate noticed how gnarled Aunt Julia's hands had become in the passing year. Her old friend never complained though. When asked how she was, there was always the same reply.

"After all the suffering I seen, a few aches and pains are small bothers in the long life the Lord has seen to bless me with."

Omie bit down on a cloth her mamma had soaked in a mix of rosewater, honey and white willow bark to help with nausea and pain. Aunt Julia shifted the baby in small movements timed with Omie's exhales. Her breaths turned to groans now and then, but pressure from the baby seemed to lessen.

Kate wiped her daughter's wet forehead and murmured softly, "That's my good girl. It will all be fine soon, darlin. No one is better at turnin' a baby the right way than Aunt Julia." Then she turned to look out the window, so as not to show her concern.

How many times can Omie could go through this without wearing her body out? She's still young, but sooner or later the making of children takes a toll. If she and Nate don't slow down long enough for Omie's body to truly heal and restore itself, I fear the next one might not make it into this world. I could lose my daughter as well.

Kate determined to have a talk with Nate, whether Omie liked it or not.

Omie closed her eyes as time seemed to slow and the world was reduced to a sharp ball of pain between her legs. Suddenly, Aunt Julia gave a cackle, grinning wide enough to show the few good teeth that remained to her.

"He's ready now!" she cried, and the baby came sliding out, blinking like he didn't quite know if he was in the right place.

Shortly after, Ephram came riding back into the yard. Phoebee went out to tell him about the baby. She listened to his story of finding no one home at Aunt Julia's, and Phoebee explained how the old woman had already been making her way there since the middle of the night.

"She's got paths through them woods we don't even know 'bout."

Ephram just shook his head, then went to the barn to unhitch the wagon and see to the horse.

Kate called Nate and the children to come meet the newest member of the family. The children gathered around the baby and Omie as she gave them a tired smile. Frank Thomas reached his small hand out to touch Ezra's smaller one, and the baby took hold of it like he'd never let his brother go. That was how they would go through much of life.

Chapter 30

Emmie came to the farm for the final fitting of Kate's and Omie's dresses since it was easier on Omie and the baby. Also, she admitted to herself, it would be nice to get away from the stifling heat of the city. Thomas unloaded the big trunk holding the dresses and Emmie's sewing goods, then promised to come back for her in two days' time.

"Three weeks, Emmie! I cain't believe you're going to be a bride, and I won't be there to see it all!" Phoebee cried. She was prone to unaccountable weeping these last weeks of her pregnancy, and Ephram helped her up the steps with a sigh and a quick exit.

"You know we'll tell you all about it, Phoebee. We won't leave anything out. You'll get to see me and Mamma in our dresses today, and there will be a real photographer taking pictures at the wedding. Emmie will bring them to show you," Omie soothed, as she helped Phoebee seat herself in a rocker.

This mollified the girl for a bit, and they soon made their way to the kitchen table for dinner. Phoebee begged Emmie for all the details of the wedding plans as she rested little Ezra on her large belly.

"I guess I'll never manage to be here for the birth of your babies, Omie. I'm so sorry to have missed seeing this little one come into the world," Emmie said.

"This one gave us a bit of trouble, hon, you might not have wanted to be here," her mamma said. "Aunt Julia came through though, as she always does."

"How is Aunt Julia?" Emmie asked. "Maizie has been concerned about her lately, says she's been rather crippled with rheumatoid."

"Oh, she's all right," Kate replied. "You can tell she hurts sometimes, but she's been getting Phoebee here to bring live bees to sting her. Strangest thing, but the venom seems to ease the swelling some."

Emmie thought that Caleb would be very interested to know more about this and made a mental note to tell him.

"Maybe we can be pregnant together in a year or so!" Omie said, smiling at Emmie. Emmie blushed, smiling as well. The only one who wasn't smiling was Kate, as she gave Omie a long, hard look.

Omie glanced at her mother and turned back to Emmie with a demand to hear more about Caleb's handsome brothers, who were to be his groomsmen. Emmie entertained them with stories of the young men's antics.

After lunch, the women tried on their dresses, and Phoebee burst into fresh tears.

"I ain't never seen anything the like of it, Emmie," she sniffled.

"Well, one day I'm going to make a new frock just for you, Phoebee. I'll make one to match, if you have a little girl."

"Really, you would do that for me?" Phoebee began to cry again in earnest. Emmie reached across Phoebee's swollen belly and hugged her.

The rest of the day passed in pleasant conversation with no more outbursts. Even Phoebee laughed a time or two.

It's good to hear Phoebee laugh again. Omie smiled. *More like her old self.*

By early evening, Ephram was nowhere to be found, and Phoebee began to worry.

"He says I'm drivin' him crazy with my moods and all, but I just cain't help it! And it was him that got me this way, so I don't know why he cain't be a little nicer about it."

"Don't worry about him, honey," Kate said. "He just doesn't understand what you're goin' through. If it was up to men to have babies, humans would have disappeared off the earth."

They all laughed, and Emmie put her arm around Phoebee's small shoulders.

At supper time, Ephram had still not come home. Phoebee fretted and paced, uncertain as to whether she should go home and start cooking or stay with Kate and the others.

"Nate, would you go find him? Sumpthin' musta' happened. He wouldn't leave me alone so long, even if I am a pain in the behind. Would he?" Phoebee looked around at them all for reassurance.

Nate put his hands on her trembling shoulders. "I'll get him and bring him back. Y'all go ahead with supper, just save us some. Don't worry no more, ok?"

She reached around his waist as best she could and hugged him. "Thank you, Nate. Thank you so much."

While Nate went in search of her husband, everyone did their best to keep Phoebee preoccupied.

Kate gave her the job of peeling potatoes, and the little girls helped by washing them—and themselves—keeping up a cheerful chatter. A bit of the old brightness came back to Phoebee's drawn face. Omie realized she hadn't noticed how much it had dimmed. Emmie kept them all distracted with tales of Savannah and gossip about the ladies she sewed for. Phoebee had nearly finished the task when she gasped and grabbed the edge of the table. She looked up at Kate and Omie as her water broke and ran down the chair onto the floor.

"Oh, my Lord!" Emmie cried. The little girls turned to look up at their mamma with concern.

"Well, now," Kate said. "It looks like Phoebee's pollywog wants to come to supper too!"

Phoebee started whimpering as Kate and Omie moved to action, thinking of all the jobs to do in preparation for the baby's coming. Emmie sat quiet and still, mesmerized by the fluid puddling on the floor.

"But it cain't be my time, Ephram ain't here!" Phoebee cried, her eyes beseeching them all to make the baby stop coming.

"Emmie, please tend to the little ones," Kate requested in a soothing voice.

Emmie took the children to their room so they wouldn't be frightened, relieved to have something to do. Kate sent out a silent prayer to Aunt Julia, hoping she would know it was Phoebee's time. She suspected this would be a long, difficult birth, but managed a calm expression as she spoke to Phoebee.

"Honey, you do what we tell you, and things will be just fine. Squeeze Omie's hand when you need to, and bite down on this stick if the pain gets bad. Mostly just try to breathe as deep and slow as you can."

An hour went by, then two. Nate rode up in the yard without Ephram. The person sitting behind him on the horse was, instead, Aunt Julia.

Omie ran out into the yard to help Aunt Julia down and carried the woman's old birthing bundle into the house. When she came back out, Nate was hitching his horse to the wagon.

"Did you find him, Nate? Where are you goin' now?"

"Oh, I found him all right," Nate grimaced. "Behind the store, drunk as Cooter Brown. He couldn't stand up, much less stay on his horse, so I'm gonna go put his sorry tail in the wagon and bring him home. How's Phoebee?"

Omie filled him in on the situation.

"I knowed when I saw Aunt Julia walkin' this way that it must be Phoebee's time. I'll get Ephram quick as I can."

Aunt Julia found Kate by the bedside, holding the hand of a white-faced, crying Phoebee.

"Hey, Phoebee," she said softly. "How you doin', girl?"

"It . . .hurts . . .so . . .bad," Phoebee gasped. "Is it goin' to be . . .much longer?"

"You just let me take a look, hon." Aunt Julia moved to the foot of the bed and gently spread Phoebee's trembling legs apart. She tried to feel for the baby's head but could not even get three fingers inside the girl. Her dark face looked up quickly at Kate. The seriousness of the situation passed between them.

Emmie peered in the door, carrying a sleeping Ezra. She raised her eyebrows in concern.

Omie returned to the room, giving Emmie a quick hug. "Thank you," she whispered.

Kate said, "Omie, come sit with Phoebee while I go get some fresh water to wipe her face with."

Omie looked down at the frightened girl.

"Phoebee, I've been through this four times, helped to deliver many more. Put your trust in us and your faith in the Creator. You know we'll get you and your baby safely through this. We would tell you if *the Sight* showed us it wasn't so."

Omie rubbed the girl's hands between her own, and Phoebee closed her eyes for a moment between contractions, surrendering to what was coming. Kate motioned for Emmie and Aunt Julia to join her on the porch. When they were out of Phoebee's hearing, she said, "I don't know if we can save either of them, she's just so small. This baby could tear her to pieces!"

"Mmhm," Aunt Julia muttered. "I don't know how he was able to make a baby in her to begin with. By the looks of it, he don't have much in the way of manliness at all! Run off and leave that girl like this. The Lord will surely make that boy pay. I just hope it ain't at the cost of his wife and child!"

"God would not be so cruel as to take them to spite Ephram!" Emmie exclaimed.

"I'm sure you're right Emmie, but if those two don't live, that's how he's gonna feel for the rest of his sorry days."

"I'll send for Caleb, Mamma," Emmie said. "I don't know if there's anything he can do, but either desperation or intuition tells me we have to get him here. I'll ask Nate to fetch him. Do you think he'll go?"

"Don't ask him, tell him!" Kate said, reaching for Ezra.

Emmie found Nate about to climb on the wagon.

"Nate, stop!" she cried.

Nate looked at her worried face and said, "It's bad, ain't it."

"Yes, it is." Emmie replied. "Mamma and Aunt Julia have done what they can, but . . . Nate, I need you to go as fast as possible to Savannah and get Caleb. I know you don't want to do this, but we don't have time to argue. It may mean the difference between life and death for both Phoebee and the baby."

Nate looked up at the sky for a moment and sighed.

"All right." He jumped up on the wagon seat, snapping the reins as he wheeled out onto the road.

Emmie went back into the bedroom and saw by Omie's face that she too knew the direness of the situation. The sisters joined hands in prayer as Phoebee's screams grew louder, then turned to moans as she weakened.

Kate spooned laudanum down the girl's throat.

"Best she stop pushin'," Aunt Julia said. "This baby isn't goin' anywhere. All we can do now is pray for a miracle."

Omie sat holding Phoebee's limp hand, tears sliding down her cheeks. She began softly humming a sweet song she knew Phoebee liked, until the girl's breathing relaxed. She leaned down and whispered, "Soon, this little pollywog will swim on out into the world. Won't that be wonderful?"

As the day lengthened, Omie turned to her mamma and asked quietly, "Can I speak with you outside?"

Kate nodded and the two of them went out to the back porch where they stood a moment, cooling themselves in the evening breeze.

"A few days ago, I was fetching water from the well." Omie gazed up at the sky a moment, then into her mamma's worried eyes. "The water looked dark and thick. Red, like blood. There was the reflection of two white doves flying. They settled into the tree above me so I glanced up. When I looked down again, the water was clear as usual. Mamma, what does it mean? I meant to tell you about it, but with all the fuss over Emmie coming, it slipped my mind."

Sobbing, Omie put a hand over her mouth. Kate wrapped her arms around her daughter.

"Mamma, does this mean God is going to take Phoebee and the baby? There was so much blood!"

"I can't say as I know for sure, darlin'. Just remember that when Noah set his doves free, they returned with a promise of a new beginning. Let's hold onto that."

Nate raced like a madman down the streets and avenues of Savannah until he came to the Campbell's home. He pounded at the door. Daniel opened it to find a sweat-soaked, breathless young man he finally recognized as Emmie's brother-in-law.

"I need Caleb to come with me fast!" Nate panted. "Where is he?"

"What's the matter son? Is it Emmie? Is she hurt?"

"No. It ain't Emmie." He panted. "It's Phoebee!"

Caleb came into the room.

"Get your stuff and come with me. Now!" Nate yelled.

Caleb grabbed his bag and pushed past Daniel saying, "I'll let you know what's happened as soon as I can."

Thomas had come out to see what all the ruckus was about. He managed to give the lathered horse some water before Caleb and Nate jumped back up on the buckboard, taking off at break-neck speed.

"Y'all be safe, hear? We be prayin' for Miz Phoebee."

Caleb held onto his hat with one hand and onto the seat with the other. The miles passed by quickly as Nate whipped the horse to go faster, racing the setting sun. Every muscle of the man's body seemed focused on the reins in his hands.

"You're going to kill this horse!" Caleb cried.

"Better the horse than Phoebee!" Nate shouted back. "I may just kill her damned husband too. He's laid up in town drunk while his wife and baby are fightin' to live."

Nate set his jaw and wouldn't say another word until he pulled up beside the house. "Tell them I'll bring his sorry ass back as soon as I can."

Caleb jumped down with his bag, and Nate changed horses for the trip to get Ephram.

The young doctor hurried to the bedroom, directed by Omie's soft humming, a more frightening sign of the state of things than any moaning or yelling would have been.

The women surrounded Phoebee with their hands joined, heads bowed in prayer. When Emmie heard Caleb come into the room, she jumped up to give him a hard embrace. Her tear-stained face implored him to do something.

He pulled his stethoscope from the bag and leaned over to listen to Phoebee's heart, then put it on her belly, listening for the baby's. It seemed to them that forever passed before he said, "They're both very faint but there are still two heartbeats. Let me see what we're in for."

He quickly scrubbed his hands as Aunt Julia moved from her place at Phoebee's feet.

Kneeling down, he felt the baby's head pressing hard against the small opening of its mother's body. He closed his eyes for a moment.

Turning to the women, he said, "Mrs. Lee, Omie. And—I'm afraid I haven't made your acquaintance, Ma'am." He looked at Aunt Julia who waved him to go on. "There is only one thing I know to try. I haven't done this surgery myself, but I've seen it done in extreme cases like this. I'll have to make an incision across her abdomen and remove the baby from her womb."

Emmie gasped, "But won't that kill her?"

"Not if it's done right," he said. "I will do my best but I can't promise to be successful."

"You do what you can, son. We don't have much time to consider it," Kate replied.

Caleb gave directions for preparing the instruments in boiling water as he cleaned an area just below Phoebee's navel. Emmie soon laid the sterilized instruments beside him on a clean towel and stood ready to assist. He took a deep breath as he prepared to make the incision. Just then, Nate walked in to see what news there was to give Ephram. When he saw Caleb about to cut into Phoebee, he yelled, "What the hell are you doing?"

Omie grabbed him and told him to hush, that Caleb was going to take the baby directly from the womb. "We have to trust him, Nate. They will both die for sure if we don't."

Nate leaned against the wall as Caleb's knife sliced a long bloody line across Phoebee's belly. Feeling as if he would swoon, he willed himself to watch.

If she dies, I will damn well have an excuse to kill this foul-blooded, half-brother of mine.

Caleb set his scalpel aside, mopping up the blood from the incision and prepared to remove the baby from Phoebee's body. Before he could gather himself to the task, a tiny fist reached out and feebly grabbed his finger. Nate did faint then, but the women stared in stunned fascination. Caleb reached in and pulled a tiny baby girl out into the soft lamplight.

Kate gathered the baby up in a clean blanket, then tied and cut the umbilical cord. Caleb pulled out the afterbirth, and went about the business of sewing up the incision, making sure the area was as sterile as possible. Aunt Julia bathed the infant with warm water and tucked a blanket snugly around her. Omie laid the tiny bundle at the breast of her faintly breathing mother. "Here's your pollywog, my dear girl."

She managed to get the baby to suckle, so as to get the first milk, which was so important. Omie's own breasts ached, and she went to feed Ezra while Emmie took a turn at Phoebee's bedside. Then they all settled in to wait for Fate's decision.

Nate picked himself up off the floor and looked around sheepishly. Everyone was too busy to notice. *I need some air!* He stood on the porch, amazed at what had just taken place. After checking to see that all the children were asleep, he headed for the wagon to go back to town.

Eventually, Nate found Ephram behind the farrier's shed with a new bottle of some foul whiskey he'd managed to get his hands on. He wasn't quite as drunk as Nate had found him earlier, but was on his way. Ephram looked sideways at his approaching friend.

"Are they dead?"

"No, you fool, but Phoebee is close to it. What the hell are you doin' here still drinkin' when you should be tendin' to your wife and daughter?"

"Dawter." Ephram slurred as he wiped a hand across his face. "Well, at least it's not a boy that's likely to turn out a sorry SOB like me."

"What are you speakin' of Ephram? I ain't seen nothin' of that in you so far! You been a right big help to us, and anybody can see Phoebee worships you. Why are you carryin' on like this?"

Ephram set the bottle down and said quietly, "This is twice I nearly kilt her, Nate. May have this time. We didn't leave Stone Mountain 'cause her folks' land was no account." He covered his face for a moment and exclaimed, "It was me was no 'count, and they didn't want her to have no more to do with such a loser. I was tryin' to get money ahead for us to get married, get a place of our own. The quickest way was to turn our corn into whiskey. That's about the only'est thing useful I learned from my daddy."

Nate looked away as Ephram continued, "Phoebee was with me in her folks' wagon when I went to pick up the last batch of it. It wuz goin' to be the last, Nate, I swear. She didn't know 'bout it. I'd told her we wuz going to see a man about a piece of land that might be for sale. Somehow the law had found out about the still and wuz waitin' beside it to ar'rest me. I grabbed Phoebee's hand and we ran into the woods.

Ephram seemed to sober a bit as he told his tale.

"They started shootin'. Nearly hit her, too. It was gittin' dark and they could only track us by the noise we wuz makin', so we climbed up a tree. You know how she can scamper up a tree like a racoon. They finally give us up for gone. I swore to her I had no idea that this "man" we wuz gonna meet had a still on his place, and she believed me. It was her daddy's wagon though. We knew they'd figure out who we wuz. I convinced her to leave with me, leave her family and all, 'cause they would surely put us in jail."

He took a deep breath and continued.

"I had enough money with me to get us horses and a wagon, nex' town we come to. Nuthin' left for us to marry and get a place. I should'a made her stay, Nate! Now I've done put her in danger again, plantin' a baby in her little belly. I'm jus' no damn use to her." Ephram took another swig and hung his head.

"That's about the most pitiful excuse for sorriness I ever heard," Nate said. "That girl put her life in your hands. She needs you!"

"We ain't even married," Ephram said, like that had some sort of importance in the moment.

"Well, get off your drunken ass and go clean up over at the river. Then I'm takin' you to her, and you damned well will marry her, or I'll throw you in that same river to drown!"

Nate had a look in his eyes that made Ephram throw down the bottle and put a hand out for a pull up.

When they arrived back at the house, Ephram walked in alone as Nate headed for the barn. Emmie picked Ezra up and the women quietly rose to leave the room. Ephram settled into a chair beside the bed, taking Phoebee's limp hand in his. He laid his head next to her still form and wept.

"Is she dead?" Ephram sobbed, catching Omie's sleeve as she moved past.

"Not as yet," she said. "I'm takin' the baby to feed."

She picked Polly up and closed the door behind her without another word.

Omie lay each night beside Phoebee's small body, with Ezra in the cradle beside the bed. Phoebee's tiny daughter was nestled between them against her mamma's side. Omie fed both babies as needed, sleeping when she could. Frank Thomas still nursed once a day, but Kate was trying to wean him.

A few days after Polly's arrival, Omie wandered in to the kitchen from the bedroom, desperately needing a drink of water. Her mamma had Frank Thomas on her lap, both equally covered in applesauce.

"This boy can eat near 'bout as much as me!" Kate exclaimed.

Omie squeezed out a bit of milk and rubbed it her sore, cracked nipples. "He needs to use those teeth on somethin' besides me."

"I'll get you some witch hazel and a warm compress, honey. Mrs. Scott gave me some wool from her sheep, said the oil in it was the best thing when she was nursing her twins."

Nate stayed up at the other house with Ephram, and the rest of them took turns sitting in the chair at Phoebee's side, spooning broths and blood-building teas down her throat. When Caleb felt sure the incision was healing well and Phoebee was out of danger, he returned to the city, insisting they send for him again if she changed for the worse.

As the days went by, Phoebee came back to them, slowly growing stronger. Kate and Omie looked for a return of the girl's ready humor, a sure sign her spirit was healing as well.

After one of Polly's morning feedings, Phoebee took the baby from Omie and held her close, weeping that her milk had dried up while she was recovering.

"Lord, Phoebee, I have more than enough for the both of them. Frank Thomas don't need to nurse anymore. If it weren't for Polly feeding too, I'd have to suckle those baby goats or sumthin'. I bet I got more milk than Mamma's cow. Wish I had as many teats as her too, so I could get rid of it faster."

The image of Omie as a cow tickled Phoebee, and she laughed, though it hurt, for the first time since giving birth. Omie sat on the bed beside her. "I know you want to nurse your own baby, sweetie. At least she got the first milk from you, which was most important. We can make a sugar tit for her soon. You can give her that at least. Have y'all given her a name yet?"

"*I* did. Polly."

Omie laughed. "Of course."

Ephram stayed busy on the farm, quietly coming in to check on Phoebee when he left their house in the morning, and again before he returned to it after work in the evening. The young man would not take meals with the family, preferring to spend time alone with Phoebee and Polly while they ate.

Phoebee confided to Omie one day that Ephram was still not comfortable holding the baby, afraid he might do something wrong and hurt her.

Everyone could hear the murmur of conversation between Phoebee and Ephram in the other room. Sometimes the barely-suppressed whispers spoke of recriminations more fiercely than shouting. Phoebee was struggling to forgive him for abandoning her when she needed him most, and he condemned himself even more. It was painful for everyone to witness, but finally some sort of resolution passed between them. As Phoebee grew more able to do for herself, she moved back into Kate's old house with him.

Omie assured them she would nurse Polly along with Ezra as long as she was needed. Life went back to some semblance of its former self, though a shadow seemed to hang over the small house up the hill. Omie and Kate cast worried looks in the couple's direction now and then.

Chapter 31

Kate puzzled over how to get Omie and Nate to slow down on adding to their little family. Omie was still young and healthy, but Ezra's difficult birth had taken a toll on her. Kate knew that if the body was not given due time to recover, things inside could become damaged beyond what her skills could heal. Omie knew this too, from the haggard state of some women her mother assisted with births. Women who seemed to have no idea how all those babies got there in the first place!

Omie knew how to keep babies from coming, and it didn't require abstinence from the intimacy she and Nate still shared. Kate couldn't quite understand what drove Omie to fill her womb with a new little one before the last finished nursing.

Kate held Ezra as she looked out the kitchen window. Omie had the children following her around the barnyard like little ducklings, helping scatter feed to the chickens. Bartie stopped to hold a baby chick while Frank Thomas carefully stroked the fine down of its back. He had a love for animals much like his mamma did and could not get enough of handling them. The little creatures seemed to trust him, following the child around like he was the fellow in the *The Pied Piper*.

Aunt Emmie had brought him a copy of the book for his first birthday. Several times a day he patted the book, wanting to have it read aloud while his eyes drank in the pictures. "Piper" was one of the first words Frank Thomas applied to himself. Given to humming while beating a rhythm on pots, the boy happily marched to his own drumming.

Mid-day, Nate came up on the back porch for a drink of water, dousing his head and neck as well.

Kate laid the baby down, hesitated a moment, then stepped out onto the porch with her hands in her apron pockets. It was an odd posture for her, Nate noted. She always had something in her hands.

"Well, hey there, Mrs. Lee. Looks like you got a few minutes of peace to yourself." He nodded toward the barnyard.

"Oh, I never mind the little ones hanging on to my skirts," she said. "Wish I'd had more of them myself but the Lord didn't intend that to be. So, I just enjoy these sweet babies of yours.

"Speaking of that, Nate, I do feel I need to talk to you about something. Omie will never say this to you, but in my experience, having too many children too quickly will rob you of years together as surely as workin' yourself to death will. I don't know if I would have had my husband longer if he'd taken more care of himself, but I think so. We'll never know, I reckon. Point is, son, give yourselves time to enjoy these ones you got before bein' in such a hurry to make more."

Nate's sunburned neck turned even redder as he looked away from his mother-in-law. This bedroom business was just not a subject that had been raised between them.

"Are you sayin' that Omie could be in danger if we don't stop?" he asked quietly. "Like Phoebee?"

"Oh no, Nate. Phoebee just wasn't built to have children. I'm only sayin' that a body gives so much to the makin' of another human being, and

Omie needs to build herself up in between. I've seen women who've given birth to a child nearly every year and not lived to see them grown. Frank's mamma had thirteen of them. The doctor had to operate on her female parts when she was near sixty years old. When her husband found out she couldn't bear any more, he called her an 'old spaded sow' and wouldn't have anything else to do with her." Kate gave Nate a sideways look and they both burst out laughing.

"Well, I don't reckon she minded all that much!" he said.

"She did not," Kate replied. "All I'm sayin', Nate, is just try to be mindful and watch out for her. She loves them babies so, you may have to be the one to say when enough is enough."

Nate nodded to her as he put his hat back on and headed for the field. This was an awkward burden, he reckoned.

How does a man lay beside the sweet warmth of his wife's body and not want to hold her to him? Just to feel for a time like they're one. This damn life asks so much of us."

Every morning in the winter, the five o'clock train blew its whistle, waking Nate up. After he had jumped up to bank the fire, it was too late to go back to sleep and too early to get up.

What else was a body to do?

Omie began to notice Nate rising before her in the mornings, going out to the barn as soon as the sun was up and only coming back for meals. She wondered if she had done something, said something to distance him from her, but he didn't act different any other way. His trips to town with Ephram became more frequent, and she noticed alcohol on his breath on several occasions. Omie found herself standing in front of the old mirror over the sideboard, wondering if the farm and the babies had changed her so, that Nate didn't find her desirable anymore. Maybe he had a fancy for someone else and didn't want to say it.

No. I'd know if it was that.

Frustration got the best of her, so she got up with Nate early one morning, determined to find out why he'd grown so cool with her in the bedroom. Omie walked up behind him and slid her hands under his shirt, pulling him close to breathe in his familiar smell.

He put his hands over hers and said, "Not now darlin', I got to get out there and get some things done before Ephram comes."

"What's so important that you can't take a little time for some lovin', Nate? You never do any more. Have I done somethin'? Is there someone you're not tellin' me about?"

He turned around and brushed the hair from her face.

"I love it when your hair's down like this," he said, running his fingers through it gently. "No, it ain't you or anybody else Omie, you know that. It's just...well, after Phoebee had such a hard time of it, your mamma talked to me about how dangerous it could be for you to have too many babies so close together. I just couldn't do anything to hurt you, darlin'. I wouldn't know how to live in this world without you."

Omie scowled and said, "My mamma talked to you about that?"

"Now, don't be mad at her. She's just tryin' to care for us. I can wait awhile before we start another young'un. You got your hands full now."

"Well," she sighed, "she had no business going behind my back and doin' that, Nate. We're grown and can make our own decisions."

"You will always be her baby just like these ones will always be ours, so don't be hard on her." He started to put on his britches.

"Just a minute there, mister," she said. "I do know of a tea that will keep the babies from comin' until we want more."

"You do?" he asked, surprised.

"It's not something everybody is comfortable about. Having relations when it's not to make babies, it goes against some folks' religion and some men's pride. Like my granny, she had to have surgery on her female parts after having thirteen children, and . . ."

"I know," Nate laughed. "Your mamma told me about that. Omie, you're my religion, or the closest thing I have to it." Then he grinned, "I kinda like you makin' those piggy noises when we're makin' bacon." He snorted as he nuzzled her neck and slipped the gown from her shoulders.

Afterwards they lay wrapped around each other in the soft morning light as day began to break. Nate heard a knock at the front door and kissed her again as he rose to throw his clothes on.

"That'll be Ephram. He'll give me hell all day now." Nate smiled.

"I'll bring you both some hot biscuits to the field shortly. That'll appease him some." She laughed as Nate hurried out the door. Omie lay there a few more moments, soaking up his lingering warmth in their bed. A sense of peace enveloped her, a reverence for all the love that filled her life.

If God is Love, as the Bible said, then surely Nate has plenty of religion.

After the biscuits were baked and delivered, Omie went to find her mamma in the backyard. The familiar face looked so much older these days that Omie felt most of her anger drift away on the breeze. Kate turned to look at Omie as if she had felt it anyway.

"Mornin'!" she said, with a bit of hesitation.

"Mornin', Mamma, how are you today?" Omie went to stand beside her. They both looked up the hill at Phoebee and Ephram's place.

"I'm fine. I've just got a sense of something comin' from that house. Not sure what. I hope that baby is all right." Kate sighed.

"Speaking of babies, Mamma, what did you say to Nate?" Omie's eyes began to well with tears. She had rarely been angry with her mother before and it scorched her heart.

"Oh Omie, sorry if I caused any trouble. I surely didn't mean to. I just been so worried about you. You know I wouldn't stick my nose in your business otherwise."

Mamma looked so sad, Omie reached out and embraced her, with tears sliding down her cheeks. "All right, Mamma, I will drink the moon-time tea for now. But I'll miss holdin' a little one in my arms when they stop nursing."

Kate turned and kissed Omie's cheek. "I know, baby, I know. I have some ginger, and we'll go to Aunt Julia's and get you some leaves from her acacia trees tomorrow. Her mamma brought seeds of those trees all the way from Africa. I reckon she knew what lay in store for her."

1939

JUNE 18

"It was a busy time!" Emmie exclaimed. "Two new babies and a wedding."

"I wish I could have seen y'all as brides!" Lilly exclaimed.

"Well, I can do the next best thing," Omie replied. "But then you girls need to get to bed, it's late."

She and Emmie took the girls inside and lit the lamp by the bedside. Omie carried it over to the old trunk at the foot of her bed. As she opened the lid, the soft light shone on a pale garment wrapped in paper. Omie gently lifted out the wedding dress that had been her mamma's, opened the paper and smoothed the delicate material out on the bed.

"It's so pretty." Tess sighed. "And so tiny."

"What is that?" Lilly pointed to what still lay in the trunk. Omie's eyes began to tear up as she reached in to unfold an old nightdress. Fine embroidery covered the front and Lilly drew a sharp breath at the sight of it.

"Who made this?" Her slender fingers lightly touched the faded threads.

Omie took her granddaughter's hand. "Our mamma made this as a wedding gift to me," she replied softly.

"It's so pretty. I can't imagine wearing it, I'd be afraid of messing up the flowers."

"Your grandaddy didn't let me wear it for long, I promise you!"

"Grandmamma!" Tess blushed.

Omie laughed and laid the gown aside.

"Mamma's handiwork was always beautiful. So was Mrs. Campbell's. Still is, I reckon." She looked at her sister. "The wedding gown Emmie wore was decorated by the woman she worked for, and you never saw anything so fine."

Emmie smiled at her great-niece. "Elizabeth Campbell came to be my dear friend. In fact, my Bitsy is named after her."

"You must have been a beautiful bride!" Lilly stood up and pranced around as if wearing a wedding dress and veil.

"I'll show you photographs when you visit us in Savannah," Emmie promised.

When the girls went to bed, Emmie realized how tired she was. The distraction of storytelling had been good on this sad day. It gave her little time to reflect on her own sorrow for Nate, for her sister and their family.

I hope when mine and Caleb's time comes, our children will have only fond memories of us. We certainly have loved them. A smile came to her face as she thought of the early days of her marriage to Caleb, and of the delight they'd had in each child's birth. She loved how he had respected her mamma and Omie's abilities as mid-wives, assisting them rather than resisting the old ways. His own mother had shown him the value of herbs and such, the gift of healing. She was his influence to go into medicine.

Chapter 32

1911

The day was quickly approaching for Kate and Omie to go to Savannah and ready themselves for Emmie's big day. Omie didn't know how she was going to manage the trip with all the children, including two nursing babies. Polly was so new, and Phoebee still too fragile for traveling.

Aunt Julia offered to stay on the farm and mind the babies while the wedding took place. The older woman had a soothing way with fussy infants that never failed. Two of her granddaughters, Alberta and Tilly, would be willing to stay with her to nurse Ezra and Polly, along with their own babies, while Omie was away. Frank Thomas and the girls would be much more manageable at the wedding.

Omie knew Phoebee would heal under Aunt Julia's care, too. The old woman would *See* more deeply into the girl's troubled soul than she and Kate had been able to.

"I don't know how I'm goin' to keep my milk from soaking right through my dress and ruining the satin, Mamma," Omie fretted.

"Well now, hon, your mamma might know a thing or two about that." Kate smiled and went to the cupboard to fetch some thin round pieces of cloth she had soaked in beeswax. "We will put these in front of some soft pads in that fancy new brassiere Emmie got you. They'll protect your dress just fine, I believe."

"As if I wasn't big enough already!" Omie grumbled. "I'm liable to pop out of that fancy new brassiere." She tugged at her breast bands and looked slyly at her mamma. "I believe she got one for you too, Mrs. Lee. In fact, I believe I saw you modeling yours in front of the mirror when you thought nobody was home."

Kate blushed and grinned. "That was not modeling, Miss Smarty Pants. I was tryin' to figure out how to fasten the durn thing! Never in my life did I think I'd wear undergarments that cost so much and only got worn the once. Seems a big waste of money to me. Bindin' works just fine."

Omie kissed her mamma's bright red cheek. "You know you like it!" she whispered gleefully, and with that she went to see what the children were carrying on about.

Ada Kate and Bartie were fussing about which one would walk out first as a flower girl. Ada Kate insisted that, as the oldest, she should be first.

Omie squatted on the ground beside them and gently reached for their small hands.

"You girls will walk side by side and you'll help your little sister carry a basket between you," she said. "Sisters always stand beside each other and stand up for each other, like your Aunt Emmie and I do. No one else in the world will ever be the friend to you that your sister is."

"Yes, Mamma," Ada Kate said quietly.

"All right now, go check to see if those baby chicks have hatched yet!"

Ada Kate grabbed Bartie's hand and they toddled toward the coop.

In Savannah, Emmie was madly finishing the final touches on Omie's gown. She needed to take it up a bit, as Omie had lost so much weight nursing two babies and keeping up with chores around the house. Emmie also still needed to make sure the flower girls' dresses were finished—as well as her mother's. The bridal gown was in the hands of Mrs. Campbell, who insisted on doing the final touches.

Emmie appreciated all the help Mrs. Campbell and Maizie had given her. The three of them had grown even closer through these preparations for the wedding. Staying busy helped calm the bride's nervous excitement that ran through her all the day and night, keeping sleep at bay.

She couldn't help smiling to herself, however. A few more days and she would be a married woman, deeply in love with a man who knew her in ways no one else ever had.

Such joy is surely subtracted from your share of heaven!

In his office nearby, Caleb found himself drawn to the window again and again between patients, looking at nothing so much as imagining the future.

Emmie. I love so many things about you. Your intelligence, your quick wit. Your lovely face and even lovelier heart. I am amazed at the person I've become since being with you. How you've led me to discover aspects of myself, and passions I did not know existed. I dearly hope this is true for you also.

He believed passion was something they would share in their bed as well. How could they not? The heat between them when they touched was nearly unbearable.

Shaking his head to clear such distracting thoughts, he would return to his work. A small smile would linger at the corners of his mouth, however, and would not be chased away.

The procession from the farm to Savannah was a festive one. The Campbells had sent a lovely, beribboned carriage to fetch them all. Thomas looked proud in his finest livery, bowing and doffing his hat when he'd arrived. Tomorrow, he told them, the bridal party and Emmie's carriages would be festooned with flowers, as well as wreaths for the horses necks.

Emmie had arranged for her family to stay at the Marshall House, a grand hotel that she knew would by turns enthrall and embarrass them with its extravagance. The Campbells had offered to have them dine that night in their home, as Emmie confided that her family would probably be too nervous to eat supper in the hotel's restaurant.

Kate and the Silars arrived at the hotel in the warmth of afternoon, travel worn, but happy and excited. Excepting Nate, who had reluctantly given in to pressure from the women to come. Emmie had asked him to give her away, as her closest male relative, but he turned pale at the thought, and she relented, glad to just have him there. Dr. Campbell agreed to do the honor of walking her down the aisle instead.

The children were speechless with awe, mesmerized by the bright lamps and rich colors of the lobby. After settling their belongings in their rooms, all were given a riding tour of Savannah's parks and lavish homes, especially along Victory Drive. Emmie and Caleb acted as guides, entertaining them with stories of Savannah's history before, during and after the Civil War. Omie begged Emmie for all the latest gossip along the way, saying she had promised to bring stories back to Phoebee.

Nate looked out the carriage window silently as Caleb held the children captive with stories of pirates and ghosts, but Omie could tell he was listening too. And then, it was time to return to the Campbell's for supper.

Maizie opened the front door of the Campbell's home, welcoming the family in as a combination of delicious smells set all mouths watering. Emmie's and Caleb's mentors spared no expense for this celebration, wanting to show the young couple how dear they had become to them.

Leaves had been added to the dining room table, making it long enough to accommodate the Campbells as well as Emmie's entire family. Extra staff had been hired to prepare the lavish feast, and once greetings were exchanged and all were seated, platters and bowls began arriving in front of them. Omie and Kate smiled at each other with delight, reveling in being on the other side of the kitchen door for once. The children were wide-eyed and speechless as Maizie kindly served them each a small portion of everything.

Savannah boasted some of the best culinary craft in the state of Georgia, and their cook had a stellar reputation. To start, bowls of creamy crab soup were served, followed by smoked oysters in nests of collard greens cooked with bacon.

Ada Kate leaned toward her mamma's ear. "What's that??"

Caleb turned to Ada with a twinkle in his eye and replied, "Why, these are sea creatures called oysters. They take grains of sand and turn them into pearls. You might just find one if you look closely."

Ada Kate looked up at him, then turned and asked, "Mamma, what are pearls?"

Everyone laughed. Mrs. Campbell rose, walking to the girls' end of the table to show Bartie and Ada Kate the string of pearls around her lovely neck.

Ada was distracted from her hunt for pearls when a large brisket was presented on a rolling cart by a smartly dressed waiter, who began sharpening his knife in front of them. He smiled as he expertly sliced succulent pieces and served the excited girls first. The meat had been slowly simmering since the night before in a secret mixture of spices, closely guarded by the cook. Tiny onions, carrots and potatoes swam in the rich brown broth.

Meanwhile, maids circled the table with bowls of red beans, okra, creamed corn and buttered peas, along with various breads. The meal was accompanied by relishes and pickles in cut-glass dishes which reflected the chandelier's light.

This night was the first time any of the family other than Emmie had tasted wine. Ada Kate looked eager to try some, but Kate kept an eye on her granddaughter, shaking her head as the servants brought more to their end of the table.

Just when everyone declared they couldn't hold anymore, coffee was served, along with a fairytale of desserts.

It was time to get a good night's rest before the next day's events. They all agreed to meet for breakfast in the hotel dining room, except for Emmie—she was not to be seen by the men until Dr. Campbell escorted her down the aisle.

After arriving back at the hotel, Nate felt restless and told Omie he was going to walk to the stables to see the carriage horses. He had been admiring the large animals and wanted a closer look. She knew her husband needed a sense of something familiar after a day of obvious discomfort and told him to go, but to be sure and wear his old clothes. He'd have to bathe in the morning so as not to smell like a barnyard.

"Nuthin' wrong with a barnyard," Nate muttered as he left their room.

He was brushing down one of the horses when he heard someone approaching. Nate slowly turned his head as Caleb walked in.

"Beautiful animals, aren't they? Percherons, I believe," Caleb said, as he ran a hand down the horse's flanks.

"I never seen such large horses," Nate replied. "Bet I could plow twice as much with one of these fellas." He faced the horse again, holding its bridle and brushing the long arc of its neck.

"Omie told me I would find you here, Nate. I just wanted a word before my family comes in the morning. This has all got to be a bit awkward for you."

Nate put the brush down and wiped his hands before speaking. "Listen, Caleb. I allow as how I may have judged you in a harsh way. What you did for Phoebee and the baby was nuthin' short of a miracle. I still don't know how you done it, and we are ever grateful. As Emmie's husband, I know that makes you another kind of family to me, but I cain't see how we will ever be friends, there's just too much . . ."

"I understand that, Nate. I will settle for not being enemies. Still, if there is anything I can do for you, please let me know."

"Just take good care of Emmie is all," Nate replied and bent to take up the brush again.

"That is one promise I can easily give," Caleb replied. He turned to go but stopped and looked back for a moment.

"Nate, I want you to know that my brothers have no knowledge about any of this. They have very few good memories of our father. I will never speak of what he did to you and your mother."

Nate just gave a slight nod without looking up and Caleb walked out.

The morning of the wedding arrived draped in sweet September sunshine. Omie stretched as she turned to look over at the children, still sleeping on cots provided by the hotel. The girls and their little brother had a made a late night of it, too excited to lie still until they all succumbed to exhaustion.

Omie heard Nate coming down the hall from the latrine and smiled at him as he opened the door. "I could get used to this!" she said, stretching some more.

"Oh, is that so?" He snuggled back under the covers, nuzzling her neck. "Do I smell like a barnyard now, Mrs. Fancy Pants?"

"MMM-mmm, not at all," she whispered, and laid on top of him. She kissed him, then raised her head to look into his eyes. "Thank you for being here, Mr. Nate Silar."

He returned the kiss. "You are very welcome, Mrs. Omie Silar." Just then Frank Thomas turned his head their way and smiled.

Omie looked at Nate. "Well, here we go."

He gave her a playful pat on her fanny as she got up, taking the quilt with her.

Breakfast was, like last night's supper, a feast for the eyes as well as the belly. The hotel dining room was quiet in the soft morning light as travelers trickled in, wanting their coffee before engaging in conversation.

Ada Kate and Bartie were still so shy and dumbstruck by their surroundings, they could hardly eat—but not their brother. He seemed to have as much blueberry syrup on his face as he had on his pancakes. The boy chortled at the attention he was getting from the staff and offered everyone who passed by a fistful of his breakfast. Nate had him constrained on his lap so Omie wouldn't have to worry about getting her clothes stained.

"You sure you're going to be able to handle him while I get ready for the wedding?" she asked.

"Oh, shore," Nate said. "I'll take him out to the stables and set him up on one of those giant horses. Would you like that, little man?"

Frank Thomas looked up at him with a purple grin and declared, "Horsey, horsey!"

"I know, I know." Nate grinned at Omie. "No dirty, no stinky!"

As Nate left with Frank Thomas on his shoulders, Caleb entered the dining room accompanied by his family.

"Good morning to you all! Mrs. Lee, this is my mother, Hazel Decker, and my brothers, Marion and Cyrus."

Kate stood to embrace Mrs. Decker. "So pleased to finally meet you, Hazel. We've heard nothing but good things about you all from Emmie." Then she hugged Caleb for a long moment and shook hands with his brothers.

"This is my other daughter Omie and her girls, Ada Kate and Bartie."

Ada Kate stood and curtsied, with a 'Pleased to meet you.' Cyrus Decker bowed low, saying, "The pleasure is all mine." This made both girls giggle.

Omie wondered how long Ada Kate had been practicing her curtsies.

"You just missed my husband, Nate, and our son, Frank Thomas," Omie said, as she shook hands all around. She wrapped Caleb in a sisterly embrace, whispering loudly, "If you're gonna run, this would be the time."

Caleb laughed and told her he was afraid they were permanently stuck with him, best get used to it.

Hazel had seen Omie's young husband leaving as she entered the dining room.

Thank goodness I saw him now instead of during the wedding. He looks so much like Charles at his age, I might have embarrassed myself by staring.

"Please, sit," Omie offered. "Mamma and I need to go get ourselves ready, but it was so nice meeting y'all."

Caleb's mother said, "I hope we shall see a great deal more of each other after the wedding."

Nate took the children to watch the decorating of the horses and carriages while Omie and Kate luxuriated in the large bathtubs the hotel boasted. An endless delight of hot water was provided along with French-milled soaps and warm fluffy towels. They confessed to each other afterwards that they both felt a bit shy of being naked before the house maids who replenished the water. Still, they managed to close their eyes and relax as they never had before.

"To think that people actually bathe like this all the time!" Kate exclaimed, shaking her head. "It's a wonder they get anything else done."

"I know." Omie sighed. "That soap smells so good, I don't know whether to wash with it or eat it."

"Well," Kate said, "there's a time or two you probably needed your mouth washed out with soap!"

Omie laughed, and they drank in the joy of just being in this moment, happy to have no more to concern themselves with than joining Emmie as she walked down the aisle toward her new life.

Thomas arrived at the hotel after the women were dressed, and helped Kate and Omie up into the buggy. Nate promised to bring the little girls over soon, giving the women a chance to get dressed.

"I am so glad to see you!" Maizie exclaimed as she opened the Campbell's front door. "Been running up and down these stairs all mornin'! I think I'm more nervous than the bride!"

As they stepped inside, they were met with a bedlam of happy activity. Flowers filled rooms that were to hold the reception for the bride and groom. Preparations in the kitchen were in full force.

Maizie chattered excitedly as she led them up the stairs. Entering the bedroom, they saw Emmie standing in front of the mirror in her bridal gown with tears running down her face. Elizabeth stood behind her, smiling. Kate hurried over and took Emmie's face in her hands.

"Honey, what's wrong?"

Emmie just looked at their reflections and pointed to the front of her gown. Elizabeth had created a tapestry of tiny seed pearls and silk ribbons on the bodice. Tucks and embroidery of the same pale thread wove a delicate background pattern which was repeated on the veil's crown. Kate and Omie were astounded.

Emmie held out her hands to Elizabeth and said, "She did all of this, Mamma. She wouldn't let me see it until today. Isn't it the most beautiful thing you've ever seen? How much time you must have spent on this, Elizabeth! I can't thank you enough."

Elizabeth embraced Emmie gently and said, "My affections and good wishes are in every stitch, Emmie. I wanted this to be as lovely as you are. This will be the happiest day in your life for a long time to come, and I pray that you and Caleb know the joy Daniel and I have."

Omie brushed her fingers carefully across the front of the dress and whispered, "Oh, Emmie." She glanced at their mamma's face in the mirror and said, "Do you remember the nightgown Mamma gave me on my wedding day, Emmie? All that handwork! It was the prettiest thing I had ever seen."

"Oh, but this wedding dress is beyond pretty, Mrs. Campbell. Thank you for being so good to my girl." Kate spoke quietly and turned a tearful smile toward Elizabeth.

"My thanks go to you for sharing your sweet daughter, Mrs. Lee. I cannot tell you what she means to Daniel and me." She took Kate's hands in hers, gazing into her eyes for a moment.

"Well, Emmie, I must go and make ready myself, now that your mother is here."

Elizabeth turned to go, and Maizie followed her out the door, blowing a kiss as she left.

Emmie took her mamma in her arms and laid her head on the soft, sweet shoulder that had been a source of comfort for so many years. Mamma smelled of scented soap, but also of the sun and soil of the farm, and of her herbs and flowers.

She stood back, smiling gently. "Mamma, I appreciate this beautiful dress and all the things Elizabeth has done for me. She and the doctor have not been blessed with children, and I believe my being here fills some of that emptiness for them. Please know, though, that it is you my heart and thoughts turn to when I am in need of love and comfort. You are the reason for who I am, and I'm thankful every day that God gave me to you."

Maizie came back to find all three of them in tears and said, "Now this won't do, y'all! We can't have the bridal party looking like they just came from a funeral!" She shook her head and tsk'ed them into motion. "Ada Kate and Bartie are here, now y'all smile!"

After the women were finished preparing, Omie went with Maizie to help the flower girls into their dresses. Emmie had enjoyed making them so much, she could not wait to have daughters of her own to sew for.

The scent of magnolia blossoms inside the church mingled with the fragrance of roses blooming just outside its doors. Emmie had only wanted simple sprays of the magnolia leaves and blossoms affixed to the ends of the pews along the center aisle. Trinity Methodist Church was magnificent in its own right, and she felt that anything more dramatic in decoration would be unnecessary. Splendid European windows melded the light into soft prisms of color. Quiet, elegant, and joyous, altogether. At the altar, calla lilies nestled among ferns in large vases dressed with yellow sashes. Mrs. Campbell's garden had taken a second breath in the cooler days and evenings of fall, gifting them with the callas, as well as white and yellow roses, for Emmie's bouquet.

Omie's and Elizabeth's bouquets were simple arrangements of roses and baby's breath. The flower girls' basket was full to the brim with rose petals, and was set in the basement to keep fresh.

From the upstairs window of the Campbells' home, Emmie could see that people had begun to arrive on the church lawn. She was moved to see how many friends, as well as family, had come to wish them happiness in their wedded life. She tried not to listen to the superstitious imp that whispered in her ear, *this kind of joy can only last so long*.

Her mamma moved to her side and said, "What is it, darlin'? It's almost time to go. You're not having any doubts about this, surely?"

Emmie sighed. "No Mamma, but I do wonder sometimes how I came to deserve this. Am I taking things for granted? Can you jinx your life by being too happy?"

Kate smiled and ran her hand over the back of Emmie's veil.

"Oh, my girl, never doubt that God wants us to be happy. You store up every bit of this joy you can, and it will give you strength, and lessen the pain of troubled times that surely will come. How we face hardships, what we learn from them, is up to us. Having a good man like Caleb by your side will allow you to embrace this life to its fullest, because nothing, good or bad, will be too big for you to handle. I know this to be true, Emmie. You go and walk down that aisle and know that the Lord is cradling you to His heart just as I do."

Emmie smiled and pressed her cheek to her mother's. They stood like that for a few moments until Omie burst through the door and announced, "The carriage is here for us, ladies! I can't hold Ada Kate and Bartie back much longer. Let's get you to the church, sister." Omie grabbed Emmie's hand and led her through the door. Elizabeth and the girls met them on the landing, glowing with excitement.

The staff had come to the foyer to watch the bride descend the stairs in her regal beauty. All cheered their good wishes, waving as the bridal party stepped up into their carriages and pulled away.

The entourage stopped before the church to wait for someone to signal the flower girls and bridesmaids to enter. Emmie could hear music pouring through the open doors. She closed her eyes and took a few deep breaths to calm herself. Caleb's brothers arrived to assist the ladies down, and Omie took her daughters' hands as they stepped into the vestibule.

"You remember what you're to do now, girls?" she whispered.

They nodded and took the handle of the basket between their small hands. Caleb's brothers joined Omie and Elizabeth as the organist began the first strains of their entrance music. Omie gave the girls a little push and they began their walk slowly at first, taking great care to toss the rose petals in front of them as they'd been shown. Bartie began sharing handfuls with people in the aisle seats until Ada Kate tugged her sister along, laughing and tossing the last of the petals up into the air.

Marion Decker offered his arm to Omie, and she rested her hand there as they began their walk.

The congregation turned to witness Emmie's matron of honor make her way down the aisle. Omie smiled, feeling proud, and also shy. All eyes were on her, but no one so much as Nate. He could only stare transfixed at this lovely creature he hardly recognized. Omie turned her head slightly to meet his gaze. As Omie passed by, she smiled at her mamma's beaming face.

Elizabeth followed on the arm of Cyrus Decker and came to stand beside Omie. Each woman pulled one of the flower girls close. Caleb, handsomely dressed in his dark waistcoat and gleaming white shirt, greeted them all with a warm grin as his brothers nudged past him to their places.

Everyone stood at the first strains of the bridal march, turning with anticipation, as Emmie, resplendent in her gown, entered on the arm of Dr. Campbell. She seemed to glide toward Caleb. Their eyes met and held, as if it were just the two of them.

She takes my breath away. Please Lord, make me worthy of her.

Daniel kissed her cheek, then helped her step up to take her place beside Caleb.

Nate, too, was struck by Emmie's radiant visage, but his eyes returned again and again throughout the ceremony to drink in the images of his wife and daughters. He was the luckiest man in all this world. Nothing in his life had ever been so perfect and precious as this moment. With a start, he realized the ceremony was over and everyone was filing out of the sanctuary. Omie guided the girls ahead of herself and Marion, followed by Elizabeth and Cyrus. Nate escorted Kate up the aisle, trying not to feel the stirrings of jealousy at seeing Omie on the arm of one of the Decker brothers.

Outside the church, Nate took Omie in his arms as soon as he was able and swung her around. She held onto her headdress and laughed, kissing him grandly as he set her down.

"Omie, just when I believed you could never be purtier than the day we was married, I believe you outshone the bride today!"

Her eyes glistened as she put a hand to his cheek and said, "Thank you, darlin'."

Ada Kate and Bartie grabbed at his sleeves and cried, "What about us, Daddy, aren't we pretty too?!"

"I thought I was seein' two little princesses when you walked down that aisle! You was throwing those rose petals so good, too. But you know who likes princesses to eat, don't you? Dragons!" He chased them in the sunshine, between and around the delighted guests, all readying to go to the Campbell's for the reception.

At the reception, once the toasts had been made, with Cyrus and Marion causing even Emmie to blush at their antics, the cake was cut and served. Afterwards, the family gathered to pose for photographs. Nate had to be pulled in for a group photo and, even then, turned his head as the flash went off. It was nearly too much for him to bear, being so close to the Deckers.

Omie would come to sorely wish that she could have had a photograph made of her and Nate that day. A precious day, before the tie between them began to unravel and he turned his face away again in the years that followed.

Maizie had been holding Frank Thomas, and Nate retrieved him as soon as he could get away, needing some distance from the crowd. He took his sleeping boy from her lap and carried him back to the hotel.

Caleb and Emmie left the reception amid a flurry of handshakes and kisses, and climbed into a new car, their wedding present to themselves. It was festooned with flowers and the longest trail of clattering cans anyone had ever seen. Marion and Cyrus clapped each other on the back as the newlyweds circled the square, waving to all. Finally, the two of them turned toward the road to Charleston, where they would catch a steamer for a month in Paris.

Chapter 33

A shaft of sunlight glanced off the copper being pounded and bent into shape. Tools lay scattered about in the hay. The morning was unusually quiet but for the sound of horses munching hay and the occasional call of a cow to her calf. Ephram had acquired all the parts necessary. Finally, the chance had come for him to assemble his still while the Silars were in Savannah at the wedding.

It was a thing of beauty, he reckoned, both in form and function, for it would bring to him and Phoebee the means to buy a place of their own. Not that life was unkind here with Nate and his family, but Ephram felt the women's judgmental eyes on him all the time. Phoebee was not the sweet self to him she used to be, and he believed he had to get her away from the influence of Kate and Omie.

The corn crop had been good—better than good—and he had been secretly stashing some of it away in a makeshift crib he'd constructed. He had chosen to build it in the woods near the old cemetery where no one seemed to go.

Ephram had bought sugar in small amounts at a time, so as not to cause suspicion, and now the time was right. He made sure Phoebee and Aunt Julia were occupied with the babies, then loaded the still into the wagon, covering it with feed sacks and hay. He hitched the mule as if he was about the business of the farm, then headed down the road toward the river and the shade of the cemetery.

What business was it of the law how a man profited from his corn? The revenuers only wanted to be able to tax the rewards of his hard work. It was always about the money, disguised as moral duty. Damned if he was going to give it to them.

Ephram set about putting the still in the area he had prepared, so as to show the least of it to distant prying eyes, then began the work of making whiskey. Pure creek water, some barley to hurry the process, and dried, cracked corn his own hands had brought to harvest; all these went into the mix.

Near to afternoon, he returned with the wagon and let the mule out to pasture, as if he had been working the fields.

Aunt Julia rocked on the porch with a sleeping Ezra in her lap. She *Saw* beyond the fields, far beyond what her eyes could see, a knowing of something out of sorts. Ephram. As if she could smell it on him—wickedness and deceit in a craft as old as recorded time: likker. A potion for weakness, just waiting to take a body down. Well, she'd speak with Omie about it when she returned, and then let things unfold as they would.

The ride back to the farm was a pleasant one for the family. Frank Thomas slept on Omie's lap, worn out.

"They all looks like angels when they sleepin." Thomas smiled down at the boy.

"Are you and Maizie thinking of starting a family soon, Thomas? I'm sorry if that was too personal a question."

He turned to her with a twinkle in his eyes. "We thinkin' 'bout it."

Everyone still felt lifted up by the joyousness of the day's events. In the back of the buggy, the girls and their grandmamma chatted about the wedding. Even Nate had a calm glow around him.

Sunlight caught in the sweetgums and maples along the river, casting their colors against the true, blue sky. Omie saw the change of seasons in the dry wild grasses, tousled by the wind, and in the carpet of acorns strewn beneath live oaks where squirrels gathered their bounty.

Nate will claim some squirrels for dinner soon. Omie smiled. *Much to do in preparation for winter, now that the big excitement of the wedding is over.*

Firewood would need to be split and stacked. Corn cobs needed to be set in the crib on the back porch for the cookstove. Apples would need to be gathered, sliced and hung on strings, giving the kitchen a sweet smell as they dried. That is, if the squirrels hadn't robbed the trees while they were gone.

Omie looked forward to settling into the lazier pace of winter with time to enjoy the rewards from a long busy summer. Taking note of the pumpkins in the fields they passed, she smiled to think of pies cooling in the pie safe. And jack-o-lanterns! She loved carving them as much as the children did.

They arrived back at the farm by late afternoon. Omie could hardly wait to scoop up Ezra to nurse. Aunt Julia and Phoebee met them in the yard with both babies ready to feed. Omie laughed and remarked that she was ready to nurse them at the same time! Nate helped Kate and the little girls down from the carriage. They thanked Thomas and waved goodbye as he hurried toward home, hoping to catch the last of the light.

While Omie settled the babies on a blanket, Phoebee took the girls to her house for cookies. Around her kitchen table, the girls told Phoebee their version of the wedding. Entertaining as they were, she was looking forward to a more detailed adult account of events.

There was a bit of time to for Omie to visit with Aunt Julia while Kate went to make a pot of tea.

"I want to hear all about the wedding and such, but first I need to tell you something. Omie, I hate to be the one to bring up bad news on this joyful day, but I thought you should know. Ephram is up to something. I can't say exactly what, but I think there's some likker business goin' on. More than that, y'all will have to find out yourselves, but be watchful, you hear?"

"Why, sure, Aunt Julia. Thank you for telling me. I'll bring it up with Nate in the morning. I think we're all so tuckered, we need a worry-free sleep."

Kate joined them with the tea, then the two of them took turns describing highlights of the wedding to Aunt Julia, laughing at the antics of the flower girls. Kate shed tears as she recounted what a vision Emmie was in her lovely gown. Seeing the fatigue in Aunt Julia's eyes, Kate stood up and went to the porch.

"Nate, would you give Aunt Julia a ride home now?"

"Thank you again for minding the babies." Omie kissed the woman's weathered cheek and held her close for a moment.

"Don't forget what I told you."

"I won't, Aunt Julia. I won't."

Omie mentioned Aunt Julia's concerns to Nate the next morning.

"I don't know, Omie. Seems like I would'a knowed if something was going on. I mean, we wuz only gone a couple a' days. I can't imagine what he could have gotten up to. He done all the things that needed doin' while we wuz gone. When would he have time to get in trouble?"

"Well, you know Aunt Julia's never wrong . . . ."

"Yeah, but maybe it's not what it seems. I'll see if I can smell likker on him today."

Nate left to see what needed tidying up and mending in the barn. The next few days went by much the same as always. Nate reported he hadn't noticed any smell of alcohol or change in Ephram's behavior, so Omie let it pass.

One morning, Omie woke before light to see Cecelia's ghostly form beside her bed.

"Cecelia?" she whispered sleepily.

There was a sense of unease and urgency about Cecelia's fading image. Omie knew the young woman was close to leaving this world, but she didn't seem to have appeared to say farewell, rather she had a message to convey. Omie finally fell back asleep, troubled, but uncertain of what this meant.

Nate had to shake her awake later that morning, as Ezra started whimpering to be changed and fed.

"I got us a fire goin'," Nate said. "I knowed you needed some extra sleep, and I rocked the baby as long as he'd let me. He's up for his breakfast now, though."

"Thank you, honey." She kissed him and rose to take Ezra from his arms. When she got the baby cleaned and fed, she asked Nate to sit a minute before the girls and Polly woke.

"I had a visitor last night," she said. "You remember the young woman I told you about, from the cemetery, that spoke to me one night a few years ago?"

"That dream you mean?" he laughed.

“No, Nate, it was no dream. She came to me last night. I think Ephram has set up a still in the cemetery.”

“Omie, that’s just craziness, he wouldn’t do that.”

“Well, maybe you should check it out early tomorrow morning.”

“Cecelia, huh? OK, if it makes you happy. Now I got six females to please on this farm. What did I ever do?” He laughed and walked out the back door.

Nate rose well before dawn the next day and sat in the dark beside the woodshed with eyes on the barn, enjoying the cool crispness in the air. A rain crow called from a tree at the river’s edge, and he wondered if they were in for a little bad weather. A faint figure slipped along the far fence row in the shadows, headed toward the river. Nate picked up the axe and started out in the same direction, but stopped when he heard Omie run up behind him.

“No way I’m going to let you take your temper and that axe to do this by yourself! You don’t need to make a widow of Phoebee.”

“Come on, then, but I’m still not sure this is what you think.”

The sun had begun to rise above the trees, and they could both see smoke from a fire in the grove around the cemetery. Nate stopped a moment and took a deep breath. Omie took his arm and looked in his eyes until she saw the fire in them die down a bit. He nodded, and they quietly walked up behind Ephram as he bent to his work.

“Just what the hell do you think you’re doin’?” Nate asked in a quiet voice.

Ephram straightened up and turned quickly to see the both of them standing there. “Uh. Nate, I was gonna talk to you.”

“Never you mind explainin’, Ephram. You know I never woulda’ had a part in this. We could lose this farm if the law was to find out, did you think of that?”

"They wouldn't ever find out, Nate, I swear. Not here! I'll do all the work and share the profits with you, that's what I was meanin' to do all along!"

"No, Ephram, you won't. And you will get your things and leave this farm by the end of the day."

That said, Nate swung the axe in a wide arc, taking down the still, nearly hitting Ephram, and scattering the fire. Water from the still killed most of the fire, leaving a scent of scorched corn in the air. Omie ran to stomp out the sparks and kicked dirt over the embers.

"Damn you, Nate Silar!" Ephram screamed, "I worked a long time on that still!"

"Huh, behind my back in our barn, I reckon!" Nate snorted.

"How did you even know? Did that old lady come snoopin' around to check on me? I'll teach her."

"You'll do no such thing," Nate replied. "It was not her."

Ephram looked at Omie.

"You. You with your damned knowin' of things. You and your mamma ain't nuthin' but witches, and I aim to take Phoebee away from this place," he panted angrily.

"It was her told me."

Ephram gasped, as Omie pointed to a shimmery figure standing by a gravestone not ten feet away. He stumbled backwards, then turned and took off running. Like he'd seen a ghost.

Nate just stared while Omie lifted her hand in goodbye and said, "We thank you, Cecelia. Good to see you again." Cecelia passed into the sunlight.

Nate turned an incredulous face toward Omie as she took his hand and said, "Come on, then."

Back at the house, Ephram was throwing things into a bag as fast as he could, yelling to Phoebee to get up and do the same. Polly started crying, and Phoebe said in a loud whisper, "What are you on about, Ephram? You're scarin' the baby!"

"That damn witch you call a friend is what I'm on about!" he yelled.

Omie came in the door and took Polly from Phoebee. "I'll feed her," she said quietly.

"No, you won't. You get my baby away from her!" Ephram lunged at Omie and Phoebee got between them.

"Calm down a damn minute and tell me what this is all about!" Phoebee cried.

"We found him down at the old cemetery with a still. He was making moonshine," Omie said quietly.

"Moonshine?" Phoebee asked. Her eyes suddenly narrowed, and she said, "It was you all along back home, wudn't it. There weren't no man in those woods makin' likker, it were you. All this time you let me believe it weren't your fault we had to run, had to leave my family and ever'thing I knowed. You lied. You ain't nuthin' but a damned liar, Ephram, and I don't never want to see your face again!"

"Well, that's fine. I'm gone. You and your damn bees. You're probably a witch like them others, and that girl will be too!" He pointed to Polly.

"Her name, which you cain't seem to recall, is Polly. And if you don't git soon, I'll sic my bees on you!"

Ephram flew out the door to the barn where his horse had already been hitched to the wagon, waiting for him. Nate watched him from the barn doorway with a mixture of anger and disappointment on his face. As the clatter of hooves faded, Omie put her arm across her friend's small shoulders which were shaking with sobs.

"I am so sorry, Phoebee. You don't need that sorry excuse for a man. He should have treated you so much better."

"Oh, Omie, I don't care about him so much. I think I stopped lovin' him when Polly was born. All I give up for him! I ain't seen my family in years now, all because of him. I thought what we was gonna have would be enough—a farm, a family of our own. Bastard took all that from me."

"Well, darlin', looks to me like you have a farm and a family right here. A beautiful little girl who'll grow up to be just as wonderful as her mamma. That's maybe why God put him in your life, to bring you to this very place. One day, you'll see your family again, and they'll be glad of it. They'll forgive you, Phoebee, especially when they see what you brought them."

They looked at the quiet gaze Polly fixed on them as she nursed. Phoebee leaned her head on Omie's shoulder.

In the light from the woodstove, Nate's troubled face brought Omie over to sit on his lap and run her fingers through his hair.

"What's troubling you, darlin'?" she asked quietly. The children were asleep and the night was still.

"It's gonna be tough gettin' everything done this spring with Ephram gone," he said. "I might need to plant those fields up by your mamma's with something we can manage better. Cotton's bringing a decent price, maybe we'll try that. I've not grown it before, but I hear it's not so hard. Growin' too much of one thing is not a smart idea anyways."

"Well, the chickens sure have enjoyed that corn of Ephram's, especially the mash." Omie laughed. "Had us some drunken hens there. The girls had no trouble catchin' them. They set one in Frank Thomas' lap, and it didn't move at all!"

1939

June 19

Omie was up before the morning sun teased the others awake. This was her favorite time, when doves in the porch eaves began to coo and mist hung in the overhanging branches of the big oak. The earth seemed to hold its breath, waiting to see what its creatures made of this new day.

Ezra and Polly strode into the kitchen hand-in-hand. They each bent to kiss Omie's cheek, then settled into chairs at the table. Ezra got up to pour them both a cup of coffee and returned, handing Polly hers.

"Creamy and sweet, just like me."

Polly rolled her eyes and smiled.

Ezra sat and put his hand on the back of Omie's chair. "How are you holdin' up, Mamma?"

Omie patted his hand. "I'm fine, son. How about you?"

"All right." He looked at Polly for a moment and said, "I saw him there. At the cemetery."

"Did you?" His mamma looked at him intently. "I'm not surprised, you were close to him toward the end, honey. How did he seem?"

Ezra sighed. "A bit lost, I'd say. He hung back like he was shy of all the folks who turned up for his funeral. Never took his eyes off you though."

Omie started to cry. The tears that had been building up finally burst through, and Polly went to wrap her arms around the older woman's shoulders. Emmie walked into the kitchen and kneeled beside her sister, stroking her hair. "Let them come, Sweetie. Let them come."

When Omie's tears had subsided, Emmie took her hand and led her to the bedroom. Ezra and Polly sat quietly for a few moments.

Lilly wandered in, rubbing her eyes and sat beside Ezra. "Is Grandmamma ok?"

"She needed to shed the weight of those tears, is all," Polly replied. "You ok, Punkin'?"

"I didn't sleep much. Kept feelin' like someone was at the foot of the bed. Didn't want to wake Tess, so I just laid there. It was too dark to see. Um...are there biscuits?"

Bartie came into the kitchen and walked over to give Lilly's a hug. "I'll make us some as soon as I have a cup of that coffee."

Ezra took his niece's hand. "Trust me, Lilly Bud, ghosts don't mean any harm. If that's what it was."

"Oh, I wasn't scared. They felt—I don't know, mostly sad. Whoever it was smelled like whiskey, though."

Polly and Ezra looked at each other.

Lilly said, "Aunt Polly? Would you tell me a story? Somethin' good that will calm my mind?"

Ezra said, "Tell her how you got your sight back."

"Got it back? I know you need glasses, but what do you mean?"

"Well, let me *see.*" Polly laughed at her own joke. "Not too long after Bitsy was born, Dr. Caleb found there was somethin' wrong with my eyes."

Chapter 34

1912

Polly grew slowly at first. But she grew. It was apparent she would be a tiny thing like her mamma. Otherwise, she seemed sound of health in spite of her difficult birth.

Polly and Ezra lay contentedly on a pallet while the women went about their chores. The babies found each other's toes and hair fascinating. They developed a language all their own before speaking a single word to the grown-ups around them. Ezra walked first, and Polly would follow wherever he went on her hands and knees, chattering at him. When Polly finally stood on her own, Ezra was there beside her, cheering her on, just as excited as if he realized a whole new world of mischief had opened up for them.

Kate noticed that Polly seemed to follow the sound of voices more than movements. She would dangle things in front of the baby, and Polly reached for them like any child, but she didn't seem to notice them if they weren't right in front of her. Kate brought it up to Phoebee and Omie one day, and they watched Polly as she toddled around behind Ezra. As the two wandered about, she didn't turn to look for him, so much as follow his babble. Phoebee confessed that she'd grown concerned about it but just hoped Polly was slow to develop.

Kate said, "Well, that may be, but it wouldn't hurt to have Caleb look her over when he and Emmie come next week." Smiling, she added, "I can't wait to see Emmie's belly!"

Phoebe brightened up, and they all fell to talking and laughing as they watched the light dance sweetly on the tops of the children's heads.

"My word!" Kate exclaimed, as Caleb helped Emmie down from the carriage. "You've grown so much. I never thought to see you any bigger than a minute!"

Everyone laughed, and hugs went around; the children stood at the top of the steps so Emmie wouldn't have to bend over to kiss them.

"How you feelin', darlin'?" Kate asked.

"Oh, Mamma, this man won't let me do anything. You'd think I was carrying the future queen of England the way he treats me."

Caleb bowed with a flourish of his hat.

"And so he should!" Omie smiled at her brother-in-law as they walked up onto the porch. "Y'all sit, I'll bring us some lemonade."

Emmie lowered herself down into one of the rockers.

"You may never get me out of this!" Omie placed Ezra in her sister's arms and Emmie smiled down at his chubby face.

"Oh, I was big with you, too, honey," Kate laughed. "Don't ever let them tell you that means it's a boy."

"Well, Ezra weren't no minnow," Omie said, returning with a pitcher and glasses.

She handed the little girls each a small glass of the sweet drink, then sat, pulling Frank Thomas onto her own lap so he could sip from hers.

The afternoon delivered a benevolent breeze, and the family passed the day on the porch until it was nearly supper time. Phoebee walked down from the hill with Polly and settled on the steps to talk with Emmie and Caleb, while Kate and Omie went into the kitchen to see to the meal.

"I just cannot believe how she's grown, Phoebee!" Emmie exclaimed.

"You would certainly never know she came into this life under such stressful circumstances," Caleb said. He smiled and took Polly's little hand, the same hand that had held his before she had even come into the world. She turned her head in his direction and grinned.

"I think she knows she wouldn'a been here atall if it weren't for you," Phoebee replied.

Caleb swung his watch on its chain for her to play with, but she seemed to just stare at it, mesmerized by the glint of light.

"Dr. Decker, I been a little concerned about Polly's eyes," Phoebe said slowly. "I wouldn't bother you with it, but Mrs. Lee said I should ask what you thought."

"Well, let's have a little look there, Miss Polly," he said, as he took her up onto his lap. He swung the watch like a pendulum back and forth, and she followed it slowly. Then he moved it further and further from her until she looked away at the sound of her mamma's voice.

"She don't seem to really see things unless they're right up on her," Phoebee said. "She feels her way around, mostly, and follows Ezra's voice when they play together. I think she sees some, but not everything. It worries me somethin' terrible." Phoebe looked up at Emmie with big moist eyes.

Emmie reached down and took Phoebee's hand. She knew not to offer reassurance until there was truly some to offer. Being a doctor's wife had taught her that the truth must be dealt out carefully and compassionately, but honesty was kinder than false hope.

Caleb observed Polly for a few more moments and said, "I can tell she sees the contrast between light and shadow, Phoebee, but her eyes don't seem to focus very much. Let's give her a year or so to see how she develops. I can't give you a real answer until I can do some tests at our clinic, and they will be more effective when she's old enough to speak. Do you think you could bring her to Savannah? You would be most welcome to stay with us, and I'm sure, between Dr. Campbell and me, we can sort this out."

"Really?" Phoebee asked. "Y'all would do that for us? I mean, I would pay you and all. I ain't got much right now but when the crops come in—"

"Not a word of that, Phoebee. I brought this girl into the world and, as her doctor, I am responsible for her well-being," Caleb declared.

He hugged Polly up close and brushed his mustache against her cheek, causing her to giggle. Smiling, he passed her back to her mamma.

"Y'all come eat!" Omie cried, and the three of them pulled Emmie up from her chair.

"I must visit the privy first!" Emmie laughed. Phoebee helped her down the steps and out into the yard. Polly walked between them holding both their hands.

Kate looked at Caleb's concerned face as he came in the kitchen door. Nodding her head, Kate stated, "It's so, isn't it, son. Polly is nearly blind."

"Not completely, though. She may be able to make out some familiar shapes, but I think she mostly sees light and dark playing against each other. She seems to be adapting to her situation, however."

"I reckon when it's all you've ever known, you just do," Omie said.

"I wonder if you might be able to bring her to our clinic, Omie? I offered for Phoebee and Polly to stay with us while Dr. Campbell and I give the baby a more thorough examination."

"That would be such a blessing, Caleb! I surely will," Omie replied.

Emmie returned, leaning on Phoebee's slight shoulder. Entering the kitchen, she rested her head wearily against her mamma and asked, "Mamma, you will come stay with us when it's my time, won't you?"

Kate looked shyly at Caleb and said, "I reckon this one has all the help he needs delivering his child."

Caleb said, "Are you kidding? I'm going to be as nervous as a long-tailed cat in a room full of rocking chairs! Please say you'll come, and we'll do this together."

Kate was obviously pleased and said of course she would be there.

"What about me?" Omie asked in mock indignation.

"You have to be there, too!" Emmie laughed. "Who else am I going to yell at while they're down there having all the fun!"

"Some things never change." Omie rolled her eyes. "Glad I'm good for something!"

"I'll stay here and tend these ones." Phoebee nodded toward the children. "I'll see y'all when Polly and I come to Savannah. For some reason, I just don't have a hankerin' to be at birthin's."

"Understood," Caleb said.

Phoebee smiled up at him. "Not that I wouldn't do it all over ag'in for my girl."

Chapter 35

Kate packed and repacked her valise for the trip to Savannah. She was as nervous as she'd been at Emmie's wedding.

"Mamma, that's the fourth time you've checked your birthin' bag. Looks like you have enough supplies to birth triplets!"

Omie's mamma smiled unconvincingly.

"Why are you nervous? How many times have you delivered babies without a hitch? Emmie can't be built much different than me."

"I haven't delivered one under the eyes of a doctor before."

"Really? You're worried about Caleb judging you? I think Caleb is scared to death at the thought of delivering his own baby. He's depending on you because he trusts you completely. And Emmie wouldn't want anyone else."

Kate sat on the bed and gave her daughter a tired smile.

Omie hugged her and stood. "Everything is ready, I promise you. Now, I'll go make us a cup of tea to help us sleep. We need to be rested for this trip."

"There's some fresh lemon balm in the herb room. Add some rose hips, would you?" As soon as Omie was out the door, Kate returned to inspecting her valise.

"Mamma!"

The women took their time driving the buggy to Savannah. They'd left early to avoid the afternoon heat and dust stirred up by other travelers.

Omens were good. They'd both gazed down into the old well to see if it had anything to tell them, good or bad, about the coming birth. Its surface was calm and clear. Crows pecked at leftover corn in the cut fields, but none rose to follow the women. No snakes had scribed a warning on the dirt road. All in all, things seemed to bode well.

Except for the stifling August heat. "I sure will be glad for the shade of those trees!" Kate declared, as Savannah came into view. "I hope this heat eases up before the baby comes."

Omie pulled up in front of the house where Thomas was waiting for the horse and buggy.

"Good day, Mrs. Lee, Mrs. Silar. I'll see to your bags. Y'all go visit."

"Mamma, Omie!" Emmie greeted them from the porch. "Sorry not to come down for a hug, this is as far as I could get."

Omie took a gander at her sister's belly and said, "Yes. Best you stay up there. If you come down here and fall, you won't stop rolling 'til you get to River Street!"

Emmie's contractions began in the early dawn. She struggled to her feet and waddled down the hall to the bedroom where her mamma and sister slept. They were not there.

"Mamma?" Emmie whimpered, wondering if she had only dreamed of their arrival and was really alone. "Caleb?" she called a little louder.

Omie came bounding up the stairs and took her sister's arm.

"Finally!"

"What?" Emmie replied.

"We been sittin' at the kitchen table waiting for you to get up and let us bring this baby into the world!" Omie noticed the wet hem of Emmie's gown. She called down the stairs, "Mamma, she's up and her water's broke."

Emmie panted as another pain hit. "Where is Caleb?"

"We told him it was your time and that he needed to fetch Elizabeth and Maizie. Didn't ask any questions, just went."

"Smart boy." Kate smiled as she joined them. "Don't you worry darlin'. We'll all be here for you."

The women put Emmie back into her bed. When Caleb arrived with Elizabeth and Maizie, Kate put them to tucking old sheets, brought for the occasion, under Emmie. Selecting the most threadbare, she instructed, "Tear these ones into rags,"

Pots of water were boiled and set aside. Kate drew out her herbs and salves and lined them up on a table nearby. She washed her hands and sat at the foot of the bed with a hand on Emmie's knee.

"I'm just gonna take a look hon, see how close this baby is to comin'." She went around to peer beneath Emmie's gown and inserted her fingers, feeling for the baby's head.

"Looks to be close. Want to check for yourself, Dr. Decker?"

Caleb smiled his gratitude and took her place. He soon stepped back and let Kate take the lead in the delivery, but they shared the tasks at hand.

"Seems your first birth is comin' along easy, daughter," Kate assured Emmie.

"This is easy?" was her reply, as she squeezed Maizie's hand in pain.

When the contractions grew close together, Emmie breathed like Omie showed her, and sipped from the raspberry leaf tea she was handed.

Soon, the baby crowned and Caleb called, "Emmie! What a head of black hair! The baby is almost out!"

Kate moved aside to let him catch the child as it slid out. "A girl! We have a baby girl!"

Mary Elizabeth Decker came into the world with the lungs of an opera singer. Tears ran down Caleb's face as Omie handed him the clamp and scissors to cut the cord.

When he was done, Omie took the tiny body and laid her at Emmie's breast.

"Please feed this young'un afore she makes us all deaf!" Kate begged, laughing.

The women stayed on for a couple of weeks to let the new parents catch up on sleep, bringing Mary Elizabeth to her mamma when she needed to nurse. Otherwise, they filled their own arms with her sweetness, knowing it might be a while before they would have time with baby Bitsy again.

She was, overall, a good-natured baby who loved attention, of which there was plenty. Mrs. Campbell came mornings and evenings to hold her namesake, often accompanied by Dr. Campbell. Maizie found reasons to leave the shop often, and Elizabeth knew these were just excuses to stop in at the Decker's home. Thomas had made a cradle for the baby, and Maizie lined it with a lovely quilt she'd sown herself. In between patients, her pappa visited every chance he could.

"Where's my girl?" Caleb called, coming in for lunch one day, as he took off his hat and placed it on the coat rack beside the door.

"I'm assuming you're not talking to any of us." Emmie gently handed the baby to him.

"Sorry ladies, but I'm a proud papa. Smitten. Over the moon in love!"

Emmie smiled down at the tiny girl in his arms and whispered, "You've got everybody in the cup of your little hands, don't you?"

"I wonder what color her eyes will decide to be," Caleb mused. "They seem unusually inclined toward grey or green."

"Not so unusual in this family!" Omie laughed, turning toward him. Caleb hadn't really noticed until now, but his sister-in-law's eyes were the color of spring leaves, flecked with amber.

"Ah. Mary Elizabitsy," he cooed at the baby. "I swear sometimes she seems to see the whole of you with those peepers."

The woman smiled at his baby talk, the language of adoration. Shortly, Caleb returned the child to her mamma. "I hate to leave such pleasant company, but I must return to work." He gave each of the women a peck on the cheek, then retrieved his hat and was out the door.

Kate and Omie looked at each other for a long moment, pondering Caleb's words, 'she sees the whole of you'. Emmie shook her head with a resigned sigh. The *Sight* may well have been passed along to her tiny girl. If that was the case, Emmie would no more be able to keep secrets from her daughter than she had from her own mamma and sister.

Not fair!

Caleb's mother and brothers waited to pay a visit until Emmie's mamma and sister left, not wanting to overwhelm the new parents with company.

Hazel cried when Emmie put the baby in her arms. She could not explain why, such a mixture of sweetness and sadness mingled in her heart that the tears could not be contained. Caleb wrapped his arms around them both, knowing there was something of grief involving his father in her emotions.

"She is absolutely beautiful!" Hazel sniffed. She kissed Emmie's cheek and cupped her daughter-in-law's chin in her free hand. "Thank you for all the happiness you are bringing to us, Emmie. We are so pleased for you and Caleb to be starting your own family"

Marion and Cyrus tickled little Mary Elizabeth under her chin, teasing Caleb that they *didn't know he had it in him* and *good thing she favors her mother*. Then they were off to explore the city's entertainments.

"Those two!" Hazel shook her head. Though, a soft smile gave away her pleasure in their antics.

Chapter 36

1913

Phoebee kept trying to tuck back loose strands of her hair.

"Are you shor I'm dressed all right for Savannah, Omie?" Phoebee asked for the third time that morning, raising her voice above the clatter of the carriage wheels.

"Phoebee," Omie laughed in exasperation, "you are FINE!"

"I'm jest nervous is all," Phoebee said, as she looked away. She held Polly close for comfort, feeling a mixture of fear and elation as the miles passed.

Omie had not told her friend of the new dress secretly waiting for her at Mrs. Campbell's dress shop. This was Emmie's surprise. She had delivered on her promise, working the fine linen brought from Paris into a dress diminutive, yet womanly, for Phoebee. Omie could not wait to see her in it. A smaller, frillier version awaited Miss Polly as well.

Phoebee's large eyes grew bigger and bigger as the homes of Savannah appeared along the tree-lined avenues. She was, for once, at a complete lack of words. She twisted in the seat to look at the people strolling by in their finery, causing Polly to squirm in discomfort until Omie took her onto her own lap so Phoebee would be free to ogle.

Finally, they arrived at the Campbell's home. Thomas helped the women down from the carriage as Caleb and Daniel fetched their belongings.

Phoebee turned to Thomas with her best approximation of a curtsy and said, "Thank you so much, sir."

"You are most welcome, Miss Phoebee." Thomas doffed his hat with a kind smile as he climbed back up on the carriage.

Emmie and Elizabeth met them at the door with hugs. Polly touched the baby's soft little hand and smiled up at Emmie. "Bitsy?" she asked.

"Yes, that seems to be her nickname," Emmie laughed.

Mrs. Campbell smiled and said, "That was my nickname, too." She looked at her husband with mock severity. "Don't even think about it!"

Caleb and Emmie's charming home was a bit small for company, so the Campbells' upstairs bedrooms had been made ready for the women. Polly even had a small bed beside Phoebee's. Omie wondered if it was a family heirloom, the Campbells having had no children of their own.

Phoebee remained in a state of awe and newfound shyness. As they all sat for supper however, she warmed up to Daniel and Elizabeth, and could not help expressing her curiosity about everything from the soup to the chandeliers.

"Phoebee and Omie, if it suits you, we'll meet at the clinic after lunch tomorrow," Caleb said. "I'm sure you'd like a little tour of the city first, Phoebee, and it's much cooler out in the morning." He looked to Emmie for confirmation.

"Oh, I would!" Phoebee exclaimed, then added formally, "If that suits you?"

"Of course," A slight smile played at the corners of Emmie's mouth.

Phoebee grinned and took Polly's hands for a joyful game of pattycakes.

Morning found Phoebee dressed and ready before the sun had fully risen. Hearing sounds in the kitchen, she tiptoed past Polly and made her way down the stairs to the kitchen.

"Why, good mornin'!" Maizie called with a big smile. "I don't believe we've had the pleasure of meeting. You must be Miss Phoebee. I'm Maizie."

Phoebee blushed and said, "Pleased to meet you, I'm sure," and curtsied.

"No need to be formal with me, Miss Phoebee." Maizie smiled. "Can I get you a hot cup of coffee?"

The others found Phoebee and Maizie laughing like schoolgirls when they peeked into the kitchen to see what the noise was all about.

"Maizie is teaching me all about Savannah so-ci-e-ty," Phoebee declared. "I don't know if she's makin' these stories up, but she's shore got some."

Maizie winked at Omie and shooed them out to the dining room.

Emmie arrived, and after a lively breakfast she said, "We'd best be on our way if we're to have a proper tour before your appointment, Phoebee."

"I'll get Thomas to bring the carriage around," Maizie offered, as they rose to get ready.

"Thank you, Maizie. We won't be long." Omie and Phoebee made their way upstairs.

Phoebee paced about the bedroom, wringing her hands with nervousness. She turned to Omie. "Do I look all right?"

"Stop right there, Missy," Omie said, taking Phoebee's hands in hers. "Everything is fine. YOU are fine. Now let's get going!"

Excitement won out and Phoebee grabbed Polly up, swinging her around. "Come on, my Pollywog!" Laughing, she rushed out the door.

"First, we must stop and show you Mrs. Campbell's shop," said Emmie.

The carriage dropped them beside the shop's door. On entering, Phoebee's jaw dropped at the sight of all the lovely mannequins in their finery.

"I would change places with one of them big dolls any day to look like that." Phoebee whispered with wonder.

Mrs. Campbell walked into the front room and said, "Well Phoebee, I don't think you'll have to!"

Emmie reached for a dress hanging behind the counter along with a tiny one to match. "Remember I said I would sew one for you and Polly?" Emmie said quietly, seeing the tears well up in Phoebee's eyes.

The young woman looked at them all and wept, touching the fine fabric and lace with trembling fingers.

"Really, Emmie, this is just for me? And one for Polly too?" She sniffled, and Elizabeth handed her a lacey handkerchief.

Phoebee shook her head, and said, "This is too–"

"Just do it, Phoebee!" Omie laughed, squeezing her friend's shoulders. "Now, you go behind that curtain and put on your new frock. Emmie will help you with the buttons, and Mrs. Campbell and I will dress Polly."

When Phoebee walked back out into the room, Omie and Elizabeth were the ones who couldn't find their words. Before them was a lovely young woman. Gone was the girl who ran barefoot through the woods in search of honey. Emmie had spent some time with Phoebee's hair as well. Her thick, black, waist-length tresses were pinned up in a stylish fashion that accented her heart-shaped face and dark eyes.

Emmie turned Phoebee to look in the mirror, and a hush fell over the room. Polly wiggled out of Omie's arms and tottered over to stand by her mother.

"Is that truly me?" Phoebee asked quietly.

"It surely is, Phoebee," Omie answered.

"Well, wouldn't Ephram be damned sorry if'n he saw me now!" She squealed and hugged Emmie hard enough to take her breath away. "And you look like a fairy princess, darlin'!" Phoebee took Polly's little hands, and they danced around the room.

The rest of the morning went by as if in a dream for Phoebee, as Emmie and Omie pointed out their favorite sights of the city. They turned heads in all the shops and at the restaurant where they dined for lunch. Phoebee often blushed, grinning from the unaccustomed attention.

After the meal, Emmie had Thomas leave her at the dress shop. "I'll assist Mrs. Campbell while you ladies take Polly to the clinic. Please come for me after you're done. Phoebee, I do hope all goes well."

"Thank you, Emmie. Thank you for everything."

"Pretty Polly!" Caleb exclaimed, picking the child up.

"Oh, my goodness! Phoebee, is that you?" He took in the transformation that Emmie had brought about.

"I'm not rightly shor! I think she turned me into one of them dolls in her shop!"

Caleb bent and kissed Phoebee's cheek. Omie joined them as they walked back to the examining room where Dr. Campbell waited. Daniel bowed to Phoebee, commenting on how lovely she looked, as Caleb sat Polly on the table.

"You are a beautiful girl, too!" he said to Polly, as he took her little face in his hands and looked into her eyes.

"I'm this many!" she stated, holding up two fingers.

"I know! Such a young lady."

Polly reached out and grabbed his beard, which made them both laugh.

Caleb came to stand beside him, and they conversed with words which made no sense to either Phoebee or Omie.

Dr. Campbell reached into a cabinet and pulled out a contraption with multiple lenses that reminded Phoebee of the eyes of a bee.

"This is called a Skoptometer, Phoebee. Although it is a bit large for Polly's eyes, I should be able to tell more about what she can and cannot see with it."

Phoebee stood quietly and nodded her head.

After what seemed hours, Caleb and Dr. Campbell returned the instrument to its place and handed Polly a sucker, telling her what a good, smart girl she had been.

"I hope this is all right?" Dr. Campbell asked, as Polly stuck the sucker in her mouth.

"Oh my, yes," Phoebee replied. "She deserves it. I need one, too! I think I been holdin' my breath this whole time."

He passed the sweet to her, and one to Omie as well.

"Let Dr. Decker and me discuss our findings, Miss Phoebee. It will take us a bit of time to come to a conclusion, but I assure you, we will."

"I will come find you as soon as I have anything to tell you." Caleb smiled at her reassuringly as he turned to follow Dr. Campbell.

The women returned to pick up Emmie, and spent the remainder of the day walking through parks, playing with Polly and trying to keep Phoebee's mind occupied until there was news from the doctors. Near to suppertime, Caleb found them in Washington Square and invited them to sit on the benches as he relayed his news.

"Phoebee, it is difficult to diagnose a little one like Polly who can't tell us what she is seeing in response to our tests. We have to go as much by instinct as fact. What we do know is there is nothing visibly wrong with her eyes." He looked at Emmie. "No detached retinas or obvious impairments."

Looking back at Phoebee he said, "It is as I imagined. She sees light and dark, and some forms, apparently, but that is all. Sometimes in premature babies, the eyes don't have time to fully develop."

"So, what you are telling me is that she will always be mostly blind?" Phoebe asked.

Caleb took her hand. "Further testing at an eye clinic in Atlanta may provide some answers beyond our limited resources, but giving you an educated guess, I would say that's so. We may be able to find the reasons for her condition with more testing, but I don't think that will change things much. There is a remarkable school for the blind in Macon, when Polly is old enough to go. They can teach her how to read Braille and show her ways she can navigate life more normally."

Phoebee took her hand back and said quietly, "Thank you, Dr. Caleb. I know you done what you could."

She stood up and walked Polly barefooted through the grass, holding her little hand.

"Oh my," Omie sighed. "I'm sure this is not the news she was hoping for, but Phoebee is a strong person. I know she will accept Polly's fate, given a little time."

They were all saddened by the notion that Polly would never be able to fully engage with her world. Phoebee, however, did not agree. She could not accept the doctors' hopeless condolences, would not be resigned to seeing her daughter limited in this unlimited world of wonder. Even if she had to paint their surroundings in words, in colors Polly could only imagine, her daughter would nonetheless know a bigger version of the world around her.

Chapter 37

1914

Caleb Daniel Decker was born two weeks early and slipped into the world quickly, ready to face it head-on. He was a big, boisterous baby, where Bitsy had been, well, itsy-bitsy. Kate and Omie arrived just in time to see the crown of dark hair beginning to show and knew at once that this was a boy. His 'light' preceded him, announcing that this child was coming into their lives with a special gift. Exactly what that gift was, they could not say. Kate held him tenderly, looking into eyes that were taking in the world for the first time.

Caleb Sr. was overjoyed at having a boy, though Emmie knew he would have loved another daughter as well. She was glad he had a son to carry on his name. Emmie hoped she was up to the task of raising a boy, having been surrounded mostly by women all her life. If he was anywhere as sweet as Omie's boys, though, he'd be a joy.

Omie went back home the day after the birth. She sensed Emmie and Kate would appreciate some time together alone, as Omie had when her babies came. There was something about bringing another generation into the family that created a special bond between mothers and daughters. She would wait a few weeks, until the christening, to bring her children to meet their new cousin. Emmie needed time to get her strength back. Little Danny needed time to become accustomed to the energy of all these people in his new world. Omie would make a big fuss over Bitsy, so the child would not feel left out in all the excitement about the baby.

Ada Kate will be the first to scoop him into her arms as soon as she sees him. She is quite the little mamma, that one.

Though Ada was not quite six, Omie had come to depend so much on her daughter to help with the other children. She could imagine Ada Kate one day with her own little ones clinging to her skirts.

The circle of life. She smiled to herself.

With the approach of Danny's christening, Caleb and Emmie decided it was also time to name the children's godparents. It had not occurred to them at the time of Bitsy's christening that anything might ever happen to them, but Caleb had witnessed the unexpected tragedies that befell his patients, and wanted to know the children would be well cared for in such circumstances. There was little doubt in their minds as to who they would be. The children already carried their names. Elizabeth and Daniel had done so much for both Emmie and Caleb, giving them each a chance to pursue their vocations. The older couple had welcomed them into their lives as if Emmie and Caleb were their own.

Emmie talked to Omie before asking the Campbells, worried her sister would be hurt. At first Omie was taken aback that she, or family, were not the first to be considered, but soon came to see the sense of it. The Campbells were nearly family, and they could well afford to care for the children. Perhaps, also, being godparents would ease the ache of not having children of their own.

It was another exciting excursion from the farm to Savannah for Ada Kate and Bartie. Omie felt the girls were old enough to witness Danny's christening, though she had few answers to their questions about the occasion. Phoebee stayed behind to take care of the boys, leaving Nate free to keep up with chores at the farm.

Thomas had come from Savannah to pick them up, so the women were free to relax as the carriage took them smoothly through the countryside. Ada Kate and Bartie had made themselves new corn shuck dolls and were busy telling 'Lavinia' and 'Tallulah' what they would see in the city.

"Hello Girls! Sister." Emmie kissed their cheeks as she ushered them in the door.

Kate hugged the children. "I missed you so much!"

"What about me?" Omie asked in mock indignation, then took her mamma into her arms.

Emmie said, "We're nearly ready to go to the church. The Campbells will meet us there shortly. Would you take the baby a moment while I change? I was afraid he might soil my dress if I put it on too early."

Ada Kate immediately reached for Danny, but Omie took him and said, "Why don't you sit in my lap and we'll hold him together?"

Bartie was much more interested in the new gramophone sitting in the parlour. "Oh! Unca Caleb, may I turn the handle and play it? Please?"

Caleb squatted beside his niece and took her hands. "This evening after supper we'll listen to some of our new phonograph records, and you can teach me to dance. I hear you're very good."

Bartie smiled up at him and replied proudly, "I am!"

Entering the church, Kate and Omie were struck by the serene beauty around them. The honey-colored wood of the pews and dais, the red velvet ropes along the aisles, the shafts of light shining through the lovely, stained-glass windows, illuminating it all. They felt their spirits lifted upward, rising toward the ornate arched ceiling.

"Mamma, is this heaven?" Ada Kate whispered. Even Bartie was uncharacteristically quiet as her eyed widened to take it all in.

"No, baby, but this is the house of God, and I expect you both to be quiet and respectful here. The minister will do a ceremony for Danny, then we'll all go out for supper. Can you be still that long?" Both girls nodded their heads and took a seat in a pew nearest where the baptism would take place.

The font reflected muted, watery colors that caressed Danny's tiny face. As the minister trickled water onto the baby's forehead, Danny smiled up at them all, as if he enjoyed being the center of attention and thought this to be great fun. The Campbells both wept openly as they vowed in front of God and the family to accept the duties of being godparents to both Danny and Mary Elizabeth—Bitsy—who stood solemnly beside her mother.

Elizabeth bent down to hug her namesake, then hugged Emmie and Caleb. She could not speak, but the parents understood the depth of her emotions. Daniel laughed softly as he tried to dry his eyes. Bitsy looked up and took his hand.

Before leaving, the older man took Caleb's hand in both of his, and their eyes held for a long moment. Daniel turned, then, and embraced Emmie, whispering, "You have no idea how much this means to us."

Kate and Omie opened their arms to the Campbells as well, assuring the godparents of their blessings.

After the ceremony, they all went to the Marshall House, anticipating a sumptuous feast and an evening of celebration. The little girls had made up a song together and entertained the adults, to the delight of the whole dining room.

"That was so good!" Omie cried as she hugged both Ada Kate and Bartie to her.

Looks like we have two little songwriters and the makings of a family band! When we get back home, I'll start bringing out my harmonica after supper. I don't know why I've waited so long.

It astounded her, all of a sudden, that she and Nate had created these little people. They were growing so fast. Each had their own distinct way of relating to the world, some of which they seemed to have brought into this life with them. Omie had a sudden sense of what a responsibility it was to guide these young ones toward becoming the best version of themselves, to teach them to respect and appreciate each other. *And most important of all, to champion kindness.*

Chapter 38

In the year following Polly's diagnosis, Phoebee took the matter of her child's sight into her own hands. She was determined that Polly would be not only be a part of everything around her, but a force within it. Not dependent on anyone, certainly not a man, to make her happy.

Much was identifiable by smell, by subtle sounds, by the slightest changes in temperature and resistance to pressure. There was a sixth sense that bloomed in the absence of light, and Phoebee made use of all these things.

Polly loved going with her mamma to milk Dinah, mornings and evenings. The child would begin to pull Phoebee along, recognizing the sweet smell of the cow, the hay and corn, before she even made out the dark shape of the barn against the light.

Phoebee set Polly on her lap and let the girl lay her small hands on the cow's udders while milk swished into the pail. "Done!" she would shout, as the ringing in the pail became a muted *sloosh*.

Kate and Omie helped the child learn to recognize birds by their calls. Polly delighted in saying the names, then trying to imitate their trills and warbles. The adults found themselves paying more attention to their surroundings as they took the girl on excursions.

One morning as she walked along the edge of the field with the women while they collected plants, Polly sang, "Cheewee, che up, che up. Thas a wobin!"

Omie squeezed the small hand. "Right you are little darlin! Now, what is that one?"

"A woodpecka."

"Which is your favorite bird?"

Polly thought about this for a moment, and replied. "Chicka wee! Him says his own name."

Polly learned quickly. She was bright, with a hunger to know about everything. She seemed to know intuitively how to be gentle when people placed living things in her small hands. Lizards, frogs, turtles; anything that moved made her giggle with joy.

Before Polly's third birthday, on a fresh, clear summer day, Phoebee sat Polly on a quilt beneath an old rowan tree. A line of bees had been spotted traveling from the fields to a hole in the tree's gnarled trunk, carrying pollen on their heavy haunches. She knew in her bones the bees would not harm Polly any more than they would harm her.

Phoebee removed her shoes, using toes as well as fingers to climb. She wrapped her legs tightly around the thick branch below the dark opening. She hummed her bee-charming tune and smiled as she heard Polly humming it below her. Hand deep in some honeycomb, she heard Polly giggle and looked down to see a snake sliding across the girl's lap. As the reptile crawled up her small arm, Phoebee shouted, "Polly, NO!" As the girl jerked her head up at the sudden panic in her mamma's voice, the snake opened its mouth and bit Polly on the side of the head. Phoebee skittered down, scraping skin on the rough bark, and jumped the last six feet. Running to the quilt, she pried open the serpent's jaw and kicked the snake away. It went slithering off into the grass, but not before she saw the rattles at the end of its tail.

She gathered her child up and ran as fast as she could across the field, crying, "Hold on baby. It will be all right. Mizz Kate will make it all right. Hold on, my sweet Pollywog!" Polly had closed her eyes and seemed to be having trouble breathing.

Omie caught sight of Phoebee running across the field, carrying Polly close, and called to Kate. They both ran to meet Phoebee, and Omie took the child into her strong arms.

"Snake!" was all that Phoebee managed to gasp out as they ran to the house. Omie laid Polly down as her mamma went to scrape some powder off her deer stone into a cup of water. They poured some of the mixture down Polly's throat. Kate dipped a cloth into the liquid and laid it across Polly's temple where swelling had begun, the punctures there an angry red.

"Polly!" Ezra cried.

Ada Kate took his hand. "Is she goin' to be ok, Mamma?"

Omie knelt down to look into Ada's wide eyes. "I hope so, baby. Can you and Bartie take your brothers to your bedroom?"

Ada Kate nodded and led Ezra toward her room. He looked back and whimpered as she closed the door behind them all.

Kate made some willow bark tea for pain and added St. John's Wort for shock. She dribbled it into the child's throat while Omie went to find Indian tobacco to help Polly's breathing. The small body was more relaxed by the time Omie returned. Kate quickly made tea from the Indian tobacco and spooned it into the girl's mouth. Soon, Polly was sleeping easily.

"I believe she'll recover, Phoebee," Kate said, resting her hand on the young mother's shoulder. "I don't think that snake got too much poison in her, or she'd be a lot worse by now."

All Phoebee could do was rest her head in her hands and cry. Finally, she looked up at them and said, "Thank you. Thank you so much. I don't know what I'd do if she was to die. She's all I got now."

Omie said soothingly, "She'll be fine darlin', and she is not all you've got. You've got us, you know that. And you always will." Omie exchanged a look with her mamma and said, "Why don't you try to get some sleep too, Phoebee. You've had quite a scare. We'll watch over the both of you."

Phoebee lay down beside Polly and pulled her daughter close. Soon, she too was fast asleep. Omie and Kate sat and watched the two small forms curled together until the light began to fade.

In the days that followed, Polly was weak, but in Kate and Omie's care, she came to be her amiable self again. Omie had written Emmie about the incident, assuring her that she felt all would be well, but hoping, too, that Caleb might come check on Polly.

Kate killed a chicken and cooked it with dumplings for supper. Omie let Phoebee know that they expected Caleb that evening, if she would like to bake one of her marvelous honey cakes.

In the late afternoon, they heard the sound of his car. Ada Kate and Bartie ran ahead of their mamma to meet him.

Caleb gathered the little girls up. "We just got your letter, Omie. I'm sorry I couldn't come sooner. Emmie wanted to come too, but Bitsy has a summer cold. She said you felt all was well, but I thought perhaps I had better look in on our girl."

"We appreciate that, son. Got your favorite supper on the stove right now," Kate said.

"But I didn't send word, just—" At a look from Omie, he smiled and shook his head.

"Might've known," he said, chuckling as he set the children down.

Phoebee appeared in the doorway, with Polly in one arm and a proud three-layer cake in the other.

"Made with sourwood honey I just harvested!" Phoebee boasted.

Caleb walked up the steps and Polly reached for him. Caleb picked her up, nuzzling her with his beard.

"You had a little scare there, didn't you Pretty Polly?"

"Snake!" Polly said, and pulled at his bow tie.

Caleb peered at her closely as she said, "What dat?"

He turned to give Phoebee a questioning look.

"I dunno, Dr. Decker. She seems to be makin' things out better."

"Hm," he muttered. "Let's go for a little walk, shall we missy?"

He set her down and Polly took his hand, pulling him away from the porch steps. Out in the yard, she led him to a patch of dandelions and picked one that had gone to seed.

"Fairies!" she chortled and blew the seeds into his face.

Caleb sat back on his haunches and studied her. There was just no way things could have changed this much in the year since they had examined Polly. She seemed to not only focus on small things around her, but to be aware of color.

He brought her back to the house and asked Phoebee, "How soon after we examined her did her vision begin to improve, Phoebee? It's nothing short of miraculous!"

"Since the snake bite, Caleb. I think it is a true miracle."

He was dumbfounded. Kate took his hand and said, "Miracles do happen, son. I've seen many things that defy explanation in my time, though I do admit, this beats them all."

"It's been what, five or six days since she was bittten?" Caleb asked.

"Yessir, five days. I know. Amazing, ain't it?" Phoebee beamed as she took Polly up into her arms again.

"This is certainly something I have to spend some time digesting!" Caleb declared in bewilderment.

"Maybe Polly is meant to be a snake charmer, like I'm a bee charmer!"

Caleb looked at Omie, who shrugged, then followed them all into the house for supper.

"Is Bitsy excited about the new baby?" Phoebee asked.

"Mostly," Caleb replied, as he helped himself to the chicken and dumplings. "She's a little worried about all this attention he's getting. Might lose her seat on the princess throne."

"Doubt that!" Omie said. "Once a princess, always a princess."

She put her hands on her brother-in-law's shoulders.

"Thank you for coming Caleb. I don't know what this family would do without you." Then, pausing a moment, hands still resting on his shoulders, Omie declared, "Nope, brother, Bitsy has nothing to worry about. I *See* two little boys around you."

Kate looked surprised that Omie was able to *See* this.

"Guess since he's not blood family, Mamma, the *Sight* works with him. I couldn't *See* for Emmie," she explained to Caleb. She began to move away and stopped.

"Wait. There's more. Oh my, I count four, six, eight . . . ten children! Dang Caleb, y'all do know how they're made, don't you?"

Caleb went white as the dumplings on his plate.

Kate's mouth moved but nothing came out.

Omie started laughing so hard she had to sit on the floor. Phoebee and the children joined in, as Kate and Caleb looked sheepishly at each other.

"She got us, son. She sure did!" Kate chortled.

Chapter 39

1915

"Damn deer!" Nate yelled, and threw his hat on the ground. The first several rows of corn on each side of the field had been completely stripped of leaves and stalks. He walked back and forth, surveying the damage until the sun began to slip behind the pines. Picking up his hat, Nate headed to the house. He stomped up the stairs, still muttering to himself.

Omie said, "What's got you in such a state, Nate Silar?"

"Between the deer and racoons, we'll be lucky to have any corn atall! Mrs. Lee, I've a mind to try some cotton up there on your land, if'n you'd be agreeable to that."

"Son, you plant what you think would be best. Frank trusted your judgment and I do too. Just don't ask me to pick it! I seen how tore up Aunt Julia's hands were when she helped harvest it. They were purely raw for a whole season."

Mollified a bit, Nate grabbed Omie's work roughened hands and kissed them. Straightening up, he said, "You ladies just leave that to me and keep those purty hands soft and sweet."

"Oh, sit down to supper, silly!" Omie grinned as she turned toward the stove.

When the dishes were done, Omie walked up the hill to the well, which was just visible in the dusk. She turned the water bucket over and sat on it with her back against the stones, appreciating a few moments of solitude. Mourning doves cooed in the pines.

'Quiet' sure is restful to the soul. I could stand more of this, but idle time is for fine city ladies like Emmie.

Omie smiled to think of her sister in the lovely little house facing Savannah's Forsythe Park. It was a converted carriage house, a miniature of the mansion it had served. Emmie's taste in furnishings was simple but elegant, and Omie knew her sister adored the "Doll House", as she called it.

I s'pose in a few years they will need a bigger place for their family. She'll be sad to leave it, though.

Her mind was on Emmie as she slipped the well's cover off, not noticing it was askew. Leaning forward to attach the bucket to the rope, Omie's attention was brought back sharply when something seemed to trouble the water below. A shadow traveled across her reflection. Suddenly, from the well's lip, a copperhead slid into the bucket, causing Omie to scream and jump back. The bucket clattered against the stones before falling to the ground, dislodging the serpent from its cool confines. It paused to regard her, tasting the air with its tongue before sliding into tall grass along the fence.

Her hammering heart seemed to take forever to calm. She took deep breaths until she was able to retrieve the bucket. She filled it and replaced the lid in such a way that the snake could not find its way back in.

Nate noticed her paleness as she poured the bucket of water into the wash basin on the back porch.

"Omie, you all right?"

She told him about the snake and about the dark shape moving over the water.

"I reckon you just got an awful fright, honey. Maybe that's all it was."

"Maybe," Omie replied, knowing there was more.

June had seemed at odds with itself, too much rain and then none at all. As soon as Nate, Omie, and the children got the young corn stalks hilled back up from washouts, wind and hail would spring up suddenly and undo everything, leaving pea-sized holes in the leaves. Finally, they felt things were turning in their favor, but then the skies held their rain even though swollen clouds drifted away from the river to the east.

Nate came in one evening from the fields with a furrow between his brows as deep as a corn row. Their stores of hope had begun to run low, and Nate seemed to take the weather personally.

"What am I supposed to do now?" he questioned. "Omie, at this rate, we may not have enough feed for the animals this winter or a bit of seed for next year.

"I know, darlin'. I know," she murmured. "Everybody is in the same fix. I heard at the store that the Varners are selling their place. I guess after Silas died, his folks just didn't have enough help to keep things going, even in the best of times."

"Shame," Nate replied. "That's such good bottomland too. If'n we could find a way to buy it, if—"

"Forget it. As my daddy used to say, *if a frog had wings, he wouldn't scrape his butt.*"

"Are you makin' fun of me?" Nate asked with mock indignation, tickling her.

After the children were fed and asleep, Omie and Nate took comfort in each other's arms. "Lord, I needed that," Nate exclaimed afterward, pulling Omie close to nestle her head against his shoulder.

"Me too, darlin'." She smiled up at him. "Seems we don't find the time for just us anymore."

"I reckon we'll have to make that time, Mrs. Silar," he whispered into her hair, and promptly fell asleep.

In the fall, Nate gave Omie time to herself as well. He took the children on walks through the woods and fields, teaching them about the trees and animals that lived there.

Early in their marriage, he and Omie would walk to the river after dinner and he'd point out things along the way. She was always surprised at his knowledge and felt like he knew as much about the outside world in his own way as she did. Nate told her that, as a boy, he had escaped from the misery of his home life by making the woods his own special place. He would leave for days at a time, taking nothing with him but some line and hooks and a bit of cornmeal and grease to fry fish with. He had kept a skillet and a few other belongings hidden in an oilcloth, buried beneath some tree roots where a fox once had its den.

"Add some hushpuppies with wild onions in them, a mess of poke salad, and you got a fine feast by the campfire."

He learned much of what he knew from observing his surroundings during these peaceful times alone. Occasionally, Nate met up with some of the local Creek Indians who shared their skills and knowledge with him. They taught him how to lay traps for rabbits and other small animals, how to skin them with his pocket knife, and then tan the small furs.

Nate always knew he had to go back to check on his mamma eventually. He'd bring home rabbits or a string of fish for supper, to keep the peace with his stepfather.

By harvest, there was hardly enough corn to make it worth selling. They had gotten a second picking once rain finally graced the fields, but it was small. Nate left the grange in a storm of frustration after selling what he could spare beyond the stock's share for winter. What they would start with in the spring, he had no idea.

Damn if I don't at least deserve a drink. Maybe I should'a just turned that corn into likker.

He made his way to the tavern and joined the rest of the disgruntled farmers who decided to make their complaints known to whatever god might rest at the bottom of a whiskey glass. Some had been there long enough to hold forth loudly about the unfairness of the price they'd gotten for their meager crops. Most just sat quietly.

Nate had patience for neither. He finished his glass and bought a bottle to take to the river, preferring his own company. Watching the waters swirl by, a deep despair pulled at him. All he had tried to do seemed bound to fail in the end. Without Frank there for counsel, managing both farms by himself was challenging. Omie and the others were a big help, certainly, but it took so much manpower to maintain everything needed to work the land, besides the planning, planting, and harvesting. Without Ephram's help, he just wasn't sure he was up to the task. Nate gave in to self-pity, finishing off one bottle and buying another on his way back through town.

His shuffling feet took him in the direction of Thistle Town—the colored part of town—where Aunt Julia lived. The name had come from a time when that parcel of land had been farmed to the point where nothing would grow any longer. Nothing, that is, but thistles and jimson weed.

When the thistles released their downy seeds, the roadsides were as white as cotton. Only former slaves had any use for the property, so it was sold to them at a cheap price.

Nate found himself in the lane that led to Aunt Julia's house. He could not go home like this, though he knew the sermon the old woman would give him. Across the lane from Aunt Julia, a young woman stood by her gate in the fading light.

"Why hello, sir. How are you on this fine evening?"

Nate took a couple of steps in her direction and halted, weaving and trying to focus. "Uh, hello yourself." He burped and laughed.

"I wonder if you might like to have a sit and share some of that good whiskey with me? It ain't good to drink alone you know," she said sweetly.

Nate looked around and turned back to her. "Well, don't mind if I do."

She motioned him on into the house, checking the street to see if anyone else was about. "Please have a seat," she said, motioning him to a chair at her small kitchen table. The stranger got two glass jars, and he poured them both a drink.

"Are you celebrating sumthin' or drownin' some troubles?" she asked. "I'm Minnie, by the way."

Nate shook her hand and slurred, "Nice ta meet you, Minnie. I'm Nate."

They sat for a bit, listening to the night sounds coming on, the chirp of crickets and the rhythmic hum of cicadas.

Nate rubbed his hand across his face and said, "I'm jest tired is all. Tired of workin' my fingers to the bone and havin' nuthin' to show for it. Farmin' is good when it's good, but when it ain't, there's no mercy in it. Damn weather this year has about wiped us out. I didn't hardly get enough for my corn today to buy much more than this bottle."

"I'm sorry to hear that, Nate. I can see you're a hard-workin' man." She lightly touched his back. "A strong one, too. The Lord can only ask so much of a body, though."

"Ain't that the truth of it," he replied.

Minnie stood up and walked behind his chair. She began to knead the bunched muscles of his shoulders and his neck.

Nate groaned with pleasure. "That feels like heaven, Miss Minnie."

"Well, finish your drink, Mr. Nate, and let me make you more comfortable."

She led him to her bed against the wall and took off his boots. He laid back and she began to unbutton his shirt.

"I got me a wife, Minnie," he mumbled.

"That's fine," she whispered. "We just gonna take a little rest now, and then you can be on your way home."

"That's good. A little rest," he said, and fell to snoring.

Sometime in the night he felt her warm body against his and slid his hands around to cup her breasts. Minnie lifted her gown and encouraged his explorations further. Their coupling was awkward, ordained only by drink, need, and loneliness.

In the morning light, Nate opened his eyes to strange surroundings. He turned his head, feeling someone's breath against his ear and that breath was not Omie's.

"Oh, my Lord in heaven!" he exclaimed, and eased himself to a sitting position. It felt like an anvil was sitting on his head, and someone was beating on it.

"Where the hell am I?" he asked the sleeping form beside him.

Minnie opened her eyes and stretched, yawning and staring at his naked back.

"Well, Mr. Nate, where the hell you are is in the house of Miss Minnie Jackson. I believe we had ourselves a party last night." She laughed.

"I'm a dead man." He sighed and put his face in his hands.

"Oh, you'll think of sumthin' to tell her. Here, let me get us a drink of water."

Minnie climbed out of bed and walked over to the bucket on the side board. The morning sun shone through her thin nightgown, and Nate felt himself flush with heat beneath the covers. She brought him a dipper of water. He gulped it down, then reached for his pants and shirt.

"I got to go!" he declared, "I'm sorry, Miss...?"

"Minnie." She sighed.

As he struggled into his clothes, he apologized. "Minnie, I ain't never done this before, cheated on my wife. I am so sorry, but this should'na happened. Damn my hide and damn that likker. I ain't no better than my sorry daddy. Either of them. Uh...do I owe you sumpthin?" he asked sheepishly.

"I ain't no whore, sir." Minnie glared up at him.

"I am so truly sorry, ma'am." He gulped and grabbed his hat, stumbling out the door.

Minnie watched him making his way down the lane and then turned to see how much money she had freed from his pants pockets last evening. Not much, but enough to get her by for a few days. She wondered if he would be back, and smiled to herself.

As she turned away from the screen door, she saw Aunt Julia on her porch, scowling in her direction. Minnie returned an insolent look and closed the front door.

Aunt Julia shook her head to free it from the images she foresaw coming from the direction of Omie's house. They had nothing to do with *the Sight* and everything to do with what she knew of Omie Silar.

A mumbling, stumbling Nate fell to his knees and told his troubles to the river, that river which seemed to carry all his sins and secrets. He stuck his head in the water as if to wash them all away, but his sins waited patiently for him to come up for air.

Images of Mr. Silar, coming in drunk after a night of whoring, came unbidden into his mind. His mother's stony silence. His 'stepfather's' scorn. Nate knew he was not cut from the same rotten cloth as that man, but the sorrow over what he'd done weighed on him as if each of his faithless fathers had a hand on his shoulders, laughing.

What can I tell Omie? Did Aunt Julia see me coming out of that woman's house?

Maybe he could confess to drinking, out of frustration at the little money he'd gotten. But now even that was gone. He'd felt the absence of its weight in his pockets, and that added to his burden. How could he have spent all of it on likker? Maybe he was a worthless shadow of Silar after all.

Standing in the doorway, Omie kept a watch on the road as the early morning light reached through the trees, expecting that was the direction Nate would come from. She just knew that this time something was different.

Has he got himself in with some rough men, gotten drunk and beaten senseless? Robbed and left for the buzzards to claim come morning?

Finally, she could stand the waiting and fretting no more, and asked her mamma to watch the children while she went out in search of him.

Kate said, "Of course."

Omie grabbed a handful of the mule's mane and leapt up on its back like she did as a child. In town she saw the wagon and the other mule still tied up at the grange, and her fears grew heavier. She asked around if Nate had been seen, but no one knew where he'd gone once he left the tavern.

Her senses led her in the direction of the river, the place she knew he would go when he was troubled. On the bank below, Nate was sitting back on his heels with his face pointed toward the sky.

"Nate!" she yelled, and jumped to the ground, sliding down the bank to him. "What's happened? Are you all right?"

Nate opened his eyes and turned to look at her with so much pain in them that she couldn't fathom what was wrong. She bent to hold him and then she knew. Whether she could smell her or just feel the presence of her, she knew he had lain with another woman, been sleeping in another woman's bed while she had been up half the night worrying about him.

She backed off and felt as if she'd faint, wanting to let the river take her so she wouldn't have to face this.

"How, Nate? How could you do this? Don't try to deny it, I know you've been with someone. Who is she? Some money sniffing whore from town? I never would have believed it!" An image of the snake in the well blacked out the world before her.

"Give me the money, Nate. Your children need it, and here you are spending it on likker and whores. I was wrong about you. You are just like your damned daddies!"

She held out a shaking hand. Nate tried to take it in his own, but she snatched it away.

"Omie," he cried, "it wasn't like that!" Tears streamed down his cheeks. "I didn't go lookin' for it. I don't even remember doin' it! I just woke up this morning in that woman's bed." He sobbed and covered his face.

Her silence was worse than her angry outburst. When Nate looked up again, Omie's eyes were as green and cold as the river water. He looked down again and said, "It's gone, Omie. The money is gone. I don't know where."

Omie turned and clambered up the bank. Catching hold of the mule, she swung up on its back again.

"I'll fetch the wagon and mule you left tied up all night. Don't bother to come home."

Then, she was gone.

Nate sat back and wept until the sun had crossed the sky and sunk behind the trees across the water. He made his way back to Thistle Town, not looking in the direction of Minnie's, until he came to Aunt Julia's house. She was on the porch with an expectant look on her dark face, black eyes flashing.

"Well, look what the cat dragged up," she said.

"I didn't know where else to go," Nate pleaded softly.

Aunt Julia took in the sorry sight of him and relented a little.

Every sinner has a place in God's heart. Maybe there is something good I can do here. It's going to take a miracle for Omie to forgive him, though.

Across the lane, Minnie stood behind her screen door smoking, considering what this might mean for her. If she could get Nate out of Aunt Julia's clenched fists, that is.

Self-righteous old hag.

She turned away and sat at her kitchen table listening to the night sounds coming on, wishing she had another drink of Nate's good likker.

Kate heard the wagon coming up the road and looked out to see Omie driving alone with both mules hitched to it. She pulled up to the barn and began unharnessing them.

"Ada, please watch the others so I can go help your mamma."

"Where's Daddy?" Ada asked, but her grandmamma went out the door without an answer.

She put a hand on her daughter's shoulder, but Omie shrugged it off and said, "I can't, Mamma. I just can't talk about it right now."

Kate turned Omie toward her and saw it all written on her face. "Oh God, child," she said, pulling the girl close.

Omie cried as if she would break apart. Finally, she took hold of herself and stood straight, saying, "I got to get these animals fed, Mamma. This mule was tied up all night. It had nothing to eat yesterday evening." As she forked hay into their feed troughs, her sobs echoed through the barn.

Kate fed the pigs and chickens without the children's help so they wouldn't see their mother this way. She would tell them their daddy had business in Savannah and would not be home for a little while.

In the days that followed, Nate broke open his heart to Aunt Julia, telling her about his childhood, his mother, Silar and Mr. Decker. He did not tell her about Silar's visit, nor about the man's death at his hands. That was a mark on his soul that no one else would ever know but Omie.

I am sorry she has to bear that too.

Aunt Julia just listened, and fed him when he would eat. She made him drink soothing teas, reading to him softly from her Bible. Her quiet voice assured Nate that God would not punish him for the sins of his fathers, but he must be very vigilant not to give in to their ways.

"Each of God's children is a shining new soul made in His image, Nate, and we have the free will to choose whether we will shine or become tarnished. We were not promised an easy life, but we are assured that He will be there with us in our time of need. Just as He is with us in the gifts we receive. You are blessed with many gifts, son. The very air we breathe is a gift. The earth beneath the plow, and the harvest it gives us. Be strong, Nate. Be wise and take counsel from the wise women of your family. They are one part of your life where you have been especially blessed. There's not many to be found on this earth like Omie and her mamma. Even that little bee charmer, Phoebee."

She smiled and laid the Bible in Nate's lap.

"I don't read so good, Aunt Julia," he said.

"Never mind, boy. God's book will comfort you whether you can read it or not."

Nate sat on her porch for the next few days, making out what he could of the words before him. Something had loosened the tightness in his chest, whether it was God speaking to him or him speaking to God through his confessions to Aunt Julia. There seemed to be space, now, for other things to grow. At the end of the fourth day, he asked Aunt Julia if she thought he might be baptized in the river by her preacher.

Aunt Julia took his hands in hers and looked into his eyes. There was a light in them she had not seen before, so much so that they seemed almost colorless.

"I am sure that would be quite fine with Reverend Wilson, Nate. I'll go talk to him and see if he will do that this very Sunday." She laid her hand against the side of his face, then picked up her cane and went down the steps.

Minnie watched as Aunt Julia left her house, then waited for Nate to come out to the porch. She went out to the street as if going for a walk and, feigning surprise to see him, called, "Why, hello again, Mr. Nate. Whatever brings you back to this side of town?"

Nate simply stood up and went back inside.

Well, Mr. High-and-Mighty, we'll see about that! Minnie sulked, turning back toward home.

The days passed in a blur for Omie, both wishing Nate would come home and hoping he was long gone. The nights were undeniably the worst, loneliness and betrayal leaving her pillow wet. Granting her little sleep. She imagined Nate's arms wrapped around another woman's body, one younger that was not aged by childbirth. A voice in her dreams implored her to listen, but she woke too exhausted to remember the message it was trying to give her.

Kate could only do what Omie would let her. She watched the children while Omie did the work that needed doing in Nate's absence, and tried to get her to eat and to drink some healing tea through the day.

From the barn, Omie saw Aunt Julia walking down the road and wondered if there was some emergency birthing she needed help with.

Well, Mamma can go. I am just not up to the task of helping another living being.

Aunt Julia walked past the house toward the barn, however, and Omie turned back to what she was doing.

"Omie," Aunt Julia said right off, "I know you are going through a hard time, and you are not going to want to listen to me, but I need you to."

As her resolve faltered, Omie decided she may as well sit and listen. No one refused Aunt Julia's counsel, though she didn't have to like it.

"What Nate has done is not to be excused. Now, he's been at my house, not with another woman. That wretched Jezebel lives across the road from me, and I know she lured him in when he was too drunk to know his own name. She is a snake if I ever saw one."

Omie looked away in anger. Aunt Julia took Omie's chin in her hand, turning the young woman's face back so as to look deeply in her eyes.

"I would not lie to you, child, you know that. Most men around here think it's the woman's place to stay at home and give them children while they are out doing what they please. But that is not Nate. That young man is truly in despair over his sin. He has spent the last week telling me about his life before he came here, and I have been teaching him about God's love and forgiveness. If God can forgive him, Omie, surely you can, too. He's going to be baptized this Sunday by Reverend Wilson."

"Nate . . . baptized? He's got no use for preachers or the word of God. I'm not sure he even believes there is one."

"Well, darlin', the Lord is a mighty shepherd and He wants Nate in His flock. It was Nate that asked to be baptized."

Omie did not know what to say. She sat there quietly as Aunt Julia rose to leave.

"Just try to find it in your heart to let him back in, Omie. He is the father of your children and a good man, though you may not be able to admit that right now."

Omie watched dust motes drifting in a shaft of sunlight coming through the hay loft, until she heard her mamma's call to supper. She felt numb and confused, as if she were sleep-walking toward the house. Stumbling over something in the path, she looked down to see her father's watch half-buried in the dirt. She bent to pick it up, thinking it must have fallen there when they carried his body to the wagon and had gotten trampled underfoot. Opening the cover, she read the inscription inside.

Love conquers all things.

She stood still a moment, contemplating what obstacles her parents might have had to overcome.

Omie placed the time piece in Kate's hand as she walked into the kitchen.

"Why Omie, what were you doing with your daddy's watch?"

"I found it near the barn, Mamma. I guess that's where it's been all this time."

Kate looked back at Omie and said, "No, child. I've been keeping it in my dresser drawer."

Omie knew then whose voice had been speaking to her in her dreams.

Sunday morning carried a frosty taste of fall on the breeze, promising to be a clear day once the sun had risen. Omie was in an agitated state, banging pots and pans while muttering to herself, when Kate and the girls wandered into the kitchen.

"Mamma, it's so early!" complained Bartie, as she sat down at the table. There were hot biscuits with ham, fried eggs, potatoes, and coffee, all ready for them.

"Guess I'd better get the other young'uns up..." Kate said quietly, walking back out.

"Mamma, what's going on?" Ada Kate touched her mother's sleeve and looked up into her face.

"I've got someplace to go is all," Omie replied. "I didn't want to leave your grandma with all of this to do."

She whipped off her apron and called, "Mamma, I'm going out, leave the dishes for the girls. Be back before dinner." One of the mules was already hitched to the wagon at the barn waiting. She climbed up into the seat and set off.

Kate came back to the table and looked at Ada, who just shrugged her shoulders. She shook her head.

Some things you just let be.

Omie fell in with the other wagons and walkers headed from Thistle Town in the direction of the river. A few puzzled faces glanced up at her, but most figured she had business with Aunt Julia. Some knew her from times she had assisted Aunt Julia with births of their babies, and called out a hello.

Omie pulled the wagon up among some trees at a high place on the bank where she could see the goings-on, but would be out of sight. The reverend was guiding people to be baptized to the front of the congregation, lifting his voice in a sing-song of praise and thankfulness for those who would soon be delivered from sin to start their life anew, washed in the blood of the Lamb.

Omie had witnessed many baptisms growing up, though she had not frequented church regularly, and not at all since her marriage to Nate. The reverend was a little grayer but otherwise showed no signs of aging or lack of energy, despite his years. She listened as he preached to those on the banks and to answers of "*Amen*" and "*Yes, Jesus.*" As the souls to be saved lined up, Nate's blonde head stood out from the rest. She stepped down from the wagon and moved closer, staring in disbelief as he waded into the muddy water.

How can so many things go through a person's mind in a matter of minutes?

It was as if their whole life together flashed before her in the time it took the preacher to dunk Nate under the water and raise him up with a resounding, "*Glory to God!*"

Most astounding of all, though, was the look on Nate's face as he walked out of the river. He grabbed Aunt Julia in a hug that looked as if it would break her old bones. Tearfully, she put her hands on either side of his face and kissed his forehead. Then she looked up at the bank where she sensed Omie watching. Nate followed her gaze and stared at his wife. For a moment there was no sound, no movement, just the locking of their eyes. Omie climbed back on the seat and waited.

He made his way, slowly and deliberately, up the bank, until he stood in front of the wagon, looking at her.

For a moment, she said nothing, then called down, "Well, get on up."

He did, and they started toward home.

Chapter 40

Lord, is there anything more tedious than a born-again man! Omie smiled to herself.

Nate was now given to reciting scripture and verse on any subject, or at least his version of it. Sometimes she had to turn her head and share a look with her mamma, but over-all was glad Nate had found something to guide his life. She wondered how deep this passion really ran, though. How much of it was to impress her and win her back? Forgiveness had come more easily to her mind than her heart. A line had been crossed that could not be erased, a small reservoir of doubt pooled deep inside her no matter how hard she wished it away.

Sunday school was Ada's favorite part of the week, now that the family had become regular attendees at New Abercorn's Methodist Church. The girl fancied herself a Bible scholar, correcting her daddy often.

"But, Mamma, he gets it all wrong!" Ada Kate complained.

"Well, honey, it feels right to him. Anyway, God doesn't care if we always get it right as long as we do what's right. Now don't argue with him anymore, it's disrespectful."

Ada Kate nodded with a scowl and took Bartie's hand, leading her out into the yard where she would have a more agreeable audience for her laments.

With both girls in school and only Frank Thomas, Ezra, and Polly at home, Omie and Kate had more time that winter to make new clothes for the children. They were growing out of everything that could be passed down. Polly was the proud recipient of all Ada's and Bartie's clothes, so Phoebee helped as best she could. It was a calm time, a time for Omie and Kate to entertain their neighbor with stories of the past.

The pain of losing Frank faded some with time, but his memory had not. Sometimes Kate still expected to see him come walking in the door at the end of the day, and had to remind herself that he never would again. She took comfort in knowing he was waiting for her on the other side, feeling the time for that reunion was not so terribly far away. For now, it was enough to watch her grandchildren grow, to store up tales of them to share with him in that sweet by-and-by.

The slower pace of winter also gave Omie and Nate time to do a slow dance of reconciliation. In the evenings, Nate stroked her hair with the balm of tender touch that held no expectations. One night, she turned into his embrace. Their lovemaking was slow and careful at first, but their bodies remembered what young love had taught them as they moved to a rhythm of forgiveness.

Kate saw the lazy smile on Omie's face the morning after and thanked the Lord for giving her youngest child her life back. The children immediately felt the change, too, and gathered around Omie's warmth as they might around the woodstove. When the girls were bundled up and sent to school, Kate simply kissed Omie's cheek and smiled, with no need to speak.

Together, they found ways to make do with what they had. The tobacco had done fairly well that year. The women had canned and dried a fair store of vegetables from the garden. Their other needs were bought with what Phoebee gave them in rent from her honey sales. The family managed to get through the winter, but there was little to spare.

Christmas was mostly a hand-made affair for the adults and the boys. Nate had carved toys for his sons out of cedar and pine. For Omie, he carved a deep, oval-shaped bowl for mixing biscuits. The girls, however, including Polly, each received beautiful dolls Emmie had ordered from New York. Kate and Omie had sewn extra doll dresses out of fancy scraps they'd gotten from Mrs. Campbell and Emmie back in the summer. To hide their work from Ada Kate and Bartie, they kept it all at Phoebee's house. Many happy evenings had been spent talking and stitching into the night after Polly and the other children were asleep,

Caleb, Emmie, Bitsy, and Danny arrived for an mid-afternoon dinner on Christmas day. They brought with them a ham and a chocolate torte from the Campbells, like the one the children remembered having the night before the wedding. The girls could not wait to show Emmie the dolls that Santa had brought them, so Kate scooped the baby out of Emmie's arms while Phoebee took Bitsy in hand.

After Nate's lengthy improvised prayer (during which Omie had to scowl at Ada for rolling her eyes, several times) the family spent hours eating and talking. The adults, aside from Nate, shared a bit of mulled cider

Caleb and Emmie had brought. As the children grew sleepy and Emmie went off to the bedroom to nurse Danny, the women began to clean up. Caleb followed Nate out to the barn to feed the animals.

The Decker family, happy and full, bundled into their automobile, hoping to get home before night fully set in. Everyone waved goodbye until they were out of sight. All agreed that this was one of the finest Christmases they'd had since Frank had passed, despite its simplicity. The family was growing. All were healthy and looking forward to what the new year would bring.

1939

June 19

Omie pretended to be asleep as Emmie left the room. She'd resolved not to break down in front of everyone, but her grief had been held back too long. The voices of Ezra and Polly filtered through the door, telling Lilly about Polly's snakebite. She smelled biscuits and figured they'd be fine without her for a while.

She needed time with memories she preferred not to speak of. Children Lilly's and Tess' age could not understand the gray areas between right and wrong. The times that made a marriage stronger were often based on human frailty, and none could escape that.

Did I ever really learn to forgive Nate for his times of weakness? Did I only see what I wanted to see? I must have hurt him, too. She sighed as tears slid down her face. *We do the best we can, Lord, and leave the rest to you.*

She thought of the people in her life who had made it all more bearable when she was lost to grief. Mamma, Emmie, Phoebee. Truly, she had been blessed with love.

Aunt Julia had been a godsend too. For her as well as Nate. *I'm glad we could be there for her, too. And Willie.*

Another tear found its way to the pillow. Aunt Julia had passed shortly after Omie's mamma, Kate, leaving a hole in her world no one else could fill. Sometimes she would hear both their voices in her head when she needed advice or solace, but nothing gave comfort like the feeling of their healing hands on her. Omie fell into that dreamy state between sleep and waking. Bits and pieces of the past visited her.

Among them was Willie's small dark face.

Chapter 41

1916

"Granny! Granny, you there? I need your help!"

Aunt Julia sat up and reached for her spectacles. She stood and slid her feet into slippers, then hurried to the front door.

Unlatching it to let her grandson in, she said, "Boy, what're you carrying on about this time of night? More like morning, I should say. Have you been drinking, Isaiah?"

The young man bent over trying to catch his breath. "No, Granny, I swear! I need your help, the baby's comin', and she's bleedin' bad. Please, I'll explain on the way, fetch your bag."

Aunt Julia quickly dressed and grabbed her birthing bag from behind the door where it was always kept ready. They rushed out, and Isaiah lifted her and the bag onto the horse's back, then jumped up behind her. He snugged her close with one hand and grabbed the horse's mane with the other, bolting out into the darkness.

"You got some girl in trouble?" Aunt Julia hollered back at him.

"I don't know, Granny. Maybe."

"What do you mean, you don't know?"

"Her daddy and brothers, they do what they want to her. Might be theirs. I hope not. I'd like to kill them all right now for what they done."

Aunt Julia heard him struggling for breath beneath the weight of anger, and said, "Hush now, we'll talk about it later."

They came upon an old shack by the railroad, the faint light of a lantern shining from one window. Isaiah jumped from the horse and helped his grandma down, then ran to open the door.

"Oh, my Lord, Isaiah . . ."

On a dirty pallet lay a girl with long yellow hair, her skin deathly pale. Her bent legs were made more stark by the blood saturating her dress and the blankets beneath. At her feet lay a small lump connected to a cord still attached to its mother. Aunt Julia ran to assess the situation, yelling at Isaiah to fetch some water. She looked around and saw that there was no hope of getting a fire going in the old grate for boiling.

The girl was alive. Barely. Aunt Julia cut the cord, feeling a slight movement from the baby. She cleared the infant's nose as best she could and blew into the tiny nose and mouth, trying to get some air into its lungs. She was rewarded with a small cry and, looking down, saw the child was a boy. A pale, dark-haired boy with Isaiah's nose and mouth.

Isaiah returned with a rusty pail of rainwater. He said there wasn't any other to be found.

Aunt Julia shook her head, handed him the baby, and pulled a small blanket from her bag, telling him to swaddle the infant as tight as he could. She dipped her rags into the murky water and put a cool cloth to the girl's forehead.

Burnin' up.

The pale blue eyes opened to slits and looked at Aunt Julia.

"Wha . . .is . . .it?" she asked.

"A little boy, honey. A fine, healthy baby boy," Aunt Julia replied. She was not certain the child would last until the morning light, but his mamma surely would not. There was just too much blood, and the girl too weak. Life was visibly draining from her face as Isiah came to lay the baby on the girl's breast.

Aunt Julia got up, quickly glancing to see if the baby was still alive, then left them to their final words. She went out into the dawn light, offering up a prayer for the soul who was leaving, and another for the one who she hoped would stay.

What to do, Lord?

Obviously, her grandson had feelings for the girl; this was not just a matter of lust crossing the line. She would have the story soon enough, but for now she had to get that baby some liquid nourishment, or he would die. He was obviously in distress.

Aunt Julia opened the door to find Isaiah with his head in his hands and the baby on his lap. The girl's pale face looked smooth and at peace.

Death's parting gift.

She had a delicate prettiness that Isiah must have seen beneath the grime and hardness of her circumstances. They were both children, really. Isaiah was what, sixteen now? And the girl, even younger.

They would kill him for this. The father, brother, every white man, and many of the women, would watch him hang for the sin of touching this girl, blaming him for her death. The family probably would have killed the girl too, had she lived.

"Isaiah, we have to get this baby some milk. Your cousin Alberta will nurse him along with her baby, but it has to be soon." Isaiah looked up, his face a mess of tears and blood. He nodded.

He's in shock. This is too big a burden for his slim shoulders to carry.

"What can we do for Missy? I can't leave her like this!" he cried.

"We will come back and take care of her properly, but right now, you need to see to your son."

This seemed to fortify him enough to take action. They went outside, looking around carefully for witnesses. He lifted Aunt Julia up onto the horse, then handed her the baby. He climbed on, and they made their way toward Thistle Town, trying not to jar the baby too much. When they reached her house, Isaiah dismounted and Aunt Julia handed the child to him. She put a hand on the boy's shoulder and slid to the ground. He looked like a terrified rabbit.

She took the baby back and looked into his eyes. "Listen to me. I need you to go inside and make us some strong coffee. Can you do that?"

Isaiah lifted his face to the sky while tears ran down his cheeks.

"I mean it now, Isaiah! You have got to get yourself together. I know this has been an awful thing. Terrible awful. But we've got to look out for this one. You need to give him a name."

He sniffled and laid his hand on the tiny head. "I'll think on it while I make the coffee."

"Good. Now, I'm going to take him to Alberta's, and I'll be back soon as I explain things."

She returned with Alberta's assurance that the baby would be well cared for and Isaiah need not worry.

"That's mighty kind," the boy whimpered, and started weeping as if he'd never stop. Like nothing in his young life mattered anymore. Certainly nothing had prepared him for this. "I'm glad my mamma and daddy aren't alive to see what a mess I've made."

"Boy, a new life comin' into this world is not a mess. What we do from here on is what matters."

When he was able to take some deep breaths, Aunt Julia made him drink a cup of well-sugared, milky coffee. Hesitatingly, the boy began telling her how he met Missy in passing on his way to school. From behind a tree, she had stared longingly at the negro children, envying them for receiving the gift of learning. He found himself hanging back from the others to talk with her. She spoke from behind the safety of leaf shadows, like a frightened bird ready to take flight at any moment. He began leaving her picture books that the younger children used, and she became less afraid, more trusting.

"Missy was so hungry for someone to talk to, besides her tormentin' brothers and brute of a father." Isaiah said.

The day came when the girl allowed him to sit beside her, behind the tree where no one would see them. Eventually, Isaiah found the abandoned railroad shed where he began teaching her to read. She told him her story, of how her mother died giving birth to her. Her father had never forgiven her for it, as if she were to blame. Her brothers ran wild, but she was expected to cook and clean, taking care of them as soon as she was old enough to build a fire in the stove. Her father's sister had grudgingly raised the girl until the age of five, neither sparing the whip nor her sharp tongue, even when sober. As Missy grew, the father and brothers expected her to take care of them in other ways, too.

"She didn't even know what it meant." Isaiah sighed, shaking his head. "She didn't know that's how babies were made. It was probably the only time they touched her that wasn't with the back of their hands."

Isaiah told Missy that what her family did with her was supposed to be an act of love between husband and wife, and she should tell them no if they tried it again. The next time they met, she showed up with a swollen eye and bruises on her face.

"They don't seem to cotton to the word no," she said.

He had tenderly touched the bruises as he looked into her sad eyes, and Isiah knew he was in love with her. Inevitably, there was the first kiss, and she asked him to show her how making love was supposed to be. What love felt like.

"From there, it was just a matter of time before she started to show. Her family teased her about getting fat, but I knew she was pregnant. I told her we would run away. I didn't even care if the baby wasn't mine," Isaiah sobbed. "Now I've killed her."

Aunt Julia closed her eyes a moment.

Thank the Lord her daddy and brothers were too ignorant to know.

She put a hand on her grandson's shoulder and said, "Isaiah, it would have happened sooner or later anyway. She just wasn't strong enough to give birth. At least the child was born out of love. Now, you need to go home and talk to your aunt and uncle. Tell them I will come as soon as I've taken care of this. Do you know for certain that you two were never seen together?" She looked hard into his eyes.

"We were real careful, Granny, but I reckon the other kids might'a saw us talkin' together after school."

"Isaiah, if anyone connects you with that girl, her menfolk will find you and kill you, no question. They got to have someone to take their anger out on, whether you touched her or not. Trash like that may be short on sense, but they're long on memory, and you won't be safe here. Best you go ahead and finish school up north where your mamma did."

"But what about Willie? That's his name, Willie. After Daddy."

"Honey, I promise you will see him again. It may be a long while. If you decide to stay up there, I will send him to you when he's old enough. Until then, you make somethin' of yourself so you can give him the life he deserves."

"But I don't know anybody up north! I've never left y'all before. And, Aunt Tildy and Uncle Ramon don't have anybody else to look out for them. They raised me like I was their own, I can't just leave them like that."

"Isaiah." She took his hands in hers. "If you don't go, they will spend every moment of their days worrying about what might happen to you. We are family. We all take care of each other. And they will have a hand in raising Willie too. I'll go with you to talk to them."

The boy paced, seeming to look for other answers in the knots and worn grain of the floorboards. Finally, he seemed to accept his fate. "Thank you so much." Isaiah sobbed, and wrapped her in a hug so tight she could hardly breathe.

They hurried to Isaiah's home, where Aunt Julia explained the situation as best she could, leaving the boy to fill in the details.

"I have to go see to things, quick. Isaiah, pack a bag and don't leave the lane. I'll see you all later."

Aunt Julia thought about the situation as she walked back home. The only thing to do was find the sheriff and tell him she'd found the girl. Say she'd been picking up coal along the tracks in the early morning and heard the girl's cries. With the Lord's help, he would take her at her word and not ask any questions she couldn't answer.

She was familiar with Sheriff Turner. She'd helped deliver one of his children, as a matter of fact, and he seemed a reasonable man. First, she needed to go back and make sure there was nothing in the shack to suggest anyone else had been there but herself. Carefully returning by way of the tracks, the old woman went inside. She straightened Missy's lifeless body into a more dignified repose, wiping blood from the cold face where Isaiah's fingertips had stroked it, then closed the girl's eyes. She made a baby-sized bundle of the afterbirth, wrapping it in rags and praying the bloody mess would discourage anyone from taking a closer look. Aunt

Julia then walked toward town, rehearsing the story, forcing her mind to blank out all she knew about the girl and Isaiah.

I just happened by...

Sheriff Turner was alone in his office, brewing a pot of coffee on a small kerosene stove.

"Aunt Julia, hello," he said.

The man never shows surprise. A good poker face must be what makes him good at his job.

"Hey, Sheriff, I got a sad situation to tell you about," she said.

"Well, take a seat and have some fresh coffee," he offered. "Cream and sugar?"

"Why, thank you, I will. It's been a tiresome mornin'."

The sheriff gave her a moment to fix her coffee and settle in the chair, then asked, "What is it you need to tell me, ma'am?"

"There's a girl." Aunt Julia closed her eyes for a moment and concentrated on the memory of Missy's delicate face. "She's in that old shack near the train depot. I was pickin' up coal beside the tracks this mornin', and I heard screamin'."

She opened her eyes and tears coursed down her cheeks. "When I looked inside, this girl was givin' birth all by herself. I ran in to see what I could do, Sheriff, but she was too far gone. There was a terrible amount of blood, and the baby..." she had to look away as she told him, "The poor baby was born dead. All that pain, all that sufferin' by herself and nothin' to be done for neither of them."

Sheriff Turner sat quietly a moment, just looking at her. "That is some sad news, Aunt Julia. If you couldn't save her, then no one could. I reckon you better go there with me to look at things. Any idea who she might be?"

"I've never seen her before, Sheriff. Young white girl, fair hair, blue eyes." She closed her eyes again and shook her head. "Such a shame. Pretty girl, too."

The sheriff walked the old midwife out and helped her onto the buggy seat. Then he climbed up beside her. In silence, they made their way along the road that followed the train tracks until the shack came into view. The sheriff got down and looked around, asking her to wait a moment in case there were tracks or any other evidence he might see before it was covered up by their footprints. After a walk around the shack, he assisted her to the ground and they headed for the door.

"Reckon whose horse might've been here recently?" he asked. "Did you hear anyone ride by?"

"Not while I was here, nossir," Aunt Julia replied.

The less I say, the better.

Inside, Sheriff Turner took in the surroundings carefully and looked down at the dead girl's face. "Missy Boyette," he said quietly. "A hard life and a hard death. Her father and brothers ain't worth the trouble of hangin', but if this was their doin', it would be a pleasure. I knew things weren't good for her at home and have no doubt any of them might have gotten her pregnant. No way to prove it, though. They'll just make claims that she was loose and deserved what she got. Sons-a-bitches. Sorry, Aunt Julia."

"No offense taken."

He wiped his face with a handkerchief and said, "I'll get the undertaker over here and find her family. I'm glad you happened by, Aunt Julia. At least a kind face was the last thing she saw. Anything else you can tell me? Did she have any final words?"

"She just wanted to know if it was a boy or a girl. I didn't tell her it was gone."

"What was it?" he asked, and her heart skipped a beat.

Lord, please don't let him ask to see it!

She looked at the bundle on the pallet and said, "A boy, Sheriff. A little boy."

He shook his head and walked toward the door.

The sheriff offered her a ride home, but she said the walk would do her good. He thanked her and said he'd let her know what he found out. As soon as the man was out of sight, she sat down beside the tracks and caught her breath, feeling as if her old heart would give out.

It wasn't hard to find the Boyette father and brothers. Sheriff Turner had never seen men work so hard at not working. They always had some kind of scheme going on how to get rich, while their house was falling down around them, and their small plot of land lay fallow.

The brothers tensed up and looked at their daddy as Turner drove up into their yard. Rayford Boyette stood his ground and spat a stream of tobacco as the sheriff looked down at them all.

"What call you got to come 'round here, Sheriff?" the father growled. "We just mindin' our own business, like usual."

"Well, whatever that business might be, this is not about it." Sheriff Turner got down from the buggy and stood in front of Mr. Boyette. "You got a daughter, Missy. Am I right?"

"Yeah, what business is she of your'n?"

Turner looked at the brothers and then back at the father. "She was found in a shack by the railroad depot this mornin'. Died giving birth, and the baby died, too. Any idea who the father might be?"

Boyette chewed on his plug of tobacco while a number of expressions crossed his face. He finally decided on the one he thought best suited the situation and snarled, "No, and I'd kill the bastard if I did know. Missy wadn't no more than a whore, so could be anybody. How'd you know she was there?"

"Brakeman on the train heard screamin' as they went by the shack. Sent someone to find me to investigate. She was dead when I got there. Looked like she suffered pretty bad, lost a lotta' blood, and the baby was just a mess, too." He looked for some reaction from the men, but the brothers just cast furtive glances at their daddy.

Rayford said. "Well, one less mouth to feed. Two if you count the brat."

The sheriff gritted his teeth and said, "I'll tell the undertaker to bring her body to you."

"We ain't got no place to plant her here!" the father yelled. "He can take her someplace else. Let those snooty church types bury her. Don't make no difference to me."

Turner stepped closer to Boyette and said, "I cain't prove it, but I know you and those boys took her whenever you wanted, and that poor baby would have been one of yours. A blessing it didn't live. And you don't even have the decency to give her a Christian burial."

"Well, I guess she weren't no Christian, wuz she? You cain't prove nuthin'. You brung us the news, so I reckon we're done here, and you can get off'n our property!" Boyette grinned at his boys.

"Oh, I'll never be done with you all," the sheriff growled. "I plan to make your life hell ever chance I get!" With that, he put his hat back on and returned to the buggy. "Don't doubt it!" he called back.

Sheriff Turner rode to Thistle Town and down along the lane to Aunt Julia's house. She was working in her flower beds, chopping at weeds. He stopped and climbed down, then stood by the gate, appreciating the care she took with her yard.

Aunt Julia looked up, wiping sweat from her face. "Did you find her folks?"

"I surely did. Warmer today, ain't it?" He fanned himself with his hat.

"It is, but a body needs to see some beauty after what we witnessed this morning. Got to remember the Lord's blessings are everywhere around us, no matter what our troubles may be."

"You're surely right about that," he replied, and got down to business. "Listen, Aunt Julia, I'm in a bit of a bind here. Missy's sorry family doesn't want to bury her. You'd think I just told them it was their dog found dead, for all the feelings they showed. Probably would have cared more if it'd been the dog. So, I got to figure out where to put her. She didn't attend church, I guess. Poor thing. Got no one to see she gets a decent burial."

"Don't you worry over it one bit, Sheriff. I know of an old cemetery over by the Rhymes' place. Well, the Silar place now, I guess. I think there's all manner of God's children buried in that spot, and I'm sure Nate and Omie would be glad for her to be laid to rest there, too. I'll meet the undertaker at the Silars' when he's done and show him where it is. Nate will help dig the grave."

"Sure do appreciate your help, Aunt Julia, and won't forget it. I'll go to Obermeyer's now and arrange things. Hopefully we can bury her tomorrow. I'll take care of the costs, it's the least I can do. Reckon if I had stepped in sooner when I saw how it was for her. . .."

"It's a difficult thing to interfere in a family's business, Sheriff. Try not to take too much blame," Aunt Julia said. "God will see to them. Yes, He will."

Aunt Julia headed off to Alberta's to ask about borrowing the wagon. As she walked in, Alberta shifted Willie to her other breast and patted the baby's back.

"Isaiah came by and talked to me." She saw how tired Aunt Julia was and said, "What can I do?"

"Just take care of that child, is all. Though I will need someone to go buy a ticket for Isaiah and take him to the train station early as they can. I'll post a letter to the folks in Pennsylvania and write one for the boy to carry with him in case he gets there first."

Alberta nodded. "Why you need the wagon?"

"I want to get to Kate and Omie's first thing. That's where we're going to bury Willie's mamma, in that old graveyard they got."

"Who you want to take you there?"

"I can drive myself, Alberta."

Her granddaughter started to object, but Aunt Julia raised her hand. "I'll be fine. I need to do this alone, Alberta. I just do."

Aunt Julia saw Isaiah off at dawn the next morning. His aunt and uncle looked like they had not slept at all, sadness etched into the lines of their faces. It wrenched her heart to make the boy go, but she knew he would see the sense of it when he got settled up north. There was little to say, so they held each other for as long as they could, then he got back on the wagon.

Lord, please watch over my grandson. I leave him in your precious hands.

By breakfast, Sheriff Turner came to tell Aunt Julia that Mr. Obermeyer would bring the coffin to the Silar's about noon. She went to get the wagon, anxious to be on her way to let Omie and Kate know of the situation. Several folks offered to drive her, but she needed solitude to think best how to tell her friends the events of the last two days. She needed time to gather herself, to talk to her maker about the weight in her heart.

Give me strength this day, I pray, Oh Lord. Help me find the words.

The mule turned her ears and listened as Aunt Julia found solace in song.

Walk with me, walk with me
In sweetness and sorrow
Walk with me

Know that you're mine
And always will be
Walk with me, walk with me

Thankfully, only Omie and Kate were home. Nate was working in the fields, and Aunt Julia had seen Phoebee and the children on a honey hunt. The women were surprised to see the old midwife, knowing she rarely drove by herself. The urgency of her mission was apparent. Aunt Julia usually had a calm turquoise light about her, but Kate saw a frenzied muddiness buzzing around her friend's brow.

"This story needs to be told quick," Aunt Julia confided. "It won't be long before the undertaker is here."

Kate and Omie looked at each other and leaned in closer. Aunt Julia told them the story as calmly as she could, and they didn't interrupt with questions. When it was done, they told her that of course the girl could be laid to rest there. Omie would go fetch Nate to help, he need not know any of the details.

Aunt Julia and Kate stayed at the house to wait for the undertaker while Omie went to talk to Nate. The old friends watched as Omie and her husband walked down to the cemetery with a hoe and shovel.

There was a peaceful spot near Cecelia's grave where the dirt was soft, and Nate began digging. When the undertaker drove up to the house, Kate and Aunt Julia climbed up onto the rear seat. At the cemetery, the assistant helped them off the wagon, then joined Nate.

"Sad thing, this is," Mr. Obermeyer said. "Such a young girl, and the baby. . . ." He put a hand on Aunt Julia's shoulder and looked into her eyes. "Well, I could not bear to look. I just put the bundle in the box with its mamma."

For a moment, Aunt Julia's dark face blanched at the mention of the baby, then she let out a shaky sigh of relief. Now, she could get to the task of finding the words that might give this young soul some comfort. When the grave was finished, they solemnly lowered the pine box into the hole, and Aunt Julia began.

"This girl was born into a hard life, harder than we can know. That baby, no matter who placed it in her womb, was probably her most cherished possession. We pray they make this journey together in peace, knowing they go straight to the bosom of our Lord, who will welcome His children home with open arms. Their time on earth was short, but they will have everlasting life in heaven."

"Amen."

They all prayed, and took a moment of silence to think about Aunt Julia's words. How little they often knew of other's lives around them. The suffering unseen.

The women stayed behind to gather flowers for the grave, and Nate went to make a marker. He'd asked if Missy had named the baby before she died, Aunt Julia simply shook her head.

As the women walked toward the house, Omie asked, "What will you do about the baby now?"

Aunt Julia took a moment before she replied. "Omie, I need to make it look like this baby belongs to a black mother and a white father. There's no other way." Omie nodded her head. "There's only one colored woman I know who could possibly play the part, if she'll do it."

Omie stopped as she realized who Aunt Julia meant.

"That whore?" she exclaimed.

"Well, Omie, who else in this town would lie with a white man? And Nate is not the only one, but there may be talk that it's his. I know that will be hard to hear, but I hope you can see my need for Isaiah to be free of suspicion. We don't know for certain that he and this girl were not seen together, so there may be talk about that too, especially if folks get a look at the baby. He's bound to be seen sooner or later. The women in Thistle Town and I will care for him. I can trust that none of them will talk."

They walked on in silence for a bit, and Kate asked, "What will become of Isaiah?"

"I'm sending him off to school like I did his mamma. If he chooses to stay up there, I'll send his son to him when the boy's of an age to travel."

Omie stopped and hugged Aunt Julia. "Of course, we won't tell anyone, you know that. And if Nate suspects he might be the daddy, well so be it. Guilt is a mighty useful tool."

Kate swatted her daughter on the backside, and they smiled at one another.

"We'll be here for anything you need, Aunt Julia. Just send for us, no need to come all this way. We'll feel you," Kate said, and kissed the old woman's forehead.

"Let me drive you home." Omie offered. "Nate can follow me in our wagon."

"Don't mind if I do," Aunt Julia said. "It's been a day, that's for sure. I feel every one of my years and more.

Chapter 42

Minnie saw Aunt Julia strolling together with Alberta and some of the other women from the lane. The old busybody was carrying a small bundle in her arms. As they drew near her gate, Minnie called out, "What you got there, Aunt Julia? You a bit old for makin' babies, ain't you?"

Alberta glared at her, and Minnie glared back from behind the safety of her fence. Aunt Julia's granddaughter was not a woman to be trifled with. She was big boned and tall of stature, with a voice to match. Alberta had her own baby in a sling and two other children trailing behind.

Aunt Julia walked over to Minnie and said, "Yes'm, a brand-new baby boy."

Minnie stepped through the gate and pulled the blanket back for a peek and cried, "Oh my, somebody done peed in the buttermilk! Who he belong to?"

Alberta spoke up, "Well, here's the thing, Minnie. This baby's mamma was white, not colored, and she died havin' him. Never mind who the daddy is, but this child needs all the help he can get. It's a situation where white folks that see him need to think his mamma is one of us, and that's where you come in."

Minnie stepped back and said, "Whoa, I don't want no baby or I'd a had one by now. Just lucky I ain't. Don't be thinkin' this girl's gonna raise that brat!"

"Lord knows, we'd never do that to the poor boy, have a no-good whore like you . . . ." Alberta snarled. Aunt Julia reached out to her granddaughter and put a hand on her arm.

"No, Minnie, that's not what we're askin'," she said calmly. "We just need you to take him with you to town sometimes when he's older, make folks think he's yours. We'll do the rest."

"And what's in it for me?"

Aunt Julia replied, "I believe he was conceived about the same time as you had a visit from Nate Silar. I may be able to get you a little help if Nate was to think it was his. Not much though, he's got his own family to take care of, but a little somethin'. And I can make you a tea that will keep you from ever havin' to worry about getting pregnant."

"You can, huh?" Minnie asked, still casting a wary eye toward the baby.

Alberta moved closer. "And the rest of us won't run your sorry ass out of town for tryin' to tempt our husbands, you Jezebel!"

"Well, long as that's all I gotta do," Minnie relented. "But I ain't changin' no diapers, or nuthin' like that."

"I'll get you the tea and let you know when he's ready for goin' to town," Aunt Julia assured her.

"I wouldn't mind makin' Nate Silar sweat a bit neither." Minnie smirked. "Serve him right for treatin' me . . . ."

"Like a whore?" Alberta sneered as they turned to go.

When Willie was a few months old, Aunt Julia thought it might be time for Minnie to put their plan in action.

"I ain't goin' carry no stinkin' baby 'round town. What if he was to mess hisself! What then? No Ma'am, that ain't goin' ta' happen."

Aunt Julia's eyes flashed. "Now you listen here Minnie, we made a deal. You make a show of bein' this baby's mamma, and you'll get what you want. An easy life. Isn't that what we agreed on?"

"Don't seem like no easy life haulin' a squalin' brat in my arms. You go with me and hold him, that's the deal. I'll smile at him like the sun shine out his ass, but I ain't carryin' him."

The old woman sighed. "All right then, but you've got to be convincing or the deal's off. Hear me?"

The two of them made their way toward town, with Minnie dressed in her best, acting like Aunt Julia was her maid. The women drew little attention except for occasional fuss over little Willie from other colored folks in town. They all knew Aunt Julia. If they had questions about the baby's origins, they kept them to themselves.

Minnie noticed a white couple across the street and said, "Give him to me."

Aunt Julia asked, "Why? I thought you didn't. . .." She had no time to finish her question before the woman snatched up the baby and was charging across the road with him in her arms. She walked along the sidewalk, keeping just enough distance to seem respectful of the couple, but close enough that they could see the baby. The man seemed startled and took his wife by the elbow, moving her quickly along. Once they were out of sight, Minnie crossed back over, thrusting Willie back into his grandma's arms.

"Did you see the look on his face!" Minnie laughed. "Maybe this ain't so bad an idea after all. Might skin me more than one cat with the brat."

"You mean you been with another white man?" Aunt Julia asked, frowning.

"You don't see all the comin's and goin's at my house, old woman. I know you sleep sometimes!"

Minnie was quite pleased with herself and remained in a good mood all the way back home.

Aunt Julia took the baby back down to Alberta's house, muttering to herself as she stroked Willie's soft pale skin. If it weren't for the lips and nose so like her precious Isaiah's, the child could have passed for white. The world was not going to be very welcoming to a child so obviously not belonging solely to one race or the other. Not in this part of the country, where his very existence was a crime.

Best I can do is get you to your daddy as soon as you're able to travel on your own. We got to put up with that hussy for now, little man, but not forever. Your grandmamma promises you that.

As the boy grew, it became a game for Minnie to take Willie into town and cause a few of the town's respected men to pass her with nervous looks. One gentleman had his driver approach Minnie and confront her about whether he was the child's father.

"Well, I would never tell tales on someone like Mr. Mason, if that's whut he's worried about. Or beg anything from him for his boy either. I have my pride, you know."

Occasionally, Aunt Julia would see Mr. Mason's driver parked in front of Minnie's house, pressing a package from his boss into her hands as she opened the door. Sometimes he was invited to stay the night. Aunt Julia wondered if the man ever asked where Minnie's child was, but it never seemed to matter.

Yes Ma'am, Minerva Jackson, you done hit the big time! Minnie smiled smugly across the street at Aunt Julia from the comfort of a new porch swing the driver had hung for her.

Yes Ma'am, indeed.

Chapter 43

Reluctantly, Omie had agreed to Nate's proposition of borrowing enough from the Farmer's Exchange to buy seed for the year. He felt so sure about the profitability of growing cotton as well as tobacco and corn, that Omie had been willing to give it a try. Provided they would start out smaller, in case it did not grow well.

Once the tobacco seedlings were past the need of frost protection, Nate had tilled and planted a section of the Lee's farm with cotton. The elements were kind that spring, balancing warmth and wet, so the eager sprouts seemed to reach for the heavens overnight. By July, the field was covered in bloom, and Omie had to agree it was a lovely sight. Early on, the chopping of weeds in the rows had been nearly a full-time job for her and the older girls, who whined about their blisters. Now that the leaves helped shade out the weeds, the rows were more manageable.

"Couple months and we'll have a fine crop, darlin'." Nate put his arm around Omie's waist, hugging her to him. "I know how tough picking cotton is on your back and hands. I'll find us some help for that. No need for you and the young'uns to wear yourselves out with this; it was my idea."

She replied, "We'll help as much as we can, hon, you know that, but mamma and I have mixed many a jar of salve for the folks who farm big fields of cotton, and I don't envy them a bit."

Nate began asking around town if there was anyone willing to come help on his small patch when the time came. Most folks preferred finding work harvesting corn or tying tobacco.

Eventually, a day came when someone directed him to a family just leaving the dry goods store. Nate introduced himself and stated his need for workers to help him when the cotton was ready to be picked.

"Charles Higgins is my name," the fellow said. "This is my wife, Irene, and our young'uns. We'd all be grateful for the work, sir. Irene could help your women folk in the kitchen while she's minding the baby."

The father was a tall, rangy man of indeterminate years. By the deep lines on his face, it was obvious he had spent a great deal of time in the sun and wind. Beside him was a woman with flaming red hair, surrounded by a stair-step of red-haired boys ranging from six to eleven years of age, Nate reckoned. On the woman's hip was a little girl who stared up at him with the same green eyes as her mamma's.

The mother has a haunted kinda' beauty. Before children and farmin' wore her down, she must have been somethin' to see. She's like some sad wilted flower now.

He could not imagine how she had come to be with an older man of small means like Charles, but who was he to judge?

"We're helpin' on the O'Dells' farm right now," Charles said. "Workin' the tobacco. Won't last much longer, I reckon. When yer ready for us, sir, you can find us about a mile out of town at that red house near to the grange. Do you know it?"

Nate did indeed know it. It was a wonder the thing hadn't fallen over sideways by now, and the man who owned it should be shot for charging any rent at all.

"I do. I'll be comin' by soon. Good day to y'all, now." Nate touched the brim of his hat with a quick glance at the woman and headed for home.

Omie said she had heard about this family from Mrs. O'Dell at the store. "Looks to be a sad story," she mused. "Nobody quite knows where they came from, which makes you wonder if they might be tryin' to leave something behind. He's said to have a fondness for likker, and his family pays the price for it. Mrs. O'Dell says she's seen the wife with bruises on her face a number of times, but she was afraid to interfere. Often just makes it harder on the woman with a man like that, havin' his business questioned. And you know how hard it is for Mrs. O'Dell not to be in everybody's business!" She smiled. "Still, it would be a kindness to offer some work to them if we can. I'm sure the mother would like to have the company of other women."

While Nate concentrated on the cotton, the women took charge of the tobacco, topping and suckering the plants as the children dusted them with arsenic for hornworms. The girls were allowed to ride the mules, wearing kerchiefs over their noses and mouths, shaking bags of white powder from above onto the plants. Even the boys helped, getting a penny for every can of worms they picked. Fortunately, the rains came when needed, then held off long enough to get the tobacco cut and hung in the drying barn. They all took turns keeping the fire going until they judged the leaves ready for sale.

As the cotton bolls formed, the field became a sea of frothy white among the browning leaves. Nate sought out Charles Higgins and brought the whole family back with him in the wagon. It pained Omie and Kate to see the little ones pricking their small fingers on the cotton bolls, but their daddy insisted they all work. Irene was shy around them and quietly moved about helping prepare food for the workers, baby Letta riding on her hip.

At first, Omie and Kate tried to start up conversations with Irene, but it seemed so painful for her to reply that they let her be. She was more comfortable with Phoebee, who did enough talking for the both of them. Omie figured the woman would open up when she got to know them better. For now, the help in the kitchen and in the garden was much appreciated. Letta was not a bit shy, however, and bounced on her mamma's hip, gurgling anytime anyone came near. Phoebee managed to get Irene to let her entertain the baby, so the woman could tend to her husband and boys.

Dinner was taken out to the fields. The women spread blankets on the ground and passed tin plates of food to everyone. Irene's boys eyed the food like hungry animals, but had the manners to wait until told they could eat.

Beaten into them, Omie imagined.

She was glad to see the boys have a good meal before their father ordered them back to the field, They would be working till dusk.

Nate took the family back to their shack at the end of the day and returned shaking his head in dismay at their living conditions.

"He's a proud man, I'll say that for Charles," Nate said. "Seems honest enough and won't take charity. I can't quite figure him out though, why he's here, what he did before they came. Holds his cards pretty close. I can tell his wife and children have some fear of him, though. What's she doin' with a man like that?"

At a glance from Omie, he said, "They just don't seem suited, is all I'm sayin'."

"He might be all she's ever known of men," Kate replied. "Might be her daddy was the same. Many girls grow up bein' beat down and worse, then run off with some sweet talker, just to end up goin' from the fryin' pan into the fire."

"We can't get a word out of her," Omie said. "Maybe if Phoebee ever stops to draw a breath, she'll learn something."

After the cotton was picked, Nate looked for other work the Higgins could do for them. Mostly, it was hard, man-sized labor, but the Higgins boys managed some of the smaller, routine tasks that freed Nate up to take advantage of Charles' strong back. It was good to have another man around to help with things. Nate hadn't realized how much he had come to depend on Ephram until he'd gone through a whole growing season without him. He didn't share the same comradery with the older man as with Ephram, but they got along.

There came a day when the boys showed up without their daddy or mamma, the oldest carrying baby Letta on his hip. When Nate walked out of the barn to meet them, one of them said their daddy had taken sick, and their mamma needed to stay home to tend him.

"I hope the missus won't mind that we brought the baby with us," the boy said with downcast eyes. By then, Omie had seen the children and came to take Letta into her arms.

"Everything all right at home?" she asked, with a worried glance at Nate.

"I'm sure it's fine, just a little sickness, the boys say." Nate shot her a look that gave her no doubt as to what ailed the parents. "You boys walked all this way?" he asked.

"Yessir," they replied in chorus.

"Well, that's fine," Omie assured them. "We'll take good care of little miss Letta while you boys help Nate with the chores. I got some extra biscuits goin' to waste if you all want some. I was about to throw them to the chickens."

The boys looked like she'd just blasphemed the good Lord's name, and one piped up, "Well, if they's just going to waste, ma'am, we'd be glad to help. I think they's sumpthin in the scriptures about the sin of wastefulness?" He looked at his brothers who nodded in agreement.

"Well, I do thank you for savin' me from sinnin'!" Omie exclaimed. "I'll be right back, before the Lord knows what I was thinkin' of doin."

As she walked to the house with the baby on her hip, Omie had a sudden sense of being in a small dark room, wind rushing past her and the steady sound of wheels on steel rails. She stopped and looked down at the child.

Where did you all come from?

She returned with the biscuits, some sorghum syrup and a jug of cool milk from the root cellar. After the boys had eaten it all, licking their fingers for every last drop of sweetness, Omie carried the dishes inside. She shook her head when she saw Kate and Phoebee.

"I don't know what there is to be done for them. I expect Charles has got the whiskey 'sickness', and Irene is the one showing signs of it. I saw red spots on a couple of the boys' cheeks and arms. Makes me so damned mad!"

"I know, daughter. It's a touchy situation. Maybe we can send home some salve with them, tell them it's for wardin' off mosquitos or something. Irene will know what to do with it." Kate shook her head.

"Maybe we can send along some tea for her, too. Lord knows another child would be the last thing she needs," Omie fumed.

"Better find a way to talk to her about it first, Omie. She may believe it would be a sin. Find a way for her to understand that, by drinking the tea, she would have more to give to the children she has now."

"I'll take it to her," Phoebee said. "I don't think he'd pay as much attention to me comin' 'round as he would you."

"Why do you say that?" Omie asked.

"My tongue may wag a lot, but it ain't as sharp as yours." Phoebee laughed. "Got anything I could slip into his bottle? Make him sick as a dog so he ain't up to beatin' on anybody? Hard to do much harm when you cain't leave the outhouse."

"Phoebee, you are a devilment!" Kate laughed. "And I believe I have just the thing."

Phoebee rode with Nate to take the children home. She saw Irene outside at the well drawing water, and carried Letta over to her, along with the basket from Kate. Sure enough, darkening bruises showed on the side of Irene's face. Marks of fingerprints were visible on one arm, which Irene kept close to her side. As Phoebe came nearer, the bruises were impossible to hide.

"Hey there," Phoebee said. "Kate sent some things over for y'all, and I thought I'd ride along. How's Charles feelin'?"

Irene took the baby and looked out across the weedy field beside the house for a moment.

"I know you ain't stupid, Phoebee. I'm not goin' to pretend this is something besides what it is. But please believe me, Charles wasn't always like this. Things just happened . . . back where we come from. Those devils get hold of him sometimes, and the drink is all he knows to drive them away. It's not really me or the boys he's fightin when these spells are on him. I try to keep the children out of his way when he's like this. One of these times, he'll do somethin' crazy and kill hisself. Please try to understand why I cain't leave him right now. I'll come around soon as possible."

She looked into the basket Phoebee handed her rather than meet Phoebee's eyes.

"Irene, look at me," Phoebee said softly. As Irene turned to face her, Phoebee saw that one eye was swollen nearly shut.

Sighing, she nodded toward the basket. "There's some things in here I want to talk to you about."

Phoebee reported the way of things to Omie and Kate when she returned.

"I explained about the tea to Irene, and she seemed open to the idea of usin' it. She even managed a little smile when I suggested doctoring his whiskey with the castor oil."

"That were your idea, weren't it?" Irene had asked Phoebee.

"Guaranteed to tame them devils!" Phoebee had laughed. "Just be sure to dose him after he's had a few drinks, it tastes awful!"

A few days later, Charles came riding up in the wagon with the rest of the family and nodded sheepishly to the women before he headed out to the barn with Nate.

Irene and Letta came into the house, Irene apologizing for having been away so long.

"Charles seem to come down with a terrible affliction of the bowels," she said with a glint in her good eye. They all laughed, and no more was said of it. Irene seemed to feel more at ease with them afterwards, as they went about the business of feeding hungry men and boys.

"Having to hide your situation is a tiresome burden," Kate said, as they watched the Higgins leave for home in the evening. "I'm glad she doesn't have to feel that way with us anymore."

"And maybe she won't have so much to hide now, neither," Phoebee agreed.

That winter, Nate had little need of the Higgins' help on the farm, but he cut and sold firewood with Charles to give the family some small income. Emmie and Caleb helped find them customers in Savannah who were more than happy to pay a good price.

There was only one more incidence of Charles' falling off the wagon and into the whiskey bottle, when work was slowed by ice storms. It did not last long, however. Stuck to a frozen outhouse seat proved far more torturous than whatever devils he meant to kill.

Chapter 44

1917

By the first of the year, Omie had known she was pregnant. She had been nervous about telling Kate, but of course her mamma knew anyway. They were wrapped in shawls, walking through frozen mud up to Phoebee's house, when Kate asked, "You hopin' for a girl or a boy?"

"Mamma, be happy for us. The girls have gotten big enough to be such help now. The boys are growing so fast. All the children will be in school this fall. I need another little one to hold, Mamma. I hope you can understand."

Kate took Omie's hands in hers. "Daughter, you need never feel you have to explain your decisions to me. I only ever wanted you to be safe and healthy. And happy. That's all that matters. I'm lookin' forward to meetin' this little one."

"Yes, ma'am!" Omie smiled as she placed her mamma's hand on her swelling belly.

Kate stood a moment with a bemused look on her face. With a laugh, she lifted her hand and walked off grinning.

"What?" Omie called after her. "Mamma, what?"

"Well, Omie, looks like you're goin' to get your wish."

"What do you mean?"

"Emmie is pregnant, too."

As the first spring buds began to show on the trees, Omie felt energized by the life growing inside her. Things had been going so well with her and Nate that, in the fall, she'd decided to refrain from the tea and bring another baby into the family. The cool, damp earth felt lovely to Omie's feet as she stood with her face raised to the morning sun. Her hand resting on the swell of her belly, she felt in this moment to be perfectly at one with everything around her. New life stirring in the ground, in the air, in her body. She sighed.

Days like this attest to God's love for this world. I must always remember that despite troubling times, just to be here is a gift.

Nate walked up from behind and wrapped her in his arms, gently circling her belly with a calloused hand.

"You ready to go see your sister, Mrs. Silar?" He nuzzled her neck as she opened her eyes and smiled. "I reckon you better put some shoes on if you are, don't want to give those city folks the impression that I keep you barefoot and pregnant."

"If all our days were like this one, Mr. Silar, I wouldn't mind that a bit."

Kate stood at the door with a basket of food for the trip and a sparkle in her eye.

The women climbed onto the wagon seat beside Nate, waving to Phoebee and the children as they set off for Savannah.

"My turn to go next time!" Phoebee declared. "Give Emmie our love."

The children ran after the wagon laughing and waving until it was out of sight. Then they ran hand-in-hand through the newly plowed field in a fit of delicious freedom. Phoebee smiled as she watched them go, so glad that Polly had these adopted brothers and sisters to share her life with.

Phoebee sometimes marveled at her own good fortune. She knew she would never have another child to keep Polly company and was grateful her daughter need not feel the lack. To be honest, she felt no desire to be married again. There was all the love a body could hope for right here.

I would like to see my family again, though. Perhaps on one of the trips to Savannah, I could persuade Omie to take the train with me from there to Atlanta and on to Stone Mountain. It's been so long now, the boys would hardly know their little sis.

Hopefully, her parents had forgiven her. Polly would melt any hardness they might hold in their hearts, surely.

She took off her shoes and ran to join the children.

"Mamma, Omie!" Emmie exclaimed as she hurried down the steps to meet them. She was hadn't known about their visit and was overjoyed when she saw the wagon pull up. Nate had a broad grin on his face as he embraced his sister-in-law.

"I needed a break from these bossy women!" he declared in mock exasperation.

"It's us that need the break!" Omie retorted, grabbing Emmie in a bear hug, snugging their swollen bellies together.

Emmie stepped back and looked at her sister. "Oh, Omie! I always hoped this would happen!"

"Double trouble!" Kate said, as she put a hand on each daughter's stomach.

“But, how did you know? You didn't say in your letter. Caleb swears it wasn't him.”

"No, it wasn't Caleb." Omie stepped up onto the porch with Emmie following.

"No? Maizie, then. She went to visit Aunt Julia last month, I bet one of them told you. It was supposed to be my surprise!"

"Nope." Omie gave her mamma a wink.

Kate took Emmie's hands and said, “Your daddy told me. I put my hand on this one’s belly when she told me she was expecting, and I heard Frank, clear as a bell, say ‘*You got a pair of ring-tailed tooters this time, Katie. Emmie’s got one in the oven, too!*”

Emmie covered her mouth as tears began to course down her cheeks. The three of them stood a moment with arms wrapped around each other. Kate smiled. "Ain't it wonderful how love reaches out to us from heaven?"

Still grinning, Nate cleared his throat, and the women stepped out of his way as he carried their bags inside. Mrs. Campbell came from the kitchen bearing a plate of cookies, Maizie right behind her with the tea servings.

“Did you know about this?” Emmie asked her.

“I just heard that we might have visitors, is all,” Elizabeth smiled.

They commenced to share news as tea was poured. Nate begged off, saying he had work to get back to, and took his leave.

"We'll get Thomas to drive them home in the Ford in a few days." Emmie kissed him on the cheek.

The women traded fond smiles with each other, knowing that sitting down to tea with a room full of women was about as comfortable for Nate as wearing wool underwear in August.

Later in the day, the sisters talked animatedly with each other in the parlour of the Campbell’s home. Kate and Elizabeth sat on the porch watching the comings and goings of carriages, of people attending to business. Neighbors waved, and Elizabeth waved back, chatting with a few as they passed.

"My!" Kate said, "I have never in all my days seen such a bustle of folks. I can't decide if I would enjoy all this activity or if it would wear me out!"

"Well, maybe you should come stay awhile and see if it suits you." Elizabeth smiled. "I know Emmie would love your company, and the children would have more time to get to know their grandmother."

"I do feel sad not to see them more often," Kate admitted, "but Omie needs me. I wouldn't feel comfortable underfoot in Emmie's home."

"Nonsense," Elizabeth replied. "We'd all love a chance to have you here. The stories Emmie has told us about your life are fascinating, and I would love to hear more."

The two women rocked in comfortable silence as breezes blew through the Spanish moss, carrying the scent of hyacinth blooms.

At breakfast the next morning, Kate noticed Caleb's strained features. He was his usual congenial self, but Emmie made a special effort to touch his hand or cheek whenever they were speaking alone. Kate did not want to let Emmie know that she had observed these private moments, so she gave her daughter room to bring up their troubles on her own.

"It's the war, Mamma. Cyrus and Marion have enlisted in the army and are headed to Fort Screven for training." Emmie gave her mamma a sad smile. "I see you are concerned, and you're right to be. Caleb is torn between enlisting and being here for me and the baby. He believes he can make a difference if he is near his brothers, watch out for them somehow, only it's not certain they would be sent to the same area."

Omie spoke up, "He doesn't have to go, though, does he? I heard the conscription is for men between 21 and 30."

"No, he doesn't. But you know Caleb. If he feels he can help, he's compelled to go, brothers or not. His mother is beside herself with worry about Marion and Cyrus. I don't know if she could take all three of them being in harm's way."

Omie gazed at her sister. *How can she be so calm? She could lose Caleb in this war! Thousands of miles between them. Probably didn't feel so calm when she first heard the news.*

She wrapped her arms around Emmie and held her for a moment. "It will be all right, you'll see," she whispered.

The afternoon of their departure, the lilt of spring coming through the bedroom window offered a sense of hope as Kate and Omie prepared to return home. They thanked the Campbells for their hospitality and made Emmie promise to send word if there was any news about Caleb's decision to enlist or about his brothers.

"Perhaps we should pay a visit to Mrs. Decker after her boys are shipped out," Kate said, as Savannah faded behind them. "She'll need all the support we can give her. I can't imagine what it must be like to see your boys sent to war."

Omie took her mamma's hand.

Lord, I pray that's something I never have to face with my own.

1939

JUNE 19

Later in the morning, Ada Kate walked into the kitchen with Tess' younger sisters and brothers. She planted a kiss on Lilly's head, and on her sister Bartie's as well.

The boys yelled, "We want biscuits!"

Ada Kate raised a finger. "Hold on just a minute. Is my girl up yet?"

"Yes'm," came a sleepy reply, as Tess came in and sat beside her Aunt Bartie. She laid her head on the table.

Ada Kate hugged her daughter. "They missed you playing the piano for choir practice this morning."

"I know Mamma, but me and Lilly were up so late."

"I knew you would be, so I took your place."

"Thank you."

"I didn't know y'all played the piano!" Lilly exclaimed. "Can you teach me this summer?"

Ada Kate looked questioningly at her sister. Bartie answered with a small shrug.

"So, we'll have you all summer, Lilly? Wonderful. Guess I'll have to drag you both out of bed on Sunday mornings. You staying too, sister?"

Bartie shook her head. "I need to get back. I'm leaving in the morning."

Ada Kate rubbed her sister's shoulders. "We're glad to have you for as long as you can stay. I hope you'll come back again soon."

"End of the summer, to get Lilly." Bartie reached back and patted her sister's hand.

Looking around, Ada asked, "Where's Mamma?"

"I'm right here, Darlin'." Omie came in from the back porch where she'd splashed cool water on her swollen eyes after rising again. She smiled at her girls. "Maybe we can have a little music tonight when we are all together. Would you bring your autoharp, Ada?"

"Sure Mamma, that would be fun." Ada Kate looked concerned, seeing her mamma's reddened eyes, but Bartie gave her sister a reassuring look.

Lilly looked at them in surprise. "Does everybody in the family play something?"

"Pretty much," Ada Kate replied. "Excepting your mamma here."

Bartie turned a wicked grin toward her sister. "I've always been the dancer!"

Ada Kate rolled her eyes.

Lilly and Tess got up from the table and went to get dressed.

"Have you talked to Ezra and Polly?" Omie asked Ada.

"Not yet."

"They were here earlier. Ezra told me he saw your daddy at the funeral yesterday."

Bartie closed her eyes and declared, "This family!"

Chapter 45

1917

Nate was putting his hymnal back in place when Omie poked him and pointed to Ada Kate sitting on the piano stool beside the preacher's wife. There was a glow of excitement on the girl's face as she placed her small hands on top of Mrs. Surber's. They went through scales, up and down the keys.

Ada Kate saw her folks walking up toward her and cried out, "Mamma, Daddy, Mrs. Surber says she can teach me to play! Would that be all right? Please say yes, I've been wantin' to play ever since we first started coming to church."

"She certainly has an ear for music, just like her mamma," Mrs. Surber said.

Omie smiled, "I remember the times you did the same thing with me, ma'am. It was like I could see the notes floating up from the keys. It's not as easy as it looks though darlin. Mrs. Surber had years of practice before she could sit and play hymns for us."

"I know Mamma, but I promise I'll work hard to learn! I'll get my chores done every day before I come to lessons. You know I'm not lazy."

"That, you are not, little lady." Nate tussled her hair affectionately. "What might we owe you for lessons, Mrs. Surber?" he asked.

"Not a thing if Ada Kate will take over some of the playing when she's ready. I would especially like to have more music for the children, songs they could learn without being able to read a hymnal. Would you do that Ada?" Mrs. Surber asked her.

"I would be well pleased to, Ma'am."

The seriousness on her young face caused Nate and Omie to look away a moment, hiding their smiles.

"Well, I reckon we have a deal then!"

Ada Kate shook hands all round.

"Shall we begin now?" Mrs. Surber asked. "I can take you home after."

"Are you sure that's not too much trouble?" Omie asked.

"I'd be well pleased to." Mrs. Surber answered with a twinkle in her eyes.

It wasn't long before Frank Thomas began sitting beside Ada Kate as she practiced her lessons after church, his small legs swinging in rhythm. Omie figured it was just a matter of time before his hands would be holding some sort of instrument. She thought of asking some of the other musicians she knew if they thought he was ready for a small parlor guitar, something they might order from the Sears and Roebuck catalogue.

I'll speak to Nate about it soon, we've put a little money by for Christmas. Wouldn't it be wonderful to have a family band one day!

She occasionally got out her harmonica to accompany and encourage Ada Kate, as her lessons grew a bit more difficult.

One Sunday morning the whole family stayed to listen to Ada Kate practice. She would be playing for the children's Sunday school class the following week. Ada Kate let Frank Thomas put his little hands on hers, just like Mrs. Surber had done. Omie asked Nate if they might order a guitar for Frank Thomas soon.

"Bartie should be the next in line, don't you think? How 'bout it, Bartie Bug. What you want to play?"

"I don't want to play, Daddy. I want to dance!" She began to do a jig to Jesus Loves Me that mostly consisted of spinning wildly.

Nate said, "No, no darlin, let me show you how it's done!"

He began to dance, strutting about and flapping his elbows. The rest of the family broke into giggles. Kate covered her mouth but her heaving shoulders gave her away.

"Nate Silar, don't you think that's a little sacrilegious?" Omie cackled, as tears ran down her face.

"Heck Omie, they's plenty of verses in the Bible that talk about the joys of dancing for the Lord. Even David danced for Him!"

"Well, I doubt he did the Chicken Wing," she said, but pretty soon they all joined in.

Ada Kate slid off the stool, declaring, "Y'all are just a pack of heathens! Don't you dare dance when I play next week."

She left the church in a huff and they laughed even harder. "I'll go after her." Bartie wiped her eyes and followed Ada to the wagon.

Mrs. Surber approached the Silars after church the next Sunday. "Howdy folks, didn't our girl do a wonderful job today in Sunday school!" Ada Kate preened at her teacher's praise. Nate tucked his thumbs under his overall straps, flapping his elbows when Mrs. Surber wasn't looking.

She had something wrapped in a quilt which she handed to the boy at her side. "I see Frank Thomas is interested in music as well, and I wondered if he might be interested in playing this." He unwrapped the bundle to reveal a mandolin. The noon sunlight glowed on honey colored wood, causing the instrument to look as if it were lit from within.

"My brother used to play this, but his hands have gotten too stove up with arthritis now. He said he would be mighty pleased for someone else to make a joyful noise with it. What do you think Frank Thomas?"

He looked at his folks. Nate nodded, and Frank Thomas cradled the instrument in his small arms.

"I believe he's big enough to learn now, Mr. and Mrs. Silar. My brother started at age six. That's about how old you are, right Frank Thomas?" She smiled down at him.

"Yes Ma'am. Almost seven!" His little face shown with excitement as he smiled at them.

Nate said, "We'll want to give you something for the mandolin, Mrs. Surber. That's a right purty thing, and I'm shore it's worth a good penny."

The teacher thought a moment and replied, "How about, when I pick Ada Kate up for practice, I pick Frank Thomas up too. My brother Collie can give him lessons at the same time. Frank Thomas can repay us by doing small chores around the Sunday school. Would you be willing to do that?"

"Yes Ma'am, I'm a good worker!" He stuck out his small hand to shake on it.

She leaned in to speak to Omie and Nate. "Mostly, I think Collie will benefit from giving him lessons and having something to pass on. His wife died young in childbirth, and he never remarried."

Omie smiled and thanked the woman.

Another member for our family band!

Chapter 46

"Mamma, it looks like you swallowed a watermelon!" Ezra declared, as he watched her hang wash on the line.

"It surely feels like it sometimes, son. I believe this baby is going to be big enough to fill your old shoes when it comes out!"

"Can we call him George?" Ezra asked.

"Why George? And how do you know it's going to be a boy?"

"My friend George thinks so." He smiled as he pushed a wooden truck through the grass.

Omie stopped and asked. "You have a friend named George?"

"Yes Ma'am," he answered, "but only I can see him. Ain't that right George?"

She looked in the direction Ezra was speaking toward. She wasn't sure if it was a shimmer of heat or if she imagined it, but something delicate seemed to shift the air.

"Ezra, do you have other friends that only you can see?"

"No, Ma'am. George is the only one. We're the same height!" He stood up and Omie definitely sensed a presence next to him.

"Hm," she said thoughtfully. "Well, hello George!"

"He says howdy back. George wants to go play in the barn now, is that ok?"

"As long as you stay out of your daddy's way. He's shoeing the mules, and I don't want either of you getting kicked."

Omie smiled and shook her head as he ran off.

Didn't fall far from the tree, that one.

She wondered where Polly had gotten off to. Usually, she and Ezra were thick as thieves. Looking toward the porch of her mother's old house, she saw Polly sitting by herself on the steps.

Omie waddled over and said, "Hi Pollywog, it sure is hot today. Mind if I sit with you in the shade awhile?"

"No Ma'am." she said, with her head hanging down and her foot tracing circles in the dirt.

"You ok, honey? Why aren't you playing with Ezra today? Too hot?"

"No'm," she mumbled. "He says he's got a new friend, but I think Ezra has gone crazy. He just talks to the air. I cain't see anything there."

She turned her small face toward Omie. "You don't think my eyes has gone bad again, do you? I can see Ezra just fine."

"Oh darlin, there's nothin' wrong with your eyes. It's just . . .. well . . .. I don't know how to explain it exactly, but some people are just more sensitive to spirits than other people are. Ezra is one of them. I am too. They come to different folks for their own reasons. I can't see Ezra's friend, but I'm sure he's there.

"Do you mean he's playin' with a ghost?" Polly asked with a shiver.

"Aw, ghosts are nothin' to be afraid of." Omie put her arm around the child's shoulders. "They're just people who've passed away and got lost on their way to heaven. George is probably looking for his mamma and daddy and doesn't know how to go on without them. He'll figure it out soon, but for now he's probably really lonely and could use all the friends he can get, even if you can't see or hear him."

"Really?" she asked, her big eyes wide and hopeful.

"I promise. Now, go find them, and Ezra will tell you what George says. I'm sure he was a nice boy—is a nice boy," she corrected herself.

"OK." Polly smiled and ran off toward the barn. That day, and for weeks after, you could see Polly and Ezra joining hands with an invisible something between them, which made Ada Kate and Bartie roll their eyes.

Eventually, it was just Polly and Ezra again. No explanation was given or needed.

1939

June 19

Ada took the boys' hands. "Why don't you two go play out back until breakfast is ready?"

"You won't forget to call us, Mamma?"

"No, Darlin'. Now scoot." Jacob and Cyrus ran out the door, calling "First on the swing!"

They nearly knocked Phoebee down coming in. "Whoa!" She set a quart of honey on the table. "Thought y'all might need somethin' to sop up with them biscuits." Taking in their bemused expressions, she commented, "Looks like you seen a ghost. Ever'thin' ok?"

Bartie laughed. "Wasn't us. Ezra saw Daddy at the service yesterday."

"Naw!" Phoebee dropped into a chair. "Are there boy witches, Omie?"

"I am not a witch!" Omie made a face.

"As good as." Phoebee smiled. "Did he talk to Ezra?"

"No. Just watched." She sighed.

Lilly and Tess plopped down at the table once again, eyeing the jar of golden sweetness.

"I remember when you were called a witch at church, Mamma," Bartie said.

Lilly's eyes grew wide. "A witch? At church? Did they want to burn you at the stake, Grandma?"

"I wish your grandmamma Kate was here to tell this story. I mighta' laid that curse on someone, but she was the *witch* that made it come true!

Chapter 47

1917

Kate came out of the church to find her daughter face to face with an angry man she didn't recognize.

"You are a damn witch! You stay away from my family, you hear?"

She moved to Omie's side as the man herded his wife and daughters toward their wagon.

"What in the Lord's name?" Kate asked.

Omie had to take a moment to steady her breathing before she spoke.

"Mamma, something about that woman and her girls drew me to her. I took her hand to say hello and the *Sight* came on me so fast I nearly couldn't speak. I *Saw* her husband sneaking into bed with those children when he thought his wife was asleep. She is terrified of what he's doing. The man preaches the gospel to any who'll listen, but he's really the devil!"

"Well, what did you say to him?"

"I told him if he ever messed with those girls again, I would put a curse on him so his thing would fall off! I know I shouldn't have, but I was so angry! His wife is too scared of him to stop him."

"Lucky no one else heard you. I understand what you did was in the heat of the moment, but you may have made things worse for them."

"I don't know how to help, Mamma. I can't stand the thought of what he's doing."

"Let's think on this after we get home and make supper. Surely the Lord will show us a way."

As they washed the dishes, Kate said, "I've seen this woman in town. Mrs. O'Dell will know who the family is."

Omie turned toward her mamma with a concerned look.

"Believe it or not daughter, the shopkeeper doesn't spread everything she hears. Iris always means well. Just doesn't know when she's bein' pokey. Maybe she can tell us how to catch the wife alone. I believe I have an idea that will help."

When next she went to town, Kate spoke with Mrs. O'Dell, who confided she felt something was wrong in that family.

"He's a bully, no doubt. None of them will meet your eyes when he's around. When he's not, Lydia and her girls seem real sweet and friendly, but something ain't right there. The husband is not usually with them on Saturdays when they come to town. Off drinking with other no-account scoundrels, I expect."

Kate extracted a promise from her friend not to tell that she had been asking questions about them.

The following Saturday, Omie and Kate hitched the mules to the wagon and drove to New Abercorn. In town, Omie spotted Lydia and her daughters coming out of the dry goods store. She drew the wagon up alongside and greeted them.

The mother glanced around quickly to be certain no one was watching, then looked up at Kate and Omie. "If my husband sees us talking to you, it will be bad for us, Ma'am. I don't know how you knew them things about him, but he believes you are a witch." Lydia looked at her girls and back up at Omie. “I thank you for trying to help, but there ain’t nothin’ you can do.”

She started to move on, but Kate stepped down and looked into the woman’s face.

“There is something you can do, though, without him knowing. He will think he’s cursed, I promise you.”

She leaned in so the girls would not hear.

“You know where those stinging nettles grow by the creek yonder? You gather a handful of those. Be careful not to get stung. Open up a slit in the bed ticking and put them on top of the corn shucks right about where his business would be.”

The woman blushed but nodded.

“You see him doing what he shouldn’t, and you stick them in there, quick. Take them out again soon as you can. Do this every time until he’s convinced he’s been witched!”

Kate smiled at the girls and climbed back on the wagon. She turned to wave, but the woman had headed toward the creek.

Chapter 48

For a time, fortune seemed to smile on the family. Emmie and Caleb had surprised Kate and Omie with a small buggy and a horse, so they could comfortably travel to Savannah as the sisters' pregnancies advanced. Kate was then able to go with Omie on rounds of the community, caring for many of her old patients again. This seemed to breathe new life into Kate, who had sorely missed the visiting and hands-on healing of folks. Omie had been covering all the usual visitations due to her mamma's sore hip keeping her from being able to ride in the wagon. Now, the two of them were often seen by the roadside, replenishing stocks of herbs that grew further afield.

Encouraged by his success with the previous year's cotton crop, Nate had planted twice the amount this year. He reduced the size of the cornfield, growing just enough for the animals' feed and their own needs.

They were glad to see the Higgins return. The children had grown and put on a bit of weight, thanks to Irene's canned goods. She had shared much of the responsibility for the Silar's kitchen garden last year and earned every jar of it. Baby Letta was walking and into everything, so Ada Kate took it upon herself to be the toddler's shepherd whenever possible.

She showed her around the farm, letting the little hands touch the soft downy chicks. Letta giggled as they fed grass to baby goats through the fence. When the girl grew restless, Ada would sit her in the yard, dab honey on her fingers and present a feather to pass back and forth between sticky hands.

Mrs. Higgins helped Phoebee manage the rest of the children, enlisting their help to plant the kitchen garden. Phoebee seemed to work magic on the shy woman, pulling from her an occasional giggle that made them all smile.

Omie had flowers growing in every empty can or other vessel. Though this seemed frivolous with everything else that needed doing, there was such satisfaction in their beauty. She especially loved zinnias, and always had a big bunch in a mason jar on the table. Nate said his daddy used to call them 'trash flowers', refusing to let his mamma grow them.

"God's living rainbow!" she proclaimed.

As the cotton bolls began to form, Charles noticed small holes appearing in some. Upon further inspection, a tiny weevil revealed itself, burrowing into the boll and depositing small larvae inside. He began searching randomly through the rows, finding signs of damage among every one of them.

"Nate!" he cried, as the younger man brought freshly sharpened hoes into the field. Nate ran over, and Charles pulled off a damaged boll, showing him the creature inside.

"No! No, no, no, no!" Nate shouted, running through the field, looking among the plants and finding much to disappoint him. "What the hell is that?"

Charles just shook his head in dismay. "Better take some to the grange and ask if anyone else knows."

Nate saddled up the mule and rode into town as fast as she would go. Dismal visions played through his mind as they went along, fear running in rivulets down the back of his neck.

At the grange were a number of long faces, men with the certainty of disaster weighing on their bent shoulders. Nate showed them the damaged cotton bolls, and they nodded their heads in unison.

"Nobody seems to know where they come from," one man said. "They's people down in Alabama already lost their whole crop to the little bastards. I don't know that there's much we can do."

Nate turned away and got back on the mule. He found it hard to breathe as he slowly made his way back home.

What the hell am I gonna do? If we lose the cotton, we've lost the farms.

He'd borrowed twice as much this year from the bank, betting on his good luck from the previous year to bring in enough money to repay the debt. He'd hoped to get them ahead for next year so he didn't have to take out any more loans. The farms were put up as collateral. Omie would hate him.

Oh, God, what to tell Omie? And her mamma and Phoebee and the children? I lost this bet, and they'll pay the price. He stopped and looked up at the sky, praying for an answer. None came. *'Fraid there's nuthin' to be done for it but to face them.*

Nate led the mule out to the pasture and closed the gate. He met with Charles and the boys in the field to tell them the news, hardly able to speak for the lump in his throat.

Omie saw all this through the window, and it made the hair on the back of her neck stand up. Noticing the change in her daughter's face, Kate joined her at the window.

"Something bad afoot," was all she said.

Nate turned to look toward the house. He hung his head a moment, took a deep breath, then headed their way. Omie was out the door in seconds to meet him, but he waited until they'd gone back inside to speak.

"The news I have to tell you is for everyone to hear, because it hurts us all. They's a plague of weevils in the cotton, eating it up. I went to the grange to show them, and it turns out they've gotten into everybody's cotton in the county. Nobody knows how to get rid of 'em."

"Well, is it too late to plant something else they won't eat?" Omie asked. "There must be something we can grow to get us through until next year. We'll plant a late crop of corn." She took his hand and looked up at him, but he wouldn't meet her eyes.

"We cain't just 'get by' Omie. I borrowed too much money to double the cotton crop this year. I got another plow and harness so Charles could help make the planting go faster. I had to use the farms as collateral."

"YOU WHAT?" she cried and let go of his hand. "You can't mean it, Nate. We could have planted the same as last year without borrowing so much and paid it off! How could you do this without discussing it with me? With us? This land doesn't just belong to you, Nate Silar, that is my family's farm up the hill. How dare you!" She went to slap him but Kate caught her hand.

"We will figure this out, daughter. Fightin' won't do any good."

The tears in his mother-in-laws' eyes wounded Nate more than any hard words she might have said. He turned and went back out the door with Omie right behind him, yelling, "We could have borrowed money from Caleb and Emmie, if you had thought to talk it over with me, and this never would have mattered!"

"It would have mattered to me, Omie. I've never taken a cent from any Decker, loan or not, and I ain't about to now!" He stomped out to the barn. Omie followed, cursing at his back, until she saw Charles and the boys at the edge of the field.

Taking a deep breath, she walked over to them and said, "I'm so sorry, this is none of your doing. We appreciate all your hard work, and there's more to be done with the other crops for awhile. You're welcome to grow as much food as you can in the garden to see you through until there's other work." Omie touched the tops of the boys' heads and looked into Charles' eyes.

"I'm sorry for this to happen, missus," he said. "Nate was tryin' to get ahead is all."

"Well, there's a saying about counting your chickens before they hatch," she replied. "You also have to make damn sure there's a rooster in the hen house first."

Omie and Nate spent the next few days in a blistering silence. Everyone cleared the house as soon as possible and went up to Phoebee's to escape the heat of their fury. Eventually, Omie walked out in the field where Nate was hacking at the dying cotton.

He stopped and wiped his face with the back of his hand, growling, "What you want to chew me out for now?"

"Oh, where should I begin?" Omie asked angrily. Then she blew a strand of hair out of her eyes and said, "Look. We've got to figure out what we're going to do about this loan. How much are we talking about?"

Nate said, "I won't know exactly until the corn and tobacco are sold, but I'm sure that will only be enough to feed us until spring. I'm tryin' to figure out what to do, Omie. Don't you think I am, dammit?"

"So, the whole of the loan then. I'll ask again. How much is that?"

"Why, what are you goin' to do about it?" he replied evasively.

"I tell you what I'm goin' to do, Nate Silar, I'm going to talk to Emmie and Caleb about it! I will not lose my family farm and ours!"

"To hell you will!" he yelled. "You go to him and I'm gone!"

"Well, fare-thee-well!" she shouted, and stomped back to the house.

Omie returned to see her mamma's worried face still looking out the window. She went inside and put her arms around Kate's shoulders.

"Don't you worry, Mamma, we're going to take care of this. Let's send word to Emmie and go to Savannah for a few days. Mr. Hothead can see to his own cooking! I'll ask Phoebee to watch the kids, and we'll talk this all over with Caleb. He'll know what to do."

"Nate is not going to like that one bit," Kate replied.

"Guess he should have thought about what I would and wouldn't like!"

After dinner, Nate still had not come in from the barn. Omie and Kate decided to go talk to Phoebee. The children ran ahead, chasing fireflies, while their mamma and grandmamma discussed what was to be done. The women got to Phoebee's door and knocked. Phoebee ushered them in quickly, seeing the expressions on their faces.

"Y'all sit."

"We have some bad news," Omie said, with angry tears running down her cheeks. Phoebee listened with unaccustomed silence while they explained about the failure of the cotton and the bank loan. They sat in silence as sounds of the children mixed with the night chorus of insects and frogs, singing beneath a full moon.

"Oh my," Phoebee said softly. "What can we do?"

"Well, I'm going to Savannah to talk to Emmie and Caleb," declared Omie. "Much as I hate to ask for help, they won't want to see us lose this place. If you could watch the children, that would be wonderful, Phoebee."

"'Course I will!"

"We'll figure out some way to pay them back. Don't know how we'll manage enough from the corn and tobacco, though. I don't expect any help from Nate. I swear, we're cursed!"

Omie finally put her head in her hands and let the tears come. Big racking sobs for the ground she and Nate had gained that was lost again. Worry for the struggles to come with a new baby on the way. Everything seemed to pour out in a flood as her mamma and Phoebee rubbed her back, trying to console her.

"Hush now, Miss Omie, I might know of somethin' to try," Phoebee said soothingly. "My daddy grew peanuts and got a real good price for them. Of course, that was awhile back, but I remember how to grow them. It might be worth a try next year. We can feed ourselves on goober peas if nuthin' else."

Omie looked up at Phoebe with weary, hopeful eyes. "Do you think we could do that, Phoebee? Really?"

"I'm too small to get behind a mule, all I'd see is her butthole winkin' at me," she chuckled, "but if you all take care of the plowing, me and the kids will do the rest. Then we'll just sit back and wait to fill our pockets with fat greenback dollars!"

Kate smiled and offered, "We can make the kitchen garden bigger, too, so at least we'll be able to put up food for next winter."

Omie sniffed and wiped her eyes.

"I also wanted to talk to y'all about havin' a boarder," Phoebee said. "The school teacher saw me at the store with my honey, and we talked a goodly while about the different flowers that it comes from. She's one of them plant scientists, I forget what you call them. She says I'm a *a-p-o-l-i-g-i-s-t* or sumpthin' like that. Sarah—that's her name—wants to write a story about me to send back east. Also, she asked if I knew of anywhere to stay outside of town. Seems there's too many menfolk trying to court her. And some's already married!"

"Isn't she interested in having a suitor?" Kate asked.

"No, ma'am," Phoebee giggled. "Says she needs a man like a sharp stick in the eye. In fact, she'd rather have the poke in the eye, except she reads all the time and that would be a problem. Anyhow, her room and board money would help. Ever'thin' is gonna be all right, y'all." Phoebee started singing,

Peas peas peas peas
Eatin' goober peas
Goodness how delicious!
Eatin' goober peas

The children gathered on the porch and peeked through the screen door, momentarily bewildered by this change of mood. Kate smiled and waved them in. Their small voices joined with Phoebee's.

Just before the battle, the general hears a row
He says, the yanks are comin', I hear their rifles now
He turns around in wonder and what dya' think he sees?
The Georgia militia, eatin' goober peas
Peas peas peas peas
Eatin' goober peas
Goodness how delicious!
Eatin' goober peas

Sitting outside the barn, Nate heard singing and looked up the hill in confusion.

What the hell?

Chapter 49

Omie decided. She would go to the bank and find out how serious their debt was before going to Savannah.

Best to have the figures to tell Emmie and Caleb, though I do dread knowing.

Kate went also, saying her home was at stake as well, but mostly wanting to be there for Omie when she found out the truth. The Lees had been banking with Mr. Roundtree for many years. He had been in school with Frank when they were children, and Frank had considered him a friend.

Omie wore her best dress for the occasion, feeling suddenly very grown up to be taking a role in the business of their finances, which her father and Nate had always taken care of.

Mr. Roundtree looked at the women over the top of his half-spectacles and said warmly, "Why, Mrs. Lee and Mrs. Silar. What a pleasant surprise!" He invited them to have a seat, and they asked about each other's families and shared bits of local news. In a small community such as theirs, folks combined business with social niceties, and to get right down to the matter at hand would have been considered rude and Yankee-like.

"Now, what can I do for you ladies?" He smiled at them each in turn.

Omie put on her most earnest expression and said, "I need to look into our accounts with you, Mr. Roundtree. I know that Nate took out a loan for the cotton seed and such, and well, I'm sure you've heard about the plague of weevils that has destroyed everyone's crops."

"Indeed, I have, and what a terrible thing it is, too." He shook his head. "But wouldn't it be best if Nate came in to discuss this, Mrs. Silar? I'm sure you have much more important things to tend to at home?"

"Now, Mr. Roundtree," Omie said, beginning to simmer. "What part of finance requires whiskers?"

Mr. Roundtree began to color with embarrassment. Kate put a hand on Omie's arm and said, "I know you understand that this is a difficult time for us all, Benjamin. I'm sure that you and Cordelia discuss these important matters between yourselves. My goodness, you know, I haven't seen her since I helped birth your last child. When was that, three years ago? I must pay her a visit soon. We were always close. I'm sure we'll have much to talk about."

Mr. Roundtree let a sigh escape from his lips and said, "Yes, you have certainly been there for us with the children, Kate. Managing things with Frank gone cannot have been easy for you. Let me get my ledgers, and we'll see what can be done. You know I'm happy to help any way I can," he said sincerely.

After he'd left his desk, Omie began to mutter about the way women were not respected or treated as if they were as important as the men.

Kate said, "That's why we have to remind them of our importance, daughter. I'm sure the Roundtrees will have more children, and I don't think he's going to want to deliver them himself."

Omie gave Kate a conspiratorial smile as Mr. Roundtree returned with the figures.

They were not good. Although he reassured them the bank would help as much as possible, Omie knew the debt was formidable. It broke her heart to have to tell Emmie how close they were to losing everything.

On the ride home, Kate kept telling Omie that all would be well, the Lord would send them a sign of what to do. Faith was easy in the good times, but the hard times made it more precious.

"I know, Mamma, I know," Omie kept replying. But a seed of doubt was stuck in her throat, and it felt the size of a maypop.

When they pulled up to the house, Omie said, "Mamma, let's just load up and go. I know I won't sleep a wink tonight, especially under this roof, even if Nate sleeps in the barn. Emmie won't mind if we just show up, she'd want to know."

They told Phoebee they were going and asked Ada Kate to help with minding the children. Ada Kate could sense that this was a serious matter and assured them she would. The women packed a few things and set off in the buggy again.

Knowing what Omie was about to do, Nate stabbed at the hay fiercely. He decided to stay and be sure Phoebee and the children were all right, just until Omie and Kate returned. Then he would figure out where to go.

The trip to Savannah passed quietly, both women lost in their own thoughts. For Kate, memories spooled through her mind like a picture show. She and Frank moving into the farmhouse the night of their wedding. Growing a family there. All the things she had done to make it their very own home. She'd sewn curtains and braided rag rugs, all of which had faded with time and yet she couldn't bring herself to throw them out.

Kate knew the land around them, and everything that grew there, as well as she knew herself. Each had its place in God's grand design. From the healing herbs to the poisonous, something resided in them that played a critical part.

Mamma gave me more than she ever knew when she took me out in these fields and woods to learn their treasures. I found my own place among them, my own purpose. She turned her head to look at Omie. *May it be the same for my daughter.*

A great blue heron flew overhead, lazily riding the wind toward the river. Kate had always felt the solitary birds were her own personal messenger from the Creator, a reassurance that her prayers had been heard. In all her times of need, one always appeared in the sky or on a nearby creek bank to bring comfort. No one else seemed to notice them.

Thank you, Friend. I need the grace of your wings today.

Omie broke the silence with a choked sob. "Mamma, how can we lose the house you and Daddy raised us in? All I ever knew was there, until Nate came along. Maybe it would have been best if he hadn't."

Her eyes were red with dark circles beneath.

"You know that's not true, now. You got those precious babies and a whole bunch of good memories. There will be many more to come, honey. Memories, I mean, not so many babies!"

That's for durn sure. He can make his bed in the barn and sleep in it too!

It was late afternoon when they arrived.

"Mamma, Omie?" Emmie met them at the gate with a worried face when they pulled up. "Is everyone all right?"

"Everyone is fine, sister. I just needed to see you and compare bellies!"

Thomas came to move the buggy into the carriage house and take care of the horse. He greeted them warmly and helped them down.

Emmie looked into her mamma's face to see the real truth of things. Kate patted her hand and said quietly, "We'll get to it honey, but let us have a look at my grandbabies first!"

"Gamma, Aunt Omie!" Bitsy came bursting out of the house with Danny right behind.

"How are you my little darlin's?" Kate called, stretching out her arms.

"Where are our cousins?" Bitsy asked.

"Oh baby," Omie said, "I sold them to a gypsy peddler that came around. Got good money for them too!"

Bitsy looked taken aback for a moment, then grinned, "You di'nt!"

Omie laughed, "No, I would not take all the money in Savannah for them, or you either! Your grandma and I just had a little business to do here and their daddy needed them to help around the farm. They're very grown-up now, you know. We'll bring them to visit soon, I promise."

Caleb came home just in time for supper. After checking in with everyone, he sensed that whatever brought his mother- and sister-in-law to Savannah would need to wait until little ears were not listening. Conversation during the meal was unusually quiet except for Bitsy's chatter about her day.

Later, when the children were settled in bed, the adults sat in the parlor to talk. Omie explained the situation as calmly as she could. Kate held her hand, lending the strength to say what needed to be said before her daughter's tears could no longer be checked.

Emmie looked at Caleb for a few moments with tears slipping down her own cheeks.

Caleb said, "Kate. Omie. I am so sorry. Rotten luck about the cotton. I know a farmer's life is anything but certain, and I'm sure Nate was doing what he thought best."

Omie stood and began to protest.

"Wait. I know he should have discussed this with you before taking any loans out. I'm just sorry he didn't feel he could come to us. Pride can be a terrible burden, is all I'm saying. Of course, we won't let the farms go to the bank. Part of my father's inheritance was meant to go to Nate. Grandmother put that money into a trust, and I will make sure it does.

"I don't want it to go to Nate, Caleb! He'll just find a way to lose it, too."

"Omie, I will see that it goes directly into your hands. Nate doesn't have to know."

Overcome with relief, Omie walked behind his chair and flung her arms around him.

"Maybe some of our children will want to carry on working the family land together one day. At the least, they should be able to know the place they came from. Let us see how soon the transfer of funds can be done," Caleb assured them. "Don't lose any sleep over it tonight."

They rose from their chairs and he embraced them all. Kate held his face in her hands and kissed him, then declared herself ready for bed. After she left the room, Omie let her tears fall in earnest and held on to Caleb as if she would never let him go.

"I don't know how to thank you, Caleb. And your family."

"No need for that, Omie. We're family too. That money should be his—and yours. Your folks' farm means as much to Emmie as it does to you. We'd never let the bank take it. For my part in the deal, I'll take payment in boiled peanuts!"

Knowing the sisters would want some time to themselves, he said, "Now, if you'll excuse me, I need my beauty sleep."

With assurances from Emmie that things would indeed be fine, Omie felt free to talk about the babies to come.

In the morning, Omie found her mamma and sister in the kitchen drinking coffee with a child in each lap.

"Mornin' sleepy head!" Bitsy called, and Danny chortled along with her.

Omie gave kisses all around and asked, "Where's your daddy?"

"He went to do a apydecomy." Bitsy said proudly.

"I think you mean an appendectomy." Emmie corrected.

"That's what I said!" Bitsy declared.

Chapter 50

Nate slipped away early in the morning after the animals had been fed so as to avoid Omie and her mamma when they returned. Maybe Aunt Julia would let him stay for a while until he figured things out. He wanted to take care of the other crops until harvest, but did not want to stay at the farm, partly from shame, partly from wounded pride.

I need time to think of a way around this mess. Things cain't go south so quickly!

He refused to believe everything good in his life was lost.

The Higgins were a concern too. They were barely scraping by before, and he didn't know if anyone else in the county was in much better shape to take them on. Nate found himself heading in the direction of the grange, hoping his worst fears about the family weren't found at the old red shack. The boys heard him ride up and rushed out in a chorus of, "Mr. Silar! Mr. Silar!"

"Where's your mamma and daddy?" Nate got down from the mule, handing the oldest boy the reins.

"I'm here." Irene was behind the screen door holding the baby.

"Could I trouble you for a drink of water?" He peered closer.

"Cup's right there by the well, help yourself." She did not move to greet him.

Nate filled the cup and took a long drink, looking at her again.

"Why don't you come on out and say hello?" he asked quietly.

Irene tucked her head and said, "You know why, Mr. Silar."

Stepping up onto the porch, he saw that the bruises on her face were the same dark shade as the door screen, making her seem ghostly and not quite there. He felt a hot fire run up his spine as images of his mamma beneath his stepfather's fists came to him, her cries and pleas for Nate to let it be.

"Where's Charles?" he asked with a clenched jaw.

"He's gone to town. Now don't even consider doin' nuthin' about this! Charles counts you as a friend and would not want you getting into our business. He's a proud man. And truly, a good one. But when he feels helpless to take care of us like this, he takes to the bottle and strikes out at everything around him. Better me than the boys. He'll soon sober up and find us sumpthin' when the likker runs out."

She turned to move further inside, but Nate called to her, "Irene, I won't cause trouble. Don't go away, just tell me what I can do to help. Here, I got some coffee, could you just make us a cup and let's talk? Then I'll be gone. Boys, give my mule some water."

She opened the door and took the coffee from him, handing over the baby. When the coffee was brewed, she finally turned to him and saw tears running down his face. "Nate, what's wrong?"

Hearing her call him by his name in such a kind voice made him cry all the harder. She pushed the coffee toward him and took Letta into her lap.

"Troubles at home too?" she asked.

"Oh Irene, holdin' Letta just makes me miss my own babies. The smell of their hair." He ran a hand over his face. "I've ruined everything, and I cain't stay home anymore, I just cain't. Omie hates me."

"Nate, I am absolutely sure that's not true. You're in a rough patch now, I can see that, but this cain't be the first time."

"No, but I never lost us our home before." He sat quietly for a moment. "I only meant to try and get us ahead for once, Irene. I was sure that cotton crop was gonna be our way out of worryin' year to year how things was gonna go. It would have given us some room to breathe, made it so Omie wouldn't have to work so hard."

"She'll understand that in time. Right now, she's scared and mad and lashin' out. Kind of like Charles."

"No Irene, no one should ever hit you, not for any reason. A man has to fight his past, not his family. Whatever made him like this, it cain't be worse than what I come from."

He told her about his mother and the sorrow of being helpless to do anything for her. He had not spoken so openly about his childhood before, except to Aunt Julia, and felt a surprising sense of relief. Irene told him a bit about herself as well, where she came from, what led her to this marriage.

"My daddy gave me to Charles soon's I become a woman. They was just too many mouths to feed in our house and he thought he was doin' me a good turn. I knew how much older Charles was, but he seemed kind and promised he would provide. The first time he was without work, that's the first I saw of his drinkin'. And his fists. I knew it wouldn't be the last. I think he believes he doesn't deserve me, and it hurts his pride when he can't take care of us."

They talked until it was time for dinner, and Irene feared Charles would come stumbling home soon.

"Well, give him this," Nate said. "It's the last of his wages. Hide some back so's he don't spend it all on likker. If you need me for anything at all, send one of the boys to get me. I'll still be workin' on the farm during the day, not sure where I'll be stayin' yet."

Irene looked down at the table, and when she looked up, he had a glimpse of the beauty she must once have been. Her eyes had gone soft and her face had lost some of its tension, despite the discoloration.

"Nate, thank you. It was good to have someone to talk to. We'll be fine, don't worry."

He put his hat on and ducked out the door. After thanking the boys for tending to the mule and for all their hard work at the farm, Nate gave them each a penny. They ran inside to tell their mamma.

Good boys. They deserve better.

Maybe he could ask 'round about for jobs for the boys. He had given Irene the last of his own money in the guise of wages owed, but wished there was more he could do.

Coming out of the feed store later that week, Nate ran smack into Charles for the first time since he'd seen Irene and the boys at the shack. The man seemed shaky, but sober, and a bit hangdog at the sight of Nate.

"Well, hey there Nate, the missus and I thank you for bringin' by our wages. It shore did help while I was looking for work." Charles said.

Nate reminded himself of his promise to Irene and asked as cordially as he could manage, "Have you found anything yet Charles? I reckon many will need help with the harvests soon."

"Oh yes, I asked around at the grange and the store. A number of folks have offered us work, thanks to the good words you've had to say about us. I surely hope things get better for you too, Nate. The loss of that cotton. Well, it were a pure-D shame and that's all. You'll bounce back, I know you will. And when you do, we'll be right there to help, just let us know."

They shook hands and went on their separate ways. Nate thought what a shame it was that drink could reduce otherwise good men to the lowest form of human nature.

He'd never know if Silar had ever had a good side.

I suppose there was something worthwhile about him that won the heart of a woman like Mamma.

He found himself stopping by to see the Higgins whenever there was reason to go to the grange. Sometimes Charles was home, sometimes not, but was sober and seemed to be getting enough work to keep them all fed.

When Charles was absent, Nate took to teaching the boys things while he and Irene talked. He showed them how to whittle a whistle that sounded just like a train, and let them borrow his knife to make themselves each one. He took them all on walks in the woods, showing them the wild things that were edible. Even in the hardest times, he told them, the Lord provided something they could get by on. Acorns boiled until the tannins were leached out could be ground into a passable flour for hoe cakes. He showed them what mushrooms were safe to eat, and how to dig up palmetto and cat tail roots for their potato-like tubers. Poke salad they already knew about, and wild onions. He showed them how to wrap sour sumac berries in cheesecloth before boiling them, so as to get the fine, prickly 'hairs' off. Then they could turn the juice into 'Indian lemonade', sweetening it with honey.

Nate told himself he was just giving them more skills to help them get by if Charles took to drinking again, but he got a good deal of enjoyment out of the lessons himself. He wondered why he had not taken the time to teach his own children the arts of surviving off the land. This knowledge had saved him and his mother from starving.

Omie seems to have everything in hand when it comes to raising the young'uns anyhow. I don't reckon mine have a need of my lessons.

He was tired of trying to come up with reasons to give Ada Kate and Bartie for why he was not around much, excuses for sleeping in the barn. The chill between himself and Omie was taking its toll. Nate was not sure if either of them could summon the forgiveness that would let them find their way back to each other again.

Rain was pouring down the next time Nate went to check on the Higgins. He saw no lamp lit.

Maybe no one's at home. But where would they be on such a day? Surely, they'd have come by the farm to say goodbye if they were moving on.

He pulled the wagon close to the porch and got down to peer in the door. The family hadn't taken their few belongings. Dishes were still in the sink, and one of the boys' whistles was broken on the floor. A chill went up the back of his neck. Setting out to search the nearby woods for a sign of them, he heard Letta crying and saw them all walking along the train tracks picking up coal.

"What are y'all doing out here? You'll catch your death in this weather!"

Irene turned a grim face to him. She tried to lift her swollen, cracked lip into a smile of greeting. "We got caught out in the storm while we was lookin' for poke salad. Figured we'd need a fire."

"Oh, my Lord!" Nate exclaimed, and took Letta from her. After helping Irene into the house and settling her with the baby, he helped the boys bring the coal they'd gathered inside. He managed to get a small fire going in the stove to dry their clothes. The boys kept stoking it as Irene talked quietly about what had gone wrong the day before. How Charles had come home with his last day's pay and little promise of more work. He had become more and more aggravated, telling her how he'd searched everywhere without success.

"As usual," Irene said, "I could see him building up to where some small thing would set him off and give him an excuse to go for a bottle."

She looked at the broken train whistle on the floor.

"Charles seen that and wanted to know where the toy had come from. The boys tried to explain to him about the things you been teaching them.

He went crazy, wanted to know what I was doing havin' a man come around when he wasn't home. And wanted to know what else we been up to. When I tried to speak, he hit me in the mouth. He wud'n even drunk this time."

That was the last they'd seen of him. The boys were quiet, huddled up to the stove for warmth, and even good-natured Letta quietly sucked her thumb, leaning into her mamma for comfort. Silent tears streamed down Irene's cheeks.

Nate stood up and paced around in the small room, cursing himself for not seeing this coming. He told them he was going out to get dry wood for the fireplace and he'd be back shortly. The boys offered to help but he told them no, to stay by the cookstove and get dry. He jumped up on the wagon and rode into town.

The rain had let up but his mood was stormy. Nate stopped by the store to pick up some basic supplies for the Higgins, as well as a few scuttles of coal for the old cookstove. He then slipped back home to the farm and stole a ham from the smoke house. Gathering some firewood, he loaded it into the wagon as well.

Why am I sneaking around? It's only Christian kindness. Omie would be doing this herself if she knew the situation. Well, she don't get to know everything about my business. Let her wonder what I'm about, if she does see me. We don't need all this wood anyhow.

He returned to the Higgins' with the supplies, and the boys helped him unload them. Irene still sat in front of the stove, listless and defeated, with Letta on her lap.

Nate squatted down and looked into her face. "Irene, I'm stayin' out in the wagon tonight. I'm not gonna take a chance on Charles comin' back and hittin' you again, or worse. Now, I know you don't want me in your business, but I've been where these boys are. Sooner or later one of them is going to get in Charles' way to protect you. I can't stand by and let that happen."

She looked at him for a moment, then let her head drop onto his shoulder. He stroked her thick red hair while she sobbed, until Letta squirmed down to climb into his lap.

They had a quiet supper, each person doing some share of the work, as if this might be their last meal. Nate talked softly about anything and everything he thought might soothe them, like he was calming a new colt.

After the dishes were done, Nate banked up the fires and went to feed and water the mule. He crawled under some feed sacks in the wagon, tossing and turning as he tried to figure out this situation.

Why does it all have to be so damned complicated?

He tried to be a good man. He prayed. He worked hard. Still, life seemed determined to keep knocking him down.

All Irene had done was take a chance on the wrong man.

Nate heard a sound and saw Irene come around the end of the wagon.

"Nate, you still awake?"

"I am. Is everything all right? You ok?"

"Yes. I brought you a blanket. The young'uns are all asleep, plumb wore out. Me too, but I wanted to thank you again for all you done for us today. I hope you won't get into hot water with Omie for stayin' with us."

"Hell Irene, she don't know or care where I am. Come look at the stars with me awhile, the sky's cleared up and they's some shootin' stars. Nights like this, seems like you can see all the way to heaven. Here, crawl under the blanket."

Irene climbed up and lay on her back beneath the covers as Nate stretched out his arm to pillow her head.

"I wonder what the poor folks are doin' tonight." He smiled and was rewarded with a small giggle. The two of them fell asleep under a shower of meteors. As the big dipper shifted from one side of the sky to the other, they burrowed deeply into dreams until the morning sun warmed their faces.

Nate woke to the smell of coffee, rousing himself to splash some water on his face. He stretched, popped his back, then slipped open the screen door, trying not to disturb the children. He and Irene had a few quiet moments to enjoy their coffee, talking softly until the boys began to stir. Nate reckoned he should be movin' on so as not to arouse the suspicions of early morning travelers passing by. He made Irene promise to send one of the boys if anything happened.

"I'll drop back by around dinner time." He handed her the blanket. While hitching the mule to the wagon, Nate thought about the sweetness of falling asleep next to her under the night sky.

Best sleep I've had in months.

He was lost in thought as he headed to town and almost didn't see the man by the side of the road hailing him.

"Nate." One of the farmers, an older colored man Nate recognized from the grange, walked up to the wagon and removed his hat. "I shore am sorry ta' hear 'bout Mr. Higgins. The wife and I took up a collection at church fo' his fambly. Those chirren should not have to suffer for the sins of their father."

"What's happened, Abraham? I ain't heard."

"Charles Higgins went and kilt a man."

Nate turned the wagon around.

She don't know.

Omie let the girls carry supplies from the store to the buggy. There wasn't much to carry. If they were careful, maybe they could make this flour and coffee last a few months at least. After the first crop of corn was harvested, she'd have most of it ground into meal. They'd have to kill off more hogs and chickens this year to save on feed.

Once the children were out the door, Mrs. O'Dell put her hand on Omie's arm and said, "Terrible thing about the Higgins family, ain't it? I don't know what his wife and children will do now that he's in jail. Shameful."

"What's that Mrs. O'Dell? I've not heard any news about them."

"Seems Charles went on a drunk and killed a man back up in the woods where they was makin' whiskey. About a week ago, is what they say. I've not seen his family since it happened, but they must be havin' a hard time of it."

"Maybe I'll go by and check on them. Thank you for telling me."

"If there's anything I can do to help, Omie, let me know."

"I will," she answered, stepping outside. The girls were up on the buggy waiting. Omie decided she would take them home first before going to the Higgins' house. There was no telling what state things might be in, and she didn't want to upset the children.

I suppose all of us women need to help each other. Depend less on menfolk, who are going to break our hearts anyway.

"Mamma, I'm goin' on an errand but I'll be back soon. Girls, help your grandma put those groceries away, all right?"

"Yes Ma'am," they chorused, and Omie turned the buggy back toward town.

Surely Nate knows about Charles. Why would he not say something to me, or at least to Mamma or Phoebee? What are Irene and the children to do?

A rain crow called from a nearby tree. She squinted against the sun to look for its speckled plumage, a rare sight. The bird called again from a row of cottonwoods further along, seeming to stay just ahead of her.

What ails this silly bird! There's not a cloud in the sky. Dammit, if Nate had just stuck to growin' what he knows best, Charles would be working on the farm instead of getting into trouble.

Omie was in such a state of agitation that she didn't notice Nate's wagon by the red house until she was beside it. In her first moment of recognition, so many things went through her mind that she could only stop the buggy and stare.

Surely, I must be dreaming. Nate and Irene?

She heard a male voice coming from the shack. It was unmistakably Nate's.

As quietly as she could, Omie turned the buggy around and headed back home, feeling numb with disbelief.

I don't have the strength to face this. How to tell Mamma? The children? Oh Lord, was I too hard on Nate? Is this my fault, or was he wanting her this whole time? Well, now he's got his chance. Charles is gone.

Back at the barn, she took her time feeding and watering the horse, working to put on a mask of indifference. She gave vague responses when the children asked about their father. Kate saw how troubled Omie was, though.

She'll tell me when she's ready. Best to let her sort things in her own time.

Omie tried to stay away from Nate when he was working in the barn. Twice she'd started to go out there and turned back. A slurry of emotions finally took over, making her legs go where her mind did not wish to.

"Where have you been all these nights, Nate? Got you a new woman in town? Didn't take you long, did it?"

"I didn't think you took any notice of where I spend my nights, Omie." He calmly kept working at the bridle he was mending.

"Our children want to know, Nate Silar. They are the ones told me you weren't sleeping in the barn. Do you think they don't notice things?"

"Well. Maybe you should tell them you was the one to kick me out of the house. This weren't my doin'. I'd rather stay in town than to be forced out of my own damn bed just to lay in the straw. I ain't a mule."

"You sure as hell act like one!"

He snorted. "Me? Best take mind of the one who's been kickin' and brayin' through all this."

"At least I ain't whorin' around in that redhead's shack for everybody to see!"

She flounced out and left Nate shaking his head.

Wouldn't do any good to tell her it ain't like that with me and Irene. She wouldn't believe me. She don't want to believe me.

He wished he could explain things to the children though, make them understand that everything he'd been doing was meant for the good of them all. He'd only been tryin' to make the farm more profitable. He was only tryin' to help the Higgins.

Well, if he was honest with himself, he did feel somethin' for Irene. He thought it was all wrapped up in what was done to his mamma, though. Tryin' to make things right for Irene in a way he couldn't for his mamma.

And dammit, it's nice to feel appreciated.

Irene had Letta on her hip and a bucket of water in her other hand. She'd just run off another nosey bastard on his way to the grange, wonderin' if she "needed" anything.

Didn't take long for the word to get out. Why do these men think they got a right to bother me now? It ain't out of the kindness of their hearts, neither. I know what they really want.

Ever last one of them married, with a house full of young'uns, I guarantee.

She told Nate about it when he came in that evening. He made a face and said, "Probably some of 'em saw my wagon here, Irene. I knew it wouldn't look good, but I couldn't leave y'all alone. Let me think on it a bit, try to figure out sumpthin' to keep them away."

"We don't want trouble for you neither, Nate. Don't know what we'd do without your help, but I won't have you give up your wife and family for us. I been thinkin', too. Maybe my sister up in South Carolina would take us in."

Nate stood on the porch, staring out at the weedy, miserly yard. "I know Charles wanted to provide better. Sometimes bad luck rolls across your life like those thunderheads there. As much as you want to escape it, lightning strikes you like a tall tree standin' alone. There's no gettin' out of its way."

"He had choices. Charles won't be comin' back this time. I knew his anger and the likker would lead to trouble in the end, but never thought he'd kill someone." She sighed. "Wish I could talk to him, though. Let him know there's somebody in this world that knows there's more to him than this."

Around noon the following day, Sheriff Turner came to the door with a notice to evict Irene and the children. He was polite and remorseful, but knew he had no choice.

"Sorry I have to do this Ma'am, but some of the womenfolk found out about their husbands stoppin' by and want to nip it in the bud. Especially the wife of the man who owns this house."

"But I ain't done nuthin', Sheriff. I chase them off. It ain't my fault. What are me and the kids supposed to do now? Where's all this Christian charity I hear folks goin' on about in town?"

"I know, Mrs. Higgins, and I really hate to do this. But the owner says you won't be able to pay rent now. He's givin' y'all until tomorrow to get packed up and gone. Is there any place y'all can go?"

"Not with such short notice, sir."

"I'll see if I can get you more time, Mrs., but those wives are not goin' to make it easy."

When Nate returned, he was angry at the news. Angry that he had thought these church women would be any different than the ones back home.

"We'll figure sumpthin' out Irene. I'll be back tomorrow. Let me find a place for y'all."

Nate left with no idea of what to do. He figured he'd sleep in his own barn tonight, maybe keep from making things look worse for Irene.

By the next afternoon he was no closer to figuring out a plan.

I'll stop by the sheriff's office and see if he's been able to buy them more time. To hell with what the man thinks about me.

Pulling into town, he saw Irene and the children sitting beneath a tree with what little belongings they had tucked around them.

"Irene!" he hollered, pulling up beside them. As he climbed down, the boys ran to encircle him in their arms. Irene held Letta and looked away.

"Them women came theirselves and kicked us out, Nate. I couldn't make them believe I hadn't had anything to do with their men. I guess men like to brag among theirselves, even if it ain't true, and somebody heard. They tossed our clothes out in the yard. Called us filth."

Tears coursed down her cheeks as she stood, uncertain what to do.

Nate went to hug her, but she said, "No, Nate. There's already talk about you and me. I won't have it."

He hung his head and said, "Y'all put your things in the wagon. There's a place I know of by the railroad tracks that will at least be dry and safe for now."

The boys clambered up and Irene sat beside Nate with Letta on her lap. People turned to stare as the wagon passed through town, but Nate refused to look at anyone.

After he'd gotten the Higgins settled in the old railman's shack, Nate headed to the farm. His head hurt trying to think what to do, how to sort this mess. Maybe if he could talk to Omie, make her understand the situation for what it was, she would help.

As the house came into view, Nate stopped for a moment. The yard was a celebration of colors from all the flowers Omie had planted. Yellow roses still clung to the porch posts. He remembered when she planted them, cuttings from her mamma's own climbers. Azaleas flanked the house from long ago. Camellias as tall as the porch roof sported glossy green leaves, tiny buds just beginning to emerge. Mrs. Rhymes' doing, he supposed.

Drawing closer, he was met with the smell of biscuits, hot from the oven. A wave of homesickness hit Nate full on, nearly doubling him over. What he longed for most sat around that table.

He pulled the wagon up beside the barn and walked slowly to the house. The children started running out to greet him. Seeing the look on his face, Ada gathered them up and herded them to Phoebee's.

"Omie," he called through the screen door, "I got to talk to you."

"What's there to talk about? Seems to me you've got things settled for yourself just fine. Got a new woman, new family. What do you need now?"

"It ain't like that. Please let me in," he sobbed.

She hesitated a moment, and then opened the door.

Omie sat down at the kitchen table, and Nate kneeled on the floor beside her.

"They've kicked Irene and the children out of that shack now that Charles is in jail. Damn women didn't want their husbands goin' round there trying to see Irene. As if she would have them!"

"Looks like she's had you," Omie said coldly.

"No Omie, I swear it! I'm just trying to help. But I don't know what to do. What will become of them?"

Omie sat looking out the door for a few more moments as Nate cried, remembering the vision she'd had when she first held Baby Letta.

A train.

She walked to the bedroom and came back with a roll of bills in her hand.

"Take this. It's from my potions. Buy them a train ticket to wherever they've got people. Now, go."

She walked back to the bedroom and shut the door.

When Nate had gone, Kate walked into the bedroom.

"You heard everything, I guess, Mamma. Charles is in jail for murder."

"I know about that, Omie," Kate said, laying a hand on her daughter's shoulder. "I know you're angry, and you have a right to be. I'm sure you feel betrayed."

"Mamma, I was betrayed!"

"I know that child, I know. And what you did for Irene and those children was so big. Brave and kind, more than I might have been able to do. It speaks to the largeness of your heart, honey, even more to the largeness of your spirit. The Lord sees this, and He will give you what you need to find your way through this mess."

Omie put her head in her hands and sobbed, "I don't know about that, Mamma. I just don't know this time."

"Faith is not an easy thing to live up to. If it was, how would we grow in this life? We need our challenges as much as our blessings. The main thing I want to say to you daughter, is that if you don't allow this anger to pass, it will own you every day of your life. It will eat you from the inside out. Like a cancer. Don't sell yourself short, honey. You can't buy back that wasted time."

Omie cried harder.

"So please, for the children, for all of us who love you, but mostly to save your own self, forgive him. We all need forgiveness from time to time, for the big and the small things. Nate is not a bad person, you know that. He is just a person."

She kissed Omie's bowed head and left the house.

Chapter 51

Other than doing what needed to be done on the farm, Nate kept his distance. During the day, the children would come out to see him in the field or barn, bringing food and tea Omie had prepared. No one knew quite what to say during these visits, so Nate took time to play with the children, chasing them up and down the rows and swinging the littlest ones up in the air.

Omie watched their daily play but did not go out to speak to Nate. There was a stone in her throat at the very thought of it. She chose to leave him alone. She wasn't sure where he spent his nights now the Higgins were gone. He was not sleeping in the barn.

Emmie had sent a letter asking if Kate and Omie would come once more while her sister could still travel. Both their babies were due in the next month and both knew it might be some time before their next visit. Phoebee had asked to go, as well. Omie felt that taking all the children would be a bit much for Emmie at this time, so she resolved to ask Nate to stay with the girls.

She took a deep breath, then headed for the barn where Nate was brushing down the mules.

"I need to ask you something," she said abruptly. "Me and Mamma and Phoebee want to take the little ones to Savannah for a few days, and I was wondering if you could watch Ada Kate and Bartie."

Nate looked back at her and replied, "Of course. When you going?"

Even from a distance, Omie could smell alcohol in his sweat. She didn't think he'd been drinking during the day, but wherever he spent his nights, he spent them with a bottle.

"We'll go Friday and come back Monday. You can't be drinking around them, so if you can't leave off for a few days, I'll find someone else."

"Omie, I would not drink with the girls in my care. At least give me that much credit."

"I don't know what you'll do anymore." She turned back toward the house, leaving him to his work.

Nate leaned his head against the mule's flanks and sighed. He'd hardly even gotten to put his hand on Omie's belly to feel this child move. The distance between them kept Nate from asking if he could, but he ached to.

What in God's name am I gonna do?

His faith had taken a hard tumble after Irene and the children were so poorly mistreated. He'd like to believe there was a God who cared about the fate of His children, but this God didn't seem much more fatherly than Silar had been.

The girls were thrilled to have their daddy to themselves for a few days. They showed him how well they could cook and read to him at night before bed. Nate wished everything could go back to how it had been before all this business with the cotton and the Higgins. Even at nine, Ada Kate was showing signs of the young woman she would become. A caretaker like her mamma. Smart like her too. There had to be a way, he was missing out on so much.

Bartie was less inclined to hurry into womanhood. He expected she would bloom in her own time. The girl danced through life without a care, though she did her chores and the things that were expected of her. Nate thought this daughter would take flight first chance she got, eager to be part of a bigger world. Though he would not admit it, Bartie was his favorite. The child he delivered with his own hands.

Late Monday afternoon, Kate, Omie and Phoebee returned from Savannah. Nate could hear their babble and laughter before the buggy came into sight. He headed for the back door but Ada Kate took his large hand in her small one and asked him to stay. He shuffled his feet as the women pulled up to the house. Bartie took his other hand and they pulled him out to the porch. Omie nodded, the sight of the girls holding their daddy's hands swelling her throat.

Nate offered to help them down. Omie hesitated but allowed him to take her hand.

He cleared his throat and said, "I'll take care of the horse."

Later, she sent Frank Thomas to the barn to tell his daddy it was time to eat.

"Mamma says come to the table."

Afterwards, Nate thought he'd never tasted a meal so good in his life.

July was a busy jumble of chores for Kate as she readied to go to Savannah for Emmie's upcoming birth. She worried about forgetting things as she packed, nervous to be going alone. Thomas came to fetch her as the time drew closer.

"Don't stay too long." Omie took her mamma's hand and rested it on her swollen belly as the baby moved. "Or this little one might pop out without you!"

"I'll be back soon as I can, tell that young'un to hold tight." They kissed, and Thomas helped Kate into the buggy.

In the days following Kate's departure, Omie wished she could be in Savannah as well, she and her sister having their babies close together. Sharing the wonder of finally holding these tiny miracles they'd been given.

Phoebee was the one to notice the wet spot on the back of Omie's skirts.

"Oh no, this can't be! Mamma's still gone."

They stared at each other for a moment. Phoebee said, "Well, guess what. It's a-comin'!" She laughed nervously, then ran to gather the children and find Nate.

"Oh Lord," he exclaimed. "Not again! Phoebee, you'll have to help this time."

"Nosirree," she replied. "I ain't never attended a birth. I was pole-axed myself when Polly was born and don't remember a thing about it. I'll take the young'uns to my house though."

Nate hurried inside to find Ada Kate and Bartie heating water. Omie was mopping up her own water off the floor.

"Get up darlin, let me do that." He pulled her up. "Remind me what else needs doin'."

"Ada Kate knows, she's been with me and Mamma at a number of birthings."

"Let's help you to the bed. Try to relax."

Another contraction hit her and she sagged to the floor.

"Ada Kate, help me here," Nate called.

The two of them managed to get Omie in bed before the next contraction came. Ada Kate fetched her a piece of kindling to bite down on.

In between breaths, Omie said, "I believe this one is coming fast, Nate. Be ready to catch her."

"Her?" he asked, smiling.

"Mhmm," Omie murmured around the stick. She attempted to smile back, but another spasm seized her.

The girls sat on the bed with their mamma, wiping her face as the contractions came faster. Nate banked up the fire and carried in pots of water. Ada Kate went to the foot of the bed, watching for the baby's head to crown.

This was Bartie's first time to witness a birth. She was trying to be brave about her mamma's cries, but Nate could see she was distressed.

"Here baby, let's watch with Ada Kate as your little sister comes out." He squatted down, his hand on Omie's leg and Bartie in his lap.

"Ungh!" Omie cried and a tiny red bundle slipped onto the bed.

Bartie's eyes went wide for a moment, then she slid off her daddy's lap and danced around the room, singing, "We got a baby, we got a baby!"

Omie reminded Nate how to cut the cord as he'd done with Bartie.

Just then Aunt Julia walked in the door. "Well, I guess y'all didn't need me after all!"

Omie smiled tiredly at her, and Nate said, "I sure am glad to see you though."

She helped him clean the baby up, then wrapped her in a blanket. They let Ada Kate hand the infant to her mamma.

"What should we name her, do you think?" Omie reached out for Ada Kate's small hand.

"Ezra wanted to name the baby George, after his invisible friend. They were so sure she would be a boy. Can we name her Georgia?" Ada asked.

"But I wanted to name her Rose!" Bartie cried.

"I think they are both fine names." Nate smiled at them.

Bartie ran over and kissed the baby's head.

"Hello, Georgia Rose!" she exclaimed.

Though she had let Nate back into their bed, the decision of whether or not to take him into her arms again was put off by the baby's presence there. Omie knew it was simply a matter of time before she would have to face that decision.

After Irene and her children had left, Nate swore that theirs was only a friendship. He cared about the family and their struggles, but was not intimate with Irene. Something in the way he lowered his eyes when he'd said it made her wonder exactly what had passed between them, though. A friendship. Nate let very few people close to him and in some ways, allowing Irene to know him was more intimate, more hurtful than lust would have been.

Days of this round-and-round thinking finally brought about the need for a decision. She kneaded bread as she worked out her frustration, covered the loaves with a damp towel, and set them in the warming ovens to rise.

Can I fault him for wanting someone to talk with about his troubles, our troubles?

Omie paced the kitchen, from stove to window and back again, checking the bread.

Why did it have to be another woman though?

After an hour or more of arguing with herself, she sat at the table and lowered her head into her hands.

I have to make peace with this. Not just for me, but for the children too. It's time to put my pride aside and think about our family.

Staring out the window at the boys seated on their daddy's knees, she resolved to speak with him before bed that evening.

Lord, you will have to give me the strength and understanding to do so.

During supper, she imagined the words she might say over and over, trying to find some that would ease their situation.

Once the children were asleep, she dressed in the gown her mamma had given her for her wedding night and sat on the edge of the bed, waiting for Nate to come back from checking on the animals. She heard the front door close and sat on her shaking hands as Nate came through the bedroom door.

"You all right?" he asked.

She took a deep breath. "Come sit by me."

He did so, turning to look in her eyes.

"I just want to say that I think what you did for Irene and the children was a true kindness."

This was as close as she could come to offering forgiveness in that moment.

"I'll find a way to pay you back for the money..."

"No need. Glad they're safe and with family."

She blew out the lamp and turned back the covers.

Chapter 52

On Sunday, the fifth day following her arrival in Savannah, Kate felt a tingle at the base of her neck. She'd been dozing in the porch rocker, dreaming of Frank. He was laughing, but she couldn't remember about what.

Omie.

In the next moment, a voice called out, "Mamma! My water has broken."

Emmie was standing in the kitchen with Danny's small hand in hers. Bitsy was wide-eyed, looking at the puddle drenching her mother's shoes.

"Mamma," the girl exclaimed, "you pottied!"

Everything had been prepared for this moment. After getting Emmie settled into bed, Kate called Elizabeth. Her hands were shaking as she dialed the unfamiliar instrument.

Lord, guide me here. You know I'm not much smarter than a chicken about this darn thing.

However, not having to leave her daughter alone was a comfort. Perhaps in time they could have a telephone of their own at the farm.

What would Frank make of that?

Elizabeth and Maizie walked through the door moments later. After being assured all was well, Maizie took the children back to the Campbells with her. Promises of warm cookies and cocoa finally convinced Bitsy to go, but she insisted on being the first to hold the baby after her mamma "peed it out".

"Promise!" she called back as they went out the door. Everyone laughed when Bitsy was out of hearing, until a contraction took Emmie's breath.

Her contractions were coming regularly by the time Caleb arrived, but had not gained strength. Kate sat at the foot of the bed, checking progress occasionally as Elizabeth and Caleb took turns sitting with Emmie, wiping her face with cool cloths.

This birth was not progressing as quickly as the first two, and Caleb was beginning to feel concerned. He looked at his mother-in-law with worried eyes.

Emmie reached out gently to turn his face toward hers and said, "Mamma would tell you if there was something wrong. You know that." She stroked the creases in her husband's forehead. He lifted her hand to his lips for a tender kiss. "Of course."

Kate met her daughter's eyes, then said, "Son, could you look in my birthing bag for the bottle of blue cohosh. I believe we need to make some tea to bring this little one along. It will give you strength too, Em. You are doing a fine job, but a little help would be a good thing."

Caleb found the herbs and gave them to Kate for brewing. He asked questions about what other herbs she might use in birthing, where they grew and how they were administered. This seemed to calm his mind as they waited for the baby.

In less than an hour, the head began to crown. Everyone breathed along with Emmie as she pushed the tiny body into the world. Laughing and crying at the same time, Caleb caught his son.

"A boy, Emmie!" He rested the child gently on her breast.

Kate cut the cord. Elizabeth bathed and swaddled him. Seeing her friend rock the small bundle in her arms brought tears to Emmie's eyes.

She would make such a fine mother. I can't for the life of me understand why those so suited to being parents are robbed of this joy, while others abuse their blessings.

The older woman handed the child back to his mamma with a melancholy smile.

"Do we have a name for this young man?" Elizabeth asked.

Caleb looked at Emmie and she replied, "We thought we would call him Aaron."

"My brother's name." Kate smiled with pleasure.

Elizabeth and Kate looked at each other, then slipped out of the room to give the new parents privacy. Elizabeth swept Kate up into warm hug that surprised them both. When she pulled away, Elizabeth laughed and said, "I do believe we deserve a glass of port after this!"

"Don't mind if I do!" Kate agreed.

For the first few days after the birth, Emmie was given all the time she needed to sleep, as many hands were ready for a chance to hold the newborn. Bitsy took it upon herself to monitor the baby's schedule. She nested him in her own small lap between feedings, imparting her new-found knowledge to visitors.

"Mamma is breastfeeding our baby," she would announce. "Daddy says it's kind of like getting a soda from the fountain at Mr. Solomon's drugstore. I think Mamma only has one flavor, though."

She looked at the adults around her, caught in fits of laughter. "What?"

Aaron became fussy within his first week, and Emmie begged her mamma to stay a bit longer. She was frantic after his third day of crying nearly non-stop. As another week went by, he began to lose more weight than was normal for a newborn, and Kate was concerned as well. She asked Maizie if Thomas might be willing to go fetch Aunt Julia.

"I'm not sure what to do, I need to get back home for Omie's baby but I can't leave Emmie like this."

"Of course, Mrs. Lee. We'll both go."

Thomas and Maizie arrived the next day with Aunt Julia. The old woman was barely visible above the window, looking like a child having their first ride. Kate realized that this probably was her friend's first automobile ride, and likely the first time she'd been to Savannah.

"Look at us!" Kate called from the porch. "Country come to the city."

Aunt Julia cackled and replied, "Near 'bout had a heart attack a few times. Thought they were going to have to bury me in that big cemetery we passed."

"Bonaventure," Maizie said.

"It was an adventure, for sure."

The sound of a crying baby got their attention. Aunt Julia made her way up the porch steps and into the parlour where Emmie paced the floor holding Aaron, her face wet with tears.

It had been months since Emmie had seen this woman she'd known all her life, and she wept as they embraced.

"Aunt Julia, I don't know what to do! Nothing seems to work, and now he doesn't want to nurse."

"You just leave it to us, child. Between me and your mamma, we'll figure this out."

The old woman took Aaron in her arms, peering into his face. "Look at you, little man!" she exclaimed. The baby stopped his whimpering and gazed up at the sound of her voice. "We are gonna' fix you up just fine, sweet boy, don't you worry none." She smiled at Emmie. "Let's take him up to your room."

Emmie took the baby back and headed up the stairs. Maizie and Kate helped Aunt Julia climb, one on either side.

"I'll get your things settled in your room, Auntie," offered Maizie.

"Thank you, child. I'll take that little one, Emmie." Turning to Kate, Aunt Julia said, "Tell me what you've done so far while I look at the boy."

Kate talked about the poultices she'd put on his belly, the onion water they'd dribbled in his mouth. No amount of rubbing his belly or burping seemed to have much effect.

Emmie peered nervously over the old woman's shoulder.

Aunt Julia soothed him with a quiet song while she got a sense of him, then laid him on the bed. Pulling up his gown, she gently explored the area around his navel. At one spot, he kicked at her touch and whimpered softly.

"So, that's it, is it?" She began to lightly rock her fingers back and forth, sinking deeper into his abdomen. Blowing gently into his face to calm his breathing, she worked the area until rewarded with a loud expulsion of gas and a tiny smile.

"Just a little twist in his tummy is all," Aunt Julia said. "Sometimes they get a little knotted up as they grow. Maybe not quite finished developing. I think he'll be fine now, though. He's a beautiful boy, Miss Emmie."

"Oh, Aunt Julia. I can't thank you enough," Emmie cried, as she hugged the slim shoulders again.

"No need, no need."

"Let's go sit on the porch and watch the fancy folks go by," Kate said. "I'll make us some coffee."

"Let Maizie make it, we've earned our rest."

The two old friends made their way to the rockers and settled in for a long talk.

"I haven't had a chance to tell you the good news," Aunt Julia said. "You have another grandbaby, a girl named Georgia Rose!"

Kate looked at her friend in surprise. "Omie's baby came early? When? Did you deliver her?"

"Easy now, everyone is fine and no, I was not there in time. Nate did a fine job, though. I got there just as he was cutting the cord."

They rocked in silence for a moment, Kate taking in the news. Then she asked again, "When was the baby born?"

"Same day as this one."

Kate nodded. *So, Frank, that's what you were trying to tell me.*

Kate sent a letter to Omie by Maizie and Thomas when they took Aunt Julia home.

Dear Omie,

I am so sorry I was not there for the birth of Georgia Rose! I am glad to hear all went well. As much as I want to hurry home and hold that little one, I feel I am more needed here. Aaron is a colicky baby and your sister is worried about him. He's small but otherwise seems fine. I will write again soon. Give my love to all.

Omie sighed and put down the letter. She felt more tired with this baby than the others, but would not complain to her mamma and cause worry. It was harder to rouse herself when Georgia cried in the night, so she and Nate slept with her little warm body between them. When the baby needed to feed, she could simply roll over and offer a breast. Usually, they both fell asleep right after, but if the baby was fussy, Omie depended on Nate to get the little one back to sleep.

Ada Kate would rock the baby in her small arms and sing to her during the day when her mamma needed to nap. Omie loved falling asleep to the sound of Ada's pure high voice.

1939

June 19

In the lull between the needs of hungry children and visiting neighbors dropping off yet more food, the women found themselves in a small pool of quiet. Tess and Lilly had taken the young ones down to the river to skim stones.

Bartie set a cup of cool coffee in front of her mamma. Omie loved to keep leftover coffee in the icebox to have in the afternoon. Phoebee and Emmie were washing peanuts to be boiled, and Bartie set glasses of cold coffee in front of them as well.

"Where has Georgia Rose got off to, Mamma? Is that the new beau I saw her talking to after the funeral?"

"Yes, that would be the O'Dell's son Micah. Georgia Rose's been helping out at the store and seems to have taken quite a shine to Mrs. O'Dell. Micah is a good boy. He'll inherit the store one of these days. I reckon your sister could do a whole lot worse."

"Except that she wants to go to art school," Emmie interjected.

Omie scowled at her sister. "Don't be trying to steal another one of my daughters to the big city, now."

Frank Thomas and Ezra came in, hunting for pie.

"Hey Y'all." Frank Thomas called.

"How are you boys?" Omie asked.

"Fine as frog's hair, Mamma. Big Sis, you got any more coffee to go with this pie?"

"I'll get you some. Now sit down and tell us what you've got up to with Aunt Emmie's boys."

Emmie smiled up at them. "Up to no good, I imagine. But then, my boys bring their own mischief. I doubt there's much you can teach them."

Omie gazed at her sons with a warm smile, admiring the men they had become.

Frank Thomas looks so much like his daddy. Those same deep blue eyes.

Omie's father had left a mark on his namesake, also. Two small dimples below each cheek that seemed to deepen whenever Frank Thomas laughed. Which was often.

Nate's other legacies? Well, I reckon his oldest son wears those beneath his skin. Ezra took after the Lee side of the family, though. Got Mamma's dark hair and my eyes. I wonder if he knows they turn more gold when the Sight is on him.

The men chatted with everyone while eating their pie. "Well, thank you all. Now we got business with your boys, Aunt Emmie." They slipped out the door with sly grins on their faces.

Bartie squinted in the direction they'd gone. "How 'bout you girls follow your uncles and see what they're up to?"

Lilly and Tess ran out the door. After a futile search, they gave up and plopped down in the grass. Above their heads, the chinaberry trees were working alive with grackles. Lilly was astounded at the raucous carrying-on of the shiny black birds. Tess' little brothers and sisters were tossing stones up toward the noisy critters.

"Wait 'til the berries start fermentin' in August!" Tess exclaimed. "They get so drunk from eatin' 'em, you can pick birds right up off the ground without a fuss. Funniest thing ya' ever did see."

"No, really?" Lilly cried.

"Yep, you'll see. I love to look into their yellow eyes. You'll be here then, right?"

"I hope so. Grandma was supposed to talk with Mamma. Maybe now that Grandaddy is gone, she'll let me stay. Do you know why Mamma left, Tess? Nobody seems to want to talk about it. I never got to know Grandaddy because of their feud. Seems like I ought to get some kind of answer from somebody. Did you know him very well?"

"Naw, not really. He was gone a lot, and when he was home, he wasn't in much of a temperament that invited your company. I'm not sure you missed out on much, Lilly."

"Look, there's cousin Danny and cousin Aaron!" Lilly exclaimed.

They jumped up and ran to see what the men were up to.

"What y'all doin' with Uncle Frank's shotguns?"

Danny winked at his brother and confided, "Don't tell nobody Lilly, but we're gonna' wait for Georgia and her new boyfriend on the porch. Just want to play a little trick on him is all."

The boys went up on the porch and sat in rockers, cleaning the guns and grinning like possums. Aaron saw Georgia and Micah walking up the road. He elbowed Danny. They put on their most severe faces.

Georgia Rose scowled at the two when she caught sight of them, but Micah just smiled and said, "Well, I guess I'm at the right place. Reckon you must be the Savannah cousins."

Everyone laughed as the men shook hands. Emmie stood at the screen door trying to look disapproving but had to chuckle with the rest of them. Omie came to stand beside her.

"Rascals," Emmie commented, shaking her head.

"But they're good boys. We're fortunate to have them."

Emmie joined hands with her sister.

"Caleb did a fine job raising them. They miss him terribly, as do I. He feels badly about missing Nate's funeral."

"I know, Emmie. Though, Caleb wouldn't be as fine a doctor if he didn't travel to where he could learn the latest in medicine."

"I just hope returning to France after the war was not a mistake. There are many ghosts there for him."

"Maybe that's the only place he can put them to rest."

Phoebee had been listening from her chair at the kitchen table and thinking on what had been occurring at home back then, while the men were at war.

"We managed to make something good come from that trouble with the cotton though, didn't we?" Phoebee asked Omie. "You and me and Sarah. All of us."

"We did indeed, Phoebee. Saved a lot of women from losing their farms during the war and after." Omie smiled. "You children were a big help too. Even little Willie."

"So many men didn't come home." Ada said quietly. "Like Uncle Caleb's brother."

"Yes, that was a true sorrow." Emmie said. "I feared every day for Caleb and Marion. And for Nate."

"War is just the most useless thing ever was!" Phoebee declared.

Emmie said, "It looks as though war is breaking out again in Europe. I read in the papers that Germany has its sights set on Poland. Who knows where they intend to go from there. Great Britain has just implemented conscription to amass troops for war."

Bartie nodded. The older women at the table were speechless for a moment as the news sank in.

"Do you suppose we will be involved as well?" Omie asked.

"Time will tell." Emmie sighed.

Chapter 53

1917

“Omie.”

Nate walked quietly into the kitchen.

“Well, hey. I wasn’t expecting you home from town so soon,” she said, pulling loaves of bread from the oven.

When she turned and saw his face, she cried, “What’s wrong?”

“I registered for the Selective Service today.”

She looked up at him. “That doesn’t mean you’ll have to go though.”

“Paper says the Germans are sinking our trade ships. I don’t know why. Mr. O’Dell says this isn’t a war about territory, it’s about commerce. I reckon he’d know.”

“And about pride,” Omie added. “But Nate, they can’t ask you to go. You’re the only man on this farm, and a father to young children.”

“I’d be one of the last ones to go for that reason. Class four, they call it. But I still have to register.” Nate sat and put his hat on the table in front of him. He ran a hand through his hair, looking out the back screen door where the children were playing in the dry leaves.

"Oh Darlin'," Omie said in a trembling voice, "We can't do without you. Not just the farm, but me and the children. Mamma. Even Phoebee. She feels like you're her brother. Tell me you won't have to go!"

"Hard to say. I'd be one of the older men going, so maybe not as soon as some. But unless this war is over pretty quick, they're gonna' take me."

Omie sat on the floor and put her head in his lap, weeping softly. Nate stroked her hair and said, "Let's keep this to ourselves for a while. The children don't need to be troubled over it until my time comes near."

They sat quietly that way until chattering voices drew near. Omie stood and wiped her eyes on her apron. Nate reached to give her hand a squeeze, then headed out to the barn, easing the screen door shut.

After supper, when the children were put to bed, Omie and her mamma sat on the porch where the children would not hear them. Kate held her daughter's hand.

"Good Lord, Mamma! Why do men have to settle their differences with bloodshed? If women were in charge, they would never send their children out to die like this."

"That's true enough. Let us hope this war is over before Nate's called to go. Mrs. O'Dell told me she's seen many a mother's tears of late." Kate sighed.

"He'll be so far away! Will I be able to *See* what's happening to him? How can I help him even if I do know things?" Omie leaned forward and put her face in her hands.

"Put your trust in the Lord, hon." Kate rubbed Omie's bent back. "You may not get the answers you're looking for, but that's the best we can do."

Crows cawed in the pines, reflecting the dark mood of the day. Worries tumbled into their minds, but to speak of them seemed to invite the worst to come true.

At bedtime, Omie pulled Nate to her and made love with him as if she would never see him again. When they were wrapped quietly in each other's arms, she gave in fully to her sorrow, thinking of all the time lost to anger and suspicion.

"Hey now. Don't worry so, I'm still here." Nate smoothed her hair back so he could see her face.

"Yes, but it's just..."

"Look at me." He kissed her gently and deeply. Soon they were moving again to a softer, sweeter rhythm that expressed all the things words could not.

News of the ongoing war in Europe hung in the air like a specter. Fear tracked Omie's footsteps, catching up to her any time she didn't have to hide it from the children.

Phoebee and Omie talked often about the peanut crop they would plant in spring. It was a welcome distraction from all the talk about the war. Nate would till the fields for them if he had not been called away for training by then. He didn't interfere with their planning. When they had questions about the tobacco and corn, or the livestock, he offered only what advice was needed. Nate was grateful to Phoebee for her knowledge about this new venture that seemed to be taking root across the south. Peanuts would save the farm if all went well. The women were eager to learn the business end of farming as well, dealing with the grange and with other farmers. In case he had to go to the war and was gone for a long time, or worse, did not return, he taught them what he could.

I hate for this all to fall on their shoulders, strong as those shoulders are. They's a bunch the children can do to help. Ada's big enough to care for the baby and cook some. He felt his throat tighten. *I reckon they'll be half grown by the time I get back.*

Nate was somber much of the time, though he tried to show a brave face. Fear of the war and dying did not drag him down so much as the thought of leaving his loved ones behind to fend for themselves. Agonizing over all the things that could go wrong in his absence, he fretted about preparations overlooked. There would be few men left to look out for the womenfolk.

Omie tried to assure him that women were stronger than he imagined and probably smarter than men anyhow. "They say that brains beat brawn any day," Omie had teased. "Though I do have a great appreciation for your brawn."

Hearing sounds from the house up the hill, Omie cleared a circle in the fogged window over the sink and watched Phoebee chopping more firewood. Her friend was as excited as Omie had ever seen her. The school teacher who had taken an interest in Phoebee's apiary knowledge was coming to meet Kate and the rest of the family. Sarah hoped to move to the farm soon if she met with their approval, having tired of town life. Phoebee was busy making supper for the two of them, along with one of her delicious honey cakes.

Omie pulled on a heavy shawl and walked up the hill. She stuck her head in Phoebee's door and smiled at the sight of her friend in an apron that reached nearly to her ankles.

"You should let me hem that apron for you. You're going to trip over it and fall in the stove one day!"

"Oh, I reckon I should learn to sew but that just never did interest me. You think she'll like what I got planned for supper? I still got all this corn we cut off the cob and canned last year. Fresh collard greens with ham hocks, fried chicken. And cake! Please come join us for cake when you're done eating. I'm nervous as that chicken was 'fore I chopped her head off. Oh, and thanks for letting Polly stay at your house so I can get my work done."

"Phoebee, you feed her this good and she's liable to expect to eat like this all the time."

They both laughed, and Omie promised to come up that evening for cake.

A short while later, as Omie was feeding the chickens, a young woman came striding up the road dressed in a wool coat with a walking stick in her hand and a floppy hat on her head. As she drew near, Omie could see her strawberry blonde hair. A freckled face peeked out beneath the brim.

"Hello," she said, offering her hand. "I'm Sarah. You must be Omie. Phoebee speaks well of you all." Gazing at the fields running down to the river, she said, "What an impressive farm you have here. I love the woods and fields, so peaceful after the dust and bustle of town."

Omie smiled and shook her hand.

If our little town seems bustling to her, wait until she sees Savannah!

"I'll take you on over to our house first. Phoebee is slaving away at the stove. You must be freezing! It's a goodly walk from town."

"I don't mind the cold. I enjoy long walks. So much to see along the way."

"Everybody's so excited to meet you! Nate is finishing up chores in the barn, but he'll be in shortly. Our boys will just sit and grin like possums, but the girls will have a million questions."

"As will I." Sarah laughed, and Omie felt a liking for her already.

Sarah proved to be a great source of entertainment for the little ones, and she listened intently as they told her stories about the farm and their pets. Thankfully their questions were not too personal. Sarah was happy to tell them about her own childhood in Virginia.

"I had a pet pig once. I named her Ruby because she had a red coat."

The children looked at each other.

Frank Thomas spoke up. "A red pig? I never seen one."

Sarah corrected him, "I have never seen one."

"Then how did you have one?" Ezra puzzled.

She laughed, "Sorry, I was correcting your grammar, Frank Thomas. I can't help it, comes with being a teacher. She was a breed named Duroc, they are all red."

Omie could understand why the woman felt called to become a teacher, she had a natural gift with children.

"Miss Sarah, would you tell us a bedtime story tonight before you go?" Ada Kate implored.

"Please!" Polly and Bartie begged.

"Maybe so, if your folks will allow me." Sarah turned to Omie and smiled.

"Lord, yes." Omie grinned, "I ran out of stories with the first two. I'm sure they would be happy to hear about something other than "Brer Rabbit."

"Well, I'm sure Phoebee has supper ready, but I'll be back afterwards to tuck you all in," Sarah promised.

Omie walked back up the hill once supper dishes were done and the children washed up for bed. Sarah and Phoebee were about to enjoy a piece of cake when she popped her head in the door.

"We was just about to start without you!" Phoebee exclaimed. "Pull up a chair."

When Omie was settled in with her own generous slice of honey cake, she asked Sarah about how she had come to Effingham County, of all places, to teach.

"This posting was on the board of my teaching college. There was a need, and I came to fill it," Sarah replied. "My parents were both teachers at city schools in Virginia. So many students and so little time for themselves. A smaller, quieter place suits me better, where I can devote as much time to researching plants as to teaching."

"Well, we're glad you did," Phoebee said. "Polly thinks you came just for her!"

"May I ask where Polly's father is?" Sarah asked. "Forgive me for being nosey. It's a bad habit of mine to dive right in about things I may not have any business knowing."

Omie looked at Phoebee, who said, "Oh no, not at all. My husband—Ephram was his name—was killed when a tornado hit the farm. He ended up head-first down the hole of the privy where he'd been doin' his business. Blew him and the outhouse way across the field. Didn't even see it coming."

Sarah put down her coffee cup and looked at Phoebee with a stricken face.

Omie choked a bit on her own coffee and managed to say, "I best get back and see if the young'uns are in bed."

"I'll be there in a moment," Sarah called to Omie's disappearing figure.

"Is she all right?"

"Omie was the one what found him. It's still hurtful for her to recollect."

Sarah helped with the dishes, then walked down the hill to tell the children a bedtime story.

Omie showed up at Phoebee's door again, moments later, and said, "Phoebee! Head first down the shithouse hole?"

Phoebee turned around, smiling, and they both fell out laughing.

Chapter 54

1918

During the past autumn, a letter had arrived from Emmie. Marion and Cyrus had completed training camp in Fort Screven and been shipped out to France. Their mother was devastated. Caleb and Emmie proposed that she come stay with them. Hazel Decker had accepted their offer, declaring that it was impossible to roam around her house with nothing but worry for company. The two brothers were being allowed to serve in the same regiment, but could not disclose in their letters where they were.

Caleb had decided to enlist too, for doctors were sorely needed. His training for administering medicine in a military environment would begin within the month. He'd hoped there was a chance to be near his brothers, if at all possible.

"It's not as if Caleb can protect them," Emmie had written, "but he feels so helpless here. I pray the Germans will be defeated soon."

Throughout the fall and early winter, news from Emmie created in Nate a simmering stew of emotions. The Decker brothers were looking like heroes, and he'd wondered if Omie was ashamed of him.

Nate sat on a pail whittling a stick. The day was frozen in place. No birds traversed the skies, squirrels stayed tucked in their leaf-lined nests, not bothering to search for hidden acorns. He'd been seized by bouts of nerves, working himself to exhaustion, until there was nothing more to be done. Prayer seemed the only path to some kind of peace.

Please Lord, let this war end soon. I'm not a coward. Just don't want to go. Omie and these young'uns are the only happiness I ever had. Don't make me die someplace I never even heard of and leave 'em alone.

Stabbing the pointed stick into the ground, he stood, then headed down the hill to sit on the bank of his old friend and confidant, staring into the muddy current.

No point pretendin' to fish.

News about the war came to Omie and her family mostly through Nate's visits to the O'Dell's store, where a copy of Savannah's newspaper was spread across the pickle barrel for anyone to read. Around the pot-bellied stove near the back, Nate talked with the few men who were left to wonder what it all meant for them. Some were eager to go. Others, like Nate, were willing to do their duty, but secretly reluctant to fight what seemed to be another country's war.

Battles and bitter cold had taken their toll on US forces in Europe. All able men were needed. By Christmas, Nate was ordered to report to Fort Screven for training.

"Omie, I cain't take anything with me. I'll be wearin' a uniform, eatin' in the mess hall."

She had been following Nate around with the baby in her arms for two days, trying to press things from home on him. "What can I do to help? There must be somethin' you need."

He turned and took her by the shoulders. "All I need is to know you and the young'uns will be ok. I won't be too far, and maybe they'll let me come back sometimes. I'll get to come home after trainin' for sure if'n they don't need me right away."

"But six months!"

"Omie, we been through plenty hard times. You and Phoebee and your mamma will do fine 'til plantin' time. Maybe they'll let me come back for a few days to help plough. Don't worry so." He stroked Georgia Rose's soft downy head.

She drew a deep breath. "School will be out by now. Guess I'd best go wash my face. I'm not the only one worried about you, you know."

"Wait, now." He placed her hand on his heart. "This is where I carry you all, whether I'm here or not. I need to know you're not spendin' all your time frettin' about me Omie, or I won't be able to bear this."

She put a hand to his cheek and said, "All right." Georgia Rose reached her little hand up and touched her daddy's chin.

The bleakness of winter and the infrequency of letters had worn the family's spirits thin. Emmie was not surprised that Omie had no news from Nate, as he'd just been at Fort Screven a few weeks. Caleb wrote from Atlanta where he was training at the Emory School of Medicine, but little word came from the younger brothers. The women prayed that February would bring an early respite, but it did not. Emmie was grateful Caleb's mother was with her when they received the telegram. Cyrus was missing in action.

"Poor Marion!" Mrs. Decker cried. "He will be devastated without Cyrus. They've never been far from one another. I fear both will be lost." She began to weep in great heaving sobs.

Emmie half-carried her mother-in-law to bed, comforting the grieving woman until Dr. Campbell arrived with a sleeping draught. Emmie lay beside Hazel until the medicine took effect. In the early hours, the two women lay wrapped in each other's arms, sleepless and miserable.

The next morning Caleb sent a telegram that he was allowed a short leave before being sent to France. He would be there as soon as he could.

On the day he was to arrive, Bitsy and Danny kept vigil by the window. A car arrived and the children cried, "Daddy!" When Emmie opened door, the sight of her handsome husband in uniform took her breath away. He knelt to embrace Danny and Bitsy, then wrapped his wife and baby in his arms. A look passed between them that said there would be private time later for them to talk. Hazel needed his attention now.

He knelt beside her trembling form. "Mother."

She wept against his chest, repeating Cyrus' name. He sat back on his heels and wiped the tears from her cheeks. "He's missing, but there's still a chance he's alive. We have to be strong and not give up hope. I will do everything in my power to find him, Mother."

"I'm so afraid I'll lose you too," his mother sobbed. "Please, don't go."

He pulled her close again and let her release her fears against his chest. Then, he murmured, "If there is any chance I can help Marion or find Cyrus, I have to try."

She finally saw the futility in her objections and sagged in resignation. She gave him a small nod, leaning her head on his shoulder.

Emmie stood at the window in the early morning, watching sunlight sift through the pale green leaves of dogwood trees.

Hard to believe such horrible things are happening in the world with so much life unfurling before us. Even more so in France.

In the short days before Caleb was to muster out, much passed within the small family, spoken and unspoken. Bitsy seemed to know something was afoot. She and little Danny clung to their daddy's legs, so that he could barely move about the house. Emmie put the baby in her husband's arms whenever he was able to hold him.

Their final evening together, he helped get Danny and Bitsy to bed and read them a story. He leaned over Aaron's cradle and inhaled the sweet scent of the baby's head.

"I fear he may be walking and talking before I return," he whispered.

"Please don't say that, darling." Emmie sat beside him on their bed and rested her hand on his. "We will be praying every day, every waking moment, for your safe return. For Marion and Cyrus as well."

On the dawn of his departure, Emmie woke and clung fiercely to the man she loved, cherished, could not imagine living without. Their tears mingled on the pillow. At last, Caleb kissed her once more and rose to dress.

Emmie felt as if she were moving in a dream. She went through the motions of greeting the children, dressing and feeding them, the way she did each day.

Please, Dear Lord. Do not let this be the last time they rise and see their father's face.

Thomas arrived in the Campbell's automobile. The groomsman had reluctantly agreed to learn how to drive 'the Beast', as he called it, but soon became quite enamored of the machine. His employers had given him a handsome new hat to wear when behind the wheel.

After clutching his family tightly to his heart, Caleb climbed into the vehicle. Thomas pulled out into the lane, taking the young doctor to join others heading for a world they knew little about.

Letters were few and far between. Caleb and Marion could tell them little, but at least the letters proved they were still alive. No mention of Cyrus was made, which kept their mother dangling between hope and despair.

Chapter 55

Omie did her best to keep her word once Nate left. She hid her emotions from the children and put a positive face to their situation. Everyone pitched in to keep firewood cut, tend the animals and carry out whatever chores had been Nate's responsibilities. She praised them often, especially Frank Thomas and Ezra, making them feel like the little men of the family.

Evenings, Omie left the children in Kate's care as she walked up the hill for a small cup of Phoebee's homemade honey wine. Phoebee rarely partook herself, but Sarah often joined Omie for a cup.

One mild evening in March, the three women sat on Phoebee's porch enjoying the first fireflies of the season.

"I'm thinking Phoebee needs to sell a new line of products along with her honey, don't you Omie? Nectar of the Bees, she could call it. For medicinal purposes, of course."

Phoebee squinted at the two of them to see if they were serious.

Omie nodded. "Mamma and I could put it in some of our potions, too. Bet we'd put a lot of women's troubles to rest. Lord knows we all need somethin' these days."

"True," Sarah agreed.

Omie and Kate opened the windows and doors to air out the house. The spring sunshine gave a lift to everyone's spirits. In the fields, dew collected in cradle-spider webs dotting the grass. There were so many, they looked like a sparkling quilt spread on the ground. Omie sighed with pleasure at the sight. Georgia Rose giggled as a new batch of baby goats kicked and frolicked in the feedlot.

"Mamma, could you hold her while the girls and I fetch eggs?"

Kate took the baby and held her by the arms as she trailed her tiny toes through the cool grass.

Your daddy will be home soon, Little One. I hate to admit I'm of two minds about it. Your mamma has come to rely on herself and seems happier for it.

Kate watched her daughter laughing and chasing the girls around the chicken pen. Frank Thomas and Ezra were stacking up crates to make a playground for the goats.

Let's pray all goes well. Only time will tell.

Omie had been preparing teas and poultices for Nate to carry with him to France.

Kate mostly left her alone while she performed these tasks, hoping they lessened her daughter's feelings of helplessness. She was grateful, though, when Omie came to her one day, asking, "Mamma, can you help me with these?"

"What can I do?"

"I need these squares of cloth to be dipped in beeswax before I fill them. When they've cooled, you could help me portion the herbs and seal the packets."

"I see this mixture contains chamomile and mint. Is that passion flower as well?"

"And hawthorn. I thought these might ease his fears a bit. He doesn't admit to any, but his spirits say otherwise."

"Of course. Who would not be afraid? Men are so burdened with their ideas of what looks like weakness."

Omie nodded.

Kate continued, "Plenty of white willow bark and devil's claw. Good. Perhaps he will have little need of these and can share them with others in pain. Poultices too. Looks to me like you've thought of everything."

They worked in silence then, drawing comfort from the familiar labors and the closeness of one another. Kate saw colors shift and change around Omie. She imagined troubling thoughts must be plaguing the girl. Fear for Nate's life. Fear of a life without him. Fear that he would return a different man. There seemed no words to offer that did not sound like false hope.

"This wax smells of Phoebee's wildflower honey."

Omie was so deep in her thoughts, she started at her mamma's voice.

"What? Oh yes, it surely does."

Kate kissed her daughter's furrowed brow and quietly turned back to the work.

The twentieth of June finally arrived, and the family was in high spirits. Nate had sent a telegram the previous week to let them know when he'd be returning. Omie was preparing a feast: chicken and dumplings, field peas, fried okra, and of course, biscuits. Two kinds of pies—apple and sweet potato—were in the oven, sending out a sweet message of homecoming.

Just before suppertime, a familiar whistle was heard coming up the road. The children flew out the door and raced to be the first their daddy scooped up in his arms. They all hung off him until he fell on the grass from the weight of them.

"Where'd this bunch of monkeys come from? Where are my young'uns?"

They laughed and tussled until Omie called them all in to eat. Nate was pulled along to the house and up the porch steps. He caught his wife around the waist as he entered the kitchen and planted a kiss on her lips. The children giggled and Kate gave a quiet sigh of relief. Maybe peace would reign after all.

Phoebee and Sarah came down to join in the celebration, bringing a jug of honey wine. The grown-ups all had a sip and toasted Nate's return. He smacked his lips and gave Phoebee an appreciative smile.

"That's mighty fine, Miss Phoebee!"

Omie leaned toward Sarah and pretended to whisper, "Better hide it!"

Once all the merrymaking was done and the children put to bed, Omie and Nate sat at the table with cups of coffee.

"This came for you." Omie handed him an envelope with a government stamp on it. "I thought about feeding it to the goats."

He reached for the letter and looked at her.

"You don't have to open it tonight," she said softly.

"I won't sleep 'til I do."

He slowly pried the envelope apart and pulled out the paper inside.

Omie took a deep breath as she watched him read it. "How long?"

"Two weeks," he replied. Nate laid the letter on the table and took her hand as he led her to bed.

The early morning light shadowed the creases in Nate's worried face. Omie reached up to smooth his forehead.

"You'll be fine, Nate. This war won't last much longer."

He kissed her hand and gave her a half-smile before rising from the bed.

Omie did not tell him that the *Sight* had little bearing on her former statement, while offering some foreknowledge of the latter. All her senses told her that this would be the final year the war played out, and men would soon be coming home.

The day Nate left, everyone gathered around him with small gifts and embraces.

Omie explained to him which of the packets of tea were for calming and which for pain, should he need them. Some packets held herbs to mix with water for making healing poultices.

Phoebee gifted him with a small jar of honey, knowing he could not carry much. Sarah had flavored it with mint from the garden to remind him of home.

Nate looked at the children grouped in a solemn bunch. Ada Kate was already a budding young lady at ten. Bartie would soon follow right behind her. His sons Ezra, who stood holding Polly's hand, and Frank Thomas, put on brave faces despite the tears barely contained.

Omie held baby Georgia on her hip as she cupped his face in her free hand.

"You do what needs to be done and get yourself back to us, you hear?" She kissed him deeply before he turned to go. Nate began walking toward the main road where a wagon full of other men shipping out would soon come to collect him.

The children ran down the road alongside him until he shooed them away, pretending to give chase and laughing. Out of sight, his tears were soon to follow.

Chapter 56

Dear Omie, bet u caint read my writin. Im outtta practice since school. Reckon Ill have to learn myself all over again. I rode on a train for the first time when they sent us north. It was the first time for a bunch of us. They was a few men I knew from home and many I did not. We got on a big ship headed for France. I never seen so much water. Omie we was outta sight of land for weeks. I liked to have lost my mind. Most everyone got sick. Me included. I may just swim home when this war is over! Ha Ha It is not so differnt here than home. Its hilly and would be purty land if it wasn't burned all to hell from the fightin. I caint say much else except I love you all more than you know. Kiss the younguns and your mamma for me. Im savin up a whole lotta kisses to bring home to you.

Love, your husband Nate Silar

My Darling Nate,

We were so glad to get your letter. The little ones ask me to read it to them every night before bed. They are growing so fast. Too fast. Just in the time you've been gone, Ezra has lost two teeth. I have told him to put them under his pillow so the tooth fairy can bring him a penny for them but no matter where I hide them after I leave the coin they keep showing up under his pillow!

Ada Kate is such a big help to me. She has taken to going with Mamma and me on our routes to visit the sick. I think she will be a healer in her own way. There are no signs she has the Sight, but that may be a mercy.

Bartie is, well, Bartie. She does what is asked of her but not much more. The girl would rather be in the woods looking for turtles and frogs. Just yesterday, she put a handful of half-grown pollywogs in my wash pan. She wanted to watch them turn into frogs or toads, whatever they are. Please send her news of the critters you see in France.

I don't know what to think about Frank Thomas. He's by turns moody and rowdy. Makes my head spin. I believe he misses you most, though he won't say so.

Ezra and Polly are thick as thieves. She helps him with his chores and he makes her laugh. She's such a smart little thing, but awfully serious. Phoebee and Sarah seem to enjoy their company which is a good thing, because they are up there all the time.

Georgia Rose is getting a mouthful of teeth. I'm going to have to wean this one early, she latched on yesterday and liked to have never let loose. Guess what her first words were? Gum it. Guess I've been saying dadgummit every time she bites down.

Mamma is slowing down but seems well overall. She and Aunt Julia spend more time together these days since they are not birthing babies so much. Most of those births have fallen to me. I don't mind, but sometimes wish there were two of me. I am so sorry to complain. You have much more to deal with and I won't burden you with our small worries.

Things are going well with the crops and we are canning much food from the garden. We are fortunate to have so many hands helping.

I try to think of you in a safe place far from the fighting, with plenty of food and a roof over your head. I know this may not be the case, but I can't bear thinking otherwise. We all miss you terribly.

It is my hope that you are on your way home as I write this. Best to come back by ship lest you are swallowed up by a whale, like Jonah. We are all waiting with open arms.

Your Loving Wife, Omie

Nate's hands trembled as he folded the letter once more and put it deep inside his coat pocket. This trembling came on him more of late, and try as he might, he could not stop it.

There was so much he longed to tell his wife, but didn't want to add to her worries. What could he say about war that would not burden his loved ones?

How the man he shot coming over the trench with a bayonet aimed at Nate's heart looked much like himself. Blonde hair and blue eyes. The dying soldier seemed to realize this too, as the light went out of those eyes. Piles of bodies became bunkers. In the rain and mud, uniforms became unrecognizable. He could not make sense of all this death.

In these few moments of silence between bouts of gunfire, the tips of cigarettes glowed like fireflies in the darkness. Nate had taken up the habit himself. It was one of the few things that seemed to calm his nerves.

Funny, to grow up surrounded by tobacco and not ever smoke it until I come here. When I get back, I'll have to learn to roll my own. He would not allow himself to think, *IF I get back.*

Nate leaned toward the soldier next to him for a light and sat back as he drew in the smoke, gazing at what stars were visible in the slice of sky above the trench.

Chapter 57

The telegram came early in the morning. As she opened the door, Emmie felt the chill wind blowing her skirts. She stood frozen with fear, staring at the young courier. Hazel reached out to accept the message and Emmie caught her mother-in-law as she sank to the floor, message in hand. With shaking hands, Emmie read,

CYRUS BODY FOUND –(STOP)– BRINGING HIM HOME –(STOP)– CALEB

Hazel clung to Emmie, sobbing and crying, "My boy. My baby boy."

Emmie knew her own tears were a mixture of grief, for the young man she'd barely gotten to know, and of relief, that Caleb and his other brother were alive.

Coming home!

She knew there was little Caleb could say about when they would return. Each day they remained in France was another chance that their fates might turn, and she would not cease her prayers for their safety until they walked in the door.

Emmie sent Maizie for Dr. Campbell and Elizabeth. Caleb's mother would need something for her nerves until she could absorb the tragic news of her son's death. Elizabeth would be a big help in getting Hazel to bed, soothing the grieving woman until she fell into the medicine's merciful embrace.

"Darling!"

Elizabeth Campbell hurried to Emmie and took the younger woman's hands in hers. Dr. Campbell kissed Emmie on the cheek, then knelt beside the couch where Mrs. Decker lay. He offered his condolences as the grieving woman sobbed against his shoulder. Gently, the physician lifted her head and took a bottle from his satchel.

"Emmie, would you bring us a glass of water?"

Once the laudanum began to take effect, Daniel carried Hazel to her room. Elizabeth and Emmie dressed her in a nightgown, then laid her back on the bed, tucking the counterpane close. They stayed until her breathing became deep and regular, then went downstairs to the kitchen.

Maizie had made both coffee and tea, needing to be busy at something. Her red eyes sought out Emmie's, who reported what she knew of the situation.

"Oh, thank you, Jesus!" Maizie cried. "Dr. Caleb and his brother are all right. I am so sorry about the younger one, I prayed every day he would be found alive. Lord, let this war be over soon!"

Emmie sat at the table. "We pray for that too, Maizie. I suppose everyone does. I don't know how their mother will hold up under the strain. Her boys are everything to her." As she looked at her own boys playing in the parlour, Emmie dropped her head into her hands.

Elizabeth rubbed her friend's back, and they sat in silent commiseration, hearts heavy for the woman upstairs.

In the days leading up to her sons' return, Hazel Decker had become nearly silent as a revenant. Emmie suspected that the woman's heart was not only broken emotionally but weakened physically as well. Dr. Campbell confirmed her fears when he put the stethoscope to Mrs. Decker's chest and begged her to come to his clinic for tests. She refused to leave the house, however, moving only from bed to chair, sometimes to the dining table, and back to bed, doing only what was necessary in between.

On the day of the brothers' arrival, so many people packed the train platform, there was barely room for Mrs. Decker and all of Caleb and Emmie's family to stand. Kate and Omie had arrived earlier in the day, having left the children with Phoebee, fearing this homecoming might be too emotional for them. Her own emotions were a tangle to her—sorrow for the loss of Cyrus' young life, relief that Caleb and Marion were returning. Her worry about Nate hung over everything.

I expect we're all a patchwork of feelings. The air around us is full of colors and lights.

Omie turned to her mamma and knew that she saw them too.

Marion stepped down from the train, dropped his duffel bag and swept his mother up into his arms. Caleb followed suit. Emmie waited patiently before stepping up to hold her husband's face between her hands, gazing into the eyes she had longed to see for so many months. Caleb kissed his wife as if there were no one else around, until Emmie pulled herself away, breathless.

"Move over sister. My turn." Omie gave her brother-in-law a tearful embrace.

Dr. Campbell said, "Let's move off this platform where we'll have room to properly greet these returning soldiers."

Omie kept looking back at the station as if Nate might materialize at any moment, being the last to disembark just to tease her. She noticed

Caleb's limp as he navigated the wooden steps. She also saw, amidst the hugs and handshakes, Marion's discomfort. His sorrow appeared like a shield, keeping everyone at bay. Only his mother seemed to be able to get close to him and take shelter behind that shield as well. Tears coursed down her face as she held on to the arms of her sons while the casket holding Cyrus' body was brought off of the train. It was not the only one, and her wail blended with the sorrow of other mothers. She crumpled beside it.

A hearse arrived to load the casket and take Cyrus to the undertaker in Statesboro. Caleb lifted his mother's sobbing form and carried her to a waiting automobile. Marion helped her in, and sat beside her.

Omie and her mamma were helped into the Campbell's automobile, then Thomas loaded the bags into the back. They were all to meet at Elizabeth and Daniel's house for lunch, though no one had much of an appetite.

Mrs. Decker managed to calm herself enough to show her concern for her remaining sons. She hungrily drank in the visage of their faces.

"I am so grateful to have you home. I've prayed every day for your safe return."

"We know you have." Marion kissed her forehead.

"Mother, you look terribly pale. Are you ill?" Caleb asked. Seated between him and his brother, the smallness of her frame was more apparent. "You've lost weight."

In a flat voice she replied, "Please, I don't want to talk about myself. I'm fine, I've just been so worried about you, is all."

Caleb looked to Emmie. At seeing her expression, he let it go for the moment, but knew Dr. Campbell would fill him in on his mother's condition when they could find time alone to talk.

Despite trying to keep Cyrus' funeral a quiet, family affair, many more people showed up at to pay their respects. So many had lost loved ones in the war, and they felt compelled to support other grieving families. Mrs. Decker had been a selfless, kind and charitable woman. Seeing her suffer so was heartbreaking.

A low-lying fog shrouded the cemetery. In concert with the day, Crows cawed from their hidden perches in the old oaks. Omie laid a gentle hand on Caleb's shoulder, noticing how the light around him had dimmed and Emmie's light was reaching toward him.

Emmie and Omie shared a look of love and sadness over the heads of the babies they held close to their hearts.

A military contingent arrived at the cemetery and carried Cyrus' flag-draped casket to the gravesite. As his body was lowered into the ground, a bugler played the lonely strains of *Taps,* then guns were fired in salute. Hazel tried to retain her composure through this tribute to her son's sacrifice, but when she was handed the folded flag from his casket, she could hold back her sobs no longer.

Marion and Caleb flanked her, nodding to those who would offer condolences while they held her up until they were able to seat her in the family automobile. She closed her eyes and seemed to disappear inside herself.

Chapter 58

Mrs. O'Dell hurried over to Omie as she entered the store. "There's a letter from Nate!" she exclaimed.

Omie sank down onto a barrel and quickly opened the envelope.

Dear Family

Today we moved into the forest. They is such big trees here you wuld not believe it! Most of them big as the live oaks at home. I bet I would see a bunch of sqirrels and deer if it wadnt for all the noise of the fightin. Probly wild hogs too. Bartie I aint seen any critters much atall since I been here. When we wuz on the ship tho I did see whales! Two times. They wuz as big as the ship almost. Most of the time I was sick in my bunk but I had to come up to see them.

You know I caint say much about what is hapenin here but I think we may be gainin on the Krauts. I surely hope so. I miss you all so much. Be good for your mamma, children. Make me proud.

Your loving daddy and husband, Nate Silar

Omie closed her eyes for a moment after reading his words, offering up a silent prayer of thanks.

The shop keeper laid her hand on the young woman's shoulder. "He is all right then?"

"Blessedly, yes."

Both women went about the business of the moment, in quiet communion. Words seemed unnecessary. The letter was a gift in this time of uncertainty.

Omie was glad Nate had addressed most of his words to the children, knowing she would be reading his letters to them. She did long for a few intimate words meant just for herself, however. These few months seemed like a lifetime of separation.

What I would give for one day with him, even an aggravated one. I will be more patient, Lord, I swear. Just give me that chance.

Dearest Nate,

The first frost has come and most of our fields are laid to rest. Now, we can concentrate on harvesting the peanuts. The children each planted a small pumpkin patch this summer, competing to see who could grow the largest. So far, Ezra is in the lead, much to his brother's dismay. I fear Frank Thomas may switch them at harvest time.

Emmie's family and the Campbells send greetings. We all pray for your safe return.

I have very sad news. Caleb's brother Cyrus has died in battle. He was missing for a time, but his body was found and returned to his family. Caleb and Marion accompanied him home. Caleb has a limp-I don't know exactly the nature of his wound. Marion seems whole physically but deeply saddened by the loss of Cyrus.

Mamma and I are sewing new clothes for the older children. Our profits from the crops allowed us to buy a bolt of cloth from the O'Dell's store. We have ordered shoes from the Sears, Roebuck catalogue as well. A good year indeed. The O'Dells ask after you, as do all the people we see in town.

Georgia is walking and chattering up a storm. The chickens fear they are in peril, but she only wants to pet them. The child looks more like you every day. She has your fondness for biscuits and sorghum too.

Know that we are fine and don't worry for us. Only get yourself safely back. Pie and hot coffee will be waiting for you!

All our love, Omie and the children

Chapter 59

Omie hitched the mules to the wagon. She was grateful the two had not been conscripted for the war as their horse had been.

I wonder what the chances are of the mare ending up where Nate is. Wouldn't he be surprised to see her.

She, Phoebee and Sarah found two more wagons and mules from neighboring farms, and had taken their peanut crop to the grange. Now, they felt like a celebration was in order, so the whole family piled into the wagon and headed to town. The children had worked so hard in the vegetable garden, they were allowed to bring some of the produce to trade at the store for things they'd coveted all summer long.

Mrs. Odell was so delighted to see them that she offered free licorice whips all around. As the children enjoyed their treats, the shopkeeper invited the women to sit for a few moments before doing their shopping.

"Ladies, you must be mighty pleased with the profits from your crop!"

Omie figured Mrs. O'Dell knew to the penny what they had made.

Mrs. O'Dell continued, "I'm glad that y'all are doing this well. Many are not these days, with the cotton failing and their menfolk gone. I been asked to speak to you on behalf of some of the women who would like to try turning their fields over to growing peanuts next year. Would you consider teaching them? It would be a truly Christian thing to do. I've seen some pretty hard cases these days, children going hungry, fields fallow."

Phoebee replied, "Why, 'course we would be happy to help, Mrs. O'Dell. Any folks who want to call on us at the farm are welcome."

Omie nodded and said, "We can at least discuss the growing of peanuts and help them make a plan for next spring."

Mrs. O'Dell patted Omie's hand and said, "I knew you could be counted on. Thanks Darlin'. Now, let me see what these young people need while y'all do your shopping."

For Ada Kate and Bartie, hair ribbons and cloth for new dresses was all they could talk about. Polly had her sights set on a doll sitting in the store window.

Phoebee stroked the top of her daughter's head, grateful that the child was able to see the doll's lovely porcelain face and fancy frock.

"Why sure, Pollywog. You worked hard for it."

The boys claimed they weren't sure what they wanted, but Omie had seen them eyeing a .22 rifle behind the counter. Two pairs of eyes looked up at her beseechingly.

Omie shook her head. "I don't feel good about you having a gun when your daddy is not here to make sure you know how to use it safely."

"Some squirrel and rabbit meat would be a nice change though," Phoebee offered.

"I can teach them."

Omie and Phoebee looked at Sarah in surprise.

"My father took me hunting with him often. Believe me, he made sure I knew which end to hold, and not to point it at people!" They all laughed. "Truly though, I am a pretty good shot, and I can teach the boys what they need to know."

Omie gave in, but with many admonitions.

"You do exactly as Sarah says if you want to keep the gun, hear me?"

"Don't worry," the school teacher said. "There will be a test before they're turned loose with it."

The boys pretended to grimace, but everyone could see how happy they were.

"Mamma." Ezra tugged at his mamma's sleeve. "Do you think I could get a harmonica? I want to play like you."

"Why, sure!" Omie smiled at Mrs. O'Dell and said, "Would you add one harmonica to our list, please?"

She scooped Ezra up, much to his embarrassment, and gave him a big kiss on the cheek.

On the ride home, Phoebee expressed that she felt bad for having so much when others had so little.

"Don't worry about it, Phoebee," Omie replied. "You've worked hard and deserve everything you've got. We had to see how things would turn out this first season. Now it's possible for us to share what we know with folks. Perhaps there are other ways to help them get through this year as well."

As the two women made plans, the boys took turns pointing the gun at imaginary prey from the back of the wagon. In Frank Thomas' mind, deer and bear alike froze in fear when they saw his fierce countenance. Ezra fantasized about dragons to be slayed, dangerous beasts in the tall grasses that only he could see.

Sarah talked with them about the responsible use of guns.

"Even pellet guns can be dangerous, boys. To yourself, as well as to others around you. And by no means are they meant for injuring or killing any creature you do not mean to eat."

"Even dragons?" Ezra asked. The other children rolled their eyes.

Word of Phoebee and Omie's offer of help spread quickly among the farm wives, who started showing up by the dozens, in wagons or on foot. Most brought their children with them, and Omie's girls offered to care for the ones too little to help. Phoebee was in her element, taking the women and children up and down the rows, talking as much with her hands as her words. She told them what all was involved in the growing and harvesting, what problems they might encounter and how to get the most from their plots of land the following year.

Omie was amazed at how Phoebee's shyness with strangers disappeared when having something all her own to share. Sarah's face showed pride in her friend, as well.

With more time on her hands for gathering herbs, Omie took long walks by herself. She'd woken on a cool, misty day, thinking how good a warm cup of sassafras tea would be. Omie dressed and pulled a shawl across her shoulders, then walked to the fence line near the river where a copse of sassafras was boasting some of the first fall color. As the young saplings were pulled from the ground, a scent of roots hung sweetly in the air, mixing with loamy smells of upturned earth. From there, she walked uphill toward the old live oaks draping the gravestones of the cemetery, and a patch of warm sun along the edge drew her. She spread her shawl on the grass to lay down.

Gratitude for all their good fortune this summer filled her heart. She was proud of what they had accomplished. A twinge of guilt for her own well-being tugged at her, knowing that Nate was somewhere far away at the mercy of who knew what.

Please, God, shield him from harm and bring him back to us whole and sound.

On the breeze, a faint melody came to her like a whispered prayer. Overhead, clouds drifted like slow boats toward the river. She slipped into a sun-drenched dream of golds and blues which collected themselves into silken hair and eyes the color of sky.

Missy?

A pale hand stroked Omie's cheek. Such a sad sweetness enveloped her, that she resisted surfacing toward wakefulness. When she did open her eyes, the changing light suggested an hour or more had passed.

Omie gathered her things and walked toward the farm, holding on to that powerful feeling of pure love for as long as she could. She would contemplate this connection with Missy over a cup of fragrant sassafras tea.

Chapter 60

Marion occasionally brought Bitsy and Danny to the country to see their cousins and Polly. His mother joined them when her health allowed.

"Why Marion, you seem to have become a fine nanny," Kate remarked, after giving him a warm hug. She kissed Hazel Decker on the cheeks and invited their guests to sit beside the woodstove while she and Omie made tea.

"He is a marvel with them," Hazel agreed. "They'll do for him what they refuse to do for their mother."

Omie saw how drawn the woman's face had become. A smell of lilies came to Omie, who discreetly shook her head to clear her senses.

Funeral flowers. Oh my. Marion has lost so much already.

Kate could see the wavering light around Hazel and glanced at Omie. A subtle nod from her daughter told her she saw the same.

Omie and Marion took the children on long walks, allowing their mothers time to visit. There was an easiness between them. They discussed books Marion had read, the latest news from Savannah, things Omie usually had little time to turn her attention to. She taught him about the plants she used in her potions and the children helped gather them.

When the time came for the Deckers to leave, Kate pressed a package of tea into Hazel's hands, telling her it was a rejuvenating mix that she and Omie were working on.

"Please let us know how you both like it. We'll be up to visit you soon."

"Goodbye," they all called as the Ford pulled away.

"I'm afraid this could be the last time we'll see that poor woman upright," Kate said sadly.

The children asked often if their daddy had gotten back on that big ship to come home. The boys were especially curious about the ship itself. To distract them from worrying over when Nate would return, Omie offered to take them all to see the ships at port in Savannah. She sent a letter to Emmie, asking if Thomas would come get them.

On a bright Sunday morning, Thomas arrived early, with his big smile and a basket of cookies Maizie had sent along. Kate went as well, excited to see Emmie and the children and also concerned about the state of Hazel's health. The trip was a welcome diversion, and all were in good spirits when they arrived at the Decker's home.

"Hello!" Bitsy and Danny ran out onto the porch. Emmie greeted them at the door with Aaron in her arms. "Let's have some hot cocoa, shall we?"

Caleb and his brother kissed the women's cheeks as they entered and escorted them to the table. They all sipped cocoa and munched on more of Maizie's cookies while Caleb and Marion answered questions from the boys about what it was like traveling on the sea. Soon, the children were raring to go see the ships. Omie said she would visit with the grown-ups later, for she had a promise to keep.

"Mamma, can we go?" Bitsy pleaded.

Emmie looked at Omie, who said, "Of course, we wouldn't have it any other way."

"We'll take care of Georgia Rose, you all go have a good time," Emmie said.

Marion offered to escort Omie and the children to River Street. She accepted, and the group piled into Caleb's Ford for the outing.

Marion parked alongside Johnson Square, and they bundled up in coats. As they walked through the park, the children played in the dry leaves and raced around the statue of General Nathanael Greene.

"Have you any news of your husband?" Caleb's brother asked, walking beside Omie.

Omie shook her head. "No letters for over a month now. I don't know what to do. He'd been writing at least every week. I keep thinking about that ship that went down, the Otranto. Many of those soldiers were from Georgia. I worry that the ship bringing him home may have met the same fate."

"You would get a telegram right away if something like that happened. The mail can be very slow, depending on where you are, Mrs. Silar. Also, mail gets lost in the fighting. Please don't give up hope. I'm sure it's just a matter of time before you hear from Nate."

"How are you, Marion? I hesitate to bring up Cyrus because I know his death grieves you deeply. I just want you to know that we are terribly sorry for your loss. I didn't know him well, but I could see how close you were."

"We were." Marion looked away. His gaze seemed to settle on something far from this place. Omie did not disturb his thoughts. The young man had aged in the time he'd been at war. His hair showed strands of gray at the temples.

He sighed, and returned to their conversation.

"I try to be present for Mother. She needs me now. Caleb's children are a soothing distraction from the places my mind goes when I am alone." He turned to her with a sad smile. "Not very pleasant company, am I? Apologies. Let's talk of something more interesting than my gloomy disposition. Have you had oysters at the new eating establishment on the wharf? Perhaps we could take the children there when they've had their fill of romanticizing about sea travel."

Omie said she thought that was a fine idea. Marion, Omie and the children wandered down the cobblestone streets toward the riverfront, with Cyrus' ghost alongside them.

For Halloween, the Savannah family was invited to a party at the farm, with Frank Thomas and Ezra's pumpkins being the main attraction. Ezra's had grown long whereas his brother's was round and fat. Caleb was asked to judge the winner, as he was thought to be impartial and probably the smartest, being a doctor and all.

"I win!" Frank Thomas declared, as he and Ada Kate hefted his orange orb onto a cart.

"Says who?" asked Ezra, needing a hand to lift his pumpkin up.

"I'd say it's a draw," Caleb announced. "Is there any way to weigh them?" he asked.

"Not without hauling them all the way to the grange," Omie replied.

"Tell you what, boys," Emmie offered, "why don't we judge them by how they look as jack-o'-lanterns? You can split into teams and the scariest one wins!"

"I pick Ada Kate and Polly," Ezra called, and teams were quickly chosen.

Hazel Decker smiled at the goings-on from the comfort of her rocker, draped in one of Kate's quilts. Bitsy had put a hat on her grandmamma's head, sticking straw around the edges so she'd look like a scarecrow. "Now you have a Halloween costume too, Grandma!" she declared.

As the pumpkin carvers went out to the barn, Kate returned from the festivities to sit with Hazel on the porch.

"How're you holding up, Hazel?"

"I feel like a dried-up scarecrow, Kate. I'm glad to be here, though. Glad to hear some laughter." She hesitated a moment, and then said, "You know it's my time. Don't object, I know you do, *Sight* or not. Kate, I'm ready to be with my boy, as much as I hate leaving these two. I don't feel like I'm much good to them now. I know Caleb and Emmie would never consider me a burden, but still."

Kate reached across to take Hazel's hand. "Do you have any fears around passing? I can tell you now, my husband Frank is with me almost as much as when he was alive." She sighed. "I'm ready to be with him, too."

Hazel shook her head *no* and they sat that way, just holding hands in quiet communion, until the day grew too chilly to stay on the porch. They went in to the kitchen and had tea until the jack-o'-lanterns were brought up to the porch and a candle lit inside each one.

Hazel and Kate stepped outside to admire the children's work. Kate turned to Hazel. "By golly, I think one is you and one is me!"

Everyone laughed and called it a tie.

The day of Hazel Decker's funeral was cold. A weak sun strained to reach through the clouds. The procession from Savannah to Statesboro was small. Marion, Caleb, Emmie, and the Decker children rode in one vehicle. Omie's family was split between the Campbell's automobile, and a borrowed one driven by Thomas. Maizie rode beside him, while Phoebee and Sarah settled in back with the boys.

The image of Marion's stricken face stayed with Omie as she looked out the window.

The man is broken. Whatever will he do now? Death seems determined to claim all our spirits these days. Nate, where are you? Why can't I feel you?

Caleb did his best to be strong, but Kate could see the way he leaned into Emmie as they stood at the gravesite. Danny and Bitsy were quiet, their red-rimmed eyes speaking to the love they had for their grandmamma.

Many friends and relatives came to say goodbye to this generous woman who was known for her good works. Hazel Decker had touched so many lives in the community. It was unspoken knowledge how Mr. Decker had treated her poorly. And now, the loss of her son seemed to have been more than her heart could stand.

As the family walked away from the graveside, Omie caught up to Marion. He had distanced himself from the rest, pausing to stand beside his brother's stone. She approached him quietly, trying to sense whether or not he would welcome her company.

He turned to her and dropped his head to her shoulder.

"I don't know what to do now, Omie. I don't know who I am without Cyrus, without Mother."

She let him sob into her coat, ignoring looks from passers-by. When his tears were spent, he steadied himself against the marble and apologized.

"You must think me weak," he said.

"I would think you heartless if you didn't grieve so, Marion. Please know that you have all of us by your side. Caleb and Emmie, the children. Everyone here. You're part of our family too."

"I do know that, and I thank you, Omie. I wouldn't have survived thus far if not for you." He looked at her with such raw emotion that she had to pull her eyes away.

"Come now. Let's go to the house and have some of that tea. You'll feel better."

The intimacy of their exchange did not escape Kate's gaze.

Chapter 61

"Mamma, it has to be today! I know it in my bones!"

Though the war had been declared at an end for more than a month, there was still no word from Nate.

Kate studied her daughter for a moment before responding. "You feel him, daughter?"

"I believe so. As much as I ever have. I'm going to make all his favorite things; fried chicken, squash and greens. What else have we got canned? And corn fritters. Biscuits, too. Maybe peach pies. He does love his pie!"

Omie moved around the kitchen, thinking out loud. She had not seemed like herself since Hazel Decker's funeral. Whatever storm was brewing in her daughter, Kate sensed that it was something Omie would have to weather alone.

The children came in from school, dropping their books on the floor, watching their mamma go from stove to table in a whirl of activity. Kate herded them out the door with instructions that they do their chores, then visit at Aunt Phoebee's until supper was ready. She reminded them Santa was watching. Georgia Rose sat at the table with her thumb in her mouth, taking everything in.

When they returned, washed and hungry, Omie ordered the boys to sit.

She ladled up bowls of food for Ada Kate and Bartie to carry to the table. Kate helped Georgia with her plate as Omie put more pies in the oven, glancing at the door every few minutes.

"Mamma, aren't you gonna' eat?" Frank Thomas asked.

"In a bit, son. Y'all go ahead."

He looked at his sisters, who shrugged, then at his grandmamma. Kate gave him a slight shake of her head as she served his plate.

Finally, the last two pies were out of the oven. Omie sank into a chair as the children bit into generous slices. She continued to stare at the screen door while plates were cleared and dishes washed. Suddenly, she stood up and went into her bedroom, closing the door behind her.

Omie rose before dawn, giving up on sleep. She wrapped a heavy shawl tightly around her shoulders and walked out into the morning mist. Ice clung to the branches of the old oak tree, weighing down the hanging moss. She hardly noticed the raw wind that chaffed at her exposed skin.

With no destination in mind, she went where her feet took her. Crows descended onto the pasture fence, hopping just ahead of her as she walked along. Lost in thought, it took her a moment to realize she'd arrived at the hillside looking toward the river. Fog hovering over the water had made its way up the hill, shrouding everything in its path.

A heavy numbness seemed to seep into her bones, her head, her heart.

Is this what it's like to be a ghost? Walking through life when there's none left in you?

As if reading her mind, a silhouette formed below in the old cemetery. A form paler than the swirling mist.

Cecelia.

Another figure joined Cecelia.

Missy?

Omie stared long at their visages, trying to understand what they were trying to tell her. Suddenly, a third figure emerged beside them. She recognized the shape of him immediately.

"Nate, No! Oh God, No!"

Omie sank to her knees, sobbing uncontrollably.

Memories tumbled through her mind. All the love and heartbreak between them.

It's too soon! She closed her eyes and beat the ground with her fists. *Too soon for our life to be over. Too soon to face a life without my husband! God, haven't I done right by you? Tried to be a good wife, a good mamma.* She dug her fingers into the frozen grass and hung her head. *Of all the healing work I've done for other folks, why couldn't I heal what mattered to me most?*

She heard a voice nearby softly call her name. Almost a whisper.

"No, Nate! I can't live with only your ghost. I just can't. Better you go find peace in the beyond."

He reached down and lifted her up.

"Omie, it's me! I'm no ghost!"

Her eyes flew open.

"Nate, Nate!" She took his face between her hands, then threw her arms around his neck.

They held each other as sunlight rolled the fog back toward the river. Tears filled the space that words could not. After a time, he whispered, "I would'a been home yesterday, but the fellas I was travelin' with from camp stayed in Savannah for a night of celebratin'. I slept in their wagon while they carried on, and they gave me a ride as far as the river road this mornin'."

"You're here now, that's all I care about." Omie leaned back and looked into his eyes.

Voices of the children carried down the hill. Nate saw them running toward him and knelt on the ground. All of them tried to hug him at once, falling into a laughing, crying heap.

Omie looked at her family and truly felt the preciousness of this moment. Time would bring changes, she knew, but for now they were all together and happy to be so. She looked up toward heaven, giving thanks, breathing in the air of a blessed new day.

The crows cawed and flew, one by one, into the pale blue sky.

Walking toward the house, she felt a tingle at the base of her skull. Looking back, she saw a single crow remaining. The bird's dark eyes watched her. A vision of dead corn and circling crows filled her head.

"Mamma, you ok?" Frank Thomas asked.

She closed her eyes for a moment. Opening them again, Omie saw his worried face. Beyond him, her family, joyfully making their way toward home.

I will only think about this day.

Taking him by the hand, she replied, "We're fine, son. Just fine."

Silently, the last crow took wing.

About the Author

Rebecca Holbrook grew up steeped in the rich culture of the south. Her mother's people were some of the first settlers around Savannah, Georgia. Their stories, passed down through the generations, inspired this book. Though she was raised in Florida and lived much of her life in Tennessee, these family tales are loosely draped around her own story. Rebecca has been a banjo player and songwriter for many years. This is her first novel and its sequel, The Deer Stone, is soon to follow. She now lives in the Pacific Northwest with her husband Gary and red dog, Liza Jane.